My Everything

My Everything

Denise Skelton

First Chance Publishing
Cockeysville Maryland

My Everything

First Chance Publishing
76 Cranbrook Road #232
Cockeysville MD 21030
1-443-912-8719

ISBN-13: 978-0-9790877-2-1 (pbk)
ISBN-13: 978-0-9790877-7-6 (ebk)
ISBN-10: 0-9790877-2-4 (pbk)
ISBN-10: 0-9790877-7-2 (ebk)

Printed in the United States of America

Acknowledgements

This book is dedicated to my daughters, Tamar, Teaonna, and Dominique. You were the first to read my book and said, "Hey this is good stuff." My best friends, and sisters, Terressa, and Diana. Thanks for believing in me. My sons Cory and Kyle, during all those long hours of sitting at my keyboard, you never complain, not even when I burned dinner… well not too much. My brother Donald, whenever you saw something that you thought would help me in my writing you would always call. And finally yet importantly to my husband James, you saw something in me that I did not see in myself, and encouraged me to let it surface. If it were not for you, I would not be me.

Love Denise

Chapter 1

"She's in there," he said, leaning in through the window of Deanna's silver Volkswagen bug.

"How long have they been in there?" she asked, getting out of the car.

"Fifteen, twenty minutes tops," he answered, slightly hunching his shoulders. She nodded as she reached in the car and grabbed her camera from the dashboard.

"Let's go." She stepped on the curb and began to walk down the narrow sidewalk. Walking next to her, keeping in step, he glanced in her direction looking for any sign of nervousness. They walked briskly to the back of the motel.

The fresh, crisp October air mixed with the pungent stench of the week's worth of rotten food and garbage that filled a nearby dumpster.

"Which room?" she asked, her nose instinctively crinkling.

"The one on the end," he said, pointing. "Second floor."

She looked around, checking to see if anyone was watching, then pulled him behind her as she stepped between the hedges. "Give me a boost," she said, looping the camera strap around her neck. He watched her anxiously, shoving his hands in his pockets.

"What?"

"Boost me up onto the balcony," she answered, jerking her thumb upward as she met his gaze. "How do you think I'm going to get the shots?"

Knowing not to argue with her, he held his hands out. She put her booted foot in his palm, and he hoisted her up to the balcony.

After grabbing the rail and pulling herself up, she swung one leg and then the other over and quickly ducked down. She moved closer to the sliding glass door and peered in; she saw a small desk with a chair next to a dresser with a television set on top of it. She moved over a little more so she could see the entire room, which included a full-size bed with a pea-green blanket. Her subject was sitting on the bed topless, humming carelessly to herself.

"C'mon, baby, I can't wait forever," the woman called out.

A minute later, the bathroom door opened. A man wearing light blue boxers walked out. His eyes filled with lust as he watched her full, bare breasts move with each breath. He smiled in anticipation of the excitement that was to come.

Click. Click. She took two shots.

"What was that?" he asked, looking at the window. "Did you hear something?"

"Oh shit," Deanna whispered. Standing quickly, she smiled to herself as her adrenalin began to pump. The man took four steps to the patio door and threw it open as she threw her leg over the rail. He reached for her, his fingers barely missing her jacket as she jumped. She hit the ground with a thud and started running.

"Come back here, you bitch!" he yelled, leaning over the balcony.

Deanna Meyers, private investigator and owner of Meyers Investigators, looked at her employee.

"Great job, Chris," she said breathlessly as they ran around the corner, racing back to their cars. "I'll see you at the office."

* * * *

He stepped into the elevator at his penthouse and headed down to the lobby. He had only an hour and a half before his appointment—just enough time to go to the office and get the information he needed. He stepped from the elevator to the lobby just as she reached for the UP button. She smiled, her eyes brightening at the sight of him.

"Hi, lover, I was just about to come up."

The sight of her made him angry; he blinked several times, surprised at his own reaction. "What are you doing here?" he asked as he stepped into the lobby.

"I wanted to surprise you. I thought we could have breakfast together."

He looked at the doorman and smiled. Then he took her arm and led her out the door and into the waiting limo.

"Morning, sir. Morning, Ms. Summers," the driver said.

"Good morning, Mike," he said then looked at his companion, taking note of her rudeness.

"Are we stopping for breakfast?" she asked, flashing him a smile.

"No, we're taking you home," he said, making eye contact with the driver through the rearview mirror and nodding slightly. The limo pulled away from the curb and weaved into the early-morning traffic. He looked out the window and watched pedestrians walking briskly to work and school, trying to beat the fall wind.

His mind reeled back to thoughts of the night before. They had had dinner and gone out for drinks with friends. He had seen an old girlfriend from school, and Janet had accused him of arranging to meet with the other woman. They had a terrible fight afterwards, which seemed to be happening more and more over the past few months. He was still tense, and the sound of her voice was slowly increasing his agitation.

"I'm hungry, and I came all this way to see you. The least you could do is take me to breakfast," she whined, folding her arms and pouting like a small child.

He lowered his voice to a whisper, choosing his words carefully. "Janet, we don't want to do this here."

She glared at the back of the driver's head and waved her hand dismissively. "Oh, he's only the driver. They get paid to *drive,* not listen," she said, reaching for his hand and tracing small circles in his palm. "I had a marvelous time last night. Didn't you?" she asked, glancing out the window.

He snatched his hand from her grasp, his voice still low. "No, I didn't."

"Tsk. Oh, don't be silly," she said, turning back to him. "I think the evening went—"

He raised his hand to stop her from speaking. "I don't think we should see each other anymore."

"You always take things far too seriously," she said with a laugh, thinking he was joking. Looking into his emerald eyes, she realized he wasn't. "You're serious?

Why?"

He turned away from her. "I don't think we're good for each other."

"I don't understand why you would think that. Aren't you happy?"

"We argue all the time and drive each other insane. I can't take it anymore," he said, looking out the window. "I just think we need time apart." They rode in silence. "Mike, stop at Ritz Coffee House up ahead, then we'll be dropping Ms. Summers off at home."

She looked over at his handsome profile, seeing his set jaw. Taking a deep breath, she turned away.

* * * *

Dee parked in front of the Quick Mart Dry Cleaning. She dropped off her laundry and then walked across the street to get coffee. A shiny black limo stopped in front of the door; she slowed her pace and watched as a handsome Caucasian male wearing a tailored black suit and black turtleneck stepped out. A beautiful, slim blonde accompanied him.

He walked gracefully to the door, reaching it before Dee, and held it open for her and his companion.

Dee walked to the counter and placed her order. "Hi, Grace. May I have a Swiss chocolate and a Cinnamon Viennese?"

"Cream only?" the woman asked.

Dee nodded. She heard the man from the limo speak; his voice was powerful, but smooth and soothing. She looked back, noticing how his suit wrapped around his broad shoulders and impressive biceps. She smiled, glancing at the blonde. Her face was oval, with a delicate nose and thin lips, and her makeup was perfect. Dee turned away.

"Come on, Janet," Dee heard him say. "I don't have time for this. I told you I have an appointment."

"Why are you rushing me?" Janet said, her voice shrill. "I don't like being rushed." She stepped up to the counter.

The young lady behind the counter smiled. "Good morning, ma'am. How may I help you?"

"I'll have the Swiss chocolate," Janet said impatiently.

"I'm sorry, we just sold the last cup."

Janet looked shocked; she lifted her hazel eyes to meet the cashier's. "Well, we'll just have to wait until you make some more, now, won't we?"

"I'm sorry, ma'am, we don't have any more to make," the cashier informed her.

"What does that mean? It's still morning and you've run out of coffee?"

"We have chocolate hazelnut or chocolate mint. They're both very good. I can—"

"What sort of business are you running here?" Janet asked indignantly.

"Just get something else," he said, groaning with annoyance.

"No, I want Swiss chocolate."

He shook his head, stepping around her and up to the counter. "Could you just give us three chocolate hazelnuts, please?"

"I want to see your manager," Janet said, pointing a thin finger at the girl.

"Ma'am, I'm sorry," the young woman said in a small voice, glancing nervously at Janet.

"I'm the manager," a second woman behind the counter said, standing tall before stepping forward. "Miss, I'm sorry for the inconvenience, but sometimes this happens. We can give you something else on the house."

The man in the suit looked at the manager, his eyes communicating his empathy, and he sighed heavily. He pulled out his billfold and put a twenty on the counter, smiling apologetically. "Keep the change."

Dee had watched the entire exchange while adding sugar to her coffees. The man walked over and reached around Dee to get napkins.

"Maybe your girlfriend needs to switch to decaf," Dee said.

He laughed. As he glanced at the African American woman standing next to him, and into the most beautiful brown eyes he'd ever seen, his pulse quickened. "If you would be kind enough to stab me to death with that stirrer and put me out of my misery," he gestured toward the slim straw in her hand, "I'd be so grateful."

Dee looked up into his green eyes, framed by dark, thick lashes. "I make it a habit never to kill gorgeous men." She smiled, flashing her deep dimples. Then she took the cups from the counter, turned, and walked briskly out the door.

He followed her to the door, watching her walk across the street and into the dry cleaners.

"And just what the hell was that all about?" Hearing his companion's voice, he grimaced; he looked over his shoulder, his eyes met hers. He walked to the counter and picked up two of the cups, and then he nodded to the coffee-shop employees.

"Ladies, have a good day." Then, turning to the Janet, he said, "Janet, I'm leaving in five minutes."

Returning to the limo, he handed one cup to the driver. "Here you go, Mike."

"Thank you, sir."

He looked across the street at the dry cleaners, trying to get another look at the woman with the beautiful eyes. Then he looked back at the coffee bar.

"If she's not here in five minutes," he instructed the driver, "we're leaving without her."

* * * *

Meyers' private investigator's office was inside a brownstone in upper Chicago. As the black limo stopped in front, the driver turned to his employer. "This is it, sir."

He looked up from his laptop. "Thanks, Mike." Benjamin Harrison, the thirty-two year old CEO of Harrison Enterprises, stepped out of his limo. Everything about the six foot, two-hundred-pound muscular man said successful, confident, and sexy. Entering the office, Ben noticed the distinct aroma of apples and cinnamon. The woman sitting at the front desk looked up from her work and gasped.

"Good morning." Ben replied in his melodious, rich baritone, "Benjamin Harrison, to see Mr. D. M. Meyers."

"Yes, sir," the young woman stuttered as she picked up the phone. "Dee, Mr. Harrison to see you."

Deanna walked out of her office to meet their prospective client. He turned toward the sound of her approach. Dee slowed her pace, surprised to see the raven-haired man from the coffee shop. She got a good look at him and thought, *Wow.* Ben Harrison was handsome; his hair was naturally wavy and perfectly combed, his face was square, his features chiseled. He looked like he had just stepped off the cover of a men's magazine. And he had the most amazing green eyes. "Mr. Harrison, I'm Deanna Meyers." Her heart raced. She smiled as she reached out to shake his hand.

"Mrs. Meyers," Ben said, as his hand met hers.

"*Miz,*" Dee corrected. She looked at her assistant. "Kimmy, could you ask Christopher to meet me in my office, please?" Dee turned to Ben and smiled, gesturing toward her office.

Ben never would have guessed that the young woman from the coffee shop was D. M. Meyers; he had been expecting a male and someone much older—she was so young. He was even more surprised at the way he felt when he watched her walk across the room to meet him. She was stunning. He guessed her to be about twenty-seven or twenty-eight, five feet five and 120 pounds. Her body was slender, her hips slim. She wore a fitted gray pantsuit and a black mock turtleneck, as well as a gold cross and small diamond earrings. She wore her hair swept up, with delicate curls hanging around her neck.

"Did your girlfriend make out okay?" she asked, walking down the hall.

"She's not my girlfriend," he quickly answered, as they walked into the small office.

"Please, have a seat." She motioned to the chair across from her desk. Ben looked around the small office. A shelf full of books lined one wall, and a mid-sized desk sat in front of the window. There was an executive chair behind it and two comfortable armchairs in front. On the other side were shelves with cameras and other electronic devices on them. After sitting down, Dee asked, "How can we help you?"

He watched her thick dark lashes as she looked down, reaching for a pen and pad to take notes. She met his gaze and then smiled as they sat and silently watched each other for a moment.

"Mr. Harrison?"

"Oh yes, I'm sorry. I need someone located." Ben watched her closely, impressed by her confidence.

"Harrison Enterprises is a multi-million-dollar company. Surely you have investigators on staff."

"Yes, but this is personal, and you—or I should say, your firm—came highly recommended."

Dee's father had been a Chicago police officer for fifteen years before deciding to start his own private investigation business when Dee was eight. After a few years, his brother came to work for him; they were known as the best PIs in the state.

"Who are you trying to find?"

"My father had an affair with someone twenty years ago, and I need to find her."

"May I ask why?"

"Does it matter?"

"Yes, it does. I need to know that no harm, physical or mental, will come to this person once we find her."

"There was a child as a result of the affair, and I want to find my half-brother or sister."

"And there's nothing else, no other reason?"

"No," Ben said, "it's pretty cut and dry."

Dee watched him as she tapped her index finger against her lip. Then there was a small rap at her door and Christopher walked in. "Benjamin Harrison, Christopher Loa. Chris is our best investigator." Ben rose slightly, shook Chris' hand, and then looked at Dee.

"I thought you were the best," Ben said, seeing a gleam in her eyes and a faint smile. *Modest but sure of herself,* he thought. *I like that.*

"Mr. Harrison, if you could give us whatever information you have, I'm sure we can help you." Dee said.

* * * *

Dee reviewed the information that she received from Benjamin Harrison: Nancy Greer, D.O.B. 4/6/56. Moved from Park Ridge to Chicago twenty years ago. Last known employer, Harrison Enterprises. No family in Chicago. Dee dropped the folder on her desk. She spun in her seat and gazed down at the passing pedestrians on the street below. Why would he want to find his sibling after so many years? She was sure there was more to the story; otherwise, he would have let the investigators at Harrison Enterprises handle the case. She turned back to the desk and saw Chris walk past her office. "Hey," she called. He stuck his head around the corner.

"Yeah boss?"

"I need you to do something for me."

"What's that?"

"I need you to find out everything you can about the Harrison Family of Harrison Enterprises."

Chris nodded. "Sure thing." He stepped inside the office. "Do you want me to start working on this?" he asked, pointing at the notes spread in front of her.

"No, I'll take care of it." She watched him leave the office then picked up the sheet of paper, scanned it, and whispered to herself. "Mr. Harrison, why do you really want to find Nancy Greer?"

Chapter 2

"Mr. Harrison is on a conference call," Ben's assistant, Jill said to the woman walking past her desk. The tall blonde held her head high, continuing as if she hadn't heard her. "Ms. Summers!" Jill called, rising from her seat and following her to the door.

Janet Summers opened the door, rushing into the office like a squall. "Hello, lover," she said in a high voice.

"I'm sorry, Mr. Harrison. I couldn't stop her."

Ben looked up from the papers spread out on his desk. Meeting Jill's eyes, he nodded. He waited until she left the office, and then closed the door behind her. Janet walked up behind him and wrapped her arms around his neck. She nuzzled his neck and nibbled his ear. He ignored her affection, raising his hand to silence her as he spoke.

"Yes, everything looks to be in order."

"We have a meeting with the shareholders tomorrow at nine," a voice from the speakerphone said.

"Good, I'll be there." Ben pushed a button on the phone, disconnecting the call, and removed her arms from around his neck.

"I can't believe you left me this morning," she said, leaning on the edge of his desk.

"I told you I had an appointment, Janet. I'm very busy. I don't have time for this now."

"Not too busy for me," she cooed.

"I wish you wouldn't barge in here like this."

"But I missed you."

"You saw me this morning," he said, sighing.

"Only briefly," she said, watching him gather the papers on his desk. "You never have any time for me."

"Janet, we just talked about this. I think we need time apart."

"That was earlier," she whined.

"So?"

"So, I thought maybe you had changed your mind and we might be able to spend some time together. How about this weekend? You can take me out for lunch, or dinner—maybe invite your mother and sister?"

"Janet, that's not going to happen," he said, rummaging through the desk, looking for a red pen.

"Why not? We've been seeing each other for months."

"Janet, listen to me," he said, putting his face in his hands. "You're a great person." He started to give her the "It's not you, it's me" speech but then thought better of it. "We're just not right for each other."

"I don't believe that, Benji."

He cringed visibly at her pet name for him.

"I think you're afraid of commitment. But I'll wait for as long as I have to, as long as we're together." Ben massaged his brow. She continued, "I love you, and I know deep down you love me too. That's what really matters, isn't it, Benji?"

"Please don't call me that. I've asked you a hundred times not to call me that."

"Humph." She stood indignantly, folding her arms across her small breasts. "Well, you don't seem to mind it when we're making love."

He didn't reply; he felt himself becoming agitated and he wanted her to leave. She returned to her seat on the edge of his desk and ran her fingers through his wavy hair, smiling and looking into his green eyes with insincere shyness, which only agitated him more.

"Get off my desk," he said harshly.

"Can we go out tonight?"

"I have a lot of work to catch up on," he lied.

"Oh Benji, please, just tonight?"

The muscles in the back of his neck tightened. "No."

"Just to talk, I promise. We've been going out for so many months, and you want to stop seeing me just like that? We need to talk. You owe me that much."

"I don't know." He sighed again.

"I've found this marvelous club that I want to take you to," she said. "They're not the kind of people we're used to being around, but it's an exciting place."

"No, we can't talk at some nightclub."

"Please?" she whined, looking like a wounded child. "I really want to go to this club. We can find a table away from the action to talk."

"Okay, fine," Ben said, sighing again as he waved his hand.

She clapped gleefully and walked to the door. "See you at seven for dinner first?"

He nodded, not looking at her. "Sure, whatever."

She threw him a kiss as she left the office.

He sat at his desk evaluating his relationship with Janet. 'When they first started dating, he really had cared for her—perhaps not in the way that she deserved, but he had cared. He rose from his desk, casually sliding his hands into his pockets, and leaned against the window frame. He cared about her, but he didn't like the person she was anymore, and he definitely didn't want to spend the rest of his life with her. Taking her home to meet his family was definitely out of the question. His mother and sister were the most important people in his life, and if he took a woman—any woman—home, she would have to be damned special. His father had died when he was twenty, leaving him as the man of the house and the protector of his family. It was a responsibility he took seriously.

His thoughts drifted back to Janet. Their sex life was good, but that was all they had in common. She infuriated him sometimes. No, she infuriated him most of the time. He didn't want to hurt her; he just didn't want to be with her. Often rude or selfish, she just wasn't the person he wanted to settle down with. He needed more. He really needed to end things once and for all.

The phoned buzzed. He walked over to his desk. "Yes, Jill?"

"Mr. Tate is here for your two thirty."

"Send him in."

* * * *

At that moment, Dee sat across from her client, Leonard Dobson. She hated this part of her job—but she hated Mrs. Dobson even more. Mr. Dobson was a mild-mannered, soft-spoken forty-six year old man. He was five three and maybe 115 pounds soaking wet, with childlike features and baby fine hair that made him look much younger. "Just give it to me. 'Whatever it is, I can take it," he said with a thin-lipped smile.

She solemnly gave him the file. "I'm sorry about this, Mr. Dobson," she said as he opened it. She hated giving bad news to clients, especially ones who seemed so gentle. How could his wife do this to him? She would never understand people.

"Dee, you have a call on line two," the voice from the intercom said.

She picked up the receiver. "Hello?"

"Dee, it's Maurice. I just wanted to make sure we're still going out this evening."

“Can I call you back? I’m with a client,” she said, lowering her voice. “

No, this is important. They can wait, I can’t. I want to know if we’re going out. If not, I’m making other plans.” She hated when Maurice was like this. She lowered her tone a little more as she watched Mr. Dobson review the file.

“Yes, we’re still on.” She paused. “Dinner too?”

“Naw, I don’t want to do that. Let’s just hang out. You can grab something before I pick you up,” he said, hanging up before she got a chance to say anything else. She slowly put the phone on the receiver.

“That bitch! I’m going to kill her!” Mr. Dobson said.

Dee’s brows shot up in surprise. “Excuse me?” she said, thinking she hadn’t heard him right.

“I’m going to kill her!” he said, his voice going from a whisper to a roar, his nostrils flaring from rage.

Whoa, where’d that come from?

“All I do for that bitch, and how does she repay me? She goes and cheats on me, and with this jackass, of all people. I know him!” he said, reaching across the desk and holding the pictures toward Dee, his hand shaking. “He works for me, but not anymore, no sirree.” He rocked back and forth in his seat, shaking as if he were a rocket preparing to take off. “Oh, yes, she’ll be sorry. They both will.”

After throwing the file on the desk, he stood, knocking the chair over, and practically ran from the office.

“Damn,” she said, putting her face in her hands. She pushed the pictures around on her desk and looked at them again: in one photo, Mrs. Dobbins was sitting in a car with another man, and in another she had her head in the same man’s lap. There were other pictures of them going into and coming out of a hotel. She sighed, cursing under her breath as she picked up the phone and dialed. “Hello, may I speak to Officer James, please? Hey, Ed, it’s Dee. I need to talk to you about one of my clients.”

* * * *

“I don’t want to go to happy hour,” Dee protested.

“C’mon, Dee,” her assistant Kimmy said, leading Dee into the restaurant. Kimmy draped her arm around Dee’s shoulder. “Dee, all we’re going to do is listen to some music and get a drink. You haven’t hung out with us in a while. Come on. Don’t be a spoilsport.”

“Leave her alone, Kimmy,” Liz said, looking around nervously at the crowd gathering at the entrance of the restaurant. “Let her leave if she wants to.”

“No,” Kimmy said, thrusting her chin toward Liz and Chris. “She’s going to hang out with us, aren’t you, Dee?”

Dee sucked her teeth. "All right."

Kimmy smiled, pleased with herself, as they walked into the restaurant to find a table. Happy hour was in full swing. "I can't stay long. I'm meeting Maurice soon and I have to go home and change."

"Sure thing," Chris said. "I'll get us some drinks."

Dee hung her purse on the back of her chair, scanning the room as she listened to Kimmy talk about her new apartment. "It's only a studio, and I don't have any furniture yet, but I really love it." Dee's attention was drawn to a couple sitting at a table not far from where they sat. Her gaze settled on the profile of Ben Harrison. He was looking solemnly at the woman that she had seen him with at the coffee shop. The woman leaned close, whispered in his ear, and then placed her hand on his. After waiting a moment, he casually moved his hand without her realizing it. Kimmy's laughter brought Dee back to the table.

There were small groups of people scattered throughout the lobby and around the bar for happy hour. "Why did you have to pick this restaurant, Janet?" Ben asked.

"It's close to the club, and I thought it might be a nice change of scenery."

He nodded. After they placed their orders with the waitress, he thought this might be a good time to talk to Janet about the relationship. He cleared his throat.

"Janet, I need to talk to you."

"Can we please not do this now?" She looked at him anxiously, her hazel eyes pleading. He turned away, looking around the room and scanning the happy-hour crowd. Sitting a few tables away was the group of investigators from Meyers. Dee dropped something, and he watched as she gracefully leaned over to pick it up. Her slim fingers gently scooped up the object and put it in her pocket. Her movement hypnotized him. "Ben," Janet called, drawing his attention back to the table.

At the other end of the room, Chris walked back to the table and sat down, smiling with satisfaction.

"Where are the drinks?" Liz asked.

"The waitress will be bringing them." His smile broadened, matching the cheerful gleam in his eyes.

"Oh God," she said, turning away from him.

"Don't worry, I've got it covered." The waitress approached the table as soon as he had completed his sentence.

"First round's on the house," she said, looking back at the bartender. The bartender was a middle-aged bosomy woman; she seductively put a cocktail straw in her mouth and then pulled it out slowly while she watched Chris. Dee looked at Chris, and he smiled.

"What can I say? The women love me," he said, hunching his shoulders. Chris, a twenty-six year old Korean American, was five feet five inches and very stylish. Dee always told him he should be a model, but Chris would say anybody could look good for the cameras; he liked the challenge of extracting information from people without them even knowing it. He also had a way with women.

"Hello ladies," a tall forty-ish man said as he stood next to Liz. He leaned on the back of her chair, talking to the women at the table. "Any of you care to dance?"

"No, thanks," they all said in unison.

"Can I join you?" he said, his question directed at Dee. She smiled.

"I was just about to leave."

"That's too bad. Hey, don't I know you?" he said, squinting in the dim lighting.

"I don't think so," she said, still smiling.

He nodded. "So, pretty lady, what's your name?"

"Liz," Dee said quickly.

Liz gasped, and Kimmy busted out laughing. The guy looked at Dee suspiciously, then at Kimmy.

"What's so funny?"

Kimmy started waving her hand, trying to contain a giggle. "Nothing, really," she said, her eyes large and innocent. He eyed her suspiciously for a moment then turned his attention back to Dee.

"All right, well, if you happen to change your mind, I'm over there." He turned, walked a few steps, and then turned back. "I do know you," he said, looking at Dee, shaking his finger at her. "Oh yeah," he said. "I do know you—you're that bitch who was hiding in the cabinet at my job. You gave my wife those pictures of me and Candy! I ought to break your neck!"

Ben heard the commotion coming from his left. Looking over his shoulder, he saw Dee sitting in her chair watching some monster of a man threatening her. She sat there looking at the man as if she were amused, her pretty features lighting up as the man shook uncontrollably and advanced toward her. Three men then grabbed him and dragged him to the door. She waved at him while he ranted and cursed at her. Ben watched her with fascination. She was a small woman, and that guy could obviously have hurt her, but it didn't seem to faze her. She turned to her friends and continued talking.

"I knew this was going to happen," Liz said, covering her face as she shook like a leaf. "God, I hate going out with you."

Dee laughed at her. "Girl, calm down, everything's fine. Here, let me buy you another drink."

"It never seems to fail. I swear, you can go out with Chris and Kimmy and nothing ever happens; go somewhere with me and we see someone that you've managed to piss off," the timid brunette said, removing her glasses and brushing her hair from her face.

Liz had worked for Meyers Investigation for a little more than a year. Dee thought that, although she was very good at research, Liz was too sensitive to be an investigator. She looked at the woman sympathetically. "Liz, maybe you're not cut out for this work."

"No, I like what I do," she said, placing her hand on Dee's, "and I love you. I'm just afraid to be in public with you."

"Don't be afraid—we have Chris her to protect us," Kimmy said, looking at him.

"Hey baby," he said, holding his palms up. "Don't look at me—I'm a lover, not a fighter."

Dee laughed again. Rising from her chair, she said. "I have to go anyway." After saying her goodbyes, she left the restaurant.

* * * *

Dee and Maurice walked into Club Pacific. "I don't see Holly and Edmond," she said, looking through the crowd in search of her best friend Holly and Holly's boyfriend.

"C'mon, let them find us," Maurice said, leading her to an empty table. After sitting down, Dee waved the waitress over.

"What can I get you?"

"Rum and Coke," Maurice said, eyeing the waitress. "And tell the bartender don't be watering down my drink." Dee looked at Maurice, waiting for him to ask her what she wanted. Biting her lip, she gave the waitress her order and then turned her attention back to him.

"How was your day?" He looked at her and smiled. She leaned closer to speak over the music. "How was your day?"

"It was good. I worked out at the gym, did a little sparring. You know, the usual."

"Really?" she said, smiling at him, waiting for him to ask her about her day. She scolded herself for expecting him to ask, knowing he wouldn't. "Well, my day was fine. I closed one of my cases. We had a little excitement—"

"Hey!" A young woman burst between them, placing an arm over Dee's shoulder.

"Hi, Terry," Dee said, surprised to see her cousin there.

"You guys been here long?" Terry asked.

"No, we just got here. Who are you with?" Dee asked. She looked in the direction that Terry pointed, spotting a good-looking Hispanic male.

"His name is Ty. I met him at the Laundromat. Hi, Maurice," Terry said, peeking at him. "You're not going to speak tonight?"

"Hey, Terry," he said, leaning over and casually looking at her cleavage.

"Why don't you order me a martini?" she said brushing her fingers down his arm. He looked at her as if she were a banquet and he hadn't eaten for a week.

Dee watched them flirt. "You guys having fun?" she asked, crossing her arms.

Terry looked at her sheepishly. "Let me get back to Ty. I'll be back in a little while."

Maurice watched Terry walk away, his eyes raking boldly over her. He looked at Dee arrogantly. "What? I was just looking."

She shook her head. "I can't believe you."

"Hey, babe, I'm sorry. I just wanted to make you jealous."

"Yeah, right."

"I'm serious. Hey, are you ready to dance?" he asked, jumping to his feet. "C'mon!" He pulled her from her seat.

Dee bit her bottom lip. "Okay, sure."

The music was loud, louder than it needed to be, as far as Ben was concerned. They sat at a small table near the edge of the dance floor. After spotting a table in the back, he leaned over to speak to Janet. "Why don't we sit back there?"

"This is a great seat. Let's not move."

He scanned the crowd then looked over at Janet who was moving to the music.

"Isn't this great?" she yelled happily.

"Sure." Ben nodded indifferently.

She rose, taking his hand. "Let's dance!"

He shook his head. "No, not tonight. I'm not really up to it."

"Come on, please?" she pleaded.

He groaned, not looking forward to being bumped around by hundreds of strangers. They walked onto the dance floor and found a spot. He stepped from side to side, looking at Janet. She was having a great time. He smiled then looked around at the other dancers. He noticed a slim woman dancing a few paces away. She wore a tight indigo dress and her hair swept up in the back, showing off her slim neck. He let his eyes travel down her body, watching her move from side to side, her hips swaying as she kept in time with the music. With her arms held above her head, she turned in his direction. It was Deanna Meyers. He didn't realize he had stopped moving as he watched her. Ben felt a tightening in his pants and a quickening of his heartbeat. Janet tugged his sleeve, drawing his attention back to her. He looked at her.

"Are you all right?" she yelled.

Feeling his cheeks redden, he nodded.

"Let's get a drink," she said, grabbing his arm and pulling him back through the crowd, as Ben flagged down a waitress. After giving the waitress their orders, he turned back to the dance floor and looked around.

"So," Janet said, pulling his arm. "Does spending time together like this make you want to reconsider our relationship?"

He looked at her. "I wanted to talk to you about that."

"Good, so then you'll take me home to meet your family?"

Ben cringed. "I was serious when I said it would be best if we didn't see each other anymore."

"Why?" she asked, confused.

"I just think its best," he said.

"You know what?" she added, quickly taking his hand. "I think you're right; I am rushing things; we should take our time. Okay?" she said slowly. He didn't answer. "But you have to do something for me." He watched her, not answering. "I want you to spend the night at my place, no strings attached."

"Janet, that's not a good idea."

"I said no strings."

"No, and besides, I have a flight to catch in the morning."

"Oh Benji," she crooned, tracing her finger in the palm of his hand. Looking at her irritably, he pulled his hand away and turned to look at the dance floor.

Dee danced close to Maurice. He bumped into the guy next to him. "Hey man," Maurice said, his voice calm. "Watch it."

She looked at the guy, offering him an apologetic smile. She then looked up at Maurice, wondering what she really saw in him. Sure, he was good looking, but aside from that, they really had nothing in common. Maurice looked down at her. His well-groomed beard and the small scars he had received from boxing accented his handsome face. There was arrogance in everything about him—the way he looked and moved and, most of all, the way he treated people. Dee felt uneasy with it and had often had to smooth things over when Maurice would pick fights because someone had bumped into him or looked at him the wrong way. She knew the real reason that she was with him: he was safe; if he decided he wanted to be with someone else, as other guys from her past had, she wouldn't get hurt. She had thought about breaking things off a few times, but had decided to give it some time. She didn't want to think about that now; she pushed the thoughts from her mind, determined to unwind and have a good time. She danced around, feeling the music. Closing her eyes, she let the music take her away.

Ben watched Dee as she moved on the dance floor. Janet put her hand on his thigh, moving it slowly to his crotch. He watched the look of pleasure on Dee's face as she danced carelessly with her eyes closed. He was sure she was unaware of how captivating she was, her hips moving sensually with the music. He felt a ripple of excitement. A tall redhead tapped her on the shoulder and her face lit up with a radiant smile. She was enchanting, with beautiful dimples. Ben felt the urge to leave his seat and go to her, to touch her and kiss her all over. He wanted to hear her beg him to take her. He felt a pulse beating in his groin. He felt like he was going to explode.

Janet massaged him, kissing his ear. She whispered his name. "Ben... Ben! Are you listening to me?" She was becoming frustrated as she removed her hand. He looked at her.

"What?"

"What? What I was trying to say is... oh, never mind," she said with a wave of her hand.

Ben looked back toward the dance floor. "I'm ready to go," he said, standing.

"No, I don't want to! We just got here."

He picked up her coat and handed it to her.

"Come on, let's go."

Janet stood, grabbing her coat from him, and he took her hand, pulling her along. They walked out the door, quickly crossing the parking lot to his car where he spun her around and pushed her against it, kissing her. Moaning, she ran her hand through his hair.

"Let's go to your place," he demanded.

"I thought you said you had a flight to catch."

He covered her mouth with his. His breathing was labored. "I need you."

"Yes, you do." She smiled.

Holly walked to the table where Dee and Maurice were sitting. "Hey, guys, we've been waiting for you. Why don't you come sit with us? We have a booth." Dee smiled up at her and stood.

"No," Maurice said, "why can't you guys come over here?"

Holly leaned around Dee, looking at him. "Because the booth is more comfortable."

"We'll be there in a minute," Dee said to Holly.

"Asshole." Holly scowled at Maurice, as she turned and left the table.

"Maurice, why did you do that?"

"What?"

"We are supposed to be hanging out with them."

"So?"

"Why does everything have to be a challenge with you?"

"It's not... I just can't see why we gotta go to them, why we gotta hang out with your tired friends anyway."

"Because we can't hang out with your friends."

"Why not?"

She wanted to tell him it was because he didn't have any friends, but she wasn't up for a fight. "Come on, Maurice. Please."

He looked at her angrily. "All right, whatever. Let's just go."

They found Holly and Edmond's booth.

"Hey, Ed," Dee said, leaning in and giving him a peck on the cheek. Then she slid into the seat across from them.

"I was wondering when you were going to show up," Holly said, keeping her eyes on Maurice.

"Hi, Maurice. How's it going?" Edmond asked. Maurice turned his head.

"We closed a case today," Dee said, trying to draw their attention from Maurice.

"No confrontations?" Holly asked.

"Nope, piece of cake," she said, looking at Edmond.

"I'm sure," Holly said with a smile. She and Edmond knew that Dee liked to take chances when it came to her work, often following suspects too closely and finding herself in hot situations just to gather information.

"How's work?" she asked her friends.

"Great. Ed's come up for promotion."

"Really? That's great," Dee said. "Isn't that great, Maurice?"

"Yeah, great," he mumbled, sliding away from Dee.

"Hey, do you want to dance?" Dee asked, taking his hand.

"No!"

She sighed, shaking her head slightly. *What the hell am I doing?* She slid around Maurice and went to the dance floor with Holly and Edmond.

When she returned to the table to look for Maurice, she saw him dancing with Terry, his hands resting on either side of her brown leather miniskirt. He leaned over and whispered in her ear; she laughed, throwing her head back, then quickly let her lips brush his.

Holly came up and put her arm around Dee's shoulder. "I see she's at it again."

Dee sighed. "Sometimes I don't know what to say about her, but I do know that I'm not going to let a man come between us."

"You know what I say?" Holly said. "Let her have him. They deserve each other."

* * * *

Janet woke to find Ben getting dressed. "Where are you going?"

"I have a flight to catch in the morning."

She looked at the clock. "It's only two fifteen. Why are you leaving now?"

He stood, pulling his shirt over his head. "This was a mistake. We shouldn't have done this." He paused and added. "I shouldn't have done this."

She pulled the blanket across her breasts as she slid to a sitting position. "But I wanted to be with you."

"I know, and I wanted to be with you—but not for the right reason."

"What the hell is that supposed to mean?"

He looked around the room, feeling too guilty to meet her gaze.

"Janet, we can't see each other again." He walked to the bed, leaned over, and kissed her cheek. "I'm sorry about tonight. Good night."

"Ben!" she called as he left the room. "Ben." She hit the pillow angrily.

"Damn it."

* * * *

"Can I come in, babe?" Maurice asked, his speech a little slurred. He stumbled as he followed Dee up the steps of the apartment building.

"Not tonight, Maurice. I'm really tired." Dee stopped in front of the door, taking her keys from her purse.

"Come on babe." He stepped close to Dee, pulling her into his arms. He ran his hands down her back, resting them on her hips. "I want to be with you."

"No, Maurice. You've had too much to drink." She pulled back. "Why don't you go see Terry? You two seemed to have a lot going on at the club tonight."

"Man, why you trippin'?" he asked. "A man can't even have a good time without you getting on his back."

"Look, Maurice, I don't want to see you anymore," she said, looking him in the eye.

"Aw, baby, why you gonna be like that? I was just trying to make you jealous." He reached for her and she pushed him away.

"No, Maurice, I'm serious—it's over," she said, turning toward the door.

"What the hell is wrong with you?" he yelled. "I can get any bitch I want— even your bitch-ass cousin wants me—and you gonna push me away?

"Good night, Maurice."

"No." He grabbed her arm, spinning her around and pushing her against the wall. "You lead me on dancing all sexy and then you tell me to go home? I should have went home with Terry. She wanted me—you know that. She asked me, but I told her I was with you. Now you gonna do me like this? That's bullshit!"

He squeezed her upper arms tight, pressed her back further against the wall, and leaned in to kiss her. She glared at him with anger. His smile was nasty, and he was nodding lecherously. "I see you like it rough, huh?"

Using all her force, Dee head-butted him in the nose. He screamed, letting go of her at the same time.

"I said good night, Maurice," she said through clinched teeth. She turned slowly and went inside, closing the door behind her.

* * * *

Ben walked into his condo, hearing the swish as the elevator doors closed behind him. He felt guilty for the way he used Janet and angry with himself for feeling guilty. She had wanted to be with him, while he had *needed* to be with her, yet the entire time they were together, he was thinking of Deanna. The thought made him feel even worse.

He walked into the kitchen, opened the cabinet, took out a glass and got a drink of water from the sink. He leaned on the counter, remembering her voice when she had asked him not to leave. *You're a real jerk,* he scolded himself. *You should never have gone out with her tonight. What the hell is wrong with you, man? Janet doesn't deserve this.*

She loved him; the problem was he didn't love her.

He walked into his bedroom, dropping his shirt on the way. He needed a way to apologize to her without giving her false hope. He sat on the side of the bed, took off his shoes, set the alarm clock, and lay back. He closed his eyes, thinking of how he would apologize to Janet. When he drifted off to sleep, the only thing on his mind was Deanna Meyers.

The doorbell was buzzing. He woke up disoriented. He looked at the clock— 7:00 A.M.—and couldn't believe he had overslept. Sitting up, he regretted going out the night before when he had known he would have to get an early start the next morning. The doorbell rang again. "Who the hell could that be?" he said, rising from the bed, feeling cranky from the lack of sleep. "That had better not be Janet," he said aloud, walking down the hall. He stabbed the intercom button with his index finger and yelled, "What?"

"Mr. Harrison, Deanna Meyers..." She hesitated. "From Meyers Investigation. I need to speak to you."

He rubbed his face, trying to wipe away the sleep.

"Are you crazy? It's seven in the morning."

"It's important, sir."

He heaved an angry sigh. "Okay, come on up." He walked back to the bedroom to retrieve his robe and made it back to the living room as the elevator door opened. Deanna stepped off the elevator; she was wearing a cream coat and the same dress she'd had on the night before. Her dark brown hair was piled on top of her head.

"Ms. Meyers, this is not a good time."

"Yes, I'm aware of that. I have some information I needed to share with you."

"And it couldn't have waited until business hours?" he asked sarcastically.

"No," she said, offering him a faint smile.

He ran his fingers through his hair. "What is it?"

"I came to tell you that I've been thinking about you since you walked out of my office." She dropped her coat on the floor, taking a step closer. "I think you are the most handsome man I've ever met." She let her hair down, shaking it free, then slid her dress from her shoulders, allowing it to glide down her body and land at her feet, revealing blue lace panties and a matching bra. He felt himself grow hard instantly, his sex throbbing with intense heat. She unhooked her bra and dropped it on her dress, revealing her full, pert breasts. She stepped in front of him. Standing on her toes, she reached up and licked his lips. "I want to feel your strong arms around me," she whispered against his mouth. He felt her nipples brush against the material of his robe. He reached out and grabbed her, pulling her closer, crushing her to him. She put her arms around his neck, licking his lips again, forcing her tongue into his mouth. He gladly accommodated it. He still heard a constant buzzing; he tried to ignore it, but it wouldn't go away. He couldn't tell where it was coming from.

Struggling through the fog of sleep, he reached over and hit the snooze button on the alarm clock. His manhood was throbbing more than ever. He groaned, "Ms. Meyers, what are you doing to me?"

Chapter 3

Ben left the condo at 7:30 A.M. for the airport. All morning long, his mind kept drifting back to Deanna Meyers and the dream. The distraction made him late leaving for the airport, and he barely made his flight. He was tired and pissed off. He didn't like being late, and he definitely didn't like not being in control. He sat back in his first class seat and closed his eyes. He wanted to sit alone, to take some time and get his thoughts together. But as luck would have it, he was seated next to a woman in her early sixties whose life mission seemed to be to tell everyone about her new grandson, whether they were listening or not.

"And Taylor is the smartest baby," she said, holding up her wallet so he could get a better look at her blond-haired angel. "He's only four months, and..."

Ben groaned to himself. *For crying out loud, lady, would you please shut up?*

* * * *

"Miss, I can't give you any information," the portly woman said. "The hospital protects all of its patients' confidentiality."

"All I need is a copy of the birth—"

"No. I'm sorry. Hospital rules," she said as she walked back into the file room, closing the door behind her. Dee walked around the corner and leaned against the wall.

"Shit," she said to herself. "I should have brought Chris." Chris could get an old lady to give him her panties. She laughed to herself. He was a good employee, and they made a good team. She checked her watch. It was 10:15. She had been hanging around for an hour, hoping that the clerk wasn't the kind of woman who would let a break get past her. She heard the door creak open and peeked around the corner.

"Bingo," she whispered. She drew her head back, waiting. "Please don't lock the door," she whispered again. "Please don't lock the door." The clerk walked out of the office, letting the door close slowly behind her, leaving it ajar. "Yes!" Dee said, bringing her fist to her side like a bowler who has just gotten a strike. She watched the woman walk in the opposite direction. Then, looking in both directions, she briskly walked down the hall and into the file room. The sixteen-by-twenty-two-foot room was well lit with more than a dozen bookshelves containing thousands of files. Dee calculated that Greer would have had her baby in 1983 or 1984. She scanned the files for those years until she found the Grs; she then took the files from the shelf and began looking for Nancy Greer. After opening the folder, she took a picture of the birth-certificate application.

"Hey Kate, I have some..."

Dee looked up at a man standing in the doorway.

"Where's Kate?" he asked, pushing a cart loaded with files into the room.

Dee bit the side of mouth and replied, "She'll be back."

"Are you a temp?"

"Uh, yeah," Dee said, placing the folders back on the self and slipping the tiny camera she held in her left hand in her pocket at the same time.

"Well, you guys sure have your work cut out for you. Since they're combining the filing room downstairs with this one, you'll be lucky if you have any room to breathe," he said, causally leaning on the cart. "I'm Kenny."

"Hi, Kenny." Dee picked up another group of files, pretending to sort them.

"What's your name?" Kenny asked.

"I'm Terry," she said, looking up at him. "It's really nice meeting you, Kenny, but I really need to get back to work. I told Kate that I would have a few things done before she got back. And you know, with me being a temp and all..."

"Oh, sure. No problem. Maybe I'll see you in the cafeteria at lunch?"

"Yeah, I'm sure we'll see each other soon."

He smiled, nodding. "See you later then," he said before stepping out of the room.

Dee crossed the room. She listened at the door before opening it, and stepped into the corridor where she saw the file clerk walking toward her carrying a coffee cup and a doughnut. Dee turned and began walking in the opposite direction.

"Miss!" called the file clerk, who picked up speed, her gait shifting from a shuffle to a waddle. "What are you doing?"

"I thought this was the rest room," Dee called over her shoulder.

"I know you're up to no good," the clerk called, trying to catch up with Dee. "I'm calling security."

Dee hurried down the hall, pushed open the door leading to the stairs, and trotted down the steps. She made her way down the corridor, slipped out a side door, and walked quickly to her car.

"No sense getting hauled in today," she said aloud. "I might need to save that trip for another time."

* * * *

His meeting was brief and he was back on the plane by 11:30 A.M. He walked purposefully out of the airport to the waiting limo. Once he was inside, he sat back and closed his eyes.

"Is everything all right, sir?"

He opened his eyes, looked at the driver, and then closed them again.

"Yes, Mike, everything's fine." He felt terrible; he was tired and grumpy, and now he had a headache.

"Where to, sir?" the driver questioned. Ben rubbed his tired eyes with his thumb and forefinger.

"Meyers Investigations," he instructed, still with his eyes closed. He'd never obsessed over a woman before; he'd never even been in love. In lust, yes, at least a couple of dozen times. But love? No. He opened his eyes and looked out the window. This woman was getting under his skin, and it made him nervous. But it also excited him. He needed to figure out what it was about Deanna Meyers that mesmerized him so.

* * * *

"Hey, Leo," she called as she entered Quick Mart Dry Cleaning.

"Hi, Dee," the older man said, concentrating on his work. "Whatcha got for me today?"

"Two suits," she said, sitting the two pantsuits on the counter.

"When do you need 'em?" he asked hanging the items that Dee was picking up, on a hook.

"Yesterday."

"You always need 'em yesterday. Just once, I'd like to hear you say 'tomorrow.'"

She laughed. "I'm going to get our coffee. Be right back." She turned and left. A brisk October breeze blew by, chilling her. She shoved her hands in her coat pocket, looked both ways, and sprinted across the street to the coffee shop. She got apple cinnamon tea for herself and got Leo his usual Swiss chocolate.

"How's your mother?" Leo asked, pulling a stool from under the counter and sitting across from Dee.

"She's doing well," Dee answered.

"You look tired, still working long hours?"

Dee smiled. Leo Silverton was Dee's father's best friend, and she knew he thought of her as family.

He shook his head, "You shouldn't be doing this kind of work. You need to settle down, get yourself a nice young man and have a bunch of babies. I'm sure there is a nice young man out there that catches your fancy. Being one of those there liberated women, you can surely ask a man out on a date."

Dee laughed. "No, I'm waiting for Mrs. Helen to give you up, then we can ride off in the sunset."

He laughed, shaking his head. "My nephew Paul is still available. He's not much to look at, but he's a good boy, and he works hard."

"I'm sure he's a great guy, but I'm sort of partial to finding my own dates." She reached over and patted his hand affectionately. "See you in a couple of days." She said picking up her dry cleaning.

"See ya." The old man smiled at her, waving as she walked out the door.

Once in the car, she checked the photos. She reached into her shoulder bag, pulled out the Harrison file, and jotted down the info. Then she headed to her office.

Walking from her parking place at the side of the building, Dee stepped around the corner and saw Maurice sitting on the steps. "Oh boy," she said, squaring her shoulders. She stopped in front of him. "Maurice."

He looked up, meeting her gaze, then stood.

"I need to talk to you."

"No, you don't," she said, trying to step around him. "There's nothing left to say."

"Like hell there's not."

She stepped back as his tone became aggressive.

"Look what you did. You broke my damn nose!" he said, pointing at his nose, which was discolored and twice its normal size.

"Maurice, I don't want to do this," she said, looking up and down the street.

"I was never anything but good to you," he said. "Everything I did for you, and how do you repay me?"

She blinked, not believing her ears, and then her temper flared. "What the hell are you talking about? What have you *ever* done for me?"

"There are plenty of women who would die for the chance to go out with me, or even just to be with me, and I choose your skinny ass."

"I don't have time for this." She tried to push him out of the way.

"I know what your problem is," he said angrily. "The problem is you're a dyke."

She smirked at him. "Maurice, I'm so disappointed in you. I always knew you weren't the sharpest tack in the box, but I can't believe you couldn't come up with anything more original than that."

His eyes twitched, his sudden rage caused tears to form in the corners. "I'm gonna teach you not to mess with me." The veins in his neck tightened and he clenched his fist as he stepped closer to her.

"I don't think you want to do that, mister."

Maurice turned to see Ben standing behind him. "Who the hell are you?"

"Just a concerned citizen. I think you need to leave the lady alone," Ben said, gesturing toward Dee.

"I think your dumb ass needs to mind your damn business," Maurice said, his voice low, his tone threatening.

Ben smiled, casually standing with his hands in his pockets. "Well now," he replied, taking a step forward. "I seem to have made this my business."

Maurice turned his attention from Dee to size up the man standing before him. Ben was about an inch shorter than he was, but around the same weight. Maurice stepped closer to Ben.

"Man, I could hurt you."

"You don't say?" Ben said with confidence, his green eyes piercing Maurice's.

Maurice studied him closely. "All right, man, I'm going to let you slide this time." He turned to Dee. "This ain't over, bitch, not by a long shot. I got something for your ass."

"I'm sure," she said, giving him a look that Ben couldn't quite read. He thought it was fear but then realized it was something else.

"Are you all right?" he asked, looking at her closely after Maurice left.

"Yes, I'm fine," she said, brushing her windblown hair from her face. "Did you need to see me?"

"Yes," he said, his pulse suddenly racing.

"Let's go inside," she said, turning and walking up the steps. He followed her.

Once inside, Dee stopped briefly at the reception desk. "Any messages Kimmy?" she asked.

Kimmy looked up from her computer monitor and smiled at Ben.

"No, but Maurice was here looking for you. What happened to his nose?"

Dee ignored her, walking down the hall into her office. "Have a seat, Mr. Harrison," she said as she sat down. "What can I do for you?"

"I wanted to see how the case was coming along," he lied.

"It's only been two days," she said.

"I understand that. I just wanted to check in with you."

Dee became noticeably angry. She gave him a look that said she thought he was lying.

"If you think we can't get the job done," she said, her voice curt, "maybe you should go elsewhere."

"That won't be necessary," he said, smiling at her feistiness. Dee took a file from her handbag and slid it across the desk toward him. She sat back in her chair, watching him as he picked up the file and opened it.

"It's impossible to get information from a hospital, but we did find out that she gave birth on May 12, 1984, at Chicago General. Her baby was a girl."

"Is there anything else?"

"Not yet, but it's coming along."

"I'm impressed," he said.

Dee didn't respond, she just sat watching him. His hair was so black it looked almost blue; his features were perfect, except for a small scar on the right side of his nose. He looked up from the file, and their eyes met.

"Was that guy outside your boyfriend?"

"Mr. Harrison," she said, "I'll call you when we come up with any more information."

He looked at her questioningly. "He's not the kind of man I'd pictured you with."

"Is that so?" she said, shifting uncomfortably in her seat.

"Yes." He watched her eyes shift nervously. "So, is he your boyfriend?"

She glanced down, picking up her pen and rolling it in her fingers. "Thank you for intervening," she said, still watching the pen. "I appreciate it."

"No problem. You still haven't answered my question, though."

"No, he's not my boyfriend." She paused. "Anyway," she said, putting the pen down and leaning forward, "was there something else?"

Ben tried to think of something that would keep him in the office a little longer.

"Dee, you have a call on two," the intercom squawked.

"Mr. Harrison?" She looked at him suspiciously

"Would you have lunch with me?" he asked.

With a look of surprise on her face, she moved back in her seat, putting space between them. "Thank you, but no," she said.

"Okay," he said, nodding thoughtfully. "Maybe some other time."

* * * *

In the limo, on the way to his office, Ben sat with his arms folded across his chest, stroking his chin in thought. He had just left her office and had learned very little about her—that she wasn't married, and that she was more beautiful then he remembered.

"Mike," Ben said, "take a drive through the park."

"Yes, sir."

*   *   *   *

She was standing on the corner; she felt the warm sun on her face and felt the warm spring breeze blowing her dress around her legs. She heard someone call her name. The voice was warm, rich, and smooth, like sweet butterscotch poured over a freshly baked brownie. She turned around. Ben walked toward her. He smiled, making the sun seem brighter. Her breath caught; she reminded herself that she needed to breathe before she passed out.

"Hello, my love," he said, running his fingers down her arm, sending chills up her spine. He looked deep into her eyes. "You're so beautiful." He bent down and kissed her, his lips full and soft. She moaned, timidly reaching up to touch his cheek. She whispered his name and heard him calling hers from a distance. She opened her eyes, smiling.

Holly was standing at the door. "Are you okay? I called you three times."

Dee rubbed her eyes, trying to wipe away the grogginess. "Yeah, I'm fine."

"Must have been one hell of a dream," Holly said, laughing. "I'm leaving. I'll see you this evening."

Dee sat up. "'Kay, see you later."

"Whoa, that was one hell of a dream," she said, sitting on the side of the bed and trying to erase the image of Ben Harrison from her head. Since he had come to her office the day before, it seemed her thoughts constantly drifted back to him. *You need to get a grip, girl. This guy is a client. He probably wanted to feel you out to see what you knew about the business.* She shook her head, laughing at herself, then stretched and went into the bathroom to get ready for her day.

She zipped her skirt before answering the phone. "Hello."

"You'll never guess what happened..."

"Hi, Terry, how are you?"

"I went to the market and I met this guy. He's great. I think he's the one..."

"Oh, I'm fine, Dee, and how are you?"

There was a pause on the other end.

"What are you talking about?"

"Oh, it's nothing. It's just that it's customary to greet someone when you call them."

"Tsk. Hi, girl. How you doin'?" Terry said, dragging each word out.

"Good. So did you and Maurice have a good time the other night?"

Terry was quiet for a moment. "What?"

Dee took a deep breath. "Nothing, forget it. I'm on my way to work, and I have to get ready."

"But I want to tell you about him—he's great."

"What about David? I thought you guys were working things out."

"No, girl, he's starting to get on my nerves."

"Terry, David is a great guy—and everyone can tell he loves you. What's the problem?"

"I don't know. He just don't do it for me. He's so dry—all he ever wants to do is go to the movies or out to dinner. I want some adventure."

Dee thought about David. He was always willing to do whatever it took to please Terry. "Terry, I can't do this now. I really have to get ready for work."

"Come on, I need you. I made a date with Shawn for tonight, and I need something to wear."

"Half my wardrobe is at your house."

"C'mon!" Terry begged. "I want something new."

"Terry, why do you do this? You meet some guy and then throw caution to the wind and have a fling with him. Meanwhile, David is waiting in the wings like some lovesick puppy. Give the man a break."

"No, I'm tired of him—and Shawn is so different. He seems exciting."

"But you just met him. What do you know about this guy? David has so much going for him: He just got promoted to accounts manager, and most importantly he's the father of your son. You really need to think about what you're doing. This guy may not even like kids, or worse yet, he might be some nut. You really don't know nowadays." She waited for Terry to respond.

"So, can I borrow something or what?" Terry asked.

Dee hung up. She turned around, slipped on her boots, and let the phone ring four times before picking up the receiver, laughing.

"Don't be a smart ass. It's not cute. I know you think it is, but it's not."

"I told you I have to get ready for work. So, are you coming tonight?"

"No, I told you I have plans. Where are you guys going anyway?"

"We're getting Thai," Dee answered.

Terry made a small grunt. "So, I guess the outfit is definitely out, huh?"

Dee hung up again.

* * * *

"Mr. Harrison, Ms. Summers is on the line."

Ben wasn't in the mood to talk to Janet. After a moment, he pushed the intercom button.

"Tell her I'm busy." He sat down, flipping through some contracts.

"Mr. Harrison, she won't take no for an answer."

Picking up the phone, he pushed the button and said, "Yeah, Janet."

"Hello, lover. Why didn't you call me last night?"

"Janet, I have a million things to do and—"

"Can we have lunch?"

No."

"Please, just for an hour?"

He sighed. "No Janet."

"I don't understand why you're doing this. This is not the way people in a relationship are supposed to treat each other."

"Janet, I really have a lot of things to take care of. I have to go now." He hung up quickly and grabbed his jacket from the back of his chair. "I'm going to lunch, Jill. I'll be back in a couple of hours."

"Mr. Harrison, Ms. Summers is on the line," Jill said to his back as he waved and walked out of the office.

* * * *

Dee entered the office and glanced around the empty room. She shook her head and then picked up a stack of mail from her assistant's desk and walked down the hall to her office. She put her briefcase on her desk and started unbuttoning her jacket. A sound came from the corner of the room, causing her to jump.

Dee was startled to see Ben standing there. She had not expected anyone to be in her office, least of all him. The dream she had had of him flashed through her mind, making her blush.

"Good afternoon, Ms. Meyers."

She removed her sunglasses and looked down, fidgeting with her briefcase. *Oh, man, this is all I need right now. Where is everyone? And why is Kimmy not at her desk?*

"Good afternoon, Mr. Harrison."

"Your assistant wasn't at her desk, so I thought I'd wait in here. That's not a problem, is it?" he said as he stepped in her direction.

Please don't come over here, she said to herself. *Please don't come over here—shit.* He walked slowly toward the desk. The scent of his cologne was intoxicating, and she could have sworn his personality emitted an electricity she could feel.

Studying her with a mischievous smile and a gleam in his eyes, he said, "Tan and cream are your colors, though I doubt there are any colors that aren't right for you."

"Um, thanks... can I get you some coffee?" She turned away, trying not to look him in the eye, and walked around the desk, heading for the coffee machine in the lobby. He followed close behind, admiring her walk. "Coffee or tea, Mr. Harrison?"

"Ben."

"Excuse me?"

"Call me Ben."

"Okay, Ben, coffee or tea?"

"What are you having?"

"Tea."

"Great. I'll have the same," he said. He walked to the table, tilting his head and studying her closely. Her eyes were as dark as milk chocolate, with just a hint of innocence. "Are you feeling well? You seem a little tense."

Dee smiled. "Couldn't be better," she said. *Yeah, right. As if you don't know what that silky voice and those beautiful eyes do to women.*

"You have a beautiful smile," he said, unable to resist the urge to touch her. He reached up, his fingers lightly stroking her cheek, "with the cutest dimples I've ever seen." When his fingers brushed her cheek, she jumped. She felt electricity running from her cheek down to her toes and back to her stomach.

She wanted to scream. After spilling water on the table, she grabbed a handful of napkins to sop it up.

Ugh what are you doing, girl? Just calm down and breathe.

"Oh, I'm sorry. Let me get that," he said, taking the napkins from her and cleaning up the water. He looked at her, wondering if she had felt the electrical charge he had when he touched her. Smiling at her nervousness, he thought, *Man, is she gorgeous—big, beautiful eyes; a small, cute nose; skin the color of cocoa and the texture of silk.* He noticed just a hint of makeup. *Nice.*

"Come on and take me," she said.

"Huh?" he asked. His mouth suddenly went dry. He stared at her, taken totally by surprise at her offer.

"Cream and sugar?" She met his gaze, confused. "In your tea?"

He smiled and then blushed slightly. "However you take yours."

Dee gave him the cup, her hands still shaking. She moved her hand quickly, trying not to touch his. Taking her cup, she returned to her office. Ben watched her walk down the hall, wondering what had come over him. Putting her cup down, she sat down, pretending to look through a folder. He walked into the office and sat in the chair across from her. He leaned on the desk, holding the cup between both hands.

"So, Ben, how may I help you today?" she asked, flipping over a sheet of paper.

"Actually, I stopped by to invite you to lunch again."

She met his stare with her mouth open, not knowing what to say. Then she snapped her mouth shut and cleared her throat. "I'm sorry, but I have a really busy day planned."

"Well, you have to eat."

She shook her head. "No, thank you, anyway."

"Is there a problem with me?"

Casually, she brushed her hand on her skirt, trying to wipe her sweaty palms.

"No, I don't date clients."

He smiled. "What if we made it a business lunch?"

"I gave you all the information we had yesterday."

He nodded. "Okay." He tilted his head, watching her.

She broke eye contact, watching his hands, too nervous to look at him. *He has strong hands,* she thought, *strong yet smooth, with long fingers.* She realized she was staring. "Is there something wrong with the tea?" she asked, glancing at him.

He smiled, setting the cup down. "I don't drink tea." He then flashed the most gorgeous smile she had ever seen and winked. "I want you to know that I'll be asking you out again—soon. Have a good afternoon, Deanna." He stood, leaving the office.

Dee watched the door close, "What the hell just happened?" she asked herself.

* * * *

Ben walked out of Meyers Investigations smiling to himself. After getting into his silver BMW Z8, he closed his eyes and brought his hand up to his nose: the aroma of her perfume was still there from his gentle touch. He become instantly aroused. "Deanna Meyers, you're not going to know what hit you," he said, watching the building for a moment. Then he picked up his phone and called his assistant. "Jill, I need you to take care of something for me."

Dee was sitting at her desk trying to write a report for a case she had just finished. Her mind kept drifting back to Benjamin Harrison: his extraordinary eyes, his full lips. She wondered how it would feel to kiss those lips, how they'd taste. She closed her eyes, imagining how it would feel. There was a knock at the door. "Yes?" she said, returning her attention to her report.

"Dee, there's a delivery for you."

"Really?" Dee rose from her chair. She saw a delivery man carrying a box from Miller's Deli.

"I think this is some sort of mistake. I didn't order anything."

"No, this is the right address."

"Is this for Deanna Meyers?"

"Yes ma'am."

She frowned, trying to see inside the box. "Who is it from?"

"I don't know, ma'am. There's a card, though." He set the box down and turned to leave.

"Wait," Dee said. "Let me get you a tip."

"It's taken care of."

Dee leaned over and looked in the box. The lunch consisted of a grilled chicken Caesar salad and a lemon meringue tart for dessert. A small bottle of spring water and some sparkling cider were also included. On top was a small vase with a pink rose that had a card attached. Dee opened the card. It read:

I'd be honored if you would join me for lunch soon.
Benjamin

Dee couldn't help but smile. *Mr. Harrison, you're something else.*

* * * *

Ben sat behind his desk, remembering Deanna's nervousness when he had stood near her and the excitement he had felt. He brought his hand to his nose; he could still smell a trace of her. Smiling to himself, he rubbed the tips of his fingers together. Even now, he felt the tingle of electricity in the tips of his fingers from her touch. He knew she was reluctant to go out with him—he understood that she was a professional—but he wanted to spend time with her, to get to know her. He had to.

There was a knock on the door.

"Yes?"

Jill peeked around the door. "Sir, I have those papers you needed to sign."

He nodded, waving her in, turning his thoughts back to business.

* * * *

The hostess seated Dee and Holly. After giving the waitress their orders, Dee asked Holly, "How's Edmond?"

"He's good. I'm a little concerned for him now that he's working undercover, but I can't really say anything, because he worries about me for the same reason."

"He's a smart guy, Hol. I'm sure he's careful."

"I know, but I still worry. Where's Maurice?" Holly asked, smiling a thank you to the waitress as she set down her drink.

"I don't know. I'm through with him."

"Finally," Holly said, sipping her drink. "He is such a jerk. I never could understand what you saw in him."

"I don't know. I guess I thought I could change him. It's so hard to find the right man," Dee said, stirring her drink with her straw. "Most of the ones I meet are either too possessive or too insecure."

"You've dated a couple of good guys."

"Yeah, but they all turned out to be just friends. I wish I could meet a great guy like Ed. You guys have a great relationship—I envy you," she said, smiling at her friend. "I just want someone who loves me and respects me for who I am."

Holly reached across the table and squeezed her friend's hand. "Trust me, it'll come." The waitress brought their food. They thanked her and began eating. "So how's work?" Holly asked.

"Everything's good."

"No problems?" Holly asked, looking at her suspiciously. Dee thought of the incident at the hospital.

"No," she said, wagging her head.

"If it took you that long to answer, something must be up," Holly said, frowning.

"It's nothing," she said, waving her hand. "I have this new client who's been looking for a family member," Dee said, skirting the real issue. "I don't know if his real reason for wanting this person found is the one he gave us."

"Do you want me to check him out, see if he has a record?"

Dee thought about it for a minute.

"No, I'm sure he doesn't. He says he just wants to 'get to know' this person. I think there's more to his story, but I really don't think that he means them any harm. I guess I just get the feeling that he's not telling me the whole story."

"If you need any help, let me know."

"I will, besides, I don't think this guy is the criminal type. If he were, he would be the last person you would suspect."

"Is he the meek type?"

"No, the complete opposite: he is ambitious and strong—and gorgeous."

"Really?"

"Yes, with the blackest hair and the most beautiful green eyes I've ever seen."

"Yeah?" Holly sat up straight.

"Hol, you'd have to see this man," Dee said, shaking her head in amazement. "I don't even think gorgeous can describe him."

"Mmm. Sounds yummy. Is he single?"

"I don't know. Why do you ask?"

"I was just thinking," Holly said, stabbing a piece of broccoli with her fork. "Why don't you ask him out?"

"Girl, I can't do that," Dee said, pushing her food around on her plate. "Do you want to hear something funny, though?" she said, whispering. "I had a dream about him last night, and sometimes when he gets near me, I feel..." She looked around, searching for the right words. "I don't know—nervous, excited—I can't even describe it."

"Oh yeah?" Holly said, raising her brows.

"So today he comes to the office and asks me out to lunch," Dee said, leaning forward. "When I turned him down, he had lunch sent to me."

"No," Holly said, showing her amusement.

Dee nodded. "Sure did."

"I think you should go for it."

"No, he's a client. It wouldn't be professional."

"All's fair in love and war. I say if you find a good man, grab him by the balls no matter where you find him. Who cares if he's a client?" Holly said, making a fist.

Dee laughed. "You're a mess."

They ate in silence for a moment, and then Dee said, "I talked to Terry."

Holly grunted.

"She said she met some new guy."

"Na-uh, you don't say?" Holly said sarcastically, pretending to look surprised. "So, what's going on with her and David?"

"I don't know. They were supposed to be working things out, but from the way she sounded this morning, it might be over between them."

"You know, the only reason she went out with David was that she knew you were interested in him."

"No... I don't think so. Things just didn't work out between us," Dee said.

"Yeah with a little help from her, I might add. Every time he came around, she was right there, wagging that tail and batting those beady eyes at him." Dee laughed at that. "Seriously," Holly continued. "She's always been that way. Remember Mark and Jamul and... what was that cop's name?"

"Who, Greg?"

"Yeah, that's the one. Don't you see a pattern here? Plus, all that nonsense with Maurice." Holly shook her head as she spoke. "She's just wicked."

Dee laughed again. "You sound like grandma."

Holly giggled and said, "I know. I got that word from her."

They both laughed.

"Anyway," Dee said, "all those other guys were just friends, and Maurice was a pig."

"That's not the point," Holly said quickly.

Dee nodded, raising her hand. "It's not important, and besides, I'm not going to argue with her over some man," Dee said. "She's my cousin."

"I don't see how you can put up with it. I just tolerate her skank ass for your sake, but it means I always have to watch your back. Never know—with a vulture like that lurking around."

Dee laughed. It was true, as long as she had known her, she had always had her best interests at heart. "Girl, you're crazy. Being a cop and dealing with all those nuts is starting to mess with your mind."

"I'm serious, sometimes you are so naive when it comes to her," Holly said. "Besides, I told grandma that I would look after you when mom moved to Atlanta with her. You know grandma agrees with me that Terry lied about the reason for needing that rent money, with all that stuff about someone breaking in and robbing hers."

"She said that so-called friend of hers, Randy did it," Dee said.

Holly's arms flared outwards. "Yet she didn't even call the police."

"Maybe she was afraid?"

"No, she wasn't. I saw her at the mall with him a few weeks back, and she didn't look scared to me. She looked like she was in shopper's heaven." Dee knew that her cousin had conned her; she had just felt the need to protect her. "I don't know, I just feel sorry for her."

"That'll change one day. You're going to get tired of being used—wait and see," Holly said as she got up from her seat. "Have to go to the ladies' room. Be right back."

A few moments later, Dee saw Terry approaching.

"Hey," Terry said, smiling as she made her way to the table.

"Hey, I thought you couldn't make it."

"Change of plans. Where's the heifer?"

Dee's look scolded her. Terry sucked her teeth. She sighed and rephrased her question: "Where's Holly?"

"She went to the ladies' room."

Terry sat in Holly's recently vacated seat. "I had a fight with David," she blurted out.

"Oh, I'm sorry," Dee said. "What happened?"

"It's so confusing—let's not talk about it now," Terry said.

"Okay, but if you need to talk, I'm here."

"I know, but you know what? I ain't sweating it. Like I told you, I want someone to thrill me, someone who can move me."

"The only moving you need to do is to move your sorry ass out of my seat."

Terry looked up at Holly's smiling face. She sucked her teeth. "Heifer."

Holly turned to Terry looking her up and down. "Wench."

Terry stood, letting Holly slide into the seat.

"This seat is awful hot. Must have that burning itching thing again, huh?" Holly said, taunting Terry.

"I don't have to put up with this, you self-righteous bi—"

"Come on, Hol. She's upset. Give her a break," Dee cut in, attempting to defuse the situation.

"Sure," Holly said, laughing. Terry sat down facing Dee.

"Like I was saying before I was so rudely interrupted..." She cut her eyes over to Holly. "I need someone to move me."

Dee looked at Holly. Holly put her hands up to ward off her inevitable quip. "I'm not saying anything. That one was just too easy."

After dinner, The three of them stood outside the restaurant.

"Come on, let's hang out," Terry said.

"I have to work, Terry," Dee said, buttoning her coat against the cold October night.

"Aw man," Terry pouted, "I don't want to go home yet."

"You should go home to your son," Holly injected.

"If you must know, he's with his grandmother," Terry said, rolling her neck

"Well, you can ride with me," Dee said, "but I have work to do."

"Why would I want to do that?" Terry said indignantly.

Dee looked at Holly. "Hol, why don't you guys do something?"

Holly snorted, looking at Dee as if she had lost her mind.

"Please, I'd rather have a root canal."

"Nobody wants to hang out with your ugly ass anyway," Terry yelled.

Holly laughed, opening her mouth to respond.

"Okay, ladies, back to your neutral corners," Dee yelled, stepping between them. Terry looked at Holly angrily. Holly responded by smiling sweetly, which pissed Terry off even more. "Come on, let's go." Dee said, leading them toward the cars. "You two are going to drive me crazy yet."

Chapter 4

Dee walked into the kitchen. She looked at the time; it was 9:35 A.M.

"Hey, good morning, sleepyhead," Holly greeted her. "I just made coffee. Want some?"

"Thanks."

"Worked late again last night?" Holly asked.

"Yeah, cheating wife in a hotel room at two thirty in the morning while her husband was away on a business trip."

Holly shook her head. Dee looked over Holly's outfit; she was wearing a sage scoop-neck sweater and dark green slacks. They accented her red hair and blue eyes. "That outfit looks great on you. Do you have a date with Edmond?"

"Mm-hmm, after work."

Dee took the cup Holly offered her and went into the living room, where she sat on the sofa and pulled her legs under her. Holly followed her, sitting in the armchair across from her. "So, what did you do last night?" Dee asked.

"Ed's cousin had a get-together last night—you know, just hanging out at his house. I told him I'd meet him after our dinner." Dee nodded her understanding. "So, I get there at about nine thirty and ring the doorbell, and Ed's cousin Sam comes to the door and lets me in. As I walk in, Ed's uncle Walter is walking down the steps. When he saw me he yelled, 'Which one of you all let some white bitch in my house.' I was in such shock that I froze. Ed walked to my side and told his Uncle Walt that I was his girlfriend. The next thing I know, his uncle is yelling that no one in his family is going to be with a white so and so—and that he didn't want my white so and so ass in his house." She glanced at the cup she was holding, her blue eyes glistening as she blinked, trying to keep tears from welling on their rims. "Girl, that hurt me like you wouldn't believe."

Dee heard the pain in Holly's voice and wished she could say something to make it go away. She couldn't imagine how it must have felt to know that the family of the man she loved would reject her simply because of her race. Dee had met a couple guys who weren't black that she would have considered dating, but she had never done it. She thought people still had too much hate in their hearts to accept someone for who they were, instead of the color of their skin.

Holly took a deep breath. "Then I started crying, and Edmond freaked. He chewed his uncle out, and then Ed's sister Karen walked into the hall and started yelling at me, saying how she thought I just wanted to take one of the better black men away from a sister. She said it with such contempt..." She set her cup on the coffee table and rubbed her eyes with the pads of her hands. "We ended up leaving and going to the movies. The rest of the evening, Ed didn't say anything. I know how he is, and I can just imagine him going over there and having it out with everyone today. Things could get ugly." She looked around the room and then sighed, looking at Dee. "I just want to be happy, Dee, and Edmond makes me happy. Why can't they see that I love him and that I'm not some white woman just out for kicks?" She looked at Dee wanting the answer but knowing she didn't have it either.

"I don't know, honey... I'm sorry," Dee said, looking down at her cup. "The way I see it," she said, looking back at Holly, "you are a wonderful person with a heart of gold, and if they aren't willing to take the time to get to know you, they're just a bunch of morons who aren't good enough to be a part of your life anyway."

Holly rose from the armchair and walked over to the sofa. Sitting down, she hugged Dee. "You always know how to make me feel better."

"Hey, if I don't, you won't help keep my butt out of jail." They both laughed.

"So, what are you going to do today?" Holly asked, sitting back.

"I don't know. I thought I'd just—"

They heard a key in the door.

"Hi," Terry said as she walked in.

"Can't you knock?" Holly asked.

"I have a key."

"Only for emergencies, man," Holly said, shaking her head. Terry walked to the armchair and sat down.

"What are you guys talking about?"

Dee looked at her. "Nothing, really. What brings you out so early?"

"I needed to ask you a favor—well, two actually."

Dee smiled. "You don't say."

Terry looked at Dee and rolled her eyes, but she let the comment go. "First, can I borrow your olive scarf with the beads on it?" she rushed in. "I promise I'll take good care of it and give it right back."

Dee thought for a moment. "I guess so."

"Be right back." Terry stood, walking down the hall toward Dee's bedroom.

"You haven't even used that yet," Holly said, hoping Terry would hear her. "She's got nerve—I give her that."

Terry walked back down the hall, happily swinging the scarf in her hand. She shoved it in her purse. Then, plopping down in the armchair, she took a deep breath.

"The other thing is... I want to know if I can borrow your car for a few weeks."

"What?"

"It'll just be for a little while. My car needs some bodywork, and Wayne is going to have it fixed and painted for me."

"No."

"Come on."

"And just what am I suppose to drive?"

"You can use one of the company cars."

"No, I can't. That's the key word—company."

"Oh, come on. It'll only be for a little while—two weeks, two and a half tops."

"What if I were to let *you* use one of the company cars?"

"No," Terry whined. "Those cars are so ugly. I can't drive that."

Dee massaged her forehead. "Terry, I need my car."

Holly asked, "Who the hell is Wayne?"

"He's some guy I'm seeing. We're just having fun—no big deal."

Holly shook her head. "Oh, my goodness, what happed to Shawn and Greg and... oh, let us not forget David."

Terry sucked her teeth. "Girl, you know how I roll. I won't settle down 'til I find the *right* man."

Dee groaned. "Terry, you can't keep living your life like this. You don't only have yourself to think about—you also have your son."

"Why do you always have to give me a hard time? Every time I turn around, you're riding my back. All I did was ask you for a favor. I don't need a lecture."

"Terry, I'm only telling you this for your own good. You can't live from day to day. You need some stability. I just think you really need to reevaluate your life."

"What the hell is wrong with my life? My life is just fine. I get my bills paid, I have a roof over my head, and I have a car. What else do I need?"

"You have other people doing everything for you. That includes paying your bills and taking care of you and your son. You need to take responsibility for yourself."

"Why do you always have to tell me how to live my life every time I ask you for a simple favor?"

"Terry, I help you out wherever I can—and you know it—but you also have to help yourself."

"You don't do anything for me without making me feel like shit. What kind of help is that? I'm tired of this mess," Terry yelled, jumping from her seat. "I can't take it anymore."

Holly was becoming angry. Out of the corner of her eye, Dee saw that look on her face.

"Hol, let it go. She's upset."

"Upset about what?" Holly said, now standing too. "Upset because she can't get her fucking way all the time?" She turned to face Terry. "You have no reason to be upset or tired."

"Hol, calm down," Dee said.

Holly stepped in front of Terry, hands on her hips. "You can't possibly be tired from working—you have no job."

"Why are you up in my business?" Terry yelled. "This doesn't even concern you!"

"Hmm, could you be tired of going to school? No, I think not," Holly said, putting a finger to her chin. "Not smart enough for that." Terry looked at her, her lips pinched together, daggers shooting from her eyes. "Or could you be tired of being a freeloading, greedy, manipulative bitch."

Terry stepped toward Holly, shaking with anger. Dee was on her feet in no time. Holly looked at Terry with such rage that Dee was afraid for Terry, since she didn't seem to have enough sense to be afraid for herself.

"I dare you," Holly said through clinched teeth.

Terry looked at her then laughed. "I'm outta here," she said. She grabbed her coat and purse and headed for the door. Turning, she gave Holly one last look saying "stupid white bitch", then slammed the door.

"Holly, you need to not let her get to you, you know how she is."

"You still let her take advantage of you," Holly said.

"I just don't want to cause her any pain. She's been through so much."

"But it's not your fault her parents died when she was a child. It's not your place to fix her pitiful life."

"I know. I've just always felt that I needed to protect her, even when we were kids."

Terry's father, Thomas Meyers, worked as a PI for Dee's father, William. When Terry was eight, Thomas was working on the case of a woman who was defrauding an insurance company. Her boyfriend was a thug and was upset that she was being investigated. He threatened Thomas and the other employees at Meyers, but they got the information to prove that she was committing insurance fraud. The case went to court, and even though Dee's father told Thomas that he shouldn't go to court to testify, that the insurance company's attorneys had all the information they needed, Thomas wasn't going to let some punk intimidate him, and he decided to go anyway. The accused lost the case and was sentenced to two years probation for insurance fraud. Her boyfriend was furious. He followed Thomas and the attorneys out of the courtroom, pulled out a gun, and shot two of the attorneys and Thomas Meyers, killing them all.

"Dee, she's a twenty-five year old woman. She should be able to take care of herself. You can handle anything from nailing insurance scammers to standing up to cheating lovers that you've busted—in addition to keeping your personal life in order—but you can't say no to your parasite cousin." Holly threw her hands up. "I just don't get it. I have to go to work."

Holly grabbed her coat from the coat tree. She looked at Dee and smiled. "You know that I love you. You're the only sister I have. I just want to look out for my baby sister."

"Girl, you only have me beat by seven months."

"I'm still older." She walked up to Dee and hugged her tightly."I'll see you later."

Dee sat on the sofa thinking about the altercation between Terry and Holly. As much as she hated to admit it, Holly was right. She sighed, lying down and resting her head on the arm of the sofa. The phone rang; she lazily reached over and picked up the receiver. "Hello."

"Good morning, Deanna Meyers, please."

"Speaking."

"Hello, this is Ben Harrison." His silky voice glided through the line. Dee was quiet for a second. "Hello?" Ben said.

"Yes?" Dee answered.

"Deanna?" He waited for an answer. When he didn't get one, he continued, "How are you?"

Dee took a deep breath. "What can I do for you, Mr. Harrison?"

"Ben."

"Ben, what can I do for you?"

"You can have lunch with me."

"I don't think that's a good idea," she said, shaking her head.

"Call it a business lunch if you like. There are a few things I need to talk to you about."

Dee swung her legs from the sofa, sitting up. She looked around the living room, thinking, *What harm could it do?* There was no sense in hanging around here all day.

"Sure, why not? Where shall we meet?"

"I'll have my car pick you up in two hours."

"Let me give you my address."

"I have it. See you soon."

Dee sat holding the phone for a moment, then hung up. She went into her bedroom to get ready. She picked out a camel-colored cashmere sweater-skirt set. "No, this is a casual business lunch," she said aloud. "A little too much for a Saturday morning." She opted for a pink chunky knit sweater and black corduroys. She held the outfit in front of her, looking in the mirror. Pleased with her selection, she laid it on the bed. As she undressed, she thought about when Ben was in her office, the way he had made her feel when his fingers touched her cheek. Man, was he fine. "Okay girl," she said, scolding herself. "This is business, and we don't mix business with pleasure—no playing in that yard." Dee went into the bathroom to get ready.

One hour and forty-five minutes later, she was checking herself in the mirror. "Hello?" someone called from the living room. She walked out to see Terry sitting on the arm of the couch, a huge smile on her face.

"Terry, was there something you wanted?"

"I decided I'll take the company car."

"Hmm, really?"

"Yeah, I guess so," she said with a sigh. "Keys please." She held out her hand.

"You'll have to meet me at the office on Monday."

"But it's Saturday. What am I supposed to do until then? Oh, Dee, come on," Terry whined. Dee knew that the driver would be there any minute and didn't want Terry there to stir things up.

"Wait a minute," she said. She walked into her bedroom and returned a few moments later with her purse. She dug out her keys and handed them to Terry. "Here. Take my car and we'll work something out later this afternoon."

Terry Smiled. "Thank you." She walked to the door and then turned to look at Dee. "So, where are you going?"

"Nowhere," she said, pushing Terry towards the door. Just then, there was a knock. Dee sighed and opened the door.

"Hello, Ms. Meyers—"

"Hold that thought. Terry, don't you have somewhere to be?"

"No, not really," Terry said, smiling at the man standing in front of her.

"Yes, you do," Dee said, pushing her out the door as she invited her guest in.

"Who is that?"

"No one."

"Hi," Terry said, leaning over to get a look.

"Bye, Terry. Be careful with my car."

"But—"

"Bye," Dee said, closing the door.

"I'm sorry about my cousin. Sometimes she can be a little overwhelming, but she's harmless."

He smiled. "No problem, ma'am. Shall we?"

"I need to grab a couple of things." She ran into the bedroom and switched from a brown purse to a black one, dropping her door keys inside. After checking herself in the mirror one last time, she walked back into the living room. "Ready." She grabbed her black leather coat from the coat tree and they walked out of the apartment.

A dark gray Mercedes sat at the curb. The driver opened the rear passenger door. Dee smiled at him. "Can I ride in front?"

"It's protocol to ride in the back, ma'am."

She nodded her understanding and then slid into the back seat as the driver closed the door. After driving in silence for a while, Dee sat forward, leaning over the seat.

"So, where are we going?"

"Mr. Harrison asked me not to say."

"Ah." She looked out the front window. "Can you tell me your name?"

He looked in the rearview mirror at her and responded, "Michael Kellam ... Mike."

"Hi Mike, I'm Deanna." She reached over the seat and shook his hand. "So, Mike, how long have you worked for Mr. Harrison?"

"Six years."

"Do you like him?"

"He's a fair man—a good guy to work for."

"He seems pretty laid back."

"He has a bit of a temper."

"Oh yeah?" Dee was surprised.

Mike seemed thoughtful. "I guess he is laid back, for the most part."

Dee waited. Noticing that he wasn't going to say anything more, she asked, "Has he ever lost his temper with you?"

"No, he treats me fairly, talks to me like a person instead of a servant."

She nodded, looking around her. As they turned into the park, Dee peered at Mike.

"I thought we were having lunch."

He smiled as he pulled the car off to the side of the road. Ben was leaning against a tall white oak. When the car stopped, he walked over and opened the door.

"Good afternoon, Deanna," he said as he held his hand out. She slid across the seat, reaching for his hand. When she touched his fingers, she felt the warmth of his soft skin. His fingers gently stroked the back of hers, sending a chill up her arm and causing heat to rise in her cheeks. She looked at him, wondering if he had noticed; if he had, he didn't show it. They walked down a path to a heated gazebo with glass windows. As they walked inside, the classical sounds of Erik Satie's "Gymnopédie" and the aroma of fresh-cut roses drifted toward them. The table in the center of the room was set with a white tablecloth and elegant fine china, complete with crystal champagne glasses and crystal candleholders housing white tapered candles. Dozens of red roses sat in tall vases throughout the gazebo.

Dee looked at Ben, and he winked at her. Then he walked around to one of the chairs and pulled it out for her. "I hope you like French."

She smiled, walking to the proffered chair. "I love it," Dee said as she sat down. Three men wearing black tuxes walked into the gazebo carrying silver serving trays and begin to serve their meal. One waiter walked over to the wine bucket, from which he plucked out a bottle of Bordeaux and showed it to Ben. Ben nodded, and the waiter opened the bottle and poured some into the glass. After Ben tasted it and nodded again, the waiter filled their wine glasses. Dee sat quietly, watching everything. The waiter served hors d' oeuvres of prawn cocktail and escargots. Using her appetizer fork, Dee picked up one of the escargot, putting it in her mouth, she heard a faint squeaking as she chewed. She frowned slightly, not caring very much for the flavor, then putting her fork down, cleared her throat.

"This is a surprise."

"A pleasant one, I hope?"

"Yes, to say the least, but why are you doing this?" she asked, studying him.

He smiled, a secret thought playing on his lips. "I'll tell you later," he said, his eyes meeting hers. "How's the case coming?"

"It's coming along." She dabbed at her mouth gently with her napkin. "Can I ask you something?"

"Sure. Whatever you want."

"Why do you really want to find Nancy Greer?"

"The reason I gave you is true: my father had another child and I want to find him or her. My father died twelve years ago, and my mother just told my sister and me about the situation. We have no other family, and even though we don't know each other, we are, in fact, family."

Dee still had a feeling there was more to it, but she figured she'd let it slide for now. She watched him as he ate. She couldn't figure him out—he didn't know anything about her, yet he had gone through such trouble to have this lunch arranged.

He looked up, meeting her gaze. Her heartbeat quickened. "No more talk of business," he said, setting his fork down. "Tell me about Deanna Meyers."

She hesitated. "Okay, what do you want to know?"

"You're not what someone would expect when they think of a PI." She sat forward, resting her elbows on the table. "Tell me, what did you expect?"

"I expected some really big guy who looked like he eats nails for lunch."

"That would have been my father. I took over the business a couple of years ago."

"Do you have a large family?"

"Just my mother and grandma—they live in Atlanta—and my cousin, Terry. And there's Holly."

"Another cousin?"

"No, Holly is my best friend, but we're more like sisters. We have been since third grade."

"And your father?"

"He died four years ago in an auto accident. A year after that, my mother moved to Atlanta to help my grandma." Dee picked at her food. "What about your family?"

"My mother and sister are all I have." Dee looked into his emerald-green eyes and saw a look that she couldn't quite place, but it was gone as quickly as it had appeared. The waiters served the salad, which was a mixed organic greens with dill dressing. For the main course, they had Chicken Wellington. During the remainder of the meal, they talked about current events and their businesses. Ben waved for the waiter, who moved in and removed the plates. A second waiter moved in just as quickly and placed dessert in front of them. The raspberry soufflé looked delicious, and Dee loved it.

"Would you care to join me for a walk after dessert?"

"That would be nice."

Once they finished dessert, Ben rose from his seat and helped Dee with her chair. A hint of his cologne tickled her senses; she closed her eyes and briefly inhaled the woody oriental fragrance.

As they walked the path along Hyde Lake, Dee looked out over the water. She loved this time of year; it always reminded her of times she had spent with her family as a child. Along the path, they saw a father flying a kite with his children, the little girl looked to be about three or four. She squealed with glee as the kite did a tail spin, the colorful string hanging from the back making quick squiggles in the air. Dee smiled, glancing at Ben, and then looked ahead as they continued to walk.

"So," she said, "now can you tell me why you're doing all of this?"

"I'm trying to sweep you off your feet."

She looked at him in disbelief. "Yeah, right."

"No, I'm serious. I'm trying to sweep you off your feet," he said again, looking as if it were the most natural thing to say.

She stopped walking abruptly. She was dumbstruck, frozen for what seemed like forever before she spoke. "You can't be serious."

He slipped his hands in his coat pocket. "More serious than you know." He smiled, his eyes sparkling.

"Why?" she asked, her face a mask of confusion.

"Since the first day I met you, I've thought about you constantly; you've even invaded my dreams."

She looked at him as though he had lost his mind. Her guard went up and she took a step back, putting distance between them. "Are you one of those deranged rich people who think they can do whatever they want to whomever they want?"

The question drew a laugh from him.

"You know what? I'm outta here." She turned to walk in the direction they had just come from.

"Wait a minute," he said, following her.

"You're crazy," Dee called over her shoulder as she quickened her pace, trying to put even more space between them. He caught up with her, stepping in front of her. She moved to one side and he did the same, not letting her pass. "Get out of my way," she said, her jaw set, looking straight ahead at his chest.

"Have you ever thought of me?" Ben questioned, trying to look her in the eyes.

She glared at him. "Why would you ask me that?"

"Because I want to know. Well, have you?"

She put her hands on her hips. Then, taking a step closer to him, she took a deep breath, looked him squarely in the eyes, and lied, "No."

Ben squinted a little and smiled. "I hope you are a lot better at investigating than you are at lying."

Dee looked around, fidgeting. "You don't even know me—you know nothing about me."

His smile broadened. "But I want to get to know you."

She sighed, shaking her head slightly, taking another deep breath. "I don't date clients, Ben."

"I can change that," he said.

Her head snapped back in his direction. "Oh, my gosh! You can't be serious."

"Yes, I am. I didn't really think about it, but I can always find another PI— although not as good as you, I'm sure." He flashed an incredible, dazzling smile, and she couldn't decide what she wanted to do more, kiss him or punch him. She turned from him and headed up the path.

"You are crazy," she said, waving him away. "Don't come near me."

He followed. "No, I'm not. You intrigue me. I want to get to know you— that's all. I'm not looking for commitment, and I don't just want to get you into bed. I just want us to get to know each other." He stepped in front of her again. She looked at him, frowning.

She slid her hands into her coat pockets and then turned to look at the water. "We come from different worlds."

"I won't give up. If you keep running, I'll just keep chasing you." She heard him say it, his voice wrapping around her like a warm blanket, but she was in a daze and could not be sure of what she was hearing. She glanced at him, and he took a few steps back, spreading his arms out. "Or you could take pity on this poor, pathetic soul and give me a chance."

Dee watched this incredibly handsome man standing before her with his arms outstretched, asking her to spend time with him. This was the last thing she had anticipated that morning. She was shocked, but before she could think, her mouth started working. "Okay, let's just see where today takes us." *God I can't believe I just said that,* she thought.

"Fair enough," Ben agreed, stepping next to her. The wind picked up a little, whipping around them. Dee pulled her coat tighter around her neck. "Are you cold?" he asked.

"No, not really," she said, shaking her head, her teeth chattering. He took his scarf off and wrapped it around her neck. She glanced at him wide-eyed as he did so, but made no move to stop him. "Better?" he asked.

She nodded. He gestured toward the path and they continued their walk.

* * * *

"Thank you. I had a wonderful time. Good night," she said as she slid across the seat and stepped out of the car. Ben got out of the car and walked around her to the apartment door, opening it for her. She stopped to study him and then walked by and up the steps with him following. When she reached the door to the apartment, she turned to face him.

"Thank you again."

"May I?" He asked, holding out his hand, and looking at her keys.

"I think I can take it from here," she said. She turned, opening the door, then turned back to him. He smiled down at her. *Please don't kiss me,* she thought. *If you do, I swear I'll pass out.* Her heart started racing, and her palms became sweaty. She hoped he wouldn't notice the shakiness of her voice. "Thanks again," she whispered. "I really did have a wonderful time."

"No. Thank you." He leaned close. She stopped breathing and closed her eyes. His lips lightly brushed her right cheek and he whispered, "Good night," so low she wasn't quite sure that he had said it. She watched him walk down the steps, taking a deep breath and willing her heart to slow down.

When she walked into the apartment, the smell of roses hit her. "Whoa," she said, looking around. Holly walked down the hall, her overnight bag on her shoulder. "Hey, where did these come from?" Dee asked, pointing to all the flower arrangements.

"I should be asking you that," Holly said, eyeing her. "What did you do to earn all of this?" she asked, gesturing.

"I went out with someone and had a great time," Dee said as she took off her coat, hanging it on the coat tree.

"From the smile on your face, and all the roses that were delivered this afternoon, I'd say someone had a great time."

"You'll never guess who I went out with."

"Who?"

"No, guess. You'll never guess."

"Okay, let me see." Holly smiled mischievously. "A florist?"

"No."

"Not an undertaker!"

Dee rolled her eyes.

"Well then, just tell me."

"Okay, okay. I went out with the client I told you about."

"No. You didn't!" Holly said.

"Yes, I did."

"Oh, my God! Tell me. Tell me everything!" Holly said as she dropped her bag and sat down on the couch. "Come on—tell, tell."

Dee sat down next to Holly. "Well, he called and asked me out and had his driver pick me up. He even found out where we lived on his own. You know I like a man with ingenuity," Dee said. Holly laughed. "Anyway, we went to the park, where he had lunch catered—French." Dee wrinkled her nose. "Then we went for a walk in the park. When we got back to the car, he talked to the driver, but I couldn't hear what he said. Then we drove to the Pizza Pub and he had a pizza delivered to the car because, he said, he noticed that I didn't care for French food. Then we went to the museum and a wonderful Italian restaurant for dinner."

"So," Holly asked, shaking Dee's arm and grinning, "when are you going out again?"

"I don't know." She paused. "He's very considerate and sweet. I've never been out with someone like him. It was the little things he did, like ordering the pizza and rubbing my hands to warm them—since I forgot my gloves—and always looking into my eyes when I spoke, as if what I was saying were so important."

"Just give it time and don't start looking for anything negative," Holly said. "You never know. This could be the one."

* * * *

Terry slowed the car down to look at the apartment building. Sitting in the borrowed car, she scanned the parking lot and saw Holly's car parked on the far end. "Shit," she said softly. "I'll have to come back tomorrow." She turned the car around and drove away.

* * * *

"What?" Terry said as she snatched the ringing phone from its base.

"Terry, wake up!" Dee yelled in the phone.

"Mmm..."

"Come on, Terry, wake up."

"What?"

"I need my car."

"Dee, I'm sleeping," she said groggily.

"No, you're not sleeping anymore. You're bringing me my car."

"Dee, let me keep it till tomorrow?"

"No! I want my car now."

"Dang, girl, why you gotta be like that?"

"I have things I need to take care of."

"Why don't you get that hottie I saw in your apartment to drive you around? I'm sure he has a car."

"No. I'm not going to get anyone to do anything," she said, raising her voice. "I'm going to drive myself around when you get your butt up and bring my car."

"Okay, you don't have to yell. I hear you. I'll be there soon." Dee hung up and started getting dressed.

Three hours later, Dee heard a key in the door and rushed into the living room. "Hello," Terry said, stepping in the door.

"Well, it's about damn time. I told you I had things to do."

"Well I'm here, ain't I?" Terry said, her tone curt.

"Three hours late," Dee said, snatching the keys from of her hand and grabbing her coat from the chair.

"Can you drop me off?"

"No," Dee said, walking out the door. Terry flopped down on the sofa, folding her arms. Looking at her, Dee gritted her teeth. At the moment, it was all she could do not to strangle her cousin.

"Just come on," she yelled.

Moments later, they were pulling from the curb. "Where do you want to go?" Dee asked.

"I was going to go get my hair done, then to the mall." She looked at Dee. "Do you think you can take me both places?"

"No, I can't," Dee said impatiently, tapping the steering wheel as she waited for the light to change.

"Well, I guess I'll go to the mall then. So, who was that guy I saw at the apartment?"

"None of your business."

"Why? What's the big secret? Is it because he's white?"

"What would that have to do with it?"

"Because you have some strange white dude in your apartment and push me out the door, you know, I just figured."

Dee looked over at her, shaking her head. "You're a mess."

"Then why won't you tell me?"

"Because there's nothing to tell. Why are you so interested?"

"Because he's kind of cute."

"You think so?" Dee asked, wondering if she would have felt the same way had she known Ben's driver was the man she had seen.

"Sure, in a Barney Fife-Opie Taylor kinda way."

"Girl, you're hopeless."

"So..." Terry put her feet on the dashboard; Dee leaned over and pushed them off just as quick. "What's his story?"

"He has no story. I'm doing some investigating for the company he works for."

"What's the name of the company?"

"Harrison Enterprises."

"An executive, huh? So, hook me up."

"No way."

"Why not?"

"You have enough on your plate as it is."

"C'mon, don't be like that. Hook a sista up."

"No."

Terry sucked her teeth and crossed her arms. "Fine, be like that."

Dee dropped Terry off and was headed to the supermarket when her cell phone rang. "Hello."

"Hello, sweetheart." Ben's rich voice poured through the line like melted butter. *He has a wonderful voice,* she thought. *I could listen to it all night.*

"How are you?" he asked.

"I'm fine."

"Yes, that you are," he said.

She smiled. "So, how are you?"

"I'm great, now that I hear your voice. What are you doing right now?" he asked.

"I'm headed to the supermarket."

"Why don't you meet me for a late lunch or early dinner?"

"We had lunch together yesterday."

"There's no law that states we can't get together two days in a row."

"I don't know," she said, feeling anxious about moving so quickly.

"What can I do to talk you into it? I'll take you anywhere you want to go: New York, L.A.—I'll even take you to Italy if you want—just say the word."

"You're persistent."

"I know. When I want something, I stop at nothing."

She was quiet.

"Are you still there?"

"Is that what this is all about, getting something you want? Am I to be one of your possessions?"

"No, that was just a figure of speech. Are you always this suspicious?"

"I'm still trying to figure this out, still trying to understand what's going on here."

"Okay, I understand. You're a beautiful young woman, and I can see why you would want to be careful." He took a deep breath and paused as if he were afraid to ask the next question. "What about lunch?"

"Let me think a minute." On the other end, Ben waited patiently. He heard a horn beep, followed by Dee calling someone an idiot. "Okay," she said finally. "Do you have a car?"

"Of course."

"I mean one that you drive yourself?" she said sarcastically.

"Yes."

"Be at my place at six thirty. Leave your driver at home."

"Oh, sounds fun. See you then."

Chapter 5

Ben knocked on the door at six fifteen.

"Hi," Dee said, opening the door.

"Hello, sweetheart," Ben said. He stopped to run his eyes over her. She wore a light blue sweater and jeans. "I was hoping to catch you off guard." He smiled mischievously.

"Not a chance, buddy," she said, stepping to the side and making room for him to walk around her. "Come on in."

Ben walked in, looking around. The couch was a bright green with a high back, while the armchair was yellow with red stripes. The first thought that went through his mind was that the decor was whimsical. The walls were painted gold, bringing the odd colors of the furniture together. There was an Art Deco-style coffee table and an end table on each side of the couch; there was a small lamp on one and papers and books on the other. Colorful throw pillows were scattered on both the chair and sofa.

"Hi," Holly said, coming out of the kitchen.

"Holly, this is Ben Harrison. Ben, my best friend, Holly Lawson."

Holly looked at Ben, smiling slyly, and then at Dee, raising her eyebrows.

"Nice to meet you, Holly."

Edmond walked out of the bedroom.

"And this is Holly's boyfriend, Edmond James."

The two men exchanged greetings and then Holly offered to make drinks. She and Edmond left for the kitchen.

"Safety in numbers?" he questioned.

Dee gave him a crooked smile. "Have a seat," she said.

Edmond walked back into the living room carrying a tray of tall glasses.

"So, Edmond, what do you do?"

"I'm a police detective."

"I'm sure that's hard work."

"Yes it is, but I like it." Ben smiled at Holly.

"And you, Holly?"

"I'm a cop too."

Ben nodded. "Do you two work together?"

"We work out of the same precinct, but we don't go out on calls together," Holly said. "We'd be so busy worrying about each other that the bad guys would make off with all the loot." They all laughed.

"May I use your bathroom?" Ben asked.

"Sure," Dee said, "you can use the one next to my room." She pointed down the hall toward her bathroom.

Ben walked in and closed the door. The bathroom had cream wall tiles, black and cream floor tiles, and a black and cream claw-footed tub. The mirror looked antique, with black frame and vintage photos around it. After using the bathroom and washing his hands, he opened the door leading to Dee's bedroom. The walls were light aqua, while the furniture was cream, probably vintage. There was a small table and chair on the left side of the bed and a tall, narrow bookshelf by the right. The bedding was rust and gold, with a West Indian motif and many pillows, and a cream rocker with a large teddy bear on it sat in the corner next to the bathroom door.

A few minutes later, after Ben had not yet returned, Dee rose and went to the bathroom to check on him. "Everything okay?" she asked, knocking.

Ben quietly closed her bedroom door. He opened the bathroom door, pulled Dee in, and closed the door behind him. "Miss me already?"

He was standing inches from her. Unable to think with him standing so close, she instinctively backed up. "No, I was just checking on you. Is everything okay?" she asked, reaching for the doorknob.

"Leaving so soon?" He placed his hand over hers.

She quickly moved her hand, putting it on her hip. "Do you make a habit of lurking in other people's bathrooms?" she asked.

He smiled. "Do I make you nervous?"

"Of course not," she said, sticking her chest out and thrusting her chin up.

He laughed. "You look beautiful in blue."

"I thought cream and tan were my colors."

"If I remember, I said you'd look gorgeous in any color."

Dee looked at him, and smiled.

"Dinner's ready. We should go."

"I like it better in here." He stepped closer. "You smell great," he whispered, smelling her hair. He felt a stirring in his pants.

Dee sidestepped him, quickly opening the door, and walked out of the bathroom. She called over her shoulder. "You coming?"

Ben followed, watching her butt as she walked.

They had oven-fried chicken, zucchini pilaf, and mixed veggies. After they finished dessert, Dee's apple pie, they played a game of Pictionary. Dee was good at drawing the clues, but horrible at guessing them. Although he and Dee lost every game they played, Ben didn't care; he was just happy to be there.

"They really skunked us in there," Ben said later as they walked toward his car hand in hand.

"Yeah, but we'll get them next time," she said as they stopped next to his BMW. "Nice car."

Ben leaned on it and then pulled her gently between his legs, putting his arm around her waist.

Dee tried to look away; he put a finger on her chin and turned her face toward him. "Do I scare you?"

"No."

He watched as she bit her lower lip.

"Maybe just a little."

He smiled. "Don't be afraid." His seductive voice warmed her. Dee looked deep in his eyes and she felt as though she were falling into a whirlpool. She closed her eyes and took a calming breath. When she opened her eyes, he leaned in and kissed her. Everything started spinning.

Dee felt something swirl inside her, a sensation she had never felt before. It started in her brain and ended in her groin. *Whoa, Nelly,* she thought. She tried to pull back, but he held on to her.

"Let me take you to lunch tomorrow?" he asked.

"I have a lot of work to do."

He nodded, pulling her close again. He brushed his nose against hers, kissing her gently on the lips.

"Good night, sweetheart."

When he released her, she was shaking all over. She heard someone say "Good night" and then realized it was her. She backed away from the car. He sat there waiting for her to walk back into the building before he started the car. Inside the lobby, she watched as his car drove away. As it did, she passed her fingers across her lips.

* * * *

Ben reached for his coffee cup. He took a sip and grimaced at the cold, bitter taste. It had been four days since he had had dinner with Dee, and for the past four days he had tried to get her to spend time with him. They talked on the phone, but her schedule had made it impossible for them to get together. He could scarcely think of anything else—the way her voice sounded like music when she laughed, the softness of her lips when he had kissed them. He could still remember the delicate but intoxicating aroma of her perfume. His member sprang to life with excitement, and he shifted in his chair trying to find comfort. He'd called Dee earlier asking if she could meet him for lunch, but she had said she had a case that she was trying to finish and had given him a rain check.

The intercom came to life. "Mr. Harrison, Ms. Summers is on the line." He drummed his fingers on his desk, watching the light on the phone. When she didn't hang up after five minutes, he picked up the receiver.

"Hello, Janet."

"Hello, lover," she said, her voice sexy. "I've missed you."

Sighing, he asked, "What do you want, Janet?"

"I wanted to see if you're free later, maybe, we could get together?"

He closed his eyes. "I have plans."

"Benjamin, we have a good thing going. Why are you trying to ruin it? Come on, let me fix dinner for you."

Ben knew he should have talked to her about the night they had spent together; he just hadn't known what to say. Today, however, he jumped right in.

"Janet, I'm sorry about the other night, about what happened between us; it should never have happened." He paused. "I don't want to send you the wrong message."

"No, I didn't get the wrong message."

"I think you did," he said, spinning his chair round to face the window. "Listen to me: we are not going to see each other again. I'm sorry if that hurts you, but—"

"Okay, if you can't see me tonight, I'm not going to push you. How about some other time?"

"No, Janet."

She was quiet.

"I have to go," he said firmly. "Take care of yourself." He hung up before she had a chance to say anything else. Turning back to the desk, he flipped through his Rolodex. Picking up the phone, he punched in the numbers that he read off the card.

"Hello?" the man on the other end said. Ben identified himself, and then he put his plan to work.

* * * *

"What about the Saunders investigation? Do you know if Chris got that information yet?" Dee asked Liz, looking up from the notepad on her desk.

"Mm-hmm." She nodded as she pushed her glasses up.

"Okay, can you take care of those things on the list right away?" Dee said.

"I will," Liz replied before leaving the office.

Rubbing her eyes, Dee looked at the phone, remembering her last call, in which she had turned down another lunch invitation from Ben. She wanted to spend more time with him, but she had a lot of work to do. *Maybe it's for the best,* she thought. *This is why I can't keep a man.* Picking up the file on her desk, she put it in her bag and then slipped the bag over her shoulder. "No sense worrying about what could have been," she said aloud. Rising from her chair, she grabbed the digital SLR camera, a mini tape recorder, and a camcorder. On her way down the hall to the lobby, she called out to Kimmy, "Can you ask Chris to give me a call when he gets in?"

"Sure thing."

Dee opened the top draw of the file cabinet and took out a small tin box that held the keys to the two company cars, which was empty. "Chris has the other car," Kimmy said.

Dee walked outside, got in her car, and put the equipment and her jacket on the back seat. She would have preferred not to take her own car on this assignment and regretted lending Terry the company car. She hated taking her own car on a stakeout; whenever she did, something always managed to happen to it. As she drove, she shook her head from side to side and tapped on the steering wheel, singing with the music. After going through a yellow light that was turning red, she checked her rearview mirror for a police car. There were none, but she did notice that a blue Honda Accord had gone through the red light with her. She instinctively memorized the tag number and tried to get a look at the driver. The driver had on a baseball cap and sunglasses, and his visor was pulled down. She made a right on a side street, then two lefts, watching her rearview as the Honda did the same. She drove another mile, making a few turns here and there, and the car continued to follow. That was when she decided to pick up her cell phone.

"Hey, Hol, I need a favor—I need you to run a tag." She recited the tag number then waited. "Ah, no, everything's fine. Thanks."

Dee pulled over onto the shoulder and got out of the car. She leaned casually on the front hood, looking in the opposite direction of the approaching car. The Honda pulled in behind her. The driver took off his cap and glasses, got out, and walked toward her. Dee spoke, still looking in the other direction.

"Mr. Harrison, to what do I owe the pleasure?" She turned and looked up at him. Her heart raced a little.

He smiled. "Hello, sweetheart."

"Well?"

"I wanted to see you in action."

"Did you now?"

"I'm pretty good, aren't I?" He smiled proudly.

"I've been following you since you left your office."

Dee looked down and kicked a rock with her sneaker-clad foot. "So, Mike let you use his car?" she asked.

"Yes, and I let him use mine. He has the day off."

Dee bit her bottom lip and nodded. "Where are you off to?" she asked.

He leaned on her car. "I was hoping that I could go with you."

"Why would you want to do that?"

"I'm interested in seeing what you do."

"It's pretty boring stuff. I doubt it would interest you."

"I'm more interested than you know."

With her head cocked quizzically to the side, she asked, "Is that the only reason?"

"No," he answered, feeling suddenly nervous. "Like I said, I want us to get to know each other better. I understand you have to work, and I thought I could help."

She looked at the ground for a moment with a thoughtful expression on her face; then she looked up at him and nodded. "Okay, follow me."

He started back to the car and stopped. "How did you know this was Mike's car?"

She merely smiled and got in the car. He followed her to a shopping center. She waited for Ben to park and then pulled up beside him. "Hop in," she yelled. "Where to?" he asked once he was seated.

"Just outside La Salle," she said as she pulled out of the parking lot. He looked over at her and leaned over to kiss her cheek.

"Did you miss me?" he asked.

She hesitated. "No," she said, not taking her eyes off the road.

He laughed.

"What's in the bag?" she asked, glancing at his lap.

"I bought you lunch," he said, flashing a brilliant smile.

"Thanks." She stole a glance at him as he reached into the bag, taking out a couple of turkey sandwiches and cups of hot tea and coffee. *This man is too good to be real,* she thought.

"If you pull over, I can drive while you eat," he said, holding the sandwich in front of her.

"No, I'm good." She snatched the sandwich from him and began munching on it while she drove. They drove east on Route 64 toward Sycamore, then turned off the main route onto a remote road heading southeast.

After another twenty minutes, she pulled off to the side of the road.

"What are we doing here?" Ben questioned as they got out of the car.

"We have to head into the middle of those woods," she said, pointing to the dense forest. "Insurance fraud. Pretty cut and dry—I just need to get some shots," she said, holding up her camera. Ben nodded.

After they had walked a quarter-mile from the road, Ben asked, "So, what sort of insurance fraud case is this?"

"This guy is a welder. He's suing his former employer for fifty thousand, claiming he was hurt on the job and is unable to work," she said, pushing tree branches aside as she walked. "We found out he's been doing freelance work out of a workshop he's set up here." They stopped a few yards before the clearing. "This is it." Up ahead another forty feet was what looked like an abandoned barn with the top-floor windows boarded up. Squatting down behind some shrubbery, Dee looked over at Ben. "I need to get a little closer to take the shots."

"Do you want me to go with you?" he asked.

"No," she said as he looked at her anxiously. She smiled. "It'll be a piece of cake. You wait here." She walked quietly to the side window then peered in, after using the sleeve of her tee shirt to wipe the window clean. She saw her subject; he appeared to be welding an eight-foot-long piece of fence. She took three shots then waited, watching him bend another piece of steel. She then took a few shots of that.

While moving over a little to get a better look, Ben accidentally kicked a piece of tin. The two immediately heard barking coming from the shack. Dee turned around and ran back to where Ben was. The door opened, and the man's six foot six frame filled the doorway; he was wearing a scraggly tee shirt that looked like he had worn it for a month. He reminded Dee of a psycho killer from an old B-movie. *Oh shoot,* Dee thought. *He's a big one.*

"Who's out there?" he bellowed, looking from side to side.

"Ssh," Dee said, putting her finger to her lips and pulling Ben down a little more.

"I said, who's there?" he yelled again, craning his neck, trying to see the entire yard. "Satan, Damien, git' 'em."

Ben looked at her, confused. "What do we do now?"

"I suggest you run," she said as she jumped to her feet, taking off before Ben had time to process the information.

A moment later, he saw two black Dobermans come running out of the shack toward him. Ben spun on his heels and stumbled, but then regained his balance and started running. Dee was screaming, "Run!" at the top of her lungs, her mind willing her own legs to move faster.

With their legs pumping furiously, they ducked and weaved through the brush, crashing into tree branches all the way. Ben expected to be ripped limb from limb at any minute; his heart was beating so loud he could hear it. When they saw the car, Dee grabbed her keys out of her jacket pocket and pushed the remote to unlock all the doors at once. They ran up the embankment to the car, and Dee slid across the hood; she hit the ground on the other side then quickly got in. Ben opened the door and got in, not daring to peek behind him to see where the dogs were. Dee dropped the camera and put the key in the ignition; it turned over just as the dogs slammed into the side of the car.

"Whoa!" Ben said, jumping from the thud. Shifting the car into gear, she took off, the spinning of the wheels spraying pebbles from under the tires. Ben rested his head on the dashboard. After he had managed to convince himself that he wasn't having a heart attack, he looked back to see if the monster from the shack had decided to jump in his vehicle and follow them. He took a deep breath, trying to calm himself down. Dee glanced at him and then turned back to the window.

"Are you okay?" she asked, her voice filled with concern.

Ben looked over at her. "That's twice in a little more than a week that some man has wanted to break you in half."

She glanced at him quickly. "Yeah, it's been a slow couple of weeks."

"Do you always have this affect on men?"

"Well, it seems they either love me or hate me," she said matter-of-factly. "Sometimes one changes into the other."

Ben watched her profile, impressed at how collected she was. She noticed his look and started laughing. "You should have seen the look on your face," she said.

He threw her a bemused look, as though she had lost it, and then he started laughing too. "That was quite an adventure. I can honestly say that I've never been that scared in my life. Is it always like this?"

"No, it's mostly hurry up and wait." This seemed to puzzle him, so she explained: "You know, hurry up and get to the stakeout and then wait until something happens. It usually takes days, or even weeks."

"Have you ever been hurt?" he asked with concern.

"I've been doing this awhile. Sometimes things happen."

"So, you have been hurt."

"Not anything major. I've had people try to take my camera. I've been thrown around a little. I've even been popped a time or two." Ben was surprised at how nonchalant she was about this. "But I give as good as I get." She smiled a mischievous smile. Ben watched her closely. *I'd like to throw you around a bit,* he said to himself. He thought about throwing her on a bed covered with red satin sheets, she wearing nothing but that tee shirt she had on, while he wore red silk boxers...

"Earth to Ben," he heard her say. He looked at her with a blank stare.

"Hmm?"

"Man, what were you thinking about?" His blank stare turned to one of desire. "Never mind. I don't want to know," she said, waving her hand. The adrenaline was still pumping through her, and she felt highly aroused. Being confined in this car with him was hard enough without him adding fuel to the fire. "I need a drink to settle my nerves," she said, taking one hand from the steering wheel and rubbing her eyes.

"That's a good idea. What's your poison—sherry, scotch?"

"No, I'm going to need something stronger," she said as she pulled into a donut shop parking lot. "Hot chocolate with extra marshmallows."

She put the car in park and got out to see how much damage the dogs had done. There were deep scratches and a dent on the passenger door where one dog ran into it. "Son of a bitch," she said, sighing heavily, bending over to get a closer look at the damage.

"I'll get your hot chocolate," Ben said, heading for the donut shop.

When he got back, Dee was sitting in the car. She had just finished writing her report. "Here you are, sweetheart."

"Thanks," she said. She sipped the cocoa. "Mmm, good stuff. I'm sure you have a lot of pressing things to do and certainly a lot more interesting than running through the woods being chased by ravenous dogs."

"There are a few things I could be doing that would be more interesting." He eyed her seductively, grinning. She squirmed in her seat, looking out her window then back at him. He was still watching her. Her phone rang. *Saved by the ringer,* she thought as she flipped it open.

"Hello."

"Hi, Dee. It's Chris."

"Hey, Chris."

"I went to the pier and got those pictures. With those, and the information you have, we should be able to wrap this one up," he said.

"Great, I'll swing by and develop those photos in the morning," she said.

"Okay. Hey, by the way, I got that info on the Harrisons if you want it now."

"Sure, what do you have?" she asked.

"The Harrisons are a pretty straight-laced family: Mother and father married thirty-eight years. Two kids. Lisa, twenty-three, single, no kids, in college—law school, to be exact—until this fall. I guess she needed some time off. And Benjamin, thirty-two, now CEO of Harrison Enterprises. He took over the business when he turned twenty-five. Went to Harvard. Never married, no kids. A favorite with the ladies, though. No criminal record. No scandals to speak of. That's all I've got."

"Good job, Chris. Thanks."

"No problem, boss." Dee closed her phone. *A ladies' man,* she thought to herself. *I can see that.*

"Everything okay?" Ben asked.

"Sure, everything's fine," Dee said, starting the car. "So, are you seeing someone?" she asked unexpectedly.

"Where did that come from?" he asked.

"Nowhere. Just thought I'd ask."

"I was seeing someone for a while."

"And?"

Ben didn't want to tell her that he'd just broken up with Janet. "And we're no longer seeing each other."

"What happened?"

"Things just didn't work out."

"Why?"

"What about you?" he asked.

"Don't change the subject," she responded quickly.

"I'm not."

She eyed him closely.

"Really," he said, becoming serious. "Okay," he said, putting his cup in the holder. "We went out for a while. At first it was good, but then we began to argue about any and everything. That's when it was decided that we'd part ways."

"Were you in love with her?" Dee asked.

He shook his head. "No, I cared for her very much, but I wasn't in love with her. Now can I ask you something?"

"Sure."

He turned sideways in his seat, watching her as she drove. "What are you looking for in a man?"

After a few moments of silent thought, Dee answered, "Someone who's strong and who loves life. A leader, but someone who doesn't have a problem with me leading sometimes."

Ben smiled wickedly. "Sounds interesting."

Dee glanced at him. "The woman I saw you with at the coffee shop—that was your girlfriend."

"Yes... no... I mean, she's the woman I was seeing."

"Have you ever dated a black woman before?"

"No," he answered without hesitation.

"So why now?" She looked at him, taking her eyes off the road longer than she should have.

"I don't understand?" He shook his head slightly.

"Why now? Why me? I know you meet women all the time. Why would you want to spend your time with a middle-class black woman who would take you to work with her and almost get you mangled?"

"I still don't think I understand your question."

"You're thirty-two years old and have never dated a black woman. Why now?"

"None of them were you."

"Come on. I'm being serious here."

"I am too."

"But I'm not white."

"So, is my being white a problem?"

"Yes... I mean, not to me, but to a lot of people."

"If you and I don't have a problem, then there is no problem."

"You've never dealt with racism." She shook her head as she spoke. "You don't know what it's like. I have to live with it—not on an everyday basis, but I live with it nonetheless."

He sighed. "Look, I can't say that I know what you go through, or that we won't have problems while we're seeing each other, but I can say that I will protect you whenever I can."

"How can you protect me? Maybe you can protect me from some jerk on the street or in the supermarket, but how about someone in your family?"

"My family is not like that," he said defensively.

"How do you know?"

Ben realized he didn't; they had never really talked about interracial dating. He didn't know what their views were. "I'd like to believe my family is above that," he said tightly. When she spoke, her voice softened. "But you really don't know they are, right?"

Ben was silent, not liking the turn the conversation had taken.

"Okay, say your mother thinks you should be dating someone white, and she tells you this. What are you going to say to her?" She sighed heavily. "Look, Holly and Edmond have gone through this. Some of his family treat her like garbage, and although he tries, he can't stop them. Would you be willing to stand up to your family over something like that?"

Ben remained quiet for a long time. Dee looked over at him, feeling sorry for having brought up the subject but believing that they needed to discuss it.

"Have you ever dated someone of another race?" Ben asked as he looked out the window.

"No, I've met a couple of guys I wouldn't have minded dating. But then I see Holly when she comes home in pain because some idiot called her something awful, and I think I might have made the right choice to avoid that situation." She shook her head in disgust.

They drove the rest of the way in silence, both lost in their own thoughts but wanting to be a part of the other's.

When they got back to Mike's car, Ben asked, "Can I take you out to dinner?"

"Thanks, I really appreciate the offer, but I have another surveillance to do tonight."

"Okay," Ben said. "Be careful, sweetheart." He leaned over, letting his lips brush her cheek. She wanted to ask him not to leave, that she was willing to take a chance with him, but she couldn't bring herself to say it.

* * * *

Sitting in the back of a smoke filled lounge, Jake Williams looked over his beer mug at his mark. He watched, as the man leaned close to the woman sitting next to him, whispering in her ear. Jake checked the time: 10:45 P.M. He had been waiting two hours for this guy to leave, so that he could make his move. He heard someone laugh, and turning to his left, he saw a slim brunette, sitting with two other women. He thought she sounded a lot like his girlfriend, Peggy. She had a deep throaty voice, with short brown hair, and a small frame, just like Peg. Well, Peg use to have a small frame, Jake reminded himself. He grunted loudly, and rolled his eyes, and sat his mug down. That was until she went and got her dumb ass pregnant.

Peg had told him, that her getting pregnant was a mistake, that she had been taking the pill everyday. But Jake knew differently, he knew that she had gotten pregnant on purpose. For the past year, the only thing Peg ever talked about was them getting married and having a baby. Jake told her that he wasn't the marrying kind, but she kept right on pushing. Then a few months ago, she told him that she was going to have a baby. He took a swig of his beer as he thought back to that awful August evening. She made a big deal out of preparing a nice dinner and dressing all sexy. Then she gave him an envelope. He opened it pulling out a greeting card with a teddy bear on the front and on the inside it read, *Congratulations to a new daddy.* He was speechless; he looked from her, to the card, then back to her. She just sat there smiling at him, telling him how happy she was and how wonderful things were going to be. She just didn't know how close she had come to him strangling her to death. It was supposed to be just the two of them; a kid would only complicate things. Jake sighed heavily and shook his head slightly. Looking up, he saw his mark rise, kiss his companion on the cheek, and walk towards the exit. "Time to go to work," Jake said standing, and following the man out of the lounge.

* * * *

Ben drove back to his office. While sifting through his mail, he stopped at a large pink envelope. It didn't have a return address, and his name was written across the front in beautiful script. Knowing it had to be from Janet, he started to throw it into the wastebasket, but then, realizing that someone might see it, he decided to take it with him. He sat it on his desk. As he flipped through the rest of his mail, his mind drifted back to the conversation with Dee. He had never given much thought to the reactions others might have to their relationship. How would he handle it if his mother or Lisa had a problem with them seeing each other? What if they fell in love? Would he be willing to choose between his family and the woman he loved?

He sat down, reading one of the contracts that Jill had placed on his desk for him to sign. He dropped his pen, realizing he couldn't work now; he needed time to think. He stood, tucked the pink envelope under his arm, and walked out of the office, heading to his mother's home.

Ben walked into the study, sitting at what had once been his father's desk. This was where he had come to work and sort things out. The rich smell of leather lingered in the air. He had always liked the study; it was his favorite room in the house. It always reminded him of his father. Even though Benjamin Harrison Sr. had been a shrewd businessman and a stern father, he had also been a good father, and after all these years, Ben still missed him.

Lisa knocked on the door, peeking in. "Are you busy?"

"No." He sat up straight. "Come on in. I was just going to come up and see you."

"What are you doing in here, working?"

"No, just thinking."

"About Daddy?"

"Yeah."

"I come in here and try to think of him too sometimes," she said thoughtfully, "but the older I get, the harder it is to remember his face." Ben watched as she struggled to hold back her tears. Lisa was eleven when their father had died, and while he had spent time with her, he had spent more time at work and had missed much of her childhood. "What did you do today?" she asked, trying to lighten the mood.

"Not a whole lot."

"Mother was trying to locate you earlier. She tried your cell several times."

"I didn't have it on. Why? Is everything all right?"

"Yes, she wanted to talk to you about some woman named Janet who stopped by."

His jaw tightened. "Did she say what she wanted?"

"No," Lisa said, watching her brother closely, "but she told mother she was your girlfriend."

Ben brought his left hand up and rubbed his eye with his knuckles.

"Ah, I thought that was the case," she said after watching his reaction. "When did you break up?"

"It's not important," Ben said. "I want to ask you something."

"What's that?"

"What do you think about interracial dating?"

"Nothing, really."

"Nothing?"

"No, not really. I don't have any friends who are in an interracial relationship, so it's never been an issue."

"Okay, let's say your friend Kelly was dating a black man. How would you feel?"

"I don't know, Ben. It's hard for me to be hypothetical with a situation like that. Plus, Kelly and I are not as close as we used to be."

Ben looked at the desk, contemplating another angle, then decided to come out with it.

"What if I told you I was interested in a black woman?"

She was quiet for a moment. "Are you?"

Ben looked into her eyes, trying to gauge her reaction. "Yes, we've just started seeing each other," he answered.

"That changes things," Lisa said.

"Does it?"

"Mm-hmm." She nodded.

"How so?" Ben asked, resting one elbow on the desk and placing his fist under his chin.

"Because you're my brother and I'd be worried that you didn't know what you where getting into."

"For example?" Ben prompted.

"Well, for example, there are different cultures and beliefs."

"That's true," Ben said, "but she could be white, Dutch, and Catholic."

"Yes, but I think the difference would be more pronounced with a black person, or even an Asian, for that matter. I think you'd notice the difference more, because you see the difference. And as much as people don't want to admit it, we always see the differences in others—we just don't like to say it out loud." She looked at him earnestly. "Also, there are many narrow-minded people out there, and it could affect you professionally."

Ben was quiet for a moment. "Anything else?"

She placed her hands on the desk, sighing. "Yes, on the other hand, I've realized in the last year that life is too short; you're not promised tomorrow, and you can't let society dictate whom you can fall in love with." Her voice softened a bit. "I can't decide who is right for you. I think you should follow your heart." Ben looked at his little sister, marveling at how much she had grown up in the past two years.

"Thanks, sis," he said, smiling.

She stood up, walked around the desk, and kissed him on the cheek. "Sometimes, we all need a pep talk." She turned, leaving the study.

* * * *

As Dee sat in her car waiting for the subject to leave the nightclub, she thought about her conversation with Ben. Maybe she was being too cynical, she thought. She imagined what her mother would say if their relationship turned serious. Dee nodded as if she could hear her mother's voice saying, "Baby, if you're sure this is what you want, and the two of you have thought it through, you do what makes you happy."

Then she laughed, thinking about her grandmother. She wouldn't question her about his race, merely about when they would get married and give her a great grandchild. Her cell phone rang. She let out a long breath and then answered.

"Hello."

"Hi, sweetheart."

"Hi, Ben." Her voice perked up a bit.

"Do you have a few minutes to talk?" he asked.

She looked around the confines of the car and laughed. "Oddly enough, all I have is time."

"I've thought a lot about what you said today."

"Look, I've been doing some thinking too, and maybe I was being too cynical."

"No, you made valid points, and I want to talk about them."

"Okay."

"You asked me, 'why you'? You are the most incredible woman I've ever met. Your skin color doesn't matter to me. You're exciting, fun, and beautiful. Any man of any race would be a fool not to want to be with you." He took a breath. "And as far as my family goes, well, we'll just have to cross that bridge when we come to it. I don't know what will happen between us, but I do know that I can't turn back now, not unless I knew there could never be anything between us. And I also know that if we decide we do want a relationship, anyone who tries to come between us will have hell to pay."

Dee sat in silence, watching the people milling around in front of the club.

"Deanna, are you still there?"

"Yes," she said softly. Then she took a deep breath. "I really like spending time with you—and maybe we won't have to go through the things Holly and Edmond have to deal with." She blew out a breath. "So let's see where we go from here."

"Good," he said. "Can I ask you something?"

"Sure, what is it?"

"Will you have dinner with me tomorrow?"

"Oh, I guess that can be arranged."

"Good night, sweetheart."

"Good night, Ben."

Ben pushed down the receiver and then lifted his finger, letting it pop back up again. He dialed, then sat back listening impatiently to the ring on the other line.

"Hi, this is Janet. I'm not here to answer your call, so please leave a message and I'll call you as soon as I can." *Beep.*

"Janet, this is Ben. I need to see you—"

"Hello?" she said, picking up the phone.

"Can I come over?"

"Sure," she said, excited.

He hung up without saying goodbye.

"Hello, lover," Janet greeted him, leaning seductively on the door. "Come on in."

Ben walked past her into the living room; he turned to look at her, taking in her red see-through teddy. She walked up to him and began running her fingers down his chest. "I knew you couldn't be without me for long."

"Janet, why did you visit my mother?" Her hand stopped moving. She looked at him, not knowing what to say. "Janet, we talked about this and decided that we weren't going to see each other any longer."

"No," she said, taking a step back. "We didn't decide anything—you decided."

He brushed his hair back. He didn't want to have this conversation with her again.

"Janet, what are you doing?"

"I'm trying to show you how much I love you." She stepped close to him, sliding her arms around his neck.

He grabbed her arms and dislodged them, bringing them down to her sides. "Janet, you can't do this."

"But I know you want me."

"No, Janet. I'm seeing someone else," he blurted.

"What?" she whispered, shock and disbelief showing on her face. A moment later she spoke, her voice filled with anger. "No you're not! You're lying! You're trying to make me beg!"

"I'm sorry, Janet. I didn't want to tell you this way, but I keep telling you: it's over. I don't want you to go to my mother's home again, and I don't want you to call her. I want you to stay away from my family." He walked to the door and then turned to look back at her. "I mean it, Janet," he said, reaching for the doorknob. As he closed the door behind him, he heard a small whimper.

Chapter 6

"Mr. Harrison, you have a call on line two."

"Who is it, Jill?"

"She won't say."

His lip twitched in anger. He snatched the receiver from its base. "Yeah?"

"Hello, Mr. Harrison," Dee said. "Did I catch you at a bad time?"

He smiled at the sound of her voice. "It's never a bad time to talk to you."

"I have some free time; I was wondering what you were doing for lunch."

"Having it with you."

Dee gave him the address of a restaurant where they could meet.

"See you soon," he said. Then he put on his suit jacket and walked across the room.

"Mr. Harrison, a package just arrived for you," Jill said, standing in the doorway and holding a small package.

"Thanks, Jill," he said, taking the package and heading toward the limo.

"Afternoon, sir," Mike greeted him a moment later.

"Good afternoon, Mike." Ben slid into the back seat and tore open the package, which contained a gift box. He frowned when he opened it, seeing red lingerie and a card. He dropped it on the seat next to him, knowing immediately that it was from Janet. *What am I going to do about her,* he pondered on the ride to the restaurant. *Maybe I need to have another talk with her.* He looked at the driver. "Mike?"

"Sir?" he answered, looking in the rearview mirror.

"Have you ever had a problem breaking up with a woman?"

The other man chuckled. "I work hard enough getting them to go out with me."

Ben smiled as he watched the man's profile. Shaking his head slightly, he decided it would be best to ignore her. When the limo pulled up in front of the restaurant, he picked up the items on the seat next to him.

"Mike, could you get rid of this for me?" he said, handing him the package.

"Yes, sir."

"I'm glad you called," he said, kissing Dee's cheek.

"Is something going on at work? You sounded a little intense when I called."

"No, sweetheart, everything's fine." He gently stroked her arm. After they sat down, she reached into her purse and took out a file, handing it to him.

He opened it and read:

Nancy Greer moved to Bethel, Maine, in September 1984. She worked as an accountant for 5 years in Bethel. She then moved, leaving no forwarding address.

"We should have more in a week, maybe sooner."

The waitress returned with their food. Dee picked up one of her BBQ ribs with her fingers, taking a small bite. Ben watched her with fascination. *How can someone eat something so messy and look so sexy?* She reached for a napkin; he slowly reached for her hand.

"Here, let me," he said, pulling her hand towards him. He put her fingers in his mouth, slowly, and sensually licking the sauce off, letting his tongue linger on the tips.

"You're not eating," Dee said, her voice bringing Ben back to reality. He grinned sheepishly, as he slowly picked up one of the ribs. Groaning inwardly he took a bite.

After lunch, they found the limo waiting outside.

"Can we take you back to the office?"

"No, I have my car," she said, jerking her head in the direction of her bug. "Do you have plans this evening?" she asked.

"No, what do you have in mind?"

"Pick me up at six," she said as she turned away. "And wear something casual," she called over her shoulder as she walked toward her car.

* * * *

"Hey, I thought I was going to pick you up?" Ben said, meeting Dee at the elevator.

"Change of plans," she said, kissing him quickly. He pulled her closer before she could turn away.

"You'd never believe the dream I had about you coming here to see me."

"Yeah?"

"Oh yeah. Maybe you can make it come true," he said, tracing her jaw line with his finger.

"Are you almost ready?" she asked, moving away from him. She walked into the living room and looked at the window. "Hmm." The outside wall had an 18′ x 8′ arched window. "Magnificent view," she said, looking at the city below.

"Isn't it wonderful?" he said, standing behind her. "Would you like a tour?"

"Sure," she said, looking around the living room. Earth tones predominated, making the room seem warmer. There was a brick fireplace with a marble hearth and double size easy chair in front. The hardwood floors shined like glass. The furniture was camel colored, with tasteful pieces of art placed throughout the room. He led her to the kitchen, which was complete with a glass plated refrigerator and glass ceiling fan. The bathroom had a whirlpool tub, a granite counter-top and floor, and a built-in TV. She looked at him. "To watch the stock market," he said. He walked to the door on the opposite side of the room. "And this is my bedroom. Enter at your own risk," he said, leaning against the door-frame.

Dee paused, looking at him, then walked around him into the room. The furniture was rich maple, and the room had a black carpet. The bedding and curtains were a subdued gold and black. It suited him—it was rich and exotic.

"Do you like it?"

"It's nice," she said, looking at the artwork. He walked behind her, putting his arms around her waist. He nibbled her ear and bit her neck gently. She closed her eyes as she felt him become aroused. "We really should be going," she said, trying to pull away from him. He held her close.

"Are you sure?"

"Yes, I'm sure," she said, nodding. When he released her, he noticed her blushing as she quickly walked around him.

She waited in the living room while he got dressed. When he walked in, he was wearing a pair of dark slacks, a dark sweater, and black Prada loafers.

They walked out of the elevator and into the lobby. "Can we take your car?" Dee asked. "Sure, if you want to," he said, reaching into his pocket and pulling out his keys.

"I'll drive," she said, reaching for them with a huge smile on her face. He hesitated and then reluctantly gave her the keys. Sitting in the car, Dee looked around. "Nice, a girl could get used to this," she said.

She started the car and pulled out of the parking garage, driving to where she had parked her car. "Sit tight," she said, getting out. She walked to her car and took a box out of the trunk. Opening the back door, she put the box behind him.

"What's that?" he asked.

"No peeking," she said, sliding behind the steering wheel and driving away.

"Where are we going?"

"It's a surprise." She smiled as though entertained by a secret thought. She pulled into the parking lot of an old movie theater. "Ready?" she asked before opening the door. He looked ahead at the dark building.

"I don't know. Am I?"

She giggled. "You're in good hands. Let's go." She got out and walked to the back door. She then took the box out of the back and led him into the building. There were lights on in the lobby and in one of the theaters. Ben walked around slowly, looking at the abandoned building, wondering why they were there. "Come on," she said, looking back at him. She led him to one of the seats in the center of the theater. "Wait here. I'll be right back," she said, walking toward the back.

The lights went down low, and after a few minutes she came back with microwave popcorn and soft drinks. Sitting down, she said, "I know the couple who just bought this place, so we have it all to ourselves. Oh, I almost forgot." She reached into her purse and pulled out a box of Snow Caps and Gummy Bears. She wiggled her brows. "Can't forget the candy."

They watched the film—*The Notebook,* with Ryan Gosling and Rachel McAdams—and then went up to the roof. She spread out a blanket so they could sit. She took two thermoses from the box. "Hot chocolate and homemade beef stew," she said, holding up each as she announced what they contained. She reached into the box again and pulled out two cups and two bowls, a box of crackers, and marshmallows. She smiled, sitting on the blanket next to him. He watched her serve the food. "I thought it would be nice to go to the movies," she said, "but I also wanted to have you all to myself."

He smiled, nodding. Eating the stew slowly, he continued watching her. She blew on her stew then ate a large spoonful. He couldn't believe that she had done all this for him. He'd had women pamper him before, but never in such a sweet and simple manner. *You'd better watch out, man,* he told himself. *This one could very well steal your heart without even trying.*

Dee set her bowl in the box and looked at Ben. "All done?" she asked.

He passed her the bowl and helped put everything away. "And now we watch for shooting stars," she said. "For each shooting star you see, you get a kiss." She took another blanket out of the box and wrapped it around their shoulders.

"This is nice," he said.

"I see one," Dee said, pointing to the sky.

"I see it," Ben said, watching her.

She looked into his eyes, "No you didn't. You weren't even looking."

He looked at her longingly. "I see another one," he said, kissing her gently. "I like that you did this for me."

"Yeah?" she asked.

"Yeah," he answered.

In the dark, his eyes looked more aqua blue then green, but she still thought they were the most gorgeous eyes she had ever seen. She leaned forward, touching the small scar on the right side of his nose. "How did you get that?"

"High school football." She stroked it lightly then, leaning in close, she brushed the scar with her lips. Sitting back, she looked into his eyes.

"Did it hurt much?" He blinked. "Yeah, it hurt like hell, but I couldn't tell the guys that."

She in leaned even closer, kissing him again, her fingers lightly stroking his cheek. She sucked his lower lip gently then let the tip of her tongue brush lightly across his. He moaned. She nipped his lip playfully. His heart raced. She pulled back, her eyes still closed. Her lashes fluttered, and she opened her eyes.

"Did you see any more stars?" she asked, her breathing labored.

"Oh yeah," he said, taking her lips once more.

They drove back to the condo, arriving at eleven thirty. He had wanted to drive her home, but she had said that she needed to take her car and that it didn't make sense for him to ride with her and then have to take a cab back home. He walked into the bathroom feeling sexually frustrated. After taking a long, hot shower, he felt better. Walking to the bedroom wearing only a towel, he sat on the bed as the phone rang. "Hello."

"Hi, I just wanted to let you know that I got home all right..." She paused. "And that I'm thinking about you." He smiled at the sound of her voice.

"I'm glad you made it home safely, and I'm always thinking about you. It seems that's all I ever do these days." He closed his eyes, seeing her face. "Good night, sweetheart."

"Good night. Sweet dreams."

He hung up, running his fingers through his hair. He got up and walked into the bathroom. Dropping his towel, he stepped back into the shower.

* * * *

Russell Pemberton watched Ben from across the conference room table. Ben absent-mindedly tapped his pen on his notepad, hearing the meeting but not really listening. "Mr. Harrison?"

He looked around; everyone was watching him. He looked across the table at the man sitting opposite him. "Find out more about the merger; once you do that, we can plan our next step."

The man across from him nodded. Everyone stood, gathering their belongings and preparing to leave the conference room.

"How's it going?" Russell asked after everyone left.

Ben stood up. "Good."

"So, who is she?" Ben looked at him curiously. "The lady that's got you so out of it."

"What makes you think there's a lady?"

"Because you have the look of a man who has either met one hell of a woman or who has just won the lottery, and I'm sure it's not the latter—and in your case it wouldn't matter anyway."

Ben nodded and smiled. "Her name's Deanna."

"Sexy name." Russell paused. "Good looking?"

Ben looked down and continued gathering his notes. "Very."

"She'd have to be," Russell replied. "I haven't seen you at the club lately."

"I've been busy," Ben said.

"With Deanna, I bet?" Russell replied slyly. Ben was quiet. "Rick and Debbie are having their engagement party tonight. Are you coming?"

"I haven't given it much thought," Ben said, picking up his things.

"Well, why don't you come? You can bring your lady friend."

"Maybe."

"Come on," Russell said, leaning on the table. "I'm sure everyone would like to meet the woman who can tame the great Ben Harrison."

"Maybe. We'll see," Ben said, walking back to his office.

"Dee, Ben Harrison on line three."

Dee looked at the woman sitting across from her. "Would you excuse me please?" she said holding up her index finger. "Hello."

"Hello, sweetheart. I was calling to see if we could get together tonight?"

"I'm with a client. Can I call you back?"

"Talk to you soon."

A half hour later, Dee picked up the phone to return Ben's call as Terry walked into her office. "Hey," Dee said hanging the phone back on its base.

"Hi," Terry said, sitting across from her.

"I haven't seen you all week," Dee said. "Where have you been hiding?"

"Oh, I've been around," Terry said happily.

Dee sat back, folding her arms. "So, you came to bring the car back?" "No, I still need it for a little while. I just wanted to see how you were doing?"

"I'm good," Dee said, smiling. "How about yourself?"

"I'm okay," Terry said without much enthusiasm. Dee knew better than to ask Terry what was wrong, but before she knew it, her mouth started working.

"Is everything alright?" *Way to go dummy*, she said to herself.

"No, I really need help."

They sat looking at each other for a moment. Dee sighed. "With what?"

"Well, Wayne, the guy I told you about, you know, who was supposed to have my car fixed..."

"Yes." Dee nodded, not liking where the conversation was headed. "He got mad at me and decided he wasn't going to pay for it, but they've already done most of the work."

"What do you need, Terry?"

"Six hundred dollars."

"What?"

"That's how much it will cost to get my car back."

Dee shook her head, pressing the fingers of her right hand against her temple. "Okay. I know this guy who is looking for someone to do light filing and paper—"

"What are you talking about?" Terry said, a look of pure horror on her face.

"You can work for him for a few weeks and keep the company car until you get yours back."

"I didn't come to you looking for a job. If I had wanted a job, I would have gone to an employment agency. I need your help."

"Terry, I'm trying to help you."

"No, you're not. You're trying to run my life." She stopped abruptly. When she spoke again, her voice was softer. "Look, Dee, I just need you to lend me the money—just for a little while."

"Terry, you can't borrow money if you don't have a job."

"Man!" Terry yelled, looking around the room. "Why you gotta be sweating me all the time? Come on. I'm family."

Dee folded her arms. "Terry, I wouldn't be helping you by giving you money."

"Whatever," Terry said, waving her hand. "Fine, I don't need you, I can take care of myself." She rose from the chair and walked out of the office, slamming the door behind her.

* * * *

Dee sat on the bed, cradling the phone on her shoulder. "Is this a formal party?" she asked.

"It's at the country club, but since it's a weeknight, I'm sure it won't be formal. Besides, whatever you wear, you'll be the most beautiful woman there. I'll pick you up at seven."

"Okay. Bye."

She walked down the hall and into Holly's room, opened the closet, and took out a cream swing coat. She took a piece of paper and a pen off the nightstand and scribbled a note: *Holly, I'm borrowing your coat. Thanks, Dee.* She then returned to her room to get ready. In the bathroom, she stripped off her clothes and got in the shower. The hot water eased her tension, most of which came from the thought of going to a party at some country club. She knew she should get to know his friends, but she was nervous about it. Although she suspected they were just people like her, another part of her thought they were different. She always thought of people with money as snobbish and rude. Ben wasn't like that, but she thought he was the exception to the rule. She wanted his friends to like her the way Holly and Ed liked him. She was beginning to care a lot about him. Maybe things were moving a little too fast—they had been spending their weekends together, and now it was weekday evenings. She thought about his smile and the way her heart skipped a beat when he called her sweetheart. She thought about his eyes and the way they lit up when he laughed and how his voice became deeper when he was in the throes of desire. She reached up, brushing her fingers across her lips, thinking about the warmth and softness of his lips pressed against hers. Maybe things were moving too fast, but she didn't think she wanted to slow them down.

She stepped out of the shower, grabbed a towel and wrapped it around herself, and looked in the mirror. *Who are you trying to fool,* she asked herself. *You want to be with him every minute.* After she dressed, she put on her diamond stud earrings and looked in her jewelry box for her tennis bracelet. Taking everything out, she looked in the bottom. "Hmm," she said to herself, looking around the room. "I always put it back in here. Maybe Holly borrowed it. " She picked up the phone to call her and then changed her mind, hanging the phone up again. After checking herself in the mirror one last time, she left the bedroom.

She opened the door and stepped out into the hallway before Ben could knock. He froze, taking in her appearance. She wore a halter-style black jumpsuit.

"Whoa, you look great."

She smiled. "Thank you."

"I don't know if I want to take you out looking like that. I'll be fighting men off all night."

She looked at him with a sexy smile. "That was my plan," she said, winking at him. He ran his hand through his hair as she walked past him and down the steps. He watched her shapely body and wished he could take her home with him and make love to her for hours.

After checking their coats at the coatroom, Ben led Dee to the party room.

"Hey, glad to see you could make it," Russell said as he walked up. He shook Ben's hand.

"Evening, Russell. Russell Pemberton, Deanna Meyers."

Dee shook his hand. "Hi, how are you?"

"Nice to meet you, Deanna." Russell looked at Dee and then Ben. "Can I get you guys anything?"

"Scotch," Ben said, looking at Dee.

"White wine, please."

"Be right back." Russell turned and walked briskly toward the bar. Ben took Dee's hand and whispered in her ear, "Don't be nervous."

She looked at him. "Do I seem nervous?"

"Yes. Everything will be fine. They're just people." He squeezed her hand lightly to provide comfort. Then he led her farther into the room, in search of a table.

"Do you come here often?"

"Not in the last couple of years."

She looked around the room; everything seemed formal. "I can't picture you hanging out here."

"Really, why not?" he questioned.

"It seems so impersonal. That's not you."

He looked around, then back at her. "Some people might not agree with you on that. How do I seem to you?"

"Warm, caring—you're nothing like I would have expected someone in your position to be."

He looked at her, seeing the sincerity in her eyes. "Maybe I seem warm and caring to you, but others see me in a different light."

"I doubt that," she said, giving him a small smile.

"Do you?" he asked, raising his brows and tilting his head. She nodded.

Russell walked over. "Here you are," he said, giving them their glasses and sitting down. "So, Deanna, what do you do?"

"I'm a private investigator."

"You don't say?" he said, looking surprised. "How did the two of you meet? Did you set your sights on the big guy here and track him down until you caught him?" he asked, trying to sound humorous. Dee could tell he meant every word.

"No," Ben said, smiling, as his eyes pierced Russell's. "I pursued Dee, actually. After I had run for a while, she felt pity for me and decided to give me a chance. I'm still on probation."

"Fascinating," Russell said, amused. Ben looked somberly at him. "Well," Russell said anxiously, "I have to go find my date." He stood. "I'm sure I'll talk to the two of you later."

"Are you friends?" Dee asked, watching Russell walk away.

"We went to school together. He works for Harrison."

"Now he," she said, pointing at his retreating back, "belongs here."

After eating a light dinner, they walked around and mingled with the other guests. Rick, an attorney, was five four and slightly overweight; Debbie, his fiancée, was a couple of inches taller and very slim. Dee thought they were a nice couple. They had just built a new house on the lake in Valparaiso, Indiana, and they had invited Ben and Dee to dinner the following week.

The DJ played love songs for most of the night, and Dee made the comment that no one was dancing

Ben took her hand. "May I have this dance?"

She nodded with a smile, and he led her to the dance floor. He slowly enclosed her in an embrace, resting his hands on her hips. Dee looked around nervously, then at him as they swayed to the smooth sound of Jon B's "They Don't Know." They moved with the music, getting lost in each other's eyes. Dee felt like there was no one else in the room. This was her paradise, and they were the only ones allowed in. Ben took her hand and kissed her fingers while he looked deeply into her eyes. He was happy to have her in his arms and wished the moment could last forever. They danced into the next song. Dee looked around. "There's still no one dancing," she said.

"They usually don't dance here. They mostly mingle and make business deals. The wives come here to socialize." Dee looked at the DJ.

"Wait here. I'll be right back."

She asked the DJ to play something more upbeat and then walked back to Ben. "Dance with me," she said. As the music started, she moved from side to side, dancing to the beat. He followed her moves, keeping in time with the music. After catching the eye of one of the younger women, who was smiling and looking at Dee with adoration, she walked over to her and took her hand, leading her onto the dance floor. Before long, she had half of the women dancing. A few minutes later, Dee took a break; she and Ben sat at their table while the rest of the women continued to dance and have fun.

Debbie and her friend Sharon walked to their table. "Dee? Why don't you guys come sit with us? We have room."

"Sure, we'll be there in a moment," Dee replied, then turned to Ben. "Wanna dance?"

He looked at the dance floor, "I don't know? Looks like I'll be the only man out there."

Dee glanced over her shoulder at all of the dancing women. "I'm sure we can fix that," she said, taking Ben's hand and leading him to dance floor. A short time later, she had convinced several men to take the dance floor.

"You were a hit," Ben said proudly as they left the club. "Not really. Most women love to dance, but sometimes they're too shy. All they needed was a little encouragement. I want to take you to a real dance club."

"Okay, any time."

"How about tomorrow night? I know Holly and Edmond don't have to work, and I'm sure they'd love to go."

"Sure—whatever you want, sweetheart. Are you hungry?"

"No, I have to get home. I have a busy day tomorrow."

"Do you need me to tuck you in? I'm really good at it," Ben asked, standing outside of Dee's apartment door.

"I'm sure you are," she said, smiling at him.

"Maybe you could come to my house and tuck me in?" he said, pulling her into his arms.

"You're a big boy; I'm sure you can manage."

He pouted. "You sure?"

"Yes, I'm sure," she said.

Bending, he kissed her, trailing kisses across her cheek and nibbling her ear. He held her tightly, kissing her along her neck to her throat. She tilted her head back, moaning. He throbbed steadily between his legs from his desire to be with her.

"You are so sexy," he whispered. "You'd better go in while I still have the strength to let you." He released her, kissing her lips lightly one last time. "Good night."

"Night," she said before going inside. She closed the door, leaning on it for support. "Whew," she said, pushing off the door and going into the kitchen.

She got a glass of orange juice and was walking down the hall toward her bedroom when she heard a knock on the door. Smiling, she walked back to the door. "I don't need you to..." she said, opening the door, "...tuck...."

Maurice's frame filled the doorframe. Dee saw the look in his eyes and tried to close the door.

"Hello, Dee," he growled. "Long time no see," he said, pushing the door and knocking her off balance. "I see you replaced me already."

Dee slid back. Then, jumping to her feet, she moved quickly in the direction of the kitchen, her heels slipping on the hardwood floor. Maurice took several long strides, grabbing her hair and pulling hard, making her fall back. When her back hit the floor, it knocked the wind out of her. He stood at her side, hovering over her. "You broke my nose, you stupid bitch, and I know you didn't think you were gonna get away with that."

Think, Dee, think! Before she could come up with a plan, he kicked her in the ribs.

"Ah!" she yelled.

"You always acted like you were better than me, with your uppity-ass self. Even went and got yourself a white dude." He bent down, grabbed her hair again, and pulled her up. Dee brought her knee up, catching him in the groin. He let her go and she ran for her bedroom. He lurched forward and caught up to her quickly, grabbing her hair again and pulling her off balance. She fell back, hitting her head on the floor. "You bitch, I'm going to teach you not to mess with a real man."

"Why don't I wait here while you go find one?" she said, kicking him in the stomach.

He took a step back. She crawled back into the living room. Her ribs where killing her, but she wasn't going to go down without a fight. Scrambling to her feet, she grabbed a ceramic statue from the coffee table and swung it with all her might, missing him. He charged her, knocking her into the wall, causing her to drop the statue. She heard the phone ringing, or maybe it was the ringing in her ears—she wasn't sure. She felt her knees give out as he pulled her upright, punching her on the left temple and knocking her down again. Then she heard a loud noise and felt herself drift away.

Ben sat in his car, looking up at the living room window of Dee's apartment. This was the fourth time he had dialed the number. He had an uneasy feeling that he couldn't shake. He dropped the phone and ran to the building, taking the steps two at a time.

The door was open, and he saw some guy hit Dee on the side of her head. Filled with rage, he charged him from behind, knocking him into the wall with a thud. He stood over the man, and when he rolled over, Ben recognized him as the guy outside of Dee's office.

Maurice shifted his weight, rising to his feet. Ben didn't give him time to react. Stepping closer, he hit Maurice in the chest with all his might, knocking the wind out of him. Maurice slumped to the floor, trying to get up as Ben kicked him in the chin.

"Freeze! Police!"

He heard the voice come from behind, but in his rage, he took another step toward Maurice. Everything seemed to be going in slow motion, like a dream. He looked down, seeing that Maurice was bleeding from his mouth, and he felt a hand on his arm and heard Holly's voice whispering to him. She was calling his name, telling him that Dee needed him.

When he heard that, he became aware of his surroundings. He looked over to where Dee lay on the floor and rushed to her side. She lay unmoving; he thought he felt his heart stop. "Oh, God," he said, "please let her be all right." He slowly lowered himself to the floor beside her and took her in his arms. He held her, rocking her, whispering her name, telling her everything was going to be okay.

She then opened her eyes and smiled up at him. "Hey."

"Are you all right?" he whispered.

"I think so."

Ben closed his eyes briefly. He breathed deeply, fighting to hold back the tears of relief.

Dee tried to sit up; she grabbed her ribs and moaned. Ben held on to her, concern in his eyes. Looking down at her ribs, she said, "Oh man, that's gonna hurt like a bitch tomorrow."

Ben sighed, kissing her temple.

The police cuffed Maurice and took him away, and then Dee and Ben gave their statements.

"I think you need to go to the hospital," Ben insisted.

"No, I'll just take a hot bath. It'll be fine."

"I think you should, too," Holly said.

Dee shook her head. "No, I don't want to."

"She's such a baby sometimes," Holly said, looking at Ben. Then she pointed at Dee. "If you don't go, I'm going to call mom."

That was all Dee needed to hear.

"She has two cracked ribs, but luckily, no head injuries," the doctor told Ben and Holly before leaving the room.

"I told you my hard head would come in handy someday," Dee joked. Neither Holly nor Ben were in the mood for humor at the moment. When they returned to the apartment, Ben waited in the living room while Holly helped Dee get ready for bed.

"She's lying down," Holly said, coming into the living room. "We need to make sure she takes the sedative the doctor gave her." Holly gave Ben the pills; he nodded, heading for the bedroom. "Hey," Holly called to him. He turned. "When she takes that, you need to check under her tongue to make sure she's swallowed it." Ben smiled, shaking his head, then walked into the bathroom and got a glass of water. He walked into the bedroom and sat on the side of the bed.

"How are you feeling, sweetheart?"

"Much better." She smiled up at him.

"Here, take this. It'll make you sleep better." She looked at the pill then back at him. "Go ahead," he said, shaking the pill in his palm. After taking the pill from his outstretched hand, she put it in her mouth and swallowed a gulp of water.

"Now open wide," he said.

She frowned at him, took another sip, and then opened her mouth. "Good girl," he said, taking the glass.

"Thank you," she said softly.

"For what?" he asked

"For coming to my rescue."

"I'd never let anything happen to you," he said gently, brushing her brow with his fingers. Leaning over, he kissed her temple. "Good night, sweetheart."

* * * *

"I know you're not going to work?" Holly said.

"Yes, I am," Dee said, walking slowly into the kitchen.

"I was going to bring you breakfast in bed."

"Aw," Dee said, walking over and kissing Holly's cheek. She then walked stiffly to the table.

"Is it bad?"

"Oh yeah."

"I swear, I never liked that jerk," Holly said, shaking her head.

"What time did Ben leave?" Dee asked.

"I'm not sure. I think I heard him leave sometime around four thirty." She picked a plate up off the counter and carried it to the table. "I made French toast," she said, setting the plate in front of Dee.

"Thanks." They heard a key at the door. Dee looked at Holly questioningly. Ben walked into the kitchen.

"Hey," she said, smiling up at him.

"I gave him a key," Holly said. "We need all the help we can get to keep you out of trouble."

Dee looked at Ben. "What are you doing here?"

"I came to make sure you took the day off. You're spending it with me."

"Good for you," Holly said, looking at Ben.

Ben asked Holly if she could pack an overnight bag for Dee and then helped her to his car. "Where are we going?" she asked.

"Somewhere where you will be pampered," he said, helping her in. After driving through the city, they pulled into the side entrance of a building. A valet walked down the steps to meet them. Ben walked around the car to give the valet his keys and instructed him to send their bags up. A host welcomed them and directed them to a set of elevators that whisked them to the Four Seasons Hotel. When they walked off the elevator, the staff greeted them. Everything was beautiful, from the marble floors to the dozens of flower arrangements. They walked into a suite with a huge bay window; a baby grand piano sat in the parlor with a dozen red and white roses on top.

"This is great," she said, looking around. Ben helped her out of her coat. He looked at the young woman who had accompanied them to the room and gave her a small nod. She went in to the adjoining room and returned a few minutes later to inform Dee that her bath was ready. Dee looked at Ben.

"I had them draw a hot bath for you so you could soak in the whirlpool."

A few minutes later she was submerged, the smell of lilacs and roses drifting from the water swirling around her.

"Yes?" she answered to the knock at the door.

"Can I come in?"

She looked down at the bubble-covered water that came up to her neck before saying, "Sure."

He walked in carrying a small covered dish. Seeing her sitting in a tub full of bubbles, he licked his lips, trying to find his voice.

"You look relaxed," he said, sitting on the side of the tub.

"I feel relaxed."

He uncovered the plate to reveal chocolate-covered strawberries.

"Mmm," she said, "they look delicious."

"So do you," he added. She smiled at him. "Don't worry; I won't take advantage of you while you're wounded. I'll wait." He smiled mischievously. They laughed and talked as they fed each other strawberries. "Are you ready to get out?" Ben asked her.

"I am starting to feel like a raisin," she said, looking at her fingers and grimacing. He stood and took a large terrycloth robe from behind the door, holding it up for her. She looked at him.

"Come on. You're safe." She stood with her back to him. His eyes wandered down her body, taking in her shapely hips and round buttocks. He wrapped the robe around her, scooped her in his arms, and carried her to the bed, gently laying her down. "When you get hungry, let me know and I'll call room service," he said, lying down next to her. "Are you all right? You're not in any pain, are you?" he asked, looking for any hint of discomfort.

"No, I'm fine," she whispered.

He held her hand, looking into her eyes. "When I walked into your apartment last night and saw him hitting you, I was so scared." His voice was low. "I always want to be there for you—to protect you." He let his fingers brush her lips. "You're so beautiful," he whispered, as he gently kissed her. "I feel lucky just being with you." He kissed her again. "When I'm near you, my heart races; it feels as though it could burst at any moment." He placed her hand on his chest, letting her feel the rhythm. "Do you feel that? That's what you do to me."

"Ben."

"Ssh," he said, placing his fingers to her lips. "Go to sleep." He kissed her eyes and pulled her gently so that her head rested on his chest. For the rest of the day, he made sure she didn't do anything but rest. When she took a nap, he went to the lobby to buy magazines for her to read and DVDs for her to watch.

Later that evening, there was a knock at the door. Ben looked at Dee. "It's for you." She glanced at him, puzzled, and then rose from the bed and walk to the door. He had arranged a surprise visit from the hotel ice-cream man. On the cart, there was chocolate and vanilla ice cream with pink sprinkles, gummy bears, and all sorts of other goodies.

"Oh boy," she said in a childlike voice. She smiled broadly, joy beaming in her eyes.

The next morning, Ben woke with Dee's head lying on his chest. He smelled the scent of her freshly washed hair and enjoyed the feeling of her body lying next to him. After moving her gently so as not to wake her, he walked to the armchair, picked up his overnight bag, and carried it in the bathroom. He stripped off his clothes and stepped into the shower.

They had stayed up until 3 A.M. talking about everything from politics to pet peeves. They had talked about their families and childhoods and all the silly things they had done as teenagers. She told him about her past relationships and confided that she had never been in love before. He told her how important his family was to him and how as a young man he had resented having to become the man of the family after his father died. He had never told anyone that, and he was surprised at how easily he could share it with Dee. He couldn't remember ever feeling so comfortable with a woman. When she had fallen asleep, he had been content just to hold her.

He closed his eyes, shoving the images from his mind as he stepped out of the shower. After drying himself and dressing quickly before she woke up, he used the phone in the bathroom. He called room service and had breakfast sent up.

When Dee woke, Ben placed the tray on her lap. "Breakfast is served, my lady," he said with a bow.

She laughed. "Now all we need is a tux."

He sat at the desk making business calls. When he finished, he sat watching Dee eat. She wore lavender silk pajamas, and her hair hung loosely around her shoulders. Her slim fingers tore off a piece of the toast and put it in her mouth. He forced himself to remain in his chair and not to go to her.

"Are you feeling better?"

She looked at him and smiled. "Yes, thank you." She set the toast on the plate. "Thank you for taking such good care of me."

"That's not necessary. I like taking care of you."

"Yes it is. You don't know how much this means to me."

He sat next to her on the bed and gently stroked her back. She peered at him intently and then smiled awkwardly looking down at the tray.

"If you like, you can stay here for a few more days," he said.

"No, I really do have to get back to work."

"Are you sure?"

"Yes, I'm feeling much better than I did yesterday."

"Are you afraid to go back to the apartment? Most women would be."

"No," she said with a shake of her head. "I need to face this head on. I'm not going to give that jerk that kind of power over me."

He smiled at her strength then leaned over and kissed her brow.

Chapter 7

"Yes grandma," Dee said, speaking to her grandmother and mother simultaneously on the phone. "I am being careful. No, ma'am, I don't need you guys to come here. That was a week ago, and I feel much better." Dee felt like they were tag teaming her. "No, mom, honest, I'm fine. Holly, Ben, and Edmond have been taking really good care of me, and I do everything the doctor tells me to do," she fibbed, crossing her fingers. "Okay, mom... yes, grandma, I love you too."

"Hey," Terry said from the doorway. "Tell Aunt Jean I said hi."

"And Terry says 'hi.' Okay, bye." She hung up and looked at Terry. "Hey."

"I heard about what happened. I'm sorry I didn't come sooner, but I thought you were mad at me," Terry said, walking over to the bed and sitting down. "Are you all right?"

"I'm fine."

Terry looked down, picking her nails. "I need to talk to you. I need your advice."

"What's wrong?"

"David wants to take Little David away from me." Tears welled in her eyes.

"Dee, I don't know what to do."

Dee reached for Terry, embracing her. "I'm sorry."

"I keep trying to reason with him," Terry said, "but he won't listen. He's angry because we broke up, and now he has Little David saying and doing awful things that he never did before."

"Really? I can't imagine David being so cruel," Dee said, surprised.

"When his father takes him out, he tells him terrible things about me, and when he comes home, he is so disrespectful. When I ask him to do something, he says no—and he even calls me Terry."

"What do you need me to do?"

"Well there's nothing you can do, but I was kind of hoping you could go to this lawyer with me. I'm a little nervous about it."

"Okay," Dee nodded. "When do you want to go?"

"I can't go for a couple of weeks."

"It'll take that long before you can get an appointment?"

Terry looked up at the ceiling and heaved a big sigh. "I don't know where I'm going to get the retainer from, but when I make the appointment I'm going to call you. Next week, the social worker his attorney talked to is coming to check out my apartment."

"He has an attorney already?"

"Yeah," Terry said. She let out a loud sigh then reached for Dee's hand and squeezed it.

"I'm really scared, Dee."

"Who is this attorney that you want to see?"

"Some lawyer from downtown; I got his name from a lawyer referral service."

Dee sat quietly in thought. Terry needed a lawyer; if David took her to court and she didn't have representation, she could definitely lose her son.

"How much is the retainer?"

"Seven hundred and fifty dollars."

Dee bit her bottom lip, shaking her head. She reached across the bed and opened her nightstand drawer to get her checkbook.

"What's the name of the law firm?"

"Roberts and Burns... no, I think it's Rogers and Barnes. You know what," she said, "I'll go home and get the paper and bring it back to you."

"Never mind," Dee said. "I'll write in the amount; you fill the rest of it in when you get home."

"Thank you, Dee," she said, hugging her. "Thank you so much."

"Call me when you make the appointment," Dee said, brushing the tears from Terry's cheek.

"I will."

"We're going out later. Do you want to come?" Dee asked Terry.

"No, I just want to get this check to the attorney."

"It might make you feel better to get out." Dee stroked her back, consoling her. "I haven't seen you much lately—I've missed you."

"I've missed you too, but thanks anyway," Terry said. "I just want to spend time with my son."

"Okay, I understand," Dee said.

* * * *

The club was hopping. People where dancing everywhere, and they practically had to yell to be heard. Ben was wearing an off-white Prada sweater and black slacks. Dee guessed the sweater alone cost more than her whole outfit, and he looked great in it. When they sat down, Edmond and Ben went to get drinks.

"You guys have been going out a lot lately," Holly said.

"Yeah," Dee said, grinning from ear to ear.

"So, things are good with you two?"

"Yes, very."

"I'm glad." Holly smiled too. "I like him. He's a good guy, the kind of guy you deserve. And he's not bad to look at either." They laughed.

When the guys got back to the table, Dee took Ben's hand. "Ready to dance?" she asked him.

"Do you mind if I wait awhile?"

"Of course not. Holly, do you mind?" she asked, grabbing Edmond's hand.

"No, go ahead," Holly said with a wave of the hand. Dee and Edmond went to the dance floor. Ben watched as Dee moved around the floor, laughing and smiling. "She's something else, isn't she?" Holly asked Ben, watching him.

"Yes, she is," he said, smiling as he watched Dee's every move.

"You're in love with her." She said it as a statement, not a question.

He looked at her, confused. "What?"

"You are! You're in love with her."

He looked at her thoughtfully, and then back at Dee. At that moment, so many things were running through his mind. He felt that he wanted to be with her all the time, he wanted to protect her, to make her laugh and wipe away her tears. He was so deep in thought that he didn't hear his name when it was called. He felt a tap on his shoulder.

"Hello, Benji," Janet said. She let her eyes glide over Holly then looked at Ben again. "What are you doing here?" she asked.

"Hello, Janet," he said tightly, giving her a small smile. "I'm here with friends."

She glanced at Holly. "Aren't you going to introduce me to your friend?"

"Holly Lawson, Janet Summers."

"Hey," Holly greeted her, reaching out her hand.

"Charmed," Janet said dryly, not wanting to shake hands with the other woman. As they shook hands, her eyes tried to bore a hole through Holly. "So, Holly, is it? Ben's never mentioned you before. How long have the two of you been, um, friends?"

Holly's eyes narrowed. Looking over Janet's shoulder, she saw Dee and Edmond walking toward the table. She smiled broadly, glancing at Janet quickly.

"That took long enough," she said. "Hey, babe, my turn," she said to Edmond. She stood, looking at Janet. "Janet, it was so nice to meet you." Turning, she kissed Edmond then took his hand and led him to the dance floor. Janet watched Holly and Edmond weave through the crowd then looked at Ben, confused.

"Dee, this is Janet Summers. Janet, Deanna Meyers." Janet looked at her in disbelief but recovered quickly.

"Hello," she said, a smile pasted on her face.

"Hi," Dee said, feeling a pang of jealousy.

Janet turned her attention back to Ben. "I haven't talked to you in a while. 'When are we going to get together?"

Ben's lip twitched. He glared at her. "It's nice to see you again, Janet," he said, taking Dee's hand.

Janet glanced at their hands then looked at him; she stiffened, noticeably annoyed.

"Yes, it was nice seeing you again also. Nice to meet you, Donna."

Dee laughed, saying, "The pleasure was all mine."

'When Janet walked away, Dee looked at Ben. "She's pretty."

"Some might think that."

"You must have."

"Yes, but she's not you."

"Good answer," she said, laughing. He leaned forward, brushing her neck with his lips. She giggled, pulling away.

"Come on. Dance with me." She pulled him from his seat, making a path to the dance floor. The DJ played a reggae song and Dee started swaying to the music.

"I don't dance very much. I'm not very good."

"There's no good or bad—just do what feels good to you."

Ben danced around, watching her hips swerve as she closed her eyes. She looked like the happiest person in the world, like she was happy just to be alive, and he realized that Holly was right—he was in love with her. He thought, *This is the sexiest, most beautiful woman in the world, and I'm in love with her.*

Janet stood in the corner watching them dance, now to Guy's "Piece of My Love." She watched him as he took her in his arms. They stood in the middle of the dance floor, looking into each other's eyes for an agonizingly long time, then started moving sensually to the sound of the music. She shook her head in disbelief, not believing that her Benji would let that whore touch him. *He is going through something,* Janet thought. *That's it—he's trying to make me jealous.* She watched as Ben kissed Dee's hand and placed it over his heart, watched as she stroked his cheek. Janet's fury almost suffocated her. *It's that whore from the coffee shop,* she thought. "I'm not going to let her use him like that. I have to do something. I have to save him from her."

Russell was just paying for their drinks when Janet walked back to the table. Seeing the look on her face, he asked, "Are you all right?"

Janet threw her purse onto the small table. "I just saw Benjamin." Russell looked into her eyes; he didn't have to ask her whom he was with. "In a million years, you'd never guess what kind of people he's with." Russell merely looked down at his glass in silence. "He was with some *black girl.* Can you believe that?" She looked at him. "You don't seem surprised."

"Her name's Deanna."

She drew back from him when he said it. "Yes, how did you know?"

"He brought her to an engagement party at the club."

"He took her to the club. Oh my gosh!" She took a deep breath. "I cannot believe this." She shook her head furiously. "I want to go."

"Wait a minute," Russell said. "This is a big place. We don't even have to see them." He looked up to see Ben and Dee in the middle of the dance floor then looked at Janet. She swept the glasses from the table, grabbed her coat, and turned in one motion.

"I said I want to leave."

* * * *

Janet stood by the window, looking out at the streetlight below her third-floor apartment. All was quiet in the city below. She liked living in the city amidst the hustle and bustle. She looked back at the sound coming from the bed, and the sight nauseated her—he nauseated her. She had no idea why she had slept with him. She didn't care for him; she didn't even like him. It was because of Ben. If she hadn't seen him with that whore, she wouldn't have slept with Russell. She turned her attention back to the window. Her mind drifted back to the nightclub and Ben touching that woman. She imagined him holding her and kissing her and...

"No," she whispered, closing her eyes, chasing the images from her mind. She walked to the bed. "Russell," she said in a sharp tone. He stirred a little. She called his name again.

"Yeah?" His eyes popped open.

They had a mutual friend, Bud Kendrick. He was the kind of guy that all the girls liked and most boys hated. They were in the locker room joking about girls.

"Hey, I think that Tina Rodriguez is hot," Russell said. He stood up from the bench and began grinding against one of the lockers. "I'd do her in a minute."

Ben looked at Russell and laughed. "Yeah, Tina is pretty hot."

"Nah," Bud said, "I like older women." He looked at Ben slyly. "I think your mom's hot, Harrison. I'd do her."

"Hey, Bud—" Russell said, shaking his head.

"Yeah, I heard his dad was having an affair. Hey, Harrison, if your mom ever gets lonely, send her to my house. I'll rock her world," he said, swerving his hips as he laughed. Ben attacked him, raining fists down on him without mercy. It took several students and the coach to pull him off. Ben broke the boy's nose and was suspended for two weeks. The school wanted to press charges, but Bud's father said that he didn't want to do that. Ben had to do community service instead.

Now, Russell fidgeted nervously under Ben's gaze. "Yes, I can see that I am," he said.

Ben stood, leaving his lunch on the table, and walked away.

Janet paced in Ben's office. After going over things in her mind, everything was clear to her. That was why he had wanted to stop seeing her; it was all so clear now. The longer she waited, the angrier she grew.

How dare he dump me for some nigger? And that worthless fool Russell saying he would talk to Ben. What good would that do? All he had to do was get her to go out with some bum and I'd take care of the rest. That spineless weasel. I should tell Ben we had an affair just to make him lose his job—and it might make Ben jealous at the same time. She nodded to herself. *No,* she thought, *I might need that loser in the future. I'll wait to bring him down.* She walked to the window. *I'm going to get him back, with or without Russell's help. Ben belongs with me. I've spent too much time and energy on this to let him just turn his back on me now.* She walked over to the desk, sat in his chair, and angrily knocked some papers to the floor. Opening the desk drawers, she searched for something—anything—that would tell her about this woman. She found his keys, one of which was circled by a red key ring. She bit on her lip, beginning to form a plan.

When he reached his office, Ben was furious.

"Mr. Harrison," Jill called as he passed her desk, not slowing down.

As he opened the door and saw Janet, he heard Jill say, "Ms. Summers is in your office." Janet was sitting in his chair.

"Great."

"I'm sorry, sir," Jill said, standing behind him.

"Don't worry about it, Jill." He walked in and closed the door. "Janet, what the hell do you want?" He walked to his desk, taking her arm and pulling her from his chair.

She glared at him before speaking. "I want to talk to you about last night."

The muscles in his neck tightened; he rubbed it.

"Janet, I don't want to do this with you."

"So, is that why you haven't been calling me, because you been spending time with that... that girl?"

"Janet, say whatever it is you came here to say and leave."

"How dare you dismiss me?"

He reached for the intercom button to ask Jill if she had any messages for him, but he thought better of it.

"How dare you treat me in such a shameful way? I thought we had something."

"Janet, I care about you, but—"

"I can see that. You care so much for me that you go running around with that, that woman."

"Her name is not 'that woman.'"

"I don't care what her name is. Ben, listen to me. I know that sometimes men want to be with other women—it's in their nature. And I'll forgive you, but you can't be with one of them."

Ben massaged his neck. "Janet, go home. Look, we had a great time together, but there's no future for us. It's time to move on."

She moved to stand in the middle of the floor. He stood up and walked over to her.

"Janet, I don't want to hurt you, but you know it's true."

"You told me you wanted me to meet your family."

"No, you told me that. Janet, you're a wonderful women and—"

"No, don't you dare do this." She met his gaze. "Don't you dare talk to me in a condescending manner. You are not going to throw me away like this."

He sighed. Jill tapped on the door.

"Sir, you have a delivery." She walked into the office carrying a vase of pink and white carnations and lilies, with two bright pink roses in the middle. She set them on the desk then left the office. Janet reached over, snatching the card before Ben could.

She read the card aloud. "'To brighten your day, as you always brighten mine.' Isn't that special."

Ben took the card from her and placed it in his pocket. "Janet, I know you're better than this."

She moved without thinking, trying to slap him; he grabbed her wrist.

"I'd never hit a woman, but I won't have one hitting me either."

She looked at him boldly. Snatching her arm from him, she turned on her heels and left his office with what dignity she could muster. *Never mind,* she thought to herself. *Oh, you will come back to me. Jam not going to let that black bitch have you.*

Ben sat behind his desk, taking the card from his pocket and reading it. He picked up the phone and dialed her cell.

"Hello?"

"Hi, thank you for the beautiful flowers."

"You're welcome. I'm glad you like them."

"I've been having a pretty rough day. Thanks for making it brighter."

"Do you need me to do anything?" she asked.

"No." He sighed. "I miss you."

"I miss you too. Can you come over to my place for dinner?"

The thought brightened his mood, and he smiled.

"There's no place I'd rather be."

* * * *

Dee was in a good mood when she got home from work. All day long, she had been happy and smiling and humming. Everyone at the office had told her she was glowing—even Leo at the dry cleaners had said she seemed different. On her way home, she had stopped at the supermarket to buy the ingredients for a special dinner.

"Mmm, something smells good," she heard from the living room. Holly appeared around the corner. "Whatcha cooking?"

"Garlic chicken, curried rice, and a green bean spinach salad."

"Ooh, what's the occasion?"

"Dee turned around, smiling broadly. "Because I'm happy, and because you're my best friend and I want to do something special for you."

"And?"

"And because Ben's coming for dinner."

Holly smiled.

Dee turned back to the counter. "Hey, have you seen my tennis bracelet?"

"No."

"You haven't seen it?"

Holly shook her head. "No, not at all."

"Hmm, that's strange." Dee frowned. "I seem to have misplaced it."

"That's not like you." Holly leaned on the counter next to her.

"I'll come across it."

"What do you need me to do?" Holly asked, picking up a carrot.

"Nothing. Go ahead and rest. I have it."

Holly went to the small breakfast table in the corner and pulled out a chair. "Hol, can I ask your advice on something?" Dee said, looking over her shoulder at Holly.

"Shoot," Holly said, sitting at attention.

"Well," she said, turning around. "I really like Ben, and we've been a little intimate, but I don't know if I'm ready to go all the way. I can tell he wants to... you know what I'm saying?"

"Sure, I understand. Have you told him this?"

"No, not really."

"Have you told him you're a virgin?" Holly asked.

Dee didn't say anything. She turned back to the counter and continued cutting the onions. "Why not?"

"I don't know. Sometimes you just don't know how to bring certain things up in conversation."

"What things never come up in a conversation?" Terry asked, standing in the kitchen doorway.

"Hi," Dee said, surprised to see her standing there. "Nothing. What's going on?"

"Nothing—I just stopped by to see what you guys were doing."

"Do you want to stay for dinner?"

"Sure," she said, walking to the table and sitting opposite Holly. The two women didn't even look at each other.

"How'd it go with the attorney?"

"Everything went well; he said he thought things looked promising."

"I thought you wanted me to go with you."

"Yeah, but I realized you were going through a lot with the Maurice thing, and I didn't want to burden you."

Dee smiled at her consideration, while Holly smiled cynically at the irony of the comment.

"I'm glad you're here. I'm having a guest for dinner, and I want you two to meet."

"Really?" Terry said, leaning on the table. "Who is it?"

"Someone I'm seeing—his name is Ben."

Terry's expression turned thoughtful. "How long have you two been seeing each other?"

"For a little while," Dee said.

Holly sat watching Terry's reaction.

Terry fidgeted. "Are you ready to be with someone new so soon after breaking up with Maurice? I mean, you guys did go out for a while and all."

"No, my relationship with Maurice wasn't even like that. It's not like I needed time to mourn or anything."

Terry looked down, picking lint off her slacks. "So, are you and this guy serious?"

"I really care about him," Dee said, her back still turned to the two of them.

Terry looked up, meeting Holly's gaze, then looked away.

"You know what? On second thought, I'll pass on dinner tonight," she said, rising from her seat.

"Oh," Dee said, "that's too bad. I really wanted you to meet Ben."

"Maybe next time. I really came by to ask you if I could borrow your brown leather maxi."

"Oh, that belongs to Holly."

Terry bit her bottom lip, stepping from side to side, debating whether she wanted to swallow her pride and ask Holly for the coat. Holly smiled a faint smile. She watched Terry squirm under her gaze, seeing her lip twitch slightly. She rose from her seat, leaving the kitchen.

Terry sighed in disappointment. "Well, I'm outta here. I'll talk to you later."

Holly waited for Terry to leave before returning to the kitchen.

"Do you want me to set the table?"

"Sure. I was hoping that Terry could stay for dinner."

"I was expecting her to come in here to show off what she bought today," Holly said. "You know how she is."

Dee looked at Holly with curiosity. "What do you mean?"

"You know how she is when she gets something new, like a little kid."

"No, what do you mean 'what she bought today?'"

"Oh, I saw her on Oak Street late this afternoon; she was coming out of Barneys New York with a shopping bag."

Dee's brow furrowed, and she frowned. "Are you sure?"

"Yeah," Holly replied as she took silverware from the drawer.

Dee groaned. She had a bad feeling in the pit of her stomach about the money she had given Terry to get an attorney, and then she remembered her tennis bracelet.

Holly glanced up, noticing the look on Dee's face. "Is everything all right?"

"I hope so. Can you keep an eye on this for me?" She gestured toward the stove and then quickly walked out of the kitchen.

Terry sat in the borrowed car watching Dee's apartment building as the silver BMW pulled into an empty parking spot. Angrily, she started the car and pulled away from the curb. She didn't want to get a look at him. *You know what that's not your business,* she told herself. *Whatever Dee does is not your concern.*

Deep down, though, she knew herself better than that.

After searching the entire apartment for her bracelet, Dee had no alternative but to believe that Terry had actually taken it. "Damn her," she said, just as she heard a knock at the door. She stopped, took a deep breath, and opened it. Ben was standing there holding a bouquet of pink and white roses.

"Good evening, sweetheart."

"Hi, yourself. Why didn't you use your key?"

"I don't know. It's the weirdest thing, but I seem to have misplaced it."

"Don't worry about it," she said with a wave of her hand. "I can give you my spare. Who are those for?" she asked, smiling.

"Some sexy PI that I happened to meet on the street. She wouldn't take them, so I decided to give them to you," he teased.

"Ah, I'm flattered."

He gave her the roses and then took her into his arms for a kiss.

"Mmm, you smell good," she said.

"Good enough to eat?"

Dee laughed, pulling away from his arms. "Let me put these in water," Dee said, heading for the kitchen with him in tow.

"Hello, Holly," he said as he walked around the corner. "Do you ladies need my help?"

"No, we have everything under control."

"I'm leaving now," Holly announced after dinner. "Do you need me to help clean up?"

"No, that's fine. You go ahead," Dee replied.

Holly grabbed her coat. "See you guys later," she said, closing the door behind her. Dee stood up and began removing the dishes from the table.

"So do you want to go out?" she asked, looking at Ben nervously.

"No." He took a step closer to her, pulling her to him. She could feel the beating of his heart, despite the racing of her own. He kissed her, slowly at first, savoring the sweetness of her full lips. Then he gently forced her lips open with his warm tongue. She felt the kiss ebbing through her body, touching places she never knew existed. His hand moved to her breast, his thumb lightly brushing her nipple through her thin sweater. She moaned, tilting her head back and letting out a long, slow breath. He moved her to the sofa, sitting and pulling her onto his lap in one movement. "I need you so bad," he said, his voice raspy with desire. As she looked into his eyes, her doubt ebbed away. Her knees trembled and he slid his hand under her sweater, his fingers brushing across her belly. Moving his hand up, he let his fingers trace the outline of her bra as his tongue slipped between her lips.

"Wait a minute," she said, trying to catch her breath. She stood up and quickly moved away from him. He watched her, confused.

"What's wrong?"

"Nothing," she said, putting space between them, picking up some of the plates from the table. He moved to her side.

"There is a problem?" he said, trying to get her to look at him. "I want you to tell me what it is."

"No, there's no problem... I just don't think this is the right time." She turned from him, and he noticed that her back was rigid. He embraced her, hugging her from behind. She laid her head back on his chest, enjoying the way his cologne mingled with his own natural body odor.

"I'm sorry. I don't want to pressure you. But I want to be with you so badly that I can barely think straight. If you need more time, just tell me."

"It's not that."

"Then talk to me, sweetheart. Tell me what it is. Maybe I can fix it."

She turned to face him. "I should have told you this awhile ago."

He held her hands in his and waited for her to say what was on her mind.

"Well, I haven't actually gone all the way when it comes to sex."

"What do you mean, 'all the way'?"

"You know, all the way."

Ben frowned. "How far have you gone?"

"Well, kissing."

"And?"

"And petting."

"And?"

"And what?"

"And, what else?"

"That's it."

"You mean you've never—"

"No."

"Wow."

"I just never met the right man." She paused. "And I had this idea that I'd wait until I got married," she said, hunching her shoulders.

He laughed. "You're joking, right?" She was quiet. "You're not joking." She looked at him innocently, hunching her shoulders again.

"Why didn't you tell me?"

"When should I have told you, over dinner?" she said defensively. "Oh, can you pass the pepper, and um, by the way, did I tell you that I'm a virgin?"

Ben was quiet.

"Well, say something."

"Well, I'll be damned."

"Anything but that." She pulled her hands from his and walked to the other side of the room.

"I'm sorry, sweetheart," he said, following her. "I just would have never guessed."

"Well, I don't wear a sign on my back."

"I know, I know." He blew out a breath. "You know, I don't think I've ever met a virgin."

Dee looked at him angrily, putting her fists on her hips. "And just what is that supposed to mean?"

"Nothing," he said playfully. "I just meant, I've honestly never met a virgin before—you know, besides really young girls."

"Oh my God!" she said, throwing her arms in the air. "I can't believe you just said that."

"No, I didn't mean anything by that. It's just that you don't act like a virgin. I never would have guessed." His eyes grew large after he realized what he had said.

"I don't want to talk to you," she said, walking down the hall to her bedroom. "Go home."

"Wait a minute," he said, following her.

She walked into the room, slamming the door behind her.

"No! Go home!" she yelled.

"Damn," he whispered. He tapped on the door gently. "I'm sorry, sweetheart. I didn't mean to make you angry." She didn't say anything. "Can I come in?" he said as he opened the door. She threw a pillow, hitting him when he peeked around the door. He laughed, catching it, and then stepped into the room. "I'm sorry—really. I didn't mean to insult you." He took a step closer. "Forgive a wretch of a man his blunder."

She sighed, biting the inside of her mouth. "That's why I need a little more time."

"I understand. Really, I do." He held his arms open.

"You don't think I'm some kind of freak?"

"No, sweetheart. I could never think of you that way." She stepped closer, and he wrapped his arms around her, kissing the top of her head. He shook his head. He would never have guessed this, he thought. But even though she had always seemed confident and sure, there was always an innocence about her that he couldn't explain. He sighed, whispering, "I'll be damned."

Chapter 8

This is ridiculous, Janet thought to herself, sitting at a corner table in a Starbucks. She watched all the customers coming and going. She studied everyone closely, but was particularly interested in the male customers. She sighed. *How am I going to get a total stranger to go along with my plan? I couldn't convince that fool Russell to do it. All he had to do was get that whore into bed, and I would have taken care of the rest.* Closing her eyes, she massaged her temple, taking a deep breath. After a few moments, she smiled, nodding to herself. She dialed a number on her cell phone.

"Hello."

"Hello Russell."

"Hello Janet, how are you?"

"I'm fine," she paused. "Russell, I called to apologize for the way I behaved the last time that we were together."

"No Janet, that's not necessary. You were upset at seeing Ben with someone else. I know how you feel about him, and I should have been more understanding, that couldn't have been easy for you."

"Yes," she said, sighing dramatically. "but that's no excuse. You are my friend, and I shouldn't have taken my anger out on you. I suppose I was jealous that you're attracted to her as well."

"Attracted to who?"

"Deanna."

"Why would you think that?"

"Well, on the way to my apartment the other night, you mentioned that you thought she was a beautiful woman, and I know that she's finds you attractive. I just—"

"And why would you think that she's attracted to me?" Russell asked.

"I talked to several people that attended Rick and Debbie's engagement party, and was told that Deanna was clearly attracted to you. Why, even Wanda Anderson told me that she heard Deanna state that she wished she'd met you before going out with Ben. I can hardly blame her; you're an exceptionally handsome man, what woman wouldn't be attracted to you."

Russell remained silent.

"Listen to me, going on and on. I just wanted to call you and apologize. Will you accept my apology, Russell?"

"Yes, Janet, apology accepted."

"Thank you, Russell. I have an idea, why don't we get together later, for dinner."

* * * *

Kimmy peered around the opened door. "Holly's on the phone," she said. "I'm headed across the street to the coffee shop for a muffin. Can I get you one?"

"Banana, thanks," Dee said, picking up the receiver. "Hey, Hol, what's up?"

"Do you have my brown leather coat?"

"No, I haven't seen it."

"Damn it." Dee heard her say on the other end.

"Is everything all right?"

"My coat's gone." Holly said, sighing. "Dee, you're going to have to get our key from Terry. I didn't want to tell you this, but a lot of my things have gone missing lately, even money."

"Why didn't you tell me?"

"I really don't know. I guess I didn't want you to think I was picking on her, but we have a problem."

Dee heaved a sigh. "I know. I didn't want to accuse her without any proof, but I think she took my tennis bracelet." She massaged her brow. "I'll call her later and have her come over. Then I'll get the key from her."

"Okay."

"Are you on your way back to work?"

"Yeah," Holly said, looking at the purple box she held in her hand. "I just have something I need to take care of. See you later."

"Yeah," Dee said. "See ya." She placed her face in her hands and massaged her temples, hoping her fingertips would keep the oncoming headache at bay. Dee looked through her Rolodex, finding David's office number. She drummed her fingers on her desk while she waited for him to answer.

"David Wilkerson, please. Yes, Deanna Meyers."

"Hi, Dee," David said, sounding happy to hear from her. "How have you been? I haven't heard from you in a long time."

"Hi, David. I've been good, how about yourself?"

"Good, good," he said.

"Look, David, this might not be the best time to call, but I need to ask you something."

"Okay, sure," he said hesitantly.

"I know this is none of my business, but are you and Terry having a custody battle over the baby?"

"She told you?"

"Yeah."

"I'm surprised she would tell you."

"David, I don't understand. Why you would do this?"

"Me? Whoa, I think you have things a little turned around here," he said. "Terry wants to give custody to her grandmother. I think he needs to be with her or me—a child needs his parents—but she won't even consider letting him come live with me." Dee was quiet. "He's been living with her mother's mom for the last few months now. At first she said it was temporary; then, after a month, I started sending her grandmother money to care for him. Last week, she told me that she'd give him to me if I helped support her financially."

"That's when you got a lawyer?" Dee asked.

He laughed. "I didn't get a lawyer," he said. "She got someone from legal aid to call me. I think she thought it would scare me."

"I had no idea. Whenever I asked her about Little David, she would always tell me that he was with you."

"That's not true," he said, his tone becoming angry. "The only time I ever get to see him lately is when I drive down to Livingston."

"I thought you guys were trying to work things out?"

"No. I'm assuming she didn't tell you why we broke up?"

"She told me something," she said slowly. "I'm half-afraid to ask you the truth."

"We broke up because one day I came home from work to find another man in my bed. I still love your cousin, but I'll be damned if I'm going to put up with that. I've had enough. I'd do almost anything for her, but I draw the line at sharing my bed with another man."

Dee sighed; she could almost feel his pain. "David, I am so sorry."

"Yeah, me too. I have to go, Dee. Take care."

* * * *

When Dee opened the door to the apartment, Holly was lying on the sofa. "Hey, what's wrong? Are you sick?" Dee asked.

Holly looked up at her, and Dee saw that she had been crying.

"Oh my gosh! What's wrong?"

"I can't believe this is happening," Holly cried, rocking as she held herself. Dee sat on the end of the sofa and embraced her friend.

"Tell me what happened," Dee said slowly. Holly looked at her, fresh tears spilling from her eyes.

"I'm pregnant."

"Are you sure?"

"Yeah, I took the test earlier. I was so upset I couldn't go back to work."

"Why didn't you call me?" Holly hunched her shoulders. "Are you all right?"

"Dee, I'm not ready for this—and what about Edmond? He just got this undercover assignment. He can't be distracted. How am I going to tell him?" Dee pulled her closer, allowing Holly's head to rest on her shoulder. "I don't know what I'm going to do."

"You know what, we're going to figure this out together," Dee said in a soothing voice.

"But we've always been careful. We always used protection. This can't be happening."

"I don't know. Maybe the condom was too old."

"No, they last at least three of four years."

"Well," Dee said, "who knows how long it was on the store shelf."

Holly went into her bedroom and came back with one of the condoms, examining it. "No, it's not past the expiration date." She sat down, placing her cheeks on her palms, and groaned. She brushed her hair from her face. She looked at the condom again and furrowed her brow. She then examined it closer, running her finger across the package. "Son of a bitch!" she yelled. "This can't be happening," she said, shaking her head in denial then giving Dee the condom. "Look at that! That looks like a pinhole. Son of a freaking bitch, I can't believe this!" Holly yelled.

"Calm down," Dee said. Looking at the condom, her eyes widened. "This has to be a mistake. How could this have happened?"

"How the hell do you think this happened?" Dee didn't know what to say. She didn't want to admit it, but as soon as she saw the condom, she suspected Terry.

"Oh my God! Holly, I'm so sorry."

"No, you're not to blame," Holly said, doing her best not to cry. "It's not your fault." She paced back and forth, trying to calm down.

Dee felt sick to her stomach. "I never should have trusted her with a key."

"She's your family. If you can't trust her..." Holly trailed off. "I have to get out of here. I need time to think." She grabbed her coat.

"Hol, wait," Dee called as Holly walked out the door. "You shouldn't be alone."

"No, I'm fine."

"At least let me go with you."

"No, I'm fine," Holly said, walking briskly down the steps.

After locking the door behind Holly, Dee dialed Terry's number.

"Terry, I need to see you, right now."

"I have plans. It'll have to wait."

"No, I want your ass over here right now!" Dee yelled before hanging up.

Dee was furious. It should have taken Terry between fifteen and twenty minutes to get to her apartment, yet two hours later she still hadn't shown up. She looked at the door when she heard the bolt click open.

"Hi, what's up?" Terry said, smiling as she stepped inside. Dee stood up and walked toward her.

"What's the matter with you? I said I wanted you to come right away."

"I had to get dressed for my date," Terry said raising her tone to match Dee's. "What's so important that it couldn't wait until tomorrow?"

Dee looked at Terry's outfit. "That's Holly's coat."

"Oh yeah, I borrowed it."

"Take it off."

"No, I'm using it."

"I said take it off. Now!"

"Shit!" Terry said, taking off the coat throwing it at Dee.

"I want my tennis bracelet back too." Dee saw a spark of recognition in Terry's eyes. Then it was gone.

"I don't have it."

"Yes you do. Where is it?"

"I don't know!" Terry yelled.

From her response, Dee knew that her bracelet was gone forever. She sighed. "Terry, why did you poke holes in the condoms Holly had?"

"What? Why would I do that?"

"Don't play with me. I won't have it. I don't understand why you would be so cruel. How could you be so cruel?"

"What makes you think I did it?"

"Because I know you." They heard someone at the door. Holly walked in. She stopped when she saw Terry and then walked past them toward her room.

"Holly, Terry has something to say."

"No, I—" Terry started to say.

Holly held up her hand. "Don't even bother. I don't want to hear anything you have to say." Holly stopped and turned toward Terry. "I don't like you, and I know you don't like me, but I would never do something like this to you." Holly went into her room and closed the door. Dee looked at Terry with disgust, shaking her head.

"Why is it that every time something goes wrong, it has to be my fault?" Terry asked, her eyes brimming with tears.

"Give me the key to the apartment."

"Why?"

"Isn't it obvious?" Dee stood with her hand out. "Key."

"Fine, whatever." Terry took the key off her ring and dropped it in Dee's hand. "You know what? One day, when your pitiful life falls apart—and it will—don't come running to me. You just turn to your horse-faced friend. When she's able to put her sorry-ass life back together, maybe she can help you with yours." She then turned and stormed out the door.

Dee tried to comfort Holly, apologizing over and over. Holly didn't blame her, but Dee knew she resented the fact that she had chosen to ignore her repeated warnings about her cousin. Holly left again, this time to spend time with Edmond, to decide whether she wanted to tell him. Dee lay across her bed with her forearm across her eyes. She heaved a sigh.

What the hell was wrong with Terry? After Terry's father died, she had come to live with Dee and her parents. There were four years between them, and Dee had always tried to look out for her little cousin. Even as a little girl, she made sure Terry never felt deprived. If her mother bought them candy, she would sometimes give Terry half of hers too. In her child's mind, she thought that it would make Terry happy, but Terry always seemed to want more. She remembered the time when Terry was twelve, she stole Dee's grandma's silver bracelet.

Dee found it in her overnight bag and gave it back, taking the blame herself. Her father punished her for a month, but she could tell that her grandma knew the truth. Her grandmother kept telling her father that she didn't think Dee had stolen the bracelet, and she had asked Terry if she thought people should be punished for something they didn't do. Terry never told the truth, and neither did Dee. After that, her grandma seemed cooler toward Terry. It seemed the more people did for her, the more she demanded. Now, Dee was the only person left in her life who was willing to give her any support.

Dee reached for the phone and pressed the now-familiar sequence of buttons.

"Hello," Ben answered.

"Hi, Ben. It's Dee."

"Hi, sweetheart."

"Is this a good time?"

"Sure it is."

"Can we meet somewhere? I need to get out."

"Is everything all right?" he asked.

"Yes, it will be. Do you know Joe's on West Seventy-Ninth Street?"

"Yes," he said. "Can you give me an hour?"

"Sure, see you there."

The restaurant was small, with booths on one side and a counter down the other. The once-white walls were yellow with grime, making it seem more like a greasy spoon than a family restaurant. "Hey," Dee said, smiling, as he reached the table.

"Hi, sweetheart," he said, sliding into the seat across from her.

A buxom young waitress appeared. "What can I get you?" she said, chewing a wad of gum with her mouth open.

"Do you know what you want?" Ben asked.

"Double cheeseburger."

He looked at the waitress. "Two double cheeseburgers and fries." He glanced at Dee. "Beer?" She nodded. "Two light beers." The waitress wrote down the order and left. She returned a moment later with two beers.

Ben reached across the table and took Dee's hand in his. "What's on your mind?" Dee turned his hand over and traced the lines in the palm of his hand with her finger.

She sighed. "My cousin Terry and Holly are having problems."

"Do they involve you?"

"No."

"Maybe you should let them work it out."

"No, this definitely can't be worked out."

"Can you tell me about it? Maybe I can help."

She looked to her left, out the window. "No, it's Holly's problem. I can't share it with you—not yet."

"So, there's nothing I can do?"

"No." She turned back to him. "Terry caused the problem, but unfortunately Holly's the one who has to deal with it."

"It sounds complicated."

"It really is. Holly's so upset, and I don't blame her. I just wish I could make it all better."

"I'm sorry, sweetheart."

She massaged her eyes, trying to erase the image of Holly's devastated expression from her mind. Wanting to change the subject, she asked, "How's your mother?"

"She's good. She's working on a fundraiser for the children's hospital. They're having a ball in a few weeks. I'd love it if you would be my escort."

"I'd really like that. And how's your sister?"

He nodded. "She's doing okay." The waitress brought their food. "Looks good," Ben said, thinking about the damage he was doing to his arteries.

"It is," Dee said, taking a huge bite.

"Do you come here often?"

"Sometimes everyone from the office comes here for lunch."

Ben's cell phone rang.

"Hello." He looked at Dee. "I'm sorry. I have to take this."

"Sure." She nodded, lost in the pleasure of eating her burger.

Ben watched her for a moment and smiled. He then got up from the table and walked outside. He flipped the cell phone open quickly. "Yes, mother?"

"Benjamin, Lisa is not doing very well tonight. The doctor was here, and he says he wants her to go to the hospital. He wants to admit her, but she refuses." There was a pause. "Ben, I'm scared. We have to help her. I don't want to lose my baby."

"I know, mother. I don't want to lose her either." He heard her sob. "Mother, I'll be there as soon as I can."

"Okay. Goodbye."

"Goodbye." He walked farther away from the building, fear knotting his insides. He felt nauseated. He squatted down, taking deep breaths to calm his nerves. Tears welled in his eyes, and he blinked them back. Standing, he slowly walked back toward the restaurant.

Three black teens were sitting in a booth a few tables behind them. One of them got up when he saw Ben leave and walked over to the table. He slid into the seat across from Dee.

"Hey, what's up, sis?"

Dee examined him for a moment. She figured he was about nineteen. His thick hair was sticking out in every direction, with a pick comb in the back.

"Do I know you?"

"What are you doing with that dude?" he said, looking down at the plate in front of him. He smirked and then picked up a French fry, putting it in his mouth.

"And why would that be any concern of yours?"

"I just don't think you should be with him. Like I said, what's up with that?" He took a few more fries and shoveled them in his mouth.

"I think you should go back over there with your friends," she said, taking a mental photograph of him and the two other boys, "before I call the cops."

"If you're going to be giving it up to that white boy, why don't you break me off a piece," he said, flashing a smile laden with three gold teeth.

"Really, I think you'd better leave." One of his friends slid out of the booth. Hiking up his pants, he walked to the table. Dee wondered how he kept them from dropping to the floor. She looked at his face. He seemed a few years younger than the guy sitting across from her.

"C'mon, yo, we ain't got time for this. Let's go."

"Naw, man, chill. I'm trying to get me a little som'som."

"Look, your friend here seems really smart. I think you should listen to him."

He reached across the table and brushed Dee's cheek with his finger. "C'mon, babe, whatcha say?"

"Don't do that. I don't like that," Dee said, her voice sharp, as she pulled away from his touch.

"What? You too good for a brother? Hum bitch?" He reached across the table again, this time running his fingers between her breasts. Without thinking, Dee lashed out across the table and punched him in the eye.

"Ah, shit," he cried, grabbing his eye. His friend busted out laughing.

"Oh, damn, she got you good."

Dee stood up and walked to the counter.

"Can I pay our bill, please?" She took $20 out her wallet and told the waitress to keep the change. Ben walked back inside as Dee was leaving.

"Are we leaving?" he asked, confused.

"Yeah, I paid the bill." Ben looked at the table where they were sitting, seeing the two boys at the table; one was holding his eye and the other one was still laughing.

"Are you all right?"

"Oh, I'm just fine." She walked past him, out the door. He caught up with her, grasping her arm.

"What the hell happened in there?"

"Nothing. Let's just go."

He looked back at the restaurant door then walked with her to the cars. "Have you found anything else on Nancy Greer's child?" he asked, shoving his hands in his pockets.

"No, not since the last report I gave you. I'm checking out some leads; I should have more for you in a couple of days." He nodded. She noticed that his mood had changed since he received the phone call. He seemed tense and upset. She leaned on the car and took his hand. "Do you want to talk about it?"

"No." He looked up at the sky, watching thousands of stars dance and twinkle. Pulling her close, he hugged her as if he was afraid to let go. She could tell something was definitely wrong. He pulled back.

"I have to go. There's something I need to take care of."

She nodded. He took her keys and opened the car door for her, then kissed her lips gently.

"I'll call you later," he told her, then after waiting for her to drive away he turned, and walked to his car.

Ben walked into the house, meeting his mother on the landing. When he approached her, she smiled at him weakly and rubbed his arm. He walked past her and up the stairs, feeling as though he were carrying the weight of the world with him with each step he took. He went into Lisa's room. Thinking she was asleep, he sat down gingerly on the bed next to her. She opened her eyes and smiled up at him. "Hi. What are you doing here?"

"I just wanted to see you. How are you feeling?"

"A little tired." She looked frail and small, her blue eyes a little dull.

"Mother said that Doctor Morris wants you in the hospital."

"I know, but I'm fine. I'm just overexerted."

"Do you need anything?" Ben asked.

"No, thanks," she said, turning on her side and facing him. "Tell me about your evening. Did you have a date?"

"I went out with Deanna."

"Do I know her?"

"The woman I talked to you about, the PI."

"The one who's trying to find Daddy's child?"

He nodded.

"Is she nice?"

"Yes she is."

"What did you guys do?" she asked softly. Her voice sounded so sweet yet so weak. It was heartbreaking; it was all he could do not to cry.

"We went out to dinner," he said, smiling to push back the tears.

"What did you have?"

"Burgers."

"Were they good?"

"They were greasy."

"Yuck." She grimaced.

"I think Dee punched some guy in the eye."

"Oh?" she said, seeming to perk up at this.

"Yeah."

She laughed. "That's funny," she said, yawning slightly. She then suddenly drifted off to sleep.

"Good night, sis." He kissed her forehead. He sat in the chair next to her bed, holding her hand, drifting off to sleep himself.

He woke at 12:30 A.M. Reaching over, he covered Lisa and brushed her brow.

He then went down to the study and phoned Dee.

"Hello," she answered groggily.

"Hi, sweetheart. I'm sorry if I woke you. I just needed to talk."

"Is everything all right? Did you take care of your business?"

"I don't want to talk about that. I just wanted to hear your voice."

She could hear despair in his voice. Sitting up, she asked, "Do you want me to meet you? It's no problem."

He thought about it. "No, I don't want to get you out of bed."

"Come over then."

"You have to work tomorrow."

"I'll be fine," she said. "I'll see you when you get here."

When Dee opened the door, Ben looked ragged. On the drive over, the image of Lisa lying in bed—frail, her voice weak—had wreaked havoc on his emotions. "Come on in," Dee said, grabbing his hand and pulling him into the apartment. She took his coat and went to hang it on the coat tree.

"Wait," he said, reaching in the pocket. He pulled out an olive-colored beaded scarf. "I found it under the seat in my car. You must have dropped it. " She held it in her hand for a moment, looking at it, then hung it on the coat tree with his coat and led him to the sofa.

"If you want to talk about anything, I'm here. I'm a really good listener," she said.

"I know, sweetheart. Thank you." They sat and talked about nothing in particular. Then he patted the sofa and asked, "Do you mind if I sleep here tonight?"

"Of course not," she answered. Getting up, she went to get some linens. She dressed the bed and then sat down and guided his head into her lap. She rubbed his brow and massaged his temples as he tried to find sleep. He took her hand and kissed it.

"Thank you for being here for me," he said, his eyes still closed. A tear escaped from the corner of his eye.

She felt tears creep to the rims of her eyes and quickly brushed them away. Leaning forward, she kissed his temple. Then, sitting back, she watched his strong jaw and thick black lashes as his breathing changed, and she could tell he was sleeping. Not long after that, she fell asleep.

He woke up to the smell of coffee.

"Good morning." Holly walked around the corner carrying a cup of coffee. Ben looked at the VCR to check the time. It was 6:30. *A little early for me,* he thought. He sat up, grunting.

"Good morning, Holly." She sat the cup on the table in front of him. "The cream and sugar is on the table," she said, going back into the kitchen. Dee walked out of the bedroom looking refreshed.

"Good morning," she said, leaning over and giving him a kiss. *How can anyone look so energized before 7:00 A.M.,* he wondered. "There's a new toothbrush in the bathroom," she said. "I hope you don't mind yellow."

Holly walked back into the living room. "I'm making eggs. I'll wait until you've freshened up." She grinned at Dee, wiggling her brows. "Nice pecs."

"Yes," Dee said, "they are."

He looked up to find both women looking at him. Blushing, he stood and went into the bathroom. Dee followed Holly into the kitchen. "Are you okay?" she asked.

"Yeah, I guess so—considering."

"Did you tell Ed?"

Holly groaned. "No, not yet."

"If you like, I can go to the office for an hour then come back here and hang out. You know, we can just talk or go to the movies—whatever you want to do."

"No. Thanks anyway. I know that whatever I decide, I'm not alone. I have Ed."

Dee stepped close, wrapping her in an embrace. "And you have me."

"And I have you," Holly said, hugging her back.

A few minutes later, Ben and Dee were seated at the breakfast table. Holly was in her bedroom getting ready.

"Do you guys always rise with the chickens?" Ben asked Dee, scooping eggs into his mouth.

"Only during the week," she said.

He leaned across the table and brushed his lips against her cheek. Taking her hand, he said, "I want you to meet my family." Dee looked at him as if he were speaking a foreign language. "Dee?" He said, squeezing her hand.

"Ah, really?"

"Yes, my mother and sister are all I have, and you're very important to me. I want the three women in my life to meet." She stared at him, not knowing what to say. "Would you?" he asked.

"Uh, when?"

"Saturday morning, if you're available."

Dee looked down at her cup and then back at Ben. "Saturday is good for me."
"Great." He smiled.

After he'd left, she closed the front door, resting her forehead against it. Then she let the panic wash over her. "Holly!" she yelled. Holly came running from her bedroom, fear in her eyes and voice.

"What? What's wrong?"

Dee plopped herself down in the armchair and moaned. "He wants me to meet his family."

"What? Girl, you scared the hell out of me. I thought it was something terrible."
Dee rested her forehead on her knees. "Oh my gosh! What am I going to do?"

"You're going to meet his family—what's the problem?"

"The problem is that he's white and I'm not."

"So?"

Dee looked at Holly. "You're kidding, right? Come on. You are one of the most caring people I know, and look at what you're going through. At least half of Edmond's family hates you. I don't think I could take that."

"Look, Dee, I've been with Edmond for more than two years. Sure, I want his family to like me—especially his sister Karen—but neither of us is going to let anyone come between us. That's how much we love each other."

"But Hol, I don't know if I'm strong enough."

"Look, sweetie," Holly said, sitting on the arm of the chair. "You really like Ben—I can tell—so just follow your heart. I know he cares about you, I think even more than you realize. Everything will work out."

* * * *

Ben walked into his condo and headed straight for the bedroom. When he reached the door, he froze. Something wasn't right: he never closed the bedroom door. His mind rushed to the fight he had had with Maurice. He debated opening the door, and possibly walking into an ambush, or calling the cops. He put his hand on the knob, bracing himself, and turned it. Quietly, he pushed the door open. Janet was sitting on the middle of the bed, naked.

"What the hell are you doing here?"

"I'm waiting for you," she purred.

"Janet, you need to go home."

"I've been waiting for you all night," she said sleepily. "Where have you been?" He looked over his shoulder. Seeing her clothes lying on the chair, he picked them up and tossed them to her.

"Put your clothes on," he said, walking to the closet to select a suit.

"You were with your *whore,* weren't you?" she spat at him.

"How the hell did you get in here anyway?" he asked, his back still to her.

"The doorman knows me. After all, I have been in your bed for months."

I'm going to have to talk to them about that, Ben thought to himself.

He turned to her. "For Christ's sake, Janet, give it a rest." His tone then became harsher. "We are not together! We will never be together!" He took a deep breath, trying to calm down. Then, speaking softly, he said, "Janet, don't do this. Just go home. Please."

She sat staring at him for a moment, and then she grabbed her clothes, shoved them in her overnight bag, and put her coat on over her nude body. "Ben, I'm not going to give up on us that easily."

"Damn it, Janet. There is no 'us,'" he said as she left the room.

Chapter 9

After parking his car, Ben got out and walked up the steps and into Meyers Investigation. He saw Chris and Dee standing by Kimmy's desk and strolled casually to where they stood. "Hello, sweetheart," he said, giving her a quick kiss and caressing her cheek.

"Hey," she said, smiling.

"Hello, Chris," Ben greeted him.

"Hey, how have you been?"

"Good. Yourself?"

"No complaints. So, Dee, this Evans guy meets her at this place across from where she works," he continued. "The last couple of times, they went into the men's room."

Dee nodded. "Did you follow up on that lead we talked about yesterday?"

"I was heading out to do that now—unless you want me to come with you."

"No," she said, "I can handle this. That lead is really important."

"Okay," Chris said, turning to Ben. "Good to see you again."

"Good to see you too," Ben said.

"You're going to spoil me, coming to see me so much," Dee said, leaning on the reception desk.

"Have you had lunch yet?" he asked.

"No, I'll get something on the way."

"More surveillance?"

"Kind of," she said, standing straight and heading toward her office.

"You're not talking about that thing with the couple in the men's room?" he asked, following her.

"Yeah, what about it?"

"You can't go into the men's room."

"It's no big deal."

"Yes, but don't you think you'd be a little conspicuous heading in there?"

"I know, but what other choice do I have?"

Ben flashed a wide grin.

The two of them stood outside the men's room of the restaurant.

"I can't believe I let you talk me into this," Ben said.

"I didn't; you volunteered. Okay, I just need you to see if anyone's in there."

Ben stepped inside, took a quick look around, and walked back out.

"No one's in there."

"Okay, now all I need you to do is watch the door and keep everyone out."

"What?"

"You know, keep everyone out," she said, nodding.

"Why?"

"So I can sneak in and take a few pictures."

"Are you sure about this?" he said, looking concerned.

"Yes. Don't worry," she said, opening the door. "Just keep everyone out," she whispered. The men's room was large, with six urinals and four stalls. The end stall door was closed. She walked quietly, looking around for something to stand on. After spotting a trashcan, she put the camera in her pocket, picked up the trashcan, and carried it with her to the far end of the bathroom. She sat the trashcan down quietly and stood on the rim, holding on to the wall. Looking over, she saw the man sitting on the toilet seat, with the woman's head in his lap. He was so engrossed in what was going on that he didn't hear the camera click. Dee heard a squeak from a few stalls down, followed by the sound of a man's voice.

"What the hell are you doing?" a short bald man asked from the other end of the bathroom. She jumped from the trashcan, darting for the door.

"Sorry, I thought this was the ladies' room."

"Not with a camera in your hand. What are you doing in here?"

Evans and his girlfriend opened the stall door. When he ran out, he fell over the trashcan.

"Hey!" the bald man said. "This pervert was taking your picture."

Ben rushed into the bathroom. "Oh, this can't be good. Come on," he said, grabbing Dee's hand.

"No, wait a minute! You're with this pervert! Call the police!" the bald man yelled as Ben and Dee walked out of the restroom. They walked briskly from the back of the restaurant to the front. As they approached the door, two police officers were walking in.

"Oh shit!" Dee said under her breath.

"Officer," the bald man called out. "That lady was in the men's room taking people's pictures."

"What?" The officer looked at him, not understanding.

"That lady," he said, pointing at Dee. "She was in the men's room taking those people's picture." The officer blocked the way so Dee and Ben couldn't leave the restaurant.

"Okay, look," Dee said, "this is all a great big misunderstanding."

"Is it now?" the officer said, pushing his hat back.

"Yes officer," she said, trying to look innocent.

The officer looked at the man and woman gathering their belongings from their seat "Sir, what's your name?"

"Uh, Evans."

"And this is?" The officer gestured to the woman with him.

"Uh, this is Mrs. Evans."

Dee snorted. "Yeah right."

"Did this woman photograph you in the restroom without your knowledge?"

"I don't know anything," he said, trying to leave.

The bald man said, "That man and lady were in the stall, and she came in the men's room to take their picture. Probably for some porn magazine." He grunted. "She's a pervert, I tell you."

Dee looked at him questioningly. "So, you knew they were in there but you stayed anyway?"

"So?"

"So, what were you doing in there?"

"What?" he asked, looking surprised.

"Were you having a little fun with yourself after you saw them come in? Now who's the perv?" He was quiet, looking like a child who had been caught stealing a cookie.

"You know what? I don't have time for this." Evans said, grabbed his coat and leaving.

"Officer, you need to do your job."

"See officer?" Dee smiled sweetly. "It was just a misunderstanding."

"I don't think so, lady. Maybe you need to come downtown with us."

Ben rushed in to help. "Officer, she wasn't doing anything wrong. She didn't even know that other gentleman was in there."

"You don't say."

"That's right, I looked into the restroom myself, and I didn't see him." Dee threw him a quick sideways glance, indicating that he should shut up.

"Officer..." she said, looking at his nametag, "Styles. I can explain all of this."

"Yeah I'm sure you can too, down at the station—you *and* your friend."

* * * *

"I've never been busted before," Ben said, looking amused. "Will we have our mug shots taken?" Dee just sat looking out the window. He took her hand. "Come on, sweetheart. It'll be okay. I'm sure we'll be out of there in no time." Dee didn't say anything during the whole ride.

"Take a seat," Officer Styles told them once they were in the station. Dee sat in a chair next to the desk, and Ben sat in the chair across from her.

"Officer, this is a mistake, really," Dee said as Holly walked into the squad room. She saw Dee and walked over to where she was sitting.

"Oh my God. What did you do this time?"

"This is all a mistake," Dee said quickly.

"Officer Styles, I'll take care of this," Holly said to the officer.

He looked at Holly and nodded. "Yes, ma'am."

"You two, come on." Dee and Ben followed Holly to her desk. Edmond walked out of one of the offices. Seeing Dee, he laughed.

"What happened now?"

"Nothing," Dee said, rolling her eyes.

"Sit," Holly said. "Now, tell me."

"Well, there's this subject we're trailing, and Chris told me that at least once a week he and this woman meet at this restaurant, so we went there, and we saw the man and this woman go into the men's room. So I told Ben to watch the door, and I went in to catch them—you know. I got the shots, but this guy was in the other stall. He came out and accused me of being a pervert—imagine that."

"Yeah," Holly said dryly. "Imagine that."

"We almost got away, but just then two cops walked into the restaurant," Dee said throwing her hands up. "But we really didn't do anything."

Holly turned to Ben. "I expect this from Dee, but why would you get involved in this Ben?"

He felt like he was being chastised by his mother. "Holly, this is really just a misunderstanding."

"That's what she always says."

They then saw a stocky black man walking in their direction. Dee slid down in her seat.

"Deanna," his voice boomed.

"Oh boy." She sat up straight. "Hi, Uncle Craig." Craig Galloway was the precinct captain and Dee's godfather. She rose from her seat and kissed him on the cheek.

"Girl, what did you do?"

"Nothing! Ugh," she said, dropping back in her seat.

"Dee, you can't keep doing this," Holly said.

"I'm tired of hearing that. 'Dee, you can't do this. Dee, you can't do that. Dee, you can't climb a tree in someone's yard and take pictures through the window,'" she said in a mocking tone.

"Well, you can't!" Holly yelled.

"My client was the homeowner," she said, looking innocent, "and she gave me permission."

Ben started laughing.

"Don't encourage her. That's not funny," Holly scolded.

"Sorry," he said, trying to hold it in.

"I thought you would have known better," Holly said, looking at him. "I figured you would be the voice of reason in this relationship."

"Hey, I was just there to watch out for her."

"What's your name, son?" the elder man asked. Ben stood.

"Ben, sir. Benjamin Harrison," he said, reaching for the other man's hand and shaking it.

"Craig Galloway. I'm Dee's godfather, and I'm thinking that you don't know my goddaughter very well, do you?" He glanced down at Dee then back at Ben. "You're the young man that saved her from that attack by her ex-boyfriend?"

He nodded. "Yes, sir."

"Well, don't let her fool you; she can be sweet, kind, and caring, but she can be mean as hell when she wants to be. That guy just caught her off guard— believe me."

"You got that right," Edmond added. "Remember that time when that guy—"

"Hey, I'm still sitting here," Dee interrupted.

Craig then became serious. "Dee, seriously, I don't want you to get hurt. You mean too much to me. You need to be more careful."

"I am, Uncle Craig. I just need to train my lookout a little better," she said, smiling at Ben.

Craig laughed. "Well, you're free to go, but I'm going to tell you mother about this."

"Thanks, Uncle Craig." She gave him a quick kiss on his cheek. "See you at home, Hol," she said sheepishly.

"See you at home, crazy woman," Holly shot back.

As they walked down the steps, Dee took Ben's hand.

"I can't believe we did that," Ben said, shaking his head.

"All in a day's work," she said happily. "Do you have to be somewhere? If not I want to show you something."

They had to catch a cab back to her car. She had wanted to ask the officer to take them back to the restaurant, but she didn't want to press her luck. They drove to the beltway and pulled the car over onto the shoulder. Then she turned on the flashers. "Come on," she said, getting out of the car. She walked to his side of the car and pointed to the sunset over the horizon. It was glorious, with orange and yellow rays emerging from a magenta sky.

"This is the best spot," she said, sitting on the hood. He looked at her, seeing the sun's rays shining on her face, giving her cocoa complexion a golden undertone. Smiling, he took her in his arms.

"You're something else." She looked at him questioningly. "You barge into a men's room, get busted, and get hauled off to jail, yet you still manage to catch a sunset before dinner."

"Like I said, all in a day's work."

* * * *

After leaving Dee, Ben went to his mother's house to check on her and Lisa. He found Lisa sitting in the sunroom reading. "Hey, sis," he said as he walked in. He leaned down and kissed her forehead then sat across from her and took her hand. "How are you doing?"

"I'm feeling much better, thank you," she said. She did look a lot better. Looking at his clothes, she asked, "Where have you been? I haven't seen you wear blue jeans in years."

"I went on a stakeout."

"A what?"

"A stakeout with Deanna."

"Really?" He nodded.

She closed her book "How was it?"

"Interesting." He told her every detail, from when they got to the restaurant to when the police took them in. Seeing the amusement on her face, he became even more animated. "And then we parked on the side of the highway and watched the sunset."

"That sounds wonderful. So romantic," she said, smiling. "I think I like this Deanna. I've never seen you smile like when talking about a woman."

"She's like no one I've ever met."

"Who is like no one you've ever met?" Natalie Harrison asked as she walked into the sunroom.

"He's talking about Deanna Meyers, mother," Lisa said. "You know, the PI we hired."

"You've been seeing her?" Natalie asked.

Ben prepared himself for his mother's reaction before answering. "Yes," he finally said. She looked at Lisa then back at Ben.

"Tell me about her?"

Lisa started telling her about the events of the day. Ben wished she wouldn't, but she seemed so full of life that he let her continue.

"You got locked up?" Natalie asked, surprised.

"No, not really. We did get taken to the police station in a squad car though."

"On my," Natalie said, placing her hand on her chest.

"But her best friends are police detectives and her godfather is the captain. It was just a misunderstanding; we worked it all out."

"Hmm," Natalie said.

Ben was thoughtful for a moment. "I want to bring Deanna here to meet the two of you."

"Oh?" Natalie said, looking surprised.

"I think that's a great idea," Lisa said. "When do you want to do it?"

"Saturday morning?" Ben asked, looking at his mother. He was like his father in so many ways. She smiled at him with pride.

"That will be wonderful—we can have brunch," she said. Ben rose from the chair, kissing the two of them before leaving.

Natalie sighed, turning to Lisa. "I'm a little worried about this Deanna woman."

"Mother, Ben has good judgment. Plus, he has never brought anyone home to meet us, so she must be pretty special."

"Maybe," Natalie said, seeming anxious. "We'll see, dear."

Saturday arrived sooner than Dee would have liked. She woke up early, reaching for the phone immediately.

"Hello?" Ben answered, his voice raspy from sleep.

"Sorry to wake you," Dee said. "Go back to sleep. I'll talk to you later."

"No, I'm fine. Is everything all right?"

She was silent.

"Sweetheart, are you there?"

"Yes, everything's fine. I'm just being silly."

"No, you're not. Tell me what's on your mind."

"I'm a little nervous about today."

"There's nothing to be nervous about; Lisa thinks you're great already and mother will love you, I'm sure." She closed her eyes, letting his soothing voice calm her. "I do understand how you're feeling," he said, "but there's nothing to worry about. I promise."

She took a deep breath. "Okay, I'll be ready when you get here." After hanging up, she watched the ceiling, allowing different scenarios of brunch with Ben's family, to play through her mind. She had had plenty of boyfriends and met many of their families, but this was somehow different. She really wanted this family to like and accept her. This time, she felt, there was a real possibility that the family might try to come between them. Considering his character, however, she thought this unlikely—but she would do whatever she could to ensure they would accept her. "I know he will do whatever he can," she whispered. "I trust him. Might as well do this," she said, getting out of bed and going into the bathroom to shower.

By 10:00 A.M., she had changed clothes three times before deciding on a cream-colored cashmere dress and brown boots. She had her hair down and was wearing a gold heart locket and earrings to accent her outfit. She looked at herself in the mirror. "No," she said aloud, walking back to the closet.

"Good morning," she heard Ben call from the living room.

"Damn," she said, turning away from the closet and walking down the hall. He was standing in the middle of the floor, holding a white rose.

"Good morning, beautiful."

Dee smiled. "Good morning, handsome." He gave her the rose and kissed her cheek. "Let me put this in water," she said, walking into the kitchen to find a small vase.

"How are you this morning, sweetheart? Did you feel better after our talk?" Ben called from the living room. Dee smiled as she walked back in the living room with the vase.

"Yes, thank you."

"Are you ready for this?" he asked.

"As ready as I'll ever be."

Ben walked over and rubbed her back "They are going to love you."

"You don't know that," she said.

Ben looked into her eyes. "Yes, I do. Ready to go?"

She took a deep breath, smiling at him, trusting him.

"Yes."

* * * *

The gates were twelve feet of wrought iron. After turning into the driveway, they drove another half-mile to the house. When they pulled in front, Dee felt every muscle in her body tighten. She looked at Ben. "You grew up here?" Ben looked at her and smiled. *Oh boy,* she thought.

"I have it, Mike," Ben said to the driver, opening the door himself and getting out of the car. He then helped Dee out of the passenger side. Dee looked up at what Ben called a house; to her it was a mansion. There were twelve-foot-tall pillars on both sides of the massive front doors. They walked into the foyer, which had a vaulted ceiling with a massive chandelier, marble floors, and an enormous staircase in the center. A short, round woman emerged from one of the side doors.

"Mr. Harrison, your mother and sister are waiting for you in the parlor."

"Thank you, Sadie." They walked down the hall and then turned into one of the doors on the left. Ben's mother and sister sat on the loveseat together; it seemed to Dee that they were having an intimate conversation. Ben cleared his throat as they approached. His mother looked up.

She smiled. "Benjamin." Standing, she hugged him.

"Hello, mother," he said, kissing her cheek. His sister stood up slowly, and Ben gave her a big hug. "Lisa, how are you today?"

"I'm fine." Ben stepped back and looked at her closely.

"Are you sure?"

"Yes." She smiled faintly.

"Dee, this is my mother, Natalie Harrison, and my sister, Lisa. Mother, Lisa, this is Deanna Meyers."

"Hello, Mrs. Harrison," Dee said, stepping forward to shake Natalie's hand. Natalie was a five foot three blonde with the same green eyes that she had passed on to her son. She wore a tailored blue suit with gold buttons and gold jewelry

She was studying Dee closely. *Oh boy,* she thought, *here we go.* Then Natalie smiled.

"Deanna, I'm so pleased to meet you. Ben has told us so many wonderful things."

Dee smiled back nervously.

"Thank you," she said, turning to Lisa. "Hello, Lisa."

Lisa offered a shy smile and a quiet "hello." Lisa looked a lot like her mother, but her eyes were as blue as the sea. She wore a pair of jeans and a blue sweater and had her hair in a ponytail. Dee saw sadness in her eyes; she looked tired and withdrawn.

"Please," Natalie said, "have a seat."

Dee sat on the couch across from Natalie. As she watched Lisa sit down slowly, she realized the young woman was ill.

"So," Natalie said, "how are things coming along with the case—finding Nancy Greer's child?"

"Mother, I don't think we need to talk about that now," Ben said.

Dee shifted nervously. "I wasn't aware that you knew about it. You don't have a problem with Ben looking for your late husband's... mistress?" Dee questioned.

"Oh no," Natalie replied, "It was my idea."

"Really?" Dee said, looking at Ben.

"Shouldn't we be sitting down to brunch now? It's getting late, and I'm sure Lisa hasn't eaten yet today."

Natalie looked at Lisa. "I'm sorry, dear. You're right," she said. "We'll be having brunch in the sunroom. Shall we?"

As they walked down the hall to the sunroom, the sun shone through the row of windows that stretched from one wall to the next. The bold yellow walls reflected the sunlight, bathing the room in brightness. The loveseat and chairs were covered in floral prints, and there were miniature hibiscus trees in each corner and flowers on every table. The décor made it seem to Dee as though it were a sunny spring day, even though it was November, with the temperature outside in the thirties.

"Do you know what's for brunch, mother?" Ben asked, trying to keep the conversation light.

"Cucumber and watercress sandwiches. Sadie knows I hate them. I think she makes them just to piss me off."

"Mother," Lisa said.

Dee giggled.

"Give me a juicy hamburger with the works any day," Natalie said.

"Mother," Ben replied, "your cholesterol?"

She shrugged. "Even still." She looked at Dee and winked as they all sat down. "You know, Deanna, I was surprised to see that you were black. I suppose Ben has some of his mother's liberal tendencies after all."

"Mother," Lisa said, her cheeks blushing.

"Oh, for crying out loud," Ben said.

Dee was shocked by her remark but was also amused by everyone's reaction.

"What?" Natalie asked, looking at her children. "Anyway, what I was going to say is that I'm glad to welcome you into our home. I would like to think that we raised our children to see people for who they are." She paused. "You know, when my husband and I first met, we were quite poor. After my husband started his business, we joined the country club. When we first started going there, the other members were dreadful to us, and I told myself then that I'd never do that to anyone else."

Dee liked Natalie already; she said what was on her mind and you knew where you stood with her. She also liked Lisa, but she felt sorry for the girl; she seemed so sad and withdrawn.

"So," Lisa said, leaning intently on the table, "tell us everything about being a PI."

Dee told her about the first case she had. She had gone to an old warehouse to take pictures of some guy running an insurance scam. She had hidden in a storage room and they had locked the door for the weekend. She had been locked in there for almost two days before her father came to rescue her.

"Didn't you have a cell phone?"

"I'd left it in the car," Dee said.

Lisa smiled. "That's a wonderful story. I'm going to have to remember that one to tell my friends."

The rest of the brunch went smoothly. Dee entertained everyone with stories from her childhood. Natalie told Dee how Ben loved playing sports, and hanging out with his friends as a teen, but no matter what he had planned, he would always make time for his little sister.

"It was really nice of you to invite me to brunch," Dee said. "Thank you."

"It was my pleasure, dear," Natalie said. She stepped close to Dee and gave her a hug. "And thank you for everything you're doing for my family."

When they parted, Dee said, "Will you tell Lisa I said goodbye?"

"Of course," Natalie said.

In the car, they rode in silence. Dee looked at Ben. "Can we go somewhere private? I need to talk to you."

"Of course you do," Ben answered.

* * * *

Dee took off her coat and dropped it on Ben's sofa. "Okay, now tell me why you really want to find Nancy Greer."

Ben looked at Dee, putting his hands in his pockets. "I told you, I'm not looking for Nancy Greer; I'm looking for my half-sister."

"Ben, don't play games with me. You know what I mean. *Why* are you looking for her?"

Ben walked to the armchair and sat down. He ran his hands through his hair and sighed.

"I already knew where Nancy Greer lived—well up until last year, when she moved again."

Dee walked to the chair and sat down. "Go on."

"My mother gave me her name and number last year, and I went to see her. I asked her to put me in contact with my half-sister, and she said she wouldn't."

"So you knew the child was a girl?" Dee asked.

"Yes. She wouldn't tell me anything, but I was able to figure it out from what she'd told me."

"Let's start from the top, Ben. You need to be straight with me."

"Twenty years ago, my father had an affair with Nancy Greer. She thought he was going to leave my mother. When she told him she was pregnant, she demanded that he leave her. He was able to convince her to hide the pregnancy for a few months. I don't know all the details, and mother only knows what my father told her, but she supposedly threatened to confront my mother, tell her everything. But my father beat her to it and told my mother himself. My parents decided to pay her to leave town—they gave her enough to start over and deposited more money into an account every month to help her raise her child. When my father wouldn't leave my mother, Nancy told my father he would never see his child."

He took a deep breath.

"Two years ago, we found out that Lisa had acute leukemia. She has had blood transfusions, and she has gone through chemotherapy once. It went into remission, but she has relapsed, and now she needs a bone-marrow transplant. I was tested but I'm not a match " He paused.

"Last year, mother told me about Nancy Greer and I went to see her. I pleaded with her—I even told her of Lisa's situation—but she wouldn't tell me where her child lived. I'm pretty sure they don't live together, but I didn't know anything else. In October, Lisa became very ill, and the doctors said she needed the transplant soon. I tried to track down Nancy Greer again and found that she had moved. That was when I came to see you."

"But why didn't you tell me? I would have helped you anyway."

"Lisa doesn't want anyone to know, she didn't want anyone feeling sorry for her. That's why I didn't use the company PI. When I told her I was going to find an outside PI, she made me swear not to tell anyone. I'm sorry for not telling you, but she's my baby sister, and I have to respect her wishes."

Dee could hear the pain in his voice. He tried to blink back the tears, but they began to flow, rolling down his cheeks. Her heart broke for him. Dee walked to the chair and stooped in front of him. She took his hands in hers. "I'm sorry for not being straight with you," he said, looking into her eyes, wrenching her heart even more.

"No, I'm sorry... I'm so sorry," she said.

For the next two hours, Dee sat with Ben and let him talk. She knew he had been allowing the pain to build inside him and decided that he needed to let it out. There then came a moment of silence. He gazed at her.

"I shouldn't be burdening you with all of this. I just feel so comfortable talking to you. I think it's hard for people to understand what it's like watching someone they love die and being helpless to stop it."

Dee looked down at her hands. "I know how you feel." She swallowed hard. "When my father had his accident, the doctors said there was nothing they could do. He was in the hospital for two weeks, trying to hang on, but I knew we were losing him."

Ben reached out and she came willingly into his arms. They sat and held each other, hoping to chase each other's pain away.

Chapter 10

"I'll be gone for two, three days tops," Dee said, holding the phone on her shoulder as she shoved clothes in her bag.

"Are you sure you don't want me to go with you?" Ben asked.

"No, I'll be fine. It'll be a piece of cake."

He groaned.

"Just kidding," she said, laughing. "I'll call you later."

"Bye, sweetheart. Be careful."

"Bye."

She zipped her bag shut and walked out of the apartment to a waiting cab.

* * * *

She shoved her carry-on bag in the overhead compartment then sat down in her coach seat and looked around at the other passengers on the plane. She shifted, trying to get comfortable. She had always hated flying. She reached into her handbag and pulled out the file. It was nearly impossible to get an actual copy of someone's birth certificate, but Chris had managed it. Mother: Nancy Greer. Father: Benjamin Harrison Sr. Child's Name: Heather Greer. In the last year, Nancy Greer had moved from Bethel, Maine, to Manchester, New Hampshire, then to Burlington, Vermont, and finally to Portland, Maine. Dee had learned a number of things about the girl, as well: Heather had lived with her mother until she was sixteen; then Greer had sent her to live with her sister in Bangor, Maine, where she had graduated from high school the previous year.

She placed the file back in her bag then closed the small shutter on her window. She shut her eyes, trying to pretend that she was on a bus.

"Ma'am?" She opened her eyes. "Can I get you anything?" the flight attendant asked. Dee smiled, shaking her head. "No, thank you."

She rested her head on the seat, thinking about the events of the past few weeks. Terry's behavior, Holly's pregnancy. Holly said that she still didn't know what she was going to do, but Dee knew Holly would keep her baby. She had so much love to give that she wouldn't consider doing anything else. She would be a good mother. As for Terry, she hadn't spoken to her since that day in her apartment. She had called her once or twice to check on her, but Terry had not returned her calls. She heard the announcement instructing the passengers to fasten their seat belts. Realizing she must have dozed off, she fastened her belt, preparing for landing.

Sitting in the cab, Dee looked at the brown ranch-style house, with its deferred maintenance. The brown paint had peeled in various spots allowing the yellow that lay underneath to show through. A shutter hung from a single hinge on one window, while the other window was missing its shutters altogether. After handing the cab driver a twenty-dollar bill, Dee slipped her bag on her shoulder and walked to the house. She rang the bell. A thin woman of about fifty opened the door, peering through the screen.

"Hello, Leslie Davidson?"

"Yes?"

"My name is Deanna Meyers. May I speak to Heather, please?"

The woman looked at Dee suspiciously. "Heather doesn't live here anymore."

Dee smiled. "Can you tell me where I can find her?"

"Who are you?"

Dee thought of a lie; then, remembering that she always got into a bind when she lied, she decided to tell her the truth. "I'm a PI hired by her father's family to find her."

"I can't talk to you," she said, closing the door.

"They want to give her the inheritance her father left," she said quickly, before the door closed. The woman stopped.

"Really?"

Dee nodded. "Yes." *I'm sure the Harrisons will include her as a family heir, so it's not really a lie.*

"How much will she get?"

"I really don't know."

Leslie Davidson looked around, scratching a red spot on her neck, then brushed her oily brown hair down. "Okay, come on in," she said, moving to the side. They walked into the living room. "My sister said that you people would probably come here. Said that you don't give a damn about her family; that you only want to use them." She scratched her neck absent-mindedly.

"Mrs. Davidson, the Harrisons won't use your niece. I promise you, they're good people."

"You say you don't know how much money she's going to be getting?" Leslie asked.

Dee shook her head slightly as she watched Leslie scratch. "You know, maybe you should get that looked at."

Leslie looked at Dee, confused. She thrust her head toward the sofa. "Have a seat. I have to get my phonebook. I'll be right back."

Dee sat her overnight bag on the floor. There was a smell of musk and cat urine in the air, and she rubbed her nose. Looking around, she saw once-blue plaid furniture which was at least fifteen or twenty years old, and three-foot bookshelves along one wall with various picture frames on it. Dee walked over, scanning the photos. She saw a stack of mail and then looked over her shoulder for Leslie. She scanned the mail quickly, finding a letter addressed to Leslie from Heather Greer. She looked over her shoulder once more then put the envelope in her pocket. She turned and walked back to the middle of the floor, not wanting to sit on the grungy sofa for fear that she might catch whatever Leslie had.

"I just talked to my sister," Leslie said. "And she told me that you weren't looking for Heather for no inheritance. She told me to call the police."

Whoa, Dee thought, *time to go.*

"Ma'am, I didn't mean any harm," Dee said, picking up her bag and walking to the door. "I'm just here on my client's behalf." She opened the screen door and quickly stepped on the porch.

"Why don't you leave my family alone?" the woman yelled. "Why don't you stop?"

Dee pulled her coat around her neck while walking down the street. She was thinking about the envelope she had in her pocket—and how she didn't want to have to explain it to the cops.

When she got a few houses down, she picked up her pace, double-timing it to the corner. She put a few blocks between her and the house before she hailed a cab, and then she headed to the airport.

* * * *

Dee walked up the steps of the Brownwood, Texas, home and knocked on the door. A young woman answered. She had curly sandy-blond hair and the same blue eyes that Lisa Harrison had. "Hello, I'm looking for Heather Greer."

"That's me."

"Ms. Greer, my name is Deanna Meyers. I'm a private investigator from Chicago. May I come in and talk to you, please?"

Heather Greer paused a moment then stepped to the side.

"Sure, come on in."

* * * *

"Benjamin Harrison, please," Dee said into her cell phone as she walked briskly through the airport, heading toward baggage claim.

"Harrison here."

"Ben, it's Dee. I don't have much time. I'm at the airport. Can you meet me at your mother's house?"

"What is it, sweetheart? Is everything all right?"

"Everything's fine. Can you meet me?"

"Sure, what time?"

"I'm getting a cab now. Can you be there in an hour?"

"Okay," he answered slowly.

"Good, I'll see you then."

* * * *

Janet walked through the main door of Harrison Enterprises with a purpose. With her jaw set and her shoulders square, she walked to the elevator and stabbed the button. She had had time to think and knew what she had to do. She was tired of playing this game, tired of Ben acting like a fool. She knew what needed to be done, even if he didn't see it. She would *make* him do the right thing, and then they would get their lives back on track—but first she needed to get rid of that whore.

She stepped off the elevator and walked past the receptionist desk, down the hall toward Ben's office, her eyes averted from the young woman smiling at her.

"Good morning, Ms. Summers," the receptionist said as Janet blew by her desk, not offering her a glance, her eyes focused down the hall.

As Jill looked up she saw the look of determination on the face of the woman walking toward her, she knew she was in for a fight. She rose from her desk as the younger woman approached. Jill smiled. "Good morning, Ms. Summers."

Janet looked through her, walking around the desk and heading toward the office door. Jill stepped in front of her, causing Janet to gasp and recoil as if a snake had suddenly appeared in her path. "What are you doing?"

"Mr. Harrison doesn't want to be disturbed."

"Well, I'll go inside and wait until he's finished with whatever it is he's doing," she said, waving her hand to shoo the other woman out of her way.

"Do you have an appointment?"

"What does that have to do with anything?"

"Mr. Harrison doesn't want you barging into his office."

"Get out of my way, you twit," Janet said. Using her forearm in a sweeping motion, she tried to shove Jill to the side.

Jill pushed her arm back, sliding in front of her. "No," she said, her voice stern.

"What are you doing you, you stupid woman?" Janet's eyes narrowed as she spoke through clinched teeth. "I said," she said, her voice rising with each word, "get out of my way!"

"Mr. Harrison told me that if you tried to get into his office, I was to call security and have them escort you from the building." Jill placed her hands on her narrow hips, a slight smile drawing across her thin lips. "And I would like nothing better than to see your nasty self being dragged out of here kicking and screaming."

Janet stared at the other woman with her mouth open until the door to the office opened. When Ben stepped out, his eyes met hers. His dark green shirt made his emerald eyes seem a deeper shade of green. Her heart fluttered, as she thought he had never looked more handsome. Her voice trembled from the excitement of seeing him. "Hello," she whispered.

"Hello, Janet. Jill, I have some urgent business to attend to. I'd like you to reschedule all my appointments for the rest of the day."

"Yes, sir," she said, stepping out of the way letting him walk by. Janet followed him down the hall.

"Ben, I'd like to talk to you if you have a moment."

"I don't," he said, walking to the elevator and pushing the button.

"I really need to talk to you," Janet said, stepping in front of him. He looked up, watching the numbers over the doors roll by, willing the elevator to hurry up. "I think we should talk. I can see you're in a bit of a hurry," she added quickly. "But surely you have a few minutes for me." He quietly took a deep breath. "Ben, are you listening to me?"

"No," he said with no emotion. As the door slid open, he stepped around her and onto the elevator. She followed him, and they rode in silence to the ground floor. When she turned to him, he walked off the elevator, not giving her a chance to speak.

"You can't avoid me. I won't just go away," she said, continuing to follow him. He walked across the lobby and out of the building with her following close behind. She ran around him and stepped in front of him again. "You are not going anywhere until you listen to me." She crossed her arms, looking at him with defiance.

"I have things to—"

"I just wanted to say I'm sorry," she said quickly. He looked interested now. "Really, I am—for the way I've been behaving and the things I've said. You know that's not me."

"Okay," he said slowly.

"So, can we call a truce?" she asked, offering her perfectly manicured hand. He glanced down at it, then up, his eyes meeting hers. Finally, and reluctantly, he took her hand.

"I'm sorry, but I really must go," he said, pulling his hand away and walking around her in the direction of the garage. She smiled to herself, put her hands in her pockets, and walked up the street.

"Ben, Deanna didn't say why she wanted to meet you here?" she said, pacing the floor.

"No, mother. She was in a hurry. She should be here soon."

"I hope there's no problem," Natalie said, her voice a whisper. Ben watched her pace, wishing she would stop. She was making him even more nervous. He watched as she wrung her hands, gracefully twirling them around one another. She seemed so small when she was afraid. He walked over to her and hugged her, kissing the top of her head.

"I'm sure everything's fine, mother." He turned when he heard the doorbell and walked briskly to the door. They reached the foyer as Sadie opened the door. Dee stepped inside when she saw Ben approaching. A young woman followed her. "Hello, sweetheart," Ben said, smiling, but his eyes were filled with worry.

"Benjamin and Natalie Harrison, I'd like you to meet Heather Greer." Ben and Natalie's mouths dropped. Ben looked at Dee, and she nodded. Then she stepped slightly to the side. Natalie stepped forward.

"Hello, dear, how are you?" Natalie asked.

Heather shook her hand. "Nice to meet you."

Ben looked at her and smiled. "You have our father's eyes—happy eyes."

She bit her lip, smiling nervously. "Hi." She reached out to shake his hand. Ben stepped in and hugged her tight. He then stepped back and kissed her forehead.

"Heather has come all the way from Texas to meet Lisa," Dee said.

"Lisa will be so pleased to meet you," Natalie gushed, taking Heather's hand and leading her to the stairs. Ben looked at Dee.

"I found her yesterday, and I thought that I might be able to convince her to meet you guys. She wanted to meet Lisa, to spend some time with her and get to know her. She said she wouldn't make any promises but would at least think about being a donor."

Ben's heart swelled with joy. "Sweetheart, I can't believe you did this. Thank you." He wrapped her in a crushing embrace, swaying from side to side. "You're one hell of a woman, Deanna Meyers."

"You're not so bad yourself, Benjamin Harrison."

When Natalie walked into the foyer, Ben and Dee parted from their embrace.

"Deanna, thank you so much," Natalie said, hugging Dee as she wept openly.

Tears ran down Dee's cheeks.

"No thanks are necessary," she said, hugging her back.

"Benjamin said you were special," Natalie said, "and I knew he was right when he brought you home to meet us—he's never brought anyone home to meet his family."

As Natalie continued to hug her, Dee looked at Ben, her eyes asking whether this was true. Ben smiled and nodded.

Dee said her goodbyes to Natalie, Lisa, and Heather, as Ben had the car brought around to take her home. "They seem to be getting along well. Lisa has always wanted a sister," he said, smiling broadly. "There's even been talk of shopping sprees. Even if Heather's bone marrow isn't a match, the visit will have been good for Lisa's spirit."

"You can never have too much love," Dee said as she leaned against the car. "So," she folded her arms, "what was all that about you never bringing anyone home to meet your family?"

"No one's ever made the cut until now."

"You don't say?" she asked, biting her bottom lip.

"Nope. A few have come close, but they didn't quite make it." Ben moved close to her and took her in his arms. "You are an amazing woman, Dee. I think about you constantly—your beautiful brown eyes, their long lashes, your sweet lips... I love you." He kissed her lips softly. Dee's heart started racing. She pulled back to look at him.

He saw her surprised expression. "It's true," he said. "I've known it for weeks. I didn't tell you, because I didn't want to scare you away."

Dee looked away, not knowing what to say. As if he could read her thoughts, he said, "I don't expect you to tell me you love me. I just had to let you know how I feel about you." He pulled her closer to him again. "God how I love you." He kissed her again.

* * * *

2:17 P.M. Subject left bar with...

She looked at what she had written. "No." She shook her head, tearing the sheet of paper from the notepad and tossing it into the wastebasket. She reached over and turned the mini tape recorder off. This was her third attempt at writing the report. She dropped her pen in frustration, sighing heavily. As much as she tried to concentrate, all she could think of was what Ben had said to her. She was confused. Did he say it because he was happy that she had found Heather? Was it gratitude? Did he just get caught up in the moment? *Maybe I'm analyzing this too much,* she scolded herself.

"Dee, you have a call on line two."

She gave up attempting to write the report and decided to let Liz take care of it. She picked up the phone.

"Hello?"

"Hello, sweetheart."

"Hey," she said, smiling.

"Can you come over to my place this evening?" he asked.

"Sure—what's up?"

"I want to cook dinner for you."

"Sounds good."

"I'll see you at seven then."

"I'll be there."

Ben hung up the phone and checked the time; he only had four hours to go to the bookstore and stop at the supermarket before getting home and preparing his feast. "Have a good day, Jill," he said as he left the office. He got into the limo and leaned over the seat to look at Mike. "Can I ask you a question?"

"Sure, sir."

"Can you cook?"

"Sir?"

"Can you cook?"

"A little." Ben rested his chin on his forearm in thought. "Where to, sir?"

"I need to go to a bookstore and a supermarket." He paused. "Could you do me a favor?" he asked, glancing at Mike.

"Sure, anything, sir."

"Thanks," Ben said, patting the man's shoulder.

Ben looked through the cookbook, deciding what he wanted to make and what ingredients they needed to buy. "This sounds pretty easy," he said, pointing a picture. Mike leaned over to take a look.

"Sir, for your first time out, I think you should stick with something simple, like steak and potatoes or baked chicken."

"No," Ben said, shaking his head, "Dee likes Mexican. Besides, it looks easy enough." The two men stood in the produce aisle figuring out what they needed to buy. "It says here that we need a three-and-a-half-pound red snapper."

"That sounds like an awful big fish for just two people," Mike said, scratching his head.

Ben nodded. "Yeah, I'll get a smaller one. What about the tomatoes?"

"It says two pounds." Mike said. "I think you should get one."

"Good idea. Hmm, it says here I need to butterfly the fish. What does that mean?"

Mike leaned over, looking at the book. "No," he said, pointing at the page and shaking his head. "They mean butter *fry* it. That's a mistake; they always do that in cookbooks. That's why I never use 'em. Come on. We need some butter."

An hour later, the fish lay motionless on the counter while the two men stood watching it with their heads cocked to the side, as if they expected it to flop over into the sink and down the drain.

"I think we should've asked the man at the fish counter to cut the head off," Mike said, scratching his chin, still staring at the fish. Ben nodded.

"Yeah, we should have." He picked up a chef's knife from the counter; then, with a thump, he whacked off the head. He looked up smiling as he wiggled his brows. "That was easy enough."

Mike turned, picking up the cookbook reading it. "It says the fish has to be cleaned and scaled."

Ben poked the fish. "If I scrub it really hard when I clean it, the scales should come off," he said, looking at Mike. "What do you think?"

Mike nodded. "Good idea."

Ben searched under the sink for something to clean the fish with. He took out a scrub brush and dishwashing liquid, holding it up for Mike to see.

"Yeah, but don't scrub too hard. You don't want to damage it."

"Right." Ben put dishwashing liquid in the sink, filled it with water, and then put the fish in. Mike walked next to him, watching as he scrubbed. After washing the fish, he mixed the ingredients with Mike's help. "Wait a second," Ben said. "Aren't we supposed to fry it in butter first?"

"If we take the four sticks of butter and put it in the pan with the fish, the heat from the oven will fry it. Then all the juices will blend together and make it taste better."

Satisfied with this rationale, Ben placed the butter in the pan then slid the pan in the oven. They set the dining room table and put white and red candles of various sizes throughout the room.

"Sir," Mike said, "I'm going to leave now. This gives me an idea for my girlfriend."

"That's right—you told me awhile back that there was someone special. How's that going?"

"Great." Mike hesitated. "I think I'm in love."

"That's wonderful. Hey, I have something for you." Ben walked to the closet and reached into his coat pocket. He handed Mike two tickets to the play *West Side Story*.

"Thank you, sir... but weren't you and Ms. Meyers going to use these?"

"No, we can go anytime. I want you to have them. Have a good time—and on that evening you can take the Mercedes, if you like."

"Thank you, sir. I really appreciate it."

"No. Thank you."

"Don't mention it," Mike said, patting his back. "Have a good time. And good luck."

"Hello?" Dee called from the living room.

"I'm in the kitchen." He was pouring salsa into a festive dip bowl along with tortilla chips.

"Oh, I love to see a man being domestic," she said, walking up behind him and wrapping her arms around his waist. He turned and kissed the top of her head, holding the tray so she could get a chip.

"Let me take this to the table; then I'll serve dinner."

"Smells good," she said, following him into the dining area. The table was decorated with a bright red vase filled with chrysanthemums. Ben sat the bowl on the table. He pulled out Dee's chair for her then leaned over and kissed her neck.

"I've missed you," he whispered. He went back in the kitchen to bring the rest of the meal to the table.

"Do you need my help?"

"No, you just sit there and relax. I have everything under control." He bought in a margarita for her and one for himself. The fish was displayed attractively on the plate, surrounded by onions, peppers, and carrots. Ben took a carving knife, cut the fish in half, and placed half on Dee's plate. He poured some sauce on top and placed the plate in front of her, and then he prepared his own plate. Dee watched as he smiled proudly. "Go ahead." She scooped up a big forkful and put it in her mouth. She chewed, then stopped, as her eyes widened.

She nodded. "Mmm."

He then took a big bite of his own. After chewing for a moment, he looked at Dee. "Somehow this isn't what I expected."

"Oh?" she asked, reluctantly taking another bite. As she chewed, she felt something strange. Thinking it was a bone, she took it out and looked at it.

Ben leaned over to examine her find. "Oh, that must have come from that scrubbing thing."

"What?" she asked, laughing.

"You know, the thing you scrub the food with."

Dee set her fork down. "Uh, babe, how many times have you cooked?"

"This is my first," he boasted. "I had a little help from Mike—he mostly read the directions from the cookbook." He set his fork down. "It's not very good, is it?" She quietly looked down at her plate and pushed the food around. "Go ahead and tell me. It won't hurt my feelings."

"You just need a little more practice," she said, holding her index finger and thumb close together.

"I'll try again next week."

"No," she said with a little more enthusiasm than she intended. He laughed. "I have an idea," she said, clasping her hands and resting her chin on them. "Let's you and I cook together next week. Maybe we can cook something for Holly and Ed—and we could invite Lisa, Heather, and your mom. I think they would like that."

Ben smiled. "Yeah. I like that idea. I like cooking. Maybe when we get married, I'll cook for you every day."

"That sounds ideal to me." She smiled. "I love to see a man in an apron—it makes me hot."

"Maybe I need to keep you away from restaurants then. I wouldn't want you running off with some chef."

"No," she said, getting up and sitting on his lap. "I just like it when I come home to it."

"Ah," he said, holding her close. "How hot does it make you?"

She kissed the tip of his nose. "You'll have to get an apron to find out."

"You know what? I think I saw one in the kitchen somewhere." The buzzer for the intercom rang, drawing Dee's attention to the elevator. She looked back at Ben. "Forget it," he said. "They'll go away." He covered her lips with his. *Buzz, buzz, buzz.*

"I think you'd better get that. It might be important."

Ben walked to the buzzer. He stabbed the button and yelled, "What?"

"Benji," Janet's voice whined from the intercom. "They won't let me up. They said you told them I'm not allowed."

"Jesus," Ben said, resting his forehead against the wall.

"It's important," she said.

"Then call my office and make an appointment."

"It's not business; it's personal."

"You might want to let her up and talk to her," Dee said from behind him. "You really don't want everyone in the lobby to know your business."

He looked back at her and sighed. "Come on up."

When Janet stepped off the elevator, Dee caught a glimpse of the white teddy she was wearing under her coat. Janet saw Dee and closed her coat, tying it at the waist. Dee watched a scowl spread across Janet's face, then noticed her jaw clinch as she struggled to control her emotions.

"What do you want, Janet?" Ben asked, not letting her any farther than the front of the elevator.

"I wanted to see how you were doing," she said, watching Dee. "I didn't mean to disturb your dinner."

"No problem," Dee said.

Janet peered at the table. "I see you made fish. Ben doesn't care much for fish."

"Actually, Ben cooked dinner for me." Dee watched anger flicker in the other woman's eyes then disappear just as quickly.

"Well," Janet said, shifting from foot to foot.

"I thought that you said you had something to talk to me about?" he said.

"No," she said, not meeting his gaze. "It doesn't seem that important now."

"Janet, I'd really appreciate it if you didn't come here again. It's not fair to

Dee, and I'm sure it's uncomfortable for you as well."

"Yes, I suppose you're right." She watched Dee as she spoke. "Have a good evening," she said as she turned, stepping onto the elevator.

Ben turned to Dee. "Are you all right?"

"Sure, I'm fine."

He walked back to the table and sat across from her, taking her hand.

"I'm sorry about that," he said, looking uncomfortable.

"It's not your fault."

"Actually, in a way it is. Janet and I stopped seeing each other not long before you and I started dating. After I told her that I didn't want to see her anymore, I went out with her once more, and I'm afraid she thinks that will happen again."

"When you went out with her, were we seeing each other?"

"No," he said quickly. "This was before we started seeing each other."

They sat quietly for a few moments. She looked down at their hands, stroking the back of his with her thumb. He leaned across the table and kissed her, and then he reached up and stroked her cheek with the back of his hand. "Is there something wrong?"

"I wanted to talk to you about something," she said. He waited patiently. She took a deep breath. "I wanted to talk to you about yesterday, about what you said." She looked into his eyes. "I know I'm overanalyzing this, but I need—"

"You need to know that I wasn't speaking out of excitement."

She nodded.

He moved his chair close to hers, placing his knees on either side of hers. "I do love you. I've never felt this way about anyone. The day I walked into your office was the best day of my life. That was the day I came to life."

She rose from her seat and sat in his lap, wrapping her arms around his neck. He looked at the table. "I'm sorry about dinner. I wanted it to be special."

She ran her finger across his lips. "It was. It's the thought that counts."

"If you like, I can make you something else," he said.

She glanced into the kitchen and saw the dish liquid and pot scrubber sitting on the counter top. "Did you by any chance use soap when you cleaned the fish?" He smiled proudly and nodded.

She bit her lip. "You know what? I really could go for a burger. Let's go out."

* * * *

Lisa was feeling much better. She and Heather made a date to go ice skating and had invited Dee and Ben to join them. They walked into his mother's house, Ben wearing a dark blue wool coat and jeans and Dee wearing a brown corduroy pea coat, jeans, and a cream hat and scarf.

"Are you guys ready?" Ben asked Lisa and Heather.

"Yes," Lisa said. "I haven't been skating in a couple of years. This is going to be such fun."

They went to the Hyde Park ice skating rink. Lisa was an excellent skater, and they all cheered when she did a perfect pirouette.

"Are you all right?" Dee asked Lisa when she sat down to rest.

"I'm great. I'm having the best time."

"We don't want you to overdo it."

"No, I'm fine, honestly," she said. Her nose and cheeks were as red as cherries.

Ben skated over to them. "I'm going to get us some hot chocolate."

They watched him skate away slowly. Lisa looked at Dee. "Can I ask you something?"

"Sure," Dee said, rubbing her hands together, warming them.

"What's it like to be in love?"

Dee watched her closely and asked, "Have you ever been in love?"

"I thought I was, once," Lisa said, watching Heather, "but now that I think back, I realize that I wasn't. I see the way you and my brother look at each other, and I know it's real. I want to know what it's like. You know, just in case."

"Just in case what?" Dee asked, regretting the question as soon as she had asked it.

"Just in case I can't get the transplant for one reason or another." Dee fidgeted uncomfortably. "No, it's all right. I've come to terms with the fact that it might not happen," she said, looking down at her feet. "It's a fifty-fifty chance—I know that—but I'm not really scared anymore. Some days, I'm just very sad."

Dee slid over and slipped her arm around the younger woman's waist, allowing her to rest her head on her shoulder.

"So?" Lisa raised her head "What's it like?"

Dee looked at her. "I don't know."

"So how do you feel when you look at Ben?"

"I feel nervous and excited and happy all at the same time. What makes you think that your brother loves me?"

"I can tell by the way his face lights up whenever he hears your name and the way he hangs on to your every word. I see it in the way you two look at each other."

"It could be lust."

"No, I know what lust looks like; it's a romantic look, an 'I can't live without you' look."

Dee watched her, feeling very sorry but trying hard not to show it. Taking her hand, Dee asked, "How does that make you feel?"

"I'm happy for him, for the both of you. I love him, and he deserves to be happy." She sighed, smiling at Dee.

She drove down University and made a left on Fifty-ninth Avenue, eventually turning into the parking lot. Driving slowly, she found a spot next to a tan pickup and pulled in next to it where she could have a better view of the skate park. She watched as the foursome sat on the bench putting on their ice skates. He was with her and two young women who looked to be in their early twenties.

She figured one was his sister, while the other must have been her friend. She watched him squat down, helping her put on her skates and tying them. Then he rose, pulling her out onto the ice with him. As he skated around with her, he slipped his arm around her waist. She looked away, not wanting to watch anymore, but the scene drew her eyes back against her will. He stopped skating and pulled her into an embrace, his long fingers stroking her cheek Then, slowly, he bent down and kissed her. As she watched him kiss her, she felt a stabbing pain in her heart; she thought surely she would die at any moment. She gripped the steering wheel until her knuckles were red, tears burning in the rims of her eyes. She willed herself to calm down and breathe.

They started skating again, and the other women joined them. Sadness overtook her as she saw the look on his face. "One day he'll look at me like that," her lips said, but no sound came from her throat. She rested her head on the steering wheel, tears streaming down her face. Then she sat up straight, trying to recompose herself. She watched her as she sat next to the young blonde. They talked for a few minutes before he skated over to them. "That must be his sister," she said aloud.

She watched as he skated away, his long, muscular legs moving gracefully. She then looked at *her* again—she seemed to be comforting his sister. "No, this is not right. I'm supposed to be the one who's there for her, who comforts her like a sister. No!" She sobbed. She looked to her left and saw him skate back carrying a box filled with hot drinks. She lovingly placed her fingers on the window, trying to feel him through the glass.

She angrily swiped away her tears and started the car. As she tore out of the parking lot, she damned herself for coming.

* * * *

"Hey," Ben said, skating back to them. "Why so serious?" Lisa and Dee looked at each other and smiled. Dee squeezed her hand.

"It's nothing. Just girl talk."

They skated for another hour, not wanting Lisa to become too fatigued, then had Caribbean food for lunch at the Calypso Café.

Chapter 11

Dee entered the lobby of Harrison Enterprises. It was large; larger than her office and lobby put together. "I have an appointment with Mr. Harrison," Dee said to the receptionist.

"You can walk down that hall, ma'am. You'll find Mr. Harrison's assistant if you enter the last door on the left."

"Thanks." Dee walked down the long hall, admiring the abstract oil paintings. She turned left into an office richly decorated in earth tones. Ben's assistant looked like she could have been a high school principal. In her crisp blue blouse and neatly cut bob, she was the perfect picture of order and efficiency. Dee walked up to her desk.

"Excuse me, I have an appointment with—"

She looked up, meeting Dee's gaze. "Ms. Meyers?"

"Yes."

"Go right in."

"Um, thank you." Dee went to the inner office door and peered in. "Whoa!" she said, stepping in and closing the door behind her. *This place is bigger than our apartment.* Everything on Ben's desk was neat and orderly, with a stack of mail sitting squarely in the center. She ran her fingers along the front of the heavy desk, picturing Ben making executive decisions from his plush leather chair. She then walked over to the window to look out over the skyline. Hearing the door open, she turned toward it.

"Hello, Deanna," Russell said, looking as surprised to see her as she was to see him.

"Hi, Russell." Dee smiled, walking back over to Ben's desk.

"How have you been?" he asked. He slowly closed the door and walked toward her.

"I've been good. And yourself?"

"Great. So, what brings you here?"

"Ben and I are having lunch together."

"Ah," Russell said. Hiking up his slacks, he sat on the edge of the desk. "So, how are things between you two? I hope they're going well."

"Yes, they are." As Dee watched him, she understood why women might consider him attractive. His sandy hair was cut short and parted on the side. His striking features—piercing blue eyes and a deeply cleft chin—seemed to complement the arrogance he exuded. As Russell looked at Dee, he licked his bottom lip and let his eyes travel down her body. She immediately felt uncomfortable, averting her eyes. She folded her arms over her breasts and turned back toward the window.

"Have you been to Club Pacific lately?" he asked.

"No," Dee said, "not lately." She felt his eyes on her and turned, looking directly into them. At that moment, she realized she didn't like him. "I'm sure Ben will be back any minute."

Russell nodded. "I saw you at the club one night. You're a great dancer. Sexy—I like that."

She bit the inside of her cheek, refusing to let him get to her.

"So, how's work?" she asked, changing the subject.

"I liked watching you dance. Maybe we could go sometime?" he said, his voice low. She glared at him as he continued, "I think we'd have a lot of fun together."

"What the hell are you talking about?"

"Maybe we could get together and have a little fun?" He stood, walking toward her. "I know how you guys are, how hot you women are."

"Really?" Dee said, gritting her teeth.

"Yeah, I heard about how you black women like it nasty," he said, reaching for her, letting the tips of his fingers brush her breast. "We could have a lot of fun. Maybe we could make a trade—I give you something and you give me something."

Dee grabbed his hand and twisted his wrist in one quick motion. "Are you crazy? What do you think this is—some kind of brothel? I could break your wrist. Maybe I will," she said, applying more pressure. "Then I'll sue your sorry ass for sexual harassment."

Russell cried out in pain.

When the meeting adjourned, Ben was the first one to his feet. He gathered the papers in front of him into a folder then turned and walked to the door. One of the executives meet him in the hall, and Ben talked to him briefly, then walked swiftly to his office.

"Mr. Harrison, Ms. Meyers and Mr. Pemberton are in your office," Jill said to Ben as he walked into the outer office.

"Thanks Jill," Ben said, as he opening his office door. He stopped in his tracks when he saw Dee standing by the window, and Russell reaching out to touch her. Dee then grabbed Russell, and a moment later, he was howling in pain. He heard Dee say something about breaking his wrist.

"What the hell is going on?" Ben said, frozen in his tracks by the door.

"I'm just giving your friend here a crash course on how to treat a lady," she said, twisting his wrist a little more. Ben closed the gap between them.

"Dee, let go of him."

"No," she said, glaring at Russell. "What did you think? That I was going to melt at the feel of your grimy touch?"

"I'm sorry," Russell cried. "I don't know what came over me."

"Come on, sweetheart. Let him go." She gritted her teeth, gave his wrist a slight turn for good measure, and then pushed him away. Russell cradled his hand while stumbling into the armchair.

"I think you broke my wrist. I can't believe this. You're crazy!"

"Are you all right?" Ben asked Dee, studying her closely. She nodded.

"Her? What about me? You saw what she did," Russell yelled, thrusting his head toward her.

"I should break your neck," Ben yelled, lurching toward him.

Russell drew back, fearful.

Dee stepped next to him, grabbing his arm. "No. He's not worth it."

Ben looked at Russell, his jaw clenched. "You're fired. I want you out of your office and this building by three o'clock."

"You can't fire me. I have a contract with this company."

Ben looked at Jill, who was standing in the doorway, her mouth hanging open and her eyes wide with shock.

"Jill, have security come to my office immediately." He turned back to Russell. "Now, you have two choices: you turn in your letter of resignation in one hour, or you can go to jail for sexual assault."

Russell looked at him as if he were mad. "If I resign, I lose everything I've worked for."

"If you go to jail, you'll lose more."

"I won't go to jail. It's my word against hers," he said, sneering at Dee.

"Jill and I both saw what you did. I'll make sure you're put away."

"Look," Russell said sitting straight, his voice pleading. "I made a mistake. Can't we talk about it?"

Jill walked through the door, followed by two security officers.

"It's your choice, Russell."

Russell looked at Ben, his dismay etched in his stark features, making them seem even more pronounced. Ben turned, picking up the phone. "Okay, okay. I'll give you the damn letter."

Ben addressed the guards. "Take Mr. Pemberton to his office; let him pack up his belongings and then escort him from the building. I expect your letter on my desk in one hour," he said, not looking at Russell.

* * * *

"You're not eating," Dee said.

"I'm not very hungry." He pushed his plate away. His mind kept drifting back to the scene in the office.

"Ben, everything's fine," she said, reaching for his hand. "Really."

"I can't believed that he talked to you that way... and that he put his hands on you." Ben clenched his fists, his face reddening.

"But I handled it."

"I should have had him locked up."

"It would have been my word against his."

"I witnessed it."

"No, you witnessed me assaulting him; it could have just as easily been me getting arrested." He looked at her. "Stranger things have happened," she said, putting her elbows on the table and resting her chin on her hands. "I think you did the right thing." She smirked. "And I also don't think he'll be trying to feel up any unsuspecting women anytime soon."

"I'm not doing such a great job at protecting you, am I?"

"Ben, what are you going to do? The guy's a jerk. Big deal. You can't lock up or, God forbid, beat up every guy who says or does something to me that you don't like."

"I know, sweetheart."

"Besides, I think I handled the situation very well."

He looked into her sparkling brown eyes. He had to smile. "Yes, you did."

"So let's not let that jerk ruin our day."

He looked out the window at the pedestrians passing by. "What are you doing for Thanksgiving?" he asked.

"I'm going to visit my family. I was kind of hoping you would come with me."

"I'd love to...but we've sort of make a tradition of spending the holidays together since my father died."

Dee nodded. "I understand."

"Tell you what," he said, reaching for her hand. "What if I come to Atlanta with you on Wednesday and then come back in time for Thanksgiving dinner with my family?"

"Really? You don't mind?"

"No, not at all."

* * * *

Letting herself in with the key, Dee and Ben walked into her grandmother's house. "Hello?" she yelled, setting her bags down. Jean Meyers walked out of the kitchen. Jean was an older version of Dee, she wore a stylish short hairstyle (which she insist made her look younger) and was a few inches shorter.

"Let me get a look at my baby," she said as she held Dee at arm's length. She looked her up and down for a moment and then pulled her into a tight embrace. "How are you really?" she whispered.

"I'm fine, mom, really."

Jean released her, looking around. "Where's your cousin?"

"I don't know. I haven't talked to her in a while. We had a falling out."

"Did you?"

"Yes."

Her mother glanced at Ben. "So, this is the young man you've told us so much about?" she said eyeing him.

"Ben Harrison, this is my mother, Jean Meyers."

"Hello, Mrs. Meyers," Ben said, shaking her hand.

"Call me Jean," she said, smiling. An elderly woman just under five feet tall walked out of the kitchen sporting a bright orange apron.

"And this is my grandmother, Harriett Marsh," Dee said. "Grandma, this is Ben Harrison."

Ben shook the older woman's hand.

"Oh, he's a cute one. Big too. I like 'em big," Dee's grandmother said.

Dee laughed. "Grandma has a habit of saying what she thinks," she whispered to Ben who smiled.

"Very nice to meet you, ma'am,"

"Glad to have ya. Are you staying with us?"

"No, ma'am. I'll be staying at a hotel."

"Nonsense," Dee's grandmother said with a wave of her hand. "We have plenty of room."

"I don't want to impose," he said.

"It's no imposition. If it was, I'd tell ya," she answered.

"Yes, ma'am," he said, smiling. "I believe you would. Thank you for having me."

Ben walked into the guest room and placed his bag on the bed. He looked around, taking in the pink walls, the flowered curtains, and the matching bedspread.

"Kind of girly, huh?" He turned to the sound of the voice at the door. Jean smiled at the startled look on his face.

"Yes, ma'am."

Jean nodded, walking into the room. "Mama likes flowers. It's been like this since I was a little girl. We don't often have overnight guests, so it doesn't matter.

Dee told me how you two met, and about your sister being ill and all."

"Yes, ma'am."

"Mother and I were so sorry to hear about that. If there's anything we can do for your family—"

"Thank you. We're hoping the transplant will be a success."

"We'll keep her in our prayers."

"Thank you." She walked to the bed and sat down.

"Have a seat," Jean said, patting the spot next to her. Ben sat, giving her his full attention. "I wanted to talk to you about my baby."

"Yes, ma'am. I thought as much."

"Dee's a smart woman, and I like to think my husband and I raised her right, but the two of you being in a relationship is a little more than we prepared her for. She knows about racism—she's had to live with it—but the two of you will have to deal with a much different set of reactions." He decided to speak candidly. "Dee and I have talked about this subject. Racism, or any sort of hatred, is hard to deal with, but I can't walk away from Dee because of what someone else thinks. Dee asked me what I would do if my family was against our relationship."

Jean watched him curiously.

"I know we haven't known each other long, but she is amazing. She makes me laugh out loud and see things in entirely different ways. I feel like she's the other half of me that I never knew was missing." He looked into her soft brown eyes. "I know that I can never know what any black person goes through, but I know that I love your daughter and that I want to protect her."

Jean smiled at the tenderness in his voice.

"And I'll do my best. Considering the line of work she's in, it's not that easy."

Jean looked up at the ceiling. "Don't even get me started on that. I talked to Craig—he said you two got hauled in." Ben's spine stiffened. "Did she ever tell you about the time she decided she wanted to do a little detective work herself and her father had to save her?"

"No." He shook his head, grateful that she had dropped the subject of their adventure in the men's room.

"Well, William had this case that he had been working on for over a year, some man collecting disability and working at the same time. He said that the man had been very careful and that it had been hard to catch him. Well, Dee decided that she wanted to prove to her daddy that she would one day be a great investigator like him. She was only seventeen, mind you. So, she cut school and followed this guy for a few days. She found out where he worked, but it was at one of those factories that you couldn't get into unless you were an employee.

"One day, the guy left his window down, so she opened the trunk and got in, planning to get out and take pictures of him when he got to work. But when he got to work, she tried to open the trunk from the inside and couldn't."

Ben sat watching her with an amused expression as she told the story.

"Well, she called William from this cell phone she had—I told him she didn't need it, but later I was glad she had it, and she reported with perfect calm, like some big-time investigator, the name of the factory and the make and model of the car. He went there with the police that day and managed to get a picture of the guy at work."

"So she was able to help him?" Ben asked.

She laughed. "Yes, but William was pissed. He told her that she could have been hurt and that he didn't want her to be an investigator—he wanted her to go to law school. But she wore him down. He was so proud that his baby girl wanted to follow in his footsteps."

"He sounded like a good man."

"He was."

"I would have loved to meet him. I know I would've liked him."

Jean looked at Ben. "I think he would have liked you too." She patted his hand. Standing, she said, "let me leave you alone so you can get settled in and freshen up a bit." She walked out the door, closing it behind her.

* * * *

Ben offered to take the women out to dinner that night since they had to cook dinner the next day, but they wouldn't hear of it. They made beef stroganoff and homemade apple pie.

"The meal was wonderful," Ben said, wiping his mouth with his napkin as Harriett cut him a large slice of apple pie and set it in front of him. "Smells good," Ben said, scooping a forkful into his mouth. "Oh, this is great. I see where Dee got her recipe."

Harriett laughed, looking at her granddaughter. "Boy, you gotta be in love, because her pie is awful."

"Hey," Dee protested.

"I'm sorry, baby. You're a good cook, but your apple pie is pretty bad," Jean said, laughing.

"Holly likes it," Dee said in a singsong voice.

"That's because," Harriett said, taking a small bite of pie and closing her eyes, savoring it as she spoke, "hers is worse than yours."

After dinner, Dee and Ben sat in the living room watching TV while her grandmother and mother were in the kitchen. Ben nuzzled her neck. "Hey, I don't want to make out with them in the next room."

"They won't know," Ben whispered.

Dee's mother walked into the dining room. "Hey, no making out in the house. If I can't, no one can," she said, laughing.

"Jean, go on and let them make out—it's good for them."

"Oh boy, here we go," Dee mumbled. "Maybe if we sit really still, she'll forget we're here."

"She needs to take him for a test drive to make sure she's getting her money's worth."

"Oh my God," Dee said, standing up quickly while Ben laughed. "Grandma, do you need any help in the kitchen?"

"No, baby, we're fine. Go on and rest a spell with your beau." Dee saw her grandmother watching Ben. She knew that look and rushed in, trying to cut her off.

"I really don't mind."

"He's got cute lips too. I bet he can kiss."

"Grandma!"

"What?" Harriett said, looking at her granddaughter.

"Grandma, maybe we can go into the kitchen and you can give me your recipe for apple pie?"

Her grandmother walked over to the sofa. "So, when are you going to marry my granddaughter?" she asked Ben earnestly.

"Grandma, we just started dating."

"Well, in my day you didn't need to be courting that long before you know if you wanted to be with somebody. If you went out, you knew right then whether he was or wasn't the marrying kind."

"Grandma, things have changed."

"No, men are still men and women are still women. Do you like him?"

"Yes, grandma."

"Well, what the hell you waiting for? I want to see my great grandbabies, and I ain't getting any younger."

Dee laughed. "Grandma, you're younger than I am."

Harriett frowned. "Girl, are you sassing me?"

"No, ma'am." Dee stopped laughing and smiled.

Her grandmother nodded and then turned back to Ben. "So," she said as she sat down across from him, looking like she was preparing for a long talk.

Dee turned away, throwing her hands in the air, saying. "I give up," she said as she walked into the kitchen and stood next to her mother, who was washing a plate. "Mom, can you get grandma?"

"Nope," Jean said, handing Dee a towel and a plate to dry. "You know how she is once she gets started."

"Yes I do—that's what I'm afraid of."

"Where's your cousin?"

"I don't know. We haven't talked much lately."

Her mother nodded, passing her another plate.

"Have you talked to her?" Dee asked, wiping the plate and putting it in the cabinet.

"She says she's coming for dinner tomorrow." Dee nodded. "What's going on between you two?" Jean glanced at her daughter.

Dee sighed wearily. "I'd rather not say just yet. I can say that she has done some pretty awful things."

"How awful?" Jean questioned. Dee sighed again. "Awful for even Terry."

Dee walked Ben to the rental car. "I wish we could have dinner together," he said.

"I do too. I'm glad you could come though."

"I am too." He wrapped his arms around her. "I miss you already."

"You're not even gone yet," she said.

"Thinking about you being so far away from me makes me miss you. I like your family; your grandmother's hilarious."

"Yeah, what did she say while I was in the kitchen?"

"The usual."

"Oh boy," she said, rolling her eyes.

"It wasn't that bad," he said. "She asked my views on children, marriage, my family, my intentions with you."

"And that didn't scare you away?"

"No, I think it's great that your family loves you so much—and that they respect me enough to ask me."

She smiled, stroking his cheek and kissing him. "You'd better go, or you'll miss your flight."

He kissed her goodbye and got into the car. "I'll call you when the plane lands. I love you, sweetheart." He said.

She leaned into the car and kissed him again.

"I'll miss you," she said.

Jean's cousin Margaret and her son Phil arrived followed by Harriett's sister-in-law.

"When can we eat?" Phil asked. "I'm starving."

Margaret glared at her son, telling him without words to keep quiet.

"We *were* waiting for Terry," Jean said, "but I suppose she's not coming. Let's all go into the dining room."

They all gathered in the small, festively decorated dining room and began to sit around the oval table when they heard a yell coming from the living room. Terry opened the front door, walking into the house like a gale.

"Hello, everyone," she bellowed cheerfully. "Happy Thanksgiving."

Jean walked into the living room. "Hi, baby," she said, giving her niece a bear hug. "I thought you weren't going to make it. We were just getting ready to sit down to dinner." Jean looked behind her. "Where's the baby?"

"He's spending today with his father. I get to keep him on Christmas."

"I wish things could have worked out between the two of you. That child needs both his mama and his daddy."

"You know what, Aunt Jean? I keep trying to tell David that very thing, but you just can't talk to some people. Besides, after finding out how he really is, I think it's for the best."

Jean looked at her niece sympathetically and then led her into the dining room.

"Hi, everyone. Happy Thanksgiving," Terry said to everyone in the room. "Hello, Grandma Marsh."

Harriett looked at her and nodded. "Terry."

"Sit down everyone. Sit down," Jean instructed. After she brought the turkey from the kitchen and set it down in the middle of the table, each of them took the hands of those sitting on either side of them, and they said grace. Jean asked their cousin Phil to carve the turkey, and they began serving the meal.

"Terry," Margaret said, "I love that sweater."

"Thanks. I just bought it from Neiman Marcus." She smiled, looking at Jean. "Aunt Jean, would you please pass the potatoes?"

Dee looked at the potatoes in front of her and then at Terry. She picked up the plate and passed it to her mother, who passed it to Terry.

"So, Terry," Dee asked, "how have you been?"

Terry ignored her, turning to talk to Phil.

"Okay, whatever," Dee said to herself.

Terry looked at her. "Why are you so concerned all of a sudden? You didn't care before."

"Terry, we don't want to do this now," Dee said, biting the inside of her mouth to keep her anger in check.

"It's Thanksgiving," Jean said. "Let's not ruin it."

"No, she acts like she cares so much about me, but when I ask her for some help, she acts like it's a big deal."

"You're crazy," Dee said.

"I went to her office one day and asked her for money to get my car fixed, and she wouldn't even help me. She had the nerve to tell me I needed to get a job."

Dee looked at her with astonishment. "What?" She put her fork down. "Oh my God. Holly was right. You really are crazy."

"Oh, don't even mention that bitch."

"Terry Ann," Jean scolded.

"All Holly ever does is run around making up all these terrible stories about me."

"Do you want me to tell everyone what you did, Terry?" Dee yelled. "Do you want me to embarrass you in front of everybody sitting here?"

Terry was quiet.

"I'd like to hear," Phil said.

"Boy, keep quiet," his mother told him.

"So, now you're all against me," Terry said.

"No one's against you, Terry," Jean said.

"Yes you are. I can see it in your eyes. You don't care that I'm having a hard time and that I could lose my son. None of you care," she said, letting out a sob. "I can't even give my son a good Christmas."

"Give it a rest, Terry," Dee said. "I talked to David."

Terry jumped from her seat, her voice rising. "Oh, now you're going to believe him?"

"Sit down, Terry," Dee's grandmother said.

Terry hesitated.

"I said sit." Harriett's voice boomed throughout the small room. She looked at Dee. "What's all this foolishness about?"

Dee looked at Terry and sighed. "Terry came to me and said David was going to take Little David from her."

There were looks of shock around the table; she held up her hand before anyone else could jump in. "But I talked to David, and it seems that Terry wants to give Little David to her mother's mother. He's been living with her for a few months, and David has been giving her money to care for him. That's why he wants to take the baby—because he thinks he needs to be with at least *one* of his parents."

"I just need her to take care of him for a while, until I get back on my feet," Terry said.

"I also gave her seven hundred and fifty dollars for a lawyer after she told me that he had hired one." Dee paused. "Which, by the way, he hadn't. He says he wanted to work all this out, but Terry told him that she'd let the baby live with him only if David gave her money every month to live on."

Dee's grandmother looked at Terry. "Is that true?"

"I was going to get a lawyer, but then we talked and we decided we could work all this out."

"So what about the money?" Jean asked.

"So I didn't need the money for a lawyer after all," Terry answered, pushing the silverware around with her index finger.

"So you'll give it back," Jean said, nodding.

"I can't. I don't have it. Besides, she gave it to me."

"Not for you to spend," Jean said in disbelief.

"You know what?" Harriett said, pointing her bony finger at Terry. "You are a real piece of work, I'll tell you." She shook her head. "Girl, you're a grown woman. You need to be taking care of yourself instead of trying to get everybody to do it for you."

Dee could see the disgust on her face and hear it in every word she said.

"At least, that's what a real woman would do."

"I can't believe you," Terry said, glaring at Dee. "You make me sick. And I actually started feeling sorry for you. Well, I don't anymore. Whatever you get, you deserve."

Terry stood, pushing the chair and knocking it over as she stormed into the living room. She grabbed her coat and rushed from the house, leaving the door open behind her.

Chapter 12

"Hi, Monica," Dee said to the young receptionist as she walked past her desk. "I love your hair like that."

"Hi, Ms. Meyers," the young woman said, touching her hair subconsciously. "Thanks." Dee walked down the hall, smiling and nodding to the other employees as she passed them. "Morning, Jill."

"Good morning, Ms. Meyers. How are you today?"

"I'm good, and yourself?"

Jill smiled broadly. "Fine, thanks. Mr. Harrison should be back any minute, so go right in."

"Thanks, Jill." Dee walked into Ben's office, took off her coat, and laid it across the armchair. She walked over to the window and watched the traffic below, wrapped in her thoughts.

"Hello, beautiful," Ben said in her ear.

She jumped and turned around. "I didn't hear you."

"You smell delicious," he said.

She smiled. "Good enough to eat?"

"Most definitely."

"Sounds promising," she purred. He bent down and kissed her, his tongue softly tracing the fullness of her lips. It sent shivers through her, and she felt him harden through his dress pants.

"Woman, you don't know what you do to me."

She smiled. "I have a pretty good idea."

He claimed her mouth again, kissing her deeper this time. She moaned, feeling dizzy. He ran his hands down her back to her buttocks, squeezing gently.

Then he drew her closer, rocking his lower body against her pelvis. "Oh, God," Dee moaned, as he trailed kisses down her neck and back up again. There was a knock at the door.

Ben groaned. "Yes?" he asked. Dee moved out of his arms.

"Mr. Harrison, someone's here to see you."

"Who?"

"She says she's your sister Heather."

After Heather's visit, Ben was more relaxed than Dee had ever seen him. Heather had agreed to undergo the testing, to see if she was a donor match for Lisa. He seemed deep in thought at the moment. "Are you all right?"

"I'm fine, sweetheart—just thinking about Lisa and Heather going through the transplant. I'm a little concerned. Hey," he said, taking her in his arms, "go away with me. Why don't we just pack up and go away for a four-day weekend?"

"I don't know. I have a lot of work to do—and what about Lisa?"

"Work will be here when we get back, and Lisa seems to be doing much better. I'm sure the transplant won't be for at least another week or two. I don't think four days will matter much."

"I don't know," she said, biting the side of her mouth.

He studied her. "What's wrong?"

"Nothing," she said, shaking her head.

Ben laid his book on his chest, looking up at Dee. "What are you reading? She held the book so he could see the cover while she continued to read. "*Double Homicide* by Jonathan Kellerman? How can you read that stuff?"

She leaned over and looked at his book: *Trading Systems and Methods.* "Oh yeah, and yours is much more entertaining."

They were at her apartment. She was sitting on the couch, with his head resting in her lap. He was deep in thought, absent-mindedly running his fingers up and down her arm.

"Sweetheart."

"Hmm."

"Tell me your fantasy."

She laughed. "What?"

"Tell me your fantasy."

"Why?'

"Pretend I'm a genie—I can make your fantasy come true. Tell me what it is."

She put her book down. "I'd need to think about it."

He looked up at her. "Whatever you want, I'll get it. Wherever you want to go, I'll take you. I only want to make you happy."

"Hmm, let me see. I would like to fly to an island with white sand and palm trees. I'd sit by the water drinking Mai Tais and have cabana boys serving me whatever I want."

"That's what all women say."

"Well, I don't know. I don't fantasize much."

"Really?"

She looked at him. "Is this a trick question?"

He smiled. "I plead the fifth. Come on, tell me."

"Okay." She sat with her arms folded, one hand under her chin. "Dancing under the stars with the man I love with a slight breeze blowing and soft music playing."

"That's nice," he said.

"Boring?"

"No, just nice," he said, stroking her arm. He picked up his book and returned to his reading.

Later that evening, as Ben sat behind his desk in his office, he picked up the phone. "Hello, Holly, this is Ben. I really need you to do me a favor."

Dee went to the bank. When she returned to the office, Ben was waiting for her. "Hello, sweetheart."

"Hi," she said, giving him a kiss. "What are you doing here?"

"I've come to make your fantasy come true."

"Oh boy, what did you do?"

"Come with me." He took the papers she was carrying and put them on Kimmy's desk. Grabbing her hand, he pulled her along with him. "We're leaving now, Kimmy. Hold down the fort."

"Wait a minute!" Dee yelled. He kept walking. They went down the steps to the limo. "What's going on?"

"I talked to Chris and Liz, and they assured me they could handle everything until we got back."

"But I haven't even packed."

"Everything is packed and ready to go," he said. "All you have to do is say yes." She looked worried. "No pressure, I promise." He added, "I'm sure everything will be okay until we get back. It'll only be four days."

She nodded. "Okay, let's go."

* * * *

They flew to Miami International Airport then boarded a seaplane, which took them twenty-eight miles from Key West to the five-acre Little Palm Island. When they stepped from the plane, Dee felt as though she had entered another time. There were thatched-roofed private bungalows buried in dense foliage and tropical flowers. Each bungalow overlooked the sea. When they entered their bungalow, it had two large bedrooms with king-size beds and a Jacuzzi. Dee passed through the sliding glass doors and saw a wraparound sundeck with steps leading to a private beach, complete with a hammock hanging between two palm trees.

"This is grand," Dee said, standing on the sundeck and looking out on the white sand beach.

Ben wrapped his arms around her from behind, resting his head on hers.

"There are no televisions, no alarm clocks, and you don't have your phone."

"What if I need to check in at the office?"

"Nope, no checking in."

"What if I have an important call to make?"

He shook his head. "I have you at my mercy."

"Mmm, sounds wicked."

"I have something special planned for you."

"What is it?"

"I can't tell you. Are you tired?"

"No, excited."

He smiled. "Okay, let me make a phone call."

"I thought you said there were no phones."

"Ah," he said, holding up his cell phone, "I said *you* had no phone. You're at my mercy." He laughed, walking inside.

"Hey, that's not fair," she said, following him.

Dee pulled the mosquito net to the side as she stepped through the door. "Hello," a young lady greeted her. "Come on in." Dee walked farther into the room.

"We will be performing massage therapy," she said, smiling at Dee, "inspired by the central palaces of Java. I'll explain everything I'm doing as we go along."

She gave Dee a towel and instructed her to undress and lie on the table in the center of the room. She began with a Balinese massage with jasmine-scented flower oil Then she gave her an invigorating skin scrub with turmeric rice, sandalwood, and jasmine. After her body was slathered with a cool yogurt polish, she took an aromatic shower and soaked in a tub infused with rose petals. And finally, they applied a moisturizer with jasmine lotion to leave her skin feeling smooth and smelling sweet.

When Dee got back to the bungalow, she felt incredible. Ben walked into the sitting area when he heard her come in.

"How was it?"

"It was fantastic," Dee said, walking to him and wrapping her arms around his neck. "I can't explain how good that felt."

"I'm glad they took such good care of you."

"Yes, they did, but not as well as you do."

He smiled as he took in her exotic aroma.

"I hope you're hungry. We have reservations for dinner in an hour."

The silver satin halter dress Dee wore clung to her shapely body, attracting the attention of men throughout the restaurant. The hostess greeted them then led them out to the terrace and down to the beach, where a twenty-by-twenty-foot platform had been set up. A single table sat on it, surrounded by tiki torches.

As they walked to the table, a slight breeze blew on her face. The aroma of the sea mixed with tropical flowers filled her senses. Ben held the chair for her, gently brushed her shoulder with his lips, and then sat down across from her.

"This is so beautiful," she said, smiling.

"Not as beautiful as you are," he said, reaching for her hand. The waiter brought the menus and they placed their orders. "I hope you're in the mood for dancing," Ben said, standing and pulling her with him.

They swayed to the soft sounds of Nora Jones' *Come Away with Me.* He leaned down, whispering in her ear. "Look up." She glanced up to see thousands of stars twinkling in a vast, open sky. "It's your fantasy come true. I ordered it special, just for you."

Her heart swelled and tears threatened to well in her eyes. "Thank you."

"I couldn't find the man you loved," he said, letting the tips of his fingers stroke her cheek. "I hope I'll do?"

She stood on her toes and spoke softly, her lips brushing his. "You'll do just fine.

On the second day, they went to Key West to snorkel and swim with the dolphins. Later that day, they strolled along the beach looking for seashells. Ben spotted two kids playing with a remote-control boat who couldn't get it to sail properly. After adjusting the antenna, Ben had it in good working condition. Dee sat on the beach watching him play with the little boys for an hour. After a couple of hours, the Florida sun had given Dee a slight golden tan, making the colors in her pink floral bikini and the white sarong hanging loosely around her waist seem even brighter.

"I want to take a picture of you from that angle," Ben said, looking at the top of a rock formation. He climbed to the edge, slipping and dropping the camera.

Dee laughed. "Are you all right?"

"Fine," he said, angry with himself. Picking up the camera, he saw that the lens was gone. After finding the lens fifteen minutes later, they walked hand in hand back to the bungalow.

Dee walked out of the bathroom. "I thought we might order a pizza for lunch then go back down to the beach. Ben sat on the sofa with the broken camera in his hand, swearing to himself. She watched him as he concentrated intently on trying to repair it.

"I bet I can fix that," she said, smiling at his diligence. "Hey," she said, walking to the chair and hitting him on the head with a pillow. He looked up, agitated. She laughed. "I said, I bet I can fix that." He dropped the camera on the floor and pulled her onto the sofa. She shrieked with laughter.

"I bet you could," he said, nuzzling her neck. She turned to kiss him, thrusting her tongue in his mouth. Running her fingers through his hair, she moaned. He pulled back, heaving heavy breaths. "You will never know what you do to me." She looked into his eyes.

"It's getting close to lunchtime," she said, moving to the edge of the sofa.

"No, don't leave," he whispered, pulling her back into him so their lips met. He pulled her back with him as he lay on the sofa. He felt sparks of electricity as he rubbed her back, ran his hand down her hips to her buttocks, squeezing gently.

"You know we really shouldn't," she said, trying to rise.

"Please don't," he pleaded. "I know you're not ready, and I won't rush you. I just want to be near you," he said, looking deeply in her eyes.

She bit her lip, her body tingling all over. She lowered herself back on him, leaning closer, kissing him, sucking his lip.

"I love you," he whispered in her ear. "I can never explain how much I love you."

She laid her head on his chest, heard his heart beating like hundreds of drums being beaten by wild natives. She felt him grow hard against her thigh, and they started moving and swaying as one. She ran her hand down his bare chest, admiring the smoothness of his skin. Grabbing her hand, he shook his head. He started to sit up, moving away from her. "You don't want to do that. I might not be able to contain myself."

She smiled. "I trust you."

He chuckled. "I don't." He rose. "I'm going to take a shower; then we can go out for lunch."

"I'm sorry," she whispered, her voice small.

"No, sweetheart, there's nothing to be sorry about."

"Yes, there is," she said, looking away from him.

"No," he said, sitting down and taking her hand. "I'm the one who should be sorry. We just got a little carried away. No harm done." He turned her face toward him, gently kissing her. "Now, let's get ready for lunch." He then got up and went straight to his shower, stepping in with his swim trunks on. The water was cold—cold enough to give him goose bumps, but not cold enough to wash away his desire.

She stood on the patio looking out on the water, inhaling the smell of the sea. Ben walked up behind her and put his arms around her waist. "What's wrong, sweetheart?"

"I can't believe that four days went by so fast."

"Did you have a good time?"

"Yes, I had a fabulous time."

"Then we'll come back."

"Can we?"

"If you like. Next time, maybe Holly and Edmond can come with us."

"That would be fun," she said, turning around and kissing him, then snuggling her head under his chin. "Thank you. No one's ever made me so happy."

"That's all I want," he said. Putting his finger under her chin, he tilted her head up to meet his eyes, and then kissed her.

* * * *

"Good morning," he said, smiling as he walked into the dining room. Natalie was sitting at the table drinking coffee. She looked up at Ben.

"Good morning, dear. How was your trip?"

"It was wonderful. We..." He stopped, alarmed when he saw the worried expression on her face. "What? What is it?"

"We have a bit of a problem."

Ben felt his heart racing. "Tell me?"

Natalie looked down in her cup. "It seems Heather isn't a match for the transplant." Though it was warm in the house, Ben felt cold.

"Why didn't you call me?"

Natalie set her cup down and brought her hands to her face, rubbing her eyes. "I didn't want you to end your trip."

"I would have come the instant you called."

"I know. Son, there's nothing you could have done."

"I could have been here for you, for all of you."

"Lisa wanted you to be happy—she wanted you to spend time with Deanna. She says she has never seen you this happy." She smiled, reaching out to take his hand. "And neither have I," she said softly. "We wanted to give the two of you time to build your relationship."

"But Dee would have understood; she would have insisted that we come home."

"I know—all the more reason for us not to call you." As Ben tried to hold back the tears, Natalie stood and put her arms around her son. At that moment, she saw the little boy who still needed his mother to protect him. When his father died, Ben had held it together for his mother and sister. He had handled everything, from the funeral arrangements to the attorneys. He was the man of the house, and he needed be strong for them. But now she needed to take care of her little boy.

"I'm going up to see Lisa," he said, rising from his chair slowly as if carrying a great weight on his shoulders. Natalie followed him as he walked up the steps and into Lisa's room, closing the door behind him. Then she walked to the study and picked up the file from Meyers Investigation.

"Hello, Deanna, this is Natalie Harrison. I'm fine, dear. It's Benjamin I'm worried about. He needs you." She hung up the phone and walked over to the door, pushing it shut. Then she sat in her late husband's chair, rested her head on the desk, and wept.

"I'll get it, Sadie," Natalie said as she approached the front door.

"Hello, Deanna, come in," she said, stepping to the side.

Dee was momentarily stunned by the sight of Natalie's eyes, which were swollen and red from crying. She closed the gap between them, wrapping Natalie in an embrace.

"Tell me what happened?" she whispered.

Natalie struggled to hold on, to utter the fateful sentence without breaking down. "Heather's marrow doesn't match."

Dee heard her pain in every word. She didn't say anything—what do you say to a mother who will likely lose her child?—so she just held her. Just be here for her, she told herself. She was so deep in thought that she didn't hear Ben walk up next to them.

"Mother told you the news?"

Dee released Natalie from her embrace. "Yes," she said. Ben took a deep breath, and Dee squeezed his hand.

"You two go into the living room," Natalie said, "I'm going to bring in some hot tea."

Ben pulled Dee close.

"How is Lisa?" Dee asked.

"Her spirits are high," he said, walking over to a chair and sitting.

"How are you?" Dee asked, watching his expression.

"They didn't want to ruin our trip," Ben said, picking an imaginary piece of lint from the arm of the sofa. "You said that we should have waited, but I didn't listen; I was just thinking of myself."

"No you weren't," she said, kneeling in front of him and taking his hand. "You didn't know."

"I should have been here for them."

Natalie walked in carrying a tray with a teapot and three cups. After setting the tray on the coffee table, she looked at her son.

"Ben, I won't allow you to blame yourself for this. If you had been here, the outcome would have been the same—there is nothing you could have done." Dee stood. "I'll leave you two alone for a moment."

Natalie caught her hand. "No. He needs you," she said, looking at Dee, her eyes confirming her words. Dee sat down next to Ben, while Natalie sat in the armchair to his right. "Benjamin, I want you to listen to me," she said as she took his hand and smiled. "You have taken care of your sister and I since your father died, and you have done a wonderful job as head of the family, but you need your own life. Lisa and I wanted you to have some peace—we wanted you to be happy and worry free for a little while. Do you understand?"

"Yes," he said, nodding, "but—"

"No 'buts.' I don't want to hear any more of this foolishness about you not being here for us—you're always here for us." Ben rose, pulling his mother up with him and embracing her. "You're a wonderful son. A mother couldn't be any prouder." Natalie looked down and saw Dee smiling; she reached for her hand.

Dee walked into her office. She had one serious headache. "Hey," Kimmy said. "How was your trip?"

"It was great."

Kimmy frowned. "Is everything all right?"

Dee sighed. "Just a headache. Can you give me the Harrison file?"

"Sure."

Dee walked into her office, dropping her coat on the armchair and sitting behind her desk. Kimmy followed her in and placed the file in front of her on the desk. "Do you need me to do anything? I can get you some aspirin."

Dee looked up. "Thanks, that would be great." After Kimmy left in search of aspirin, Dee opened the file, not knowing what she was looking for. She had a nagging feeling that she had missed something. She had read everything, and then re-read it. Then she saw what she was looking for. "Oh my gosh! How could I have been so blind?" she said, picking up the phone and calling Chicago General Hospital. After a few moments, she hung up then called Chris.

"Hey, Chris, I need you to do something for me."

Dee walked up the steps of the Harrison home. She rang the bell and then waited anxiously. "Hello, Sadie," she said to the housekeeper as she walked past. Ben met her at the bottom of the steps.

"Hi," he said, walking toward her.

"Where's Heather?" she said. "I need to speak to her."

"She's upstairs with Lisa." Ben looked at the housekeeper. "Sadie, would you ask Heather to meet us in the parlor please?"

As Ben and Dee walked into the parlor, he asked, "Can you tell me what this is about?"

"I'd rather wait until Heather gets—"

"Hi, Dee. How are you?"

"I'm good, Heather. Could you close the door behind you please?"

She stepped inside, closing the door. "Is there a problem?"

"I need to ask you something," Dee asked. "Where is Kyle?"

"Kyle?" Heather asked, looking uncomfortable.

"Who's Kyle?" Ben asked.

"Her twin brother."

"What?"

"Yes, when I went to the hospital and made a copy of the birth-certificate application, it stated that Nancy Greer had a daughter. While I was reviewing the information, I noticed that the document was numbered. So I had it checked out and I discovered that years ago they would number the documents for babies from multiple births until the babies were named." Dee looked at Heather again. "Your brother—his name is Kyle, right?"

Heather looked down. "Yes."

"Where is he?"

"I'm sorry," Heather said, tears spilling down her cheeks.

Ben stepped forward. "Tell us, for God's sake."

"He won't come. I tried to get him to meet us in Chicago when you came to see me. When you left me alone to pack, I called him, and he wouldn't even consider it. He just got angry. I told him about Lisa, and he still wouldn't come. That's why I didn't tell you. I'm so sorry." She started crying.

Ben put his arms around her. "It's okay," he said, stroking her back. "It's not your fault," he said, looking over at Dee.

"We need to figure out how to get him to come here. He needs to be tested," Ben said, pacing.

"We can't make him come if he doesn't want to," Dee said, following him with her eyes.

"He'll come," Ben said angrily. "He'll come if I have to tie him up and tow his sorry butt behind the plane."

After Dee left, he went back inside to have a talk with Heather. He pleaded with her to give him her brother's address, assuring her he would be able to convince him to undergo the procedure. After a while, his confident appeal broke her resolve, and Heather reluctantly told Ben that Kyle lived with her mother in Portland, Maine.

* * * *

"Hey girl, how was the trip?" Holly said, walking into the living room when she heard Dee come in. She saw the worn look on her friend's face. "Whoa, is everything all right?"

"No. Heather wasn't a match for Lisa's transplant."

"Oh my," Holly said, covering her mouth with her hand. "How's the family?"

"They're okay—for now," Dee said. "I discovered something interesting, though—I found out that Heather has a twin."

"That's great."

"Not so fast." Dee said, holding her hand up with a sigh. "He wants nothing to do with the Harrisons, and he refuses to help."

Holly shook her head slightly. "Well, I can see his side in this all."

"Yes, and I should be able to as well—I realize he was abandoned by his family—but it's hard for me to sympathize with him when he's doing the same thing to Lisa."

"And Ben," Holly added.

Dee nodded. "And Ben."

"I wish there was something I could do," Holly started to say. "Hmm, I have a couple of days off—maybe I could talk to him. You never know."

Dee thought about this for a moment. "At this point, it's worth a try. Let me call Ben."

A minute later, after she had finished talking to Natalie, she hung up and turned to Holly. "He's gone to the airport. I need to stop him. He's too angry right now—they could end up killing each other. I've seen these kinds of situations before."

Dee grabbed her coat and purse off the coat tree and headed out the door.

"Call me," Holly yelled as she closed the door.

Dee pulled up to the departure area and got out of her car. She ran through the sliding doors, arriving just in time to see Ben striding purposefully toward the ticket counter. "Ben," she called. He turned as she rushed toward him. "Ben, you can't do this," she said, catching her breath, "not now."

"I've got to convince him to come here and help Lisa," he said sternly.

"Not the way you are now. You're too upset, and you'll only make things worse."

He looked around anxiously. "We don't have much time. I have to do something now."

"Holly and I were talking, and she thought she might be able to talk to him."

He thought about this for a moment and then shook his head. "No, I have to do this on my own."

She bit the side of her mouth. "Okay, then let me come with you."

He looked at her, then looked around and sighed. "Come on," he said, grabbing her hand and pulling her with him toward the ticket counter.

"What about my car? It's parked in the drop-off zone." He turned around and strode quickly to the valet parking counter.

"Give me your keys," he said, holding out his hand. She placed them in his hand and he turned to a valet. "I need you to take care of this," he said, handing him the keys and a one-hundred-dollar bill.

Dee called out over her shoulder as Ben dragged her toward the ticket counter, "Silver bug, license number ### ###."

"I'm checking in," Ben said to the ticket agent, placing his bag on the counter.

"I also need another first-class ticket."

"Yes, sir."

Ben stared at the agent intently, anxiously squeezing Dee's hand.

"Here you are, sir. Enjoy your flight."

Turning, he pulled Dee behind him toward their gate.

"I don't have anything to wear," she said breathlessly.

"We'll get something there," Ben said, taking long strides.

Dee didn't like being pulled along like a child, but she felt his anxiety and didn't want to add to it. "We have ten minutes until boarding," Dee said. "Let me get you something—maybe a drink of water or some coffee?"

"I'm fine, sweetheart."

As they sat in the waiting area, Ben fidgeted, looking around but not really seeing anything, feeling more helpless than he could imagine. Dee reached over and took his hand. She kissed it.

"Baby, it's going to be okay. Everything's going to be fine."

"Yes." He nodded. "I hope so."

"United Air, flight seven-zero-three-two to Portland, Maine, now boarding at gate B7."

"That's us," he said. Standing quickly, they walked to the counter, checked in and boarded the plane. They remained silent for most of the flight.

After they landed, Ben walked quickly through the terminal, with Dee struggling to keep up. They grabbed the first porter they could find, and had him hail a cab. While they waited for the cab, Dee called Holly.

"Hi, it's me."

"Hey, are you at work?"

"No, I'm in Portland with Ben."

"You're going to see his brother?"

"Yeah."

"Do you guys need me to do anything?"

"No, I just wanted to let you know where I was."

"Be safe."

"Thanks. Bye." Dee said, hanging up as the cab pulled to the curb.

"We're going to 1214 Charles Street," Ben said as they got in. The driver nodded, then turned on the meter. As they rode in silence, Ben said a silent prayer. Dee reached over, taking his hand and squeezing it.

"Can you wait here?" Dee said to the driver after they pulled up to the curb. "Leave the meter running. Please, it's very important."

"Sure, lady. It's your money," the cabbie replied.

As Ben walked purposefully toward the house, Dee put a hand on his arm. "Let me do the talking," she said. "You're a little high strung; maybe I can reason with him."

After thinking about this a moment, he nodded reluctantly.

She rang the bell, and a young man answered. "Yeah?"

"Mr. Greer? My name is Deanna Meyers. I'm a priv—"

"I know who you are; my sister told me all about you. Said you might pay me a visit."

"May I come in and spea—?"

"It's not going to make a difference."

"But I'd just like—"

"Whatever. Come on in," Kyle said, shaking his head. He walked farther into the living room, taking the remote control off the table and turning the TV volume down. Dee and Ben stepped into the house. The living room was small and tidy, a stark contrast to Nancy's sister's home. "So, what do you want?" Kyle asked, bringing her back to the living room.

"I want you to reconsider coming to Chicago with me."

"Not likely."

"I know you're angry."

"Lady, you don't know the half of it. The great Benjamin Harrison Sr., wonderful man that he was, loved my mother to death as long as he could get a piece of ass from her. But when he knocks her up, she's suddenly no longer good enough for him."

Dee cringed at his anger. *This is going to be harder than I thought.*

"Then," he continued, "dear old Dad and his perfect wife decide to chase her out of town, giving her a few scraps to feed on like she's some animal."

"Mr. Greer... Kyle. May I call you Kyle?"

"No!"

"Okay," Dee said, softening her tone. "Mr. Greer, listen to me."

"No, I don't have to. I know all I need to know. Now those people want me to put my life on hold for their precious daughter."

"But she's your sister," she said.

"No, she's not! Heather is my sister!" he yelled.

"Look," Dee said, "let's just calm down—"

"Listen here, you little prick," Ben said from behind her.

"Oh boy," Dee said. "This is not going well at all."

"Who's your goon?" Kyle looked at Ben with disgust.

"Benjamin Harrison," Ben said proudly.

"Oh?" Kyle looked at him and smiled sardonically. "Now I get to put a face to the name of the scum that abandoned my mother."

"No, if you want to see that face, you need to look in the mirror."

Kyle looked like he had just been slapped. "That's not true," he sneered.

"Actually, it's very true you are the spitting image of my father."

Dee looked at Ben, surprised, then said, "Oh yeah, that's gonna help a lot."

"You even have his mannerisms," Ben continued as he studied the young man. Kyle narrowed his eyes and spoke through gritted teeth.

"Get out of my house."

"No," Ben said, taking a step closer. "You are coming to Chicago with us, you little asshole, and I'm not taking no for an answer."

"What are you going to do, make me?" Kyle said, squaring his shoulders. "Yes, if I have to," Ben said, through clenched teeth.

"Whoa, buddy," Dee said, stepping between them. "Okay, everybody just calm down."

During all the commotion, no one heard the door being opened. "Kyle, who are these people?" a voice said.

"Mom, this is the son of the great Benjamin Harrison."

Dee turned to her. "Ms. Greer, I'm Deann—"

"Get out of my house," Nancy Greer said, before taking a deep breath. "Get out now, or I'll call the police."

Ben looked at Nancy, then Kyle.

"I said get out!"

"Ben... *Ben?"* He looked at her. "Did you reserve a room?"

"No." He shook his head.

Dee leaned forward, speaking to the cab driver. "Can you recommend a nice hotel?"

He recommended the Carlton, a plush hotel that business people frequented. "I'll take care of it," she said, walking to the counter.

Ben had never felt such anguish and uncertainty. He could make millions in a year—hell, in months even—but he couldn't convince his brother, his own flesh and blood to save his sister's life.

Dee returned with the key. "Come on," she said, taking his hand.

Ben walked into the room, dropping his bag on the floor and sitting down on the king-size bed. Bending forward, he rested his face in his hands and began weeping.

Dee brought her hands to her face, feeling his pain. She sat on the bed and rocked him in her arms gently, assuring him that they would figure something out.

"How?" he questioned. "What can we do?" His voiced cracked like glass. "How am I going to tell Lisa that her big brother let her down?"

Dee's eyes welled up and she held him tighter.

An hour later, Ben fell asleep with his head on her breast. She moved away without waking him, then grabbed her coat and left the room, walking briskly down the hall to the elevators. She walked through the lobby to the reservation desk. "Can you not disturb room 634?"

"Yes, ma'am."

She walked out of the hotel and hailed a cab.

"Take me to 1214 Charles Street," she told the driver. During the ride, she thought of what to say in order to get Kyle to reconsider. She had to do something. She couldn't let Lisa die. She couldn't let Ben go through that pain. She rested her head on the seat, remembering Ben's tears of sorrow. She'd never felt so helpless, not even when she had realized there was nothing she could do to prevent her father's death. She hadn't been able to do anything about that, but she could damn sure do something about this. As she paid the driver and got out of the cab, she took a deep breath, preparing herself.

Nancy opened the door. "It's you again," she spat. "What do you want this time?"

"Ms. Greer, may I speak to Kyle, please?"

"No."

"Ms. Greer, please."

"I said—"

"Let her in, mom," Kyle said from inside the house. Nancy glared at Dee then stepped to the side, letting her enter. She moved to the other side of the room folding her arms across her chest as she watched. Dee put her hands in her pockets as she watched Kyle stare at the TV screen.

"What?" Kyle asked.

"Kyle, please listen to me." He looked at her with indifference. "I know that you're angry with your father, but Lisa has nothing to do with that. Why should she have to pay for something her father did when she was a child, something she had nothing to do with?"

"That's not my problem," he said, flipping through the channels.

"No, I'm not saying it is. What I am saying is she's your sister—whether you want to admit it or not. Are you really going to let her die because you're angry about something that happened before you were born?"

"Why are you here?" Nancy asked. "You people took Heather from me. Now you've come to take my other child. All those people want to do is use me again. Why don't you just go away and leave us alone?"

"Ms. Greer, no one wants to take your children from you. We only want to save someone else from losing hers."

"All they want to do is take," Nancy said bitterly. "That man took my heart, and now she wants my children."

Dee looked at Nancy. "Did you know he was married?"

Nancy looked away, not answering.

"If you knew he was married, and you gave him your heart willingly, you can hardly call yourself a victim. The only victims I see here are the children, yours, who had to live without their father, and hers, for having to live without the love and support of their brother and sister."

"Look," Kyle said, "my father left us; he abandoned us. We should've had the life they had, but we were cheated."

Dee had a feeling of déjà vu, remembering something Terry had once said. She shook off the feeling and asked, "Is this about the money?"

"No, it's not about the money. I was supposed to have a father," he said angrily, poking his chest. "They did, and we had nothing. Where was he when I needed him, when I broke my arm, when I won a trophy in Little League? They had their father. Where was mine?"

"I'm sorry. I can't help ease your pain. The past is gone, and there's nothing anyone can do to change it. But the future is still to come. How are you going to live with yourself when Lisa dies? And make no mistake about it—that is exactly what will happen if she doesn't get this transplant." Dee took a business card out of her pocket. Putting the card on the coffee table, she looked at Kyle again. "Just think about it," she said before walking out the door.

Kyle looked at his mother then he reached over and picked up the business card.

"Son, don't let her pressure you. They only want to use you. Don't let her get to you."

"I know, mom. I'm not going to do anything I don't want to." He said, standing and walking upstairs to his room.

* * * *

Ben knocked on the bathroom door. "Dee? Dee, are you in there?" He pushed the door open and walked in. He looked at himself in the mirror over the sink, his green eyes looked dull, his hair tousled and limp.

He felt like crap. *What now?* He splashed some water on his face, ran his hands through his hair, and left the bathroom. Sitting on the bed, he tried to come up with an idea. He lay back, fending off despair once again. He needed Dee. As the thought entered his mind, he heard her at the door. "Where were you, sweetheart?" he said, not looking at her.

"I had to pick up a few things." He looked at the bag in her hand and nodded. She set the bag down and sat on the bed next to him. "Can I get you anything?"

"I just need you," he said, pulling her close and holding her tight. He inhaled her hair. It made him feel warm. "I miss you when you're not with me, even when it's just for a little while."

"I do too," she said, feeling his sorrow.

Tears fell from the corners of his eyes as he took a deep breath.

Dee's cell phone rang. She sat up, reaching for her purse. "Hello."

"Ms. Meyers?" Kyle Greer."

"Yes?" Dee said, holding her breath.

"I thought about what you said. I'll do it. I'll go to Chicago with you."

"Oh, thank you. Thank you so much."

"I'm not going to promise you anything. If any of those people pressure me or offend me in any way, I'm on the next thing smoking."

"I understand," Dee said. "I'll call you back with the details." She hung up, looking at Ben.

"That was Kyle Greer. He's reconsidered. He's coming to Chicago with us."

"Thank god," Ben said as he pulled Dee close to him.

* * * *

"Guys, I'm going to get some magazines," Dee said. She squeezed Ben's hand before rising from her seat. "Can I get you two anything?"

Kyle smiled. "How about a *Playboy?*"

Dee laughed. "Not a chance, buddy."

He laughed. "I guess I'll settle for a *Sports Illustrated* then."

She nodded. "Sure thing. Ben?"

"No, thank you." She walked away, as both Ben and Kyle watched her.

Kyle looked over at Ben and grinned. "Is she your girl?"

"Yeah." Ben smiled as he nodded

"She's something else. She can be very convincing."

Ben glanced at Kyle. Each time he looked at him, he was amazed at how much this young man looked like his father.

"You know," Kyle continued, "all that stuff she said about not being able to change the past and having to live with the future. It really got to me. Made me think."

Ben looked across the hall at Dee, watching her browse through the magazine rack. "Did it?"

When Dee got back from the newsstand, Ben took her hand and held it tightly. He held it until they landed in Chicago, thinking he never wanted to let go.

At the valet counter, Ben asked, "Where are you going, sweetheart?"

"Home. I have a few things to take care of."

"I'm going to take Kyle to mother's. Then I'll come over to your place."

"Okay." She kissed him before getting in her car and driving off.

Chapter 13

"Hello?" Ben called from the front door.

"Hey, I'm in the kitchen." He walked around the corner. "Hi," Dee said over her shoulder. "Can I get you something? I just made coffee."

"Yes please," he said, leaning against the doorframe, admiring her. She glanced back and smiled.

"What?" she asked.

"Kyle told me you came to see him."

"Oh." She turned and took two cups out of the cabinet, setting them on the counter.

"He said if you hadn't come, he wouldn't have changed his mind. Thank you."

"That's not necessary," she said, pouring the coffee.

"Yes it is—you may have saved Lisa's life." He turned her around and looked into her eyes. "You're an amazing woman, Deanna Meyers. Every time I say that, you do something to show me how much more amazing you are. You didn't have to go back there, but you did."

"Yes I did—I had to. I had to help Lisa." She took a deep breath. "I had to stop your pain. I love you too much to see you hurt."

"What?"

"I don't want to see you hurt."

"No, say that other part again."

"I love you."

Ben's heart felt like it was going to burst out of his chest. "You don't know how I've longed to hear you say that."

She took another deep breath. "I've loved you since the first time you held me in your arms, since the first time you danced with me and I looked into your eyes and saw who you really were. I've never felt this way about anyone before, and I guess I was afraid to say it. I was afraid of being hurt."

"You don't have to be afraid with me. I love you with all my heart and soul, with my entire being. I'd never hurt you."

This time, Dee cried. He kissed her tenderly, wiping away her tears with the pads of his thumbs. Then he kissed her more deeply. She moaned. He picked her up and sat her on the countertop. Stepping between her legs, he stroked her thighs with the tips of his fingers, ran his hand up her skirt and massaging her hips. Dee felt hot everywhere. She felt like she was on a rollercoaster ride, about to go spinning down from the top.

"Ahem."

They became aware of someone else in the kitchen and broke off their kiss. Ben stepped back, turning toward the entranceway.

"Man, what are you guys cooking?" Holly said from the doorway. "It sure is hot in here."

Dee jumped off the counter, brushing down her skirt. "Hey, I didn't hear you come in."

Holly looked at the two of them, amused. "Evidently not," she said with a Southern twang. "Why, Deanna Marie Meyers, I do believe you're blushing."

"I am not," Dee said, turning toward the counter. Ben cleared his throat. "I was just about to leave."

"Oh, don't leave on my account, big boy. I'll be out of your way in no time."

"No really, I do have to go." He turned to Dee. "Remember, we have that charity fundraiser tonight. I have a surprise for you. It should be here shortly." He kissed her. "I'll see you soon, sweetheart." He walked past Holly, then stopped and kissed her on the cheek, saying, "See you later."

"Grrr," Holly growled, then laughed at his embarrassment. She grinned at Dee after he left. "Girl, he is hot! You are so lucky."

"I am pretty lucky, but you are too."

"Oh, I know that," Holly said, waving her hand and sitting at the table. "But sometimes we all need to hear someone else say it." Dee smiled. "So, how'd the trip go?"

"It went well." Dee poured a glass of apple juice for Holly. "Kyle's at Ben's mother's house as we speak."

"No bloodshed?"

"Nope. It was kind of touch and go for a while, but it all worked out in the end."

"Great. I'm happy to hear that."

"So, have we come up with a name for my godson or daughter?" Dee asked casually.

"What makes you think that I'm going to keep it?"

"Holly, I know you better than I know myself."

"Girl, I don't know if I'm ready to be a mommy, but the time is here, so I guess I'll find out."

"You're going to make a wonderful mommy," Dee said, reaching for Holly's hand, "and Edmond is going to be a great dad."

"He's so excited," Holly said, looking down at the glass in her hand. "I didn't tell him how it happened though. He'd ring Terry's neck."

Dee nodded. "I'm sure he would—not that she doesn't deserve it."

"She hasn't called you?"

"No, I haven't talked to her since Thanksgiving."

"She needs to stop all this foolishness, settle down, and start being a mother to her son."

Holly subconsciously placed her hand on her belly. Dee noticed the gesture and smiled. *Yeah,* she thought, *you're going to be a great mom.*

"So, what are you going to wear this evening?" Holly asked.

"You know, I haven't even had time to think about it. If you don't mind going, we could run down to the mall. I'm sure I'll find something."

"Sure, I'm game," Holly said, draining her glass.

"Let me get my shoes," Dee said. As she made her way toward the bedroom, there was a knock at the door. She answered it.

"Delivery for Deanna Meyers."

"Thanks." Dee went to the couch and set the box down, running her fingers across the name on the top. Vera Wang Originals. She opened the box, folding back the black tissue paper.

"Wow, that's beautiful," Holly said, standing in the kitchen doorway.

"Yes, it is," Dee said, taking the dress out of the box. She stood holding the cream satin evening gown in front of her.

"I have the perfect shoes to go with that," Holly said, rushing down the hall. She returned with a pair of open-toed sling back pumps. They were satin and almost the same color as the dress.

"Can you help me with my hair?" Dee asked.

"You bet."

At five thirty, the limo service called to inform Dee that the car would be there at seven. At six fifty, Dee and Holly stood in front of the mirror, looking at Dee. "You look beautiful," Holly gushed.

Dee smiled. "You did a good job."

"I had a good canvas to work with." Holly hugged her from behind. "Look at you—my baby is growing up so fast," she said, emitting something between a laugh and a cry.

"It's okay, mommy," Dee said in a child's voice. "I promise I'll be home before midnight."

Holly looked at her, frowning. "You'd better not! After all that work I did to get you ready, you'd better get lucky."

Dee playfully pushed her arm. "I swear, the people from the nuthouse should be looking for you." Holly opened her mouth to reply as a knock came at the door. She left the room to answer it.

When the limo arrived at the hall, Ben was waiting out front. He walked to the door, opened it, and got in.

"Hi," Dee said, smiling shyly when she saw the look of desire in his eyes.

"You look amazing."

"Thank you," she blushed.

"I have something for you," he said, reaching in a compartment in the refreshment box of the limo. He pulled out a nine-by-nine inch box with Tiffany & Co printed across the top. She looked at him questioningly. "Open it," he urged, placing it in her hands. She opened it to find a .65-carat Tiffany heart pendant.

"Oh my gosh! This is beautiful."

"Mother and Lisa picked it out for me." He took it out of the box and fastened it around her neck.

"Thank you," she said, kissing him sweetly.

"You're welcome."

"Ready to go in?" she asked.

"Maybe we could go somewhere else?" he said, suddenly feeling hot from sitting this close to her.

"Your mother is expecting us." Ben tried to come up with a quick excuse. As he opened his mouth, she cut in, "Come on, let's go."

When they walked into the hall, Dee felt like Cinderella. Natalie rushed over to meet them. "Oh, Dee. You look so beautiful, dear."

"Thank you. So do you."

"Oh pooh. This old thing." She smiled and winked. "Come, dear. I want you to meet some of the guests." She pulled Dee along with Ben following. "Stu and Beverly Bernstein, I'd like you to meet my future daughter-in-law, Deanna Meyers." *Whoa,* Dee thought, looking at Ben.

"Mother, you're embarrassing Dee," he whispered. "We haven't even spoken of marriage."

"Oh pooh," she said, fanning him away with her hand. "That's just a formality." She turned back to the Bernsteins. "Dee is just a wonderful person, so smart and beautiful. Isn't she beautiful?" The Bernsteins agreed with Natalie. "Well, I'll be back soon. I have to make my rounds. There are so many people I want Deanna to meet." She pulled Dee toward another couple.

"Mother," Ben said

"Oh, Benjamin, don't be such a party pooper. I'm proud of Dee, and I want to show her off." Dee looked at Ben and smiled.

"Yeah, she wants to show me off."

"Sweetheart, don't encourage her," Ben said as he followed them.

After Natalie introduced Dee to practically everyone in the hall, Dee and Ben went in search of Lisa, Heather, and Kyle. Lisa walked in first, followed by Kyle and Heather. "Good evening," Ben said as he walked over, giving Lisa a hug. She looked beautiful in her gold gown, her blond hair hanging around her shoulders, framing her small face. He pulled back and kissed her on the forehead. He hugged Heather, kissing her on the cheek, then shook Kyle's hand.

Kyle looked uncomfortable. "How can you wear this monkey suit? It's so uncomfortable."

Ben laughed. "You'll get use to it."

"You look handsome," Dee remarked.

"Thanks," Kyle said shyly.

"Hi, Dee," Lisa said as she hugged her.

"How are you feeling?" Dee asked, studying her.

"I'm fine. Mother tells me you two are getting married."

"Really?" Dee looked at Ben.

He closed his eyes, shaking his head. "That woman. I'm going to have to talk to her."

"Oh, leave her alone," Dee said. "She's cute."

"Like a pit bull," he mumbled. They all laughed. Beverly Bernstein walked up to them. "Lisa, I haven't seen you in a while. How are you?"

"I'm fine, Mrs. Bernstein. Oh, do you know Dee?"

"Yes, we've met."

"Then I'd like you to meet my sister, Heather, and my brother Kyle."

"Nice to meet you."

Kyle smiled, feeling both surprise and pride.

They walked around, happily mingling with other guests. Then, Dee looked over her shoulder and saw Janet approaching them, wearing a stunning red gown that suited her sultry walk.

"Good evening," she crooned.

"Good evening, Janet," Ben said as Dee smiled and nodded.

"Oh," she said, turning to the couple who appeared at her left. "Benjamin, this is my mother and father, Mathew and Hilary Summers." She smiled slyly at Dee. "Mother, Daddy, this is Ben Harrison—you know, the man I told you about."

"Pleased to meet you," they said. Ben shook their hands.

"And this is Deanna Meyers," Ben said, placing his hand on Dee's back.

"Charmed," Janet's mother said, nodding. Dee shook Mr. Summer's hand.

"Wonderful gala, isn't it?" Janet said, smiling, but with no joy in her eyes.

"Yes," Ben said, taking Dee's arm and leading her away. "Will you excuse us?"

"I'm really surprised you would come here, Deanna," Janet said as they walked away.

Dee stopped. "Really? And why is that?"

"I would imagine that you felt you didn't belong."

Dee opened her mouth, and then snapped it shut. *No,* she thought, I *won't sink to her level.* She smiled, looking intently at Janet, letting her know that she knew her game and wasn't playing.

"Well," Janet continued, "With the history that Ben and I share, I thought for sure you wouldn't feel comfortable coming here," She waved her hand dramatically. "Why, everyone knows how in love Ben and I were; we were practically engaged. And with your, um, friendship being so new and all," Janet heaved a heavy sigh "I just assumed that..."

Natalie appeared at Dee's side. "Deanna, there's someone else I'd like you to meet."

"Hello, Mrs. Harrison," Janet said, smiling genuinely. "Janet Summers—I'm a friend of Benjamin," she said.

Natalie nodded her recognition. "Yes, I'm aware of who you are."

"Yes," Janet said, happy Natalie remembered her. "How have you been?"

"Very well," Natalie said, unsmiling.

"I was just telling Deanna that—"

"I heard what you were telling her. You know," Natalie said, meeting Janet's gaze as she took Dee's hand, "Ben is very close to his family, and its odd how he's never mentioned you to us; I mean, since you were practically engaged."

Dee watched Janet, becoming amused by the look on her face.

Ben watched his mother proudly.

"Anyway, I must introduce Dee to Judge Kimble. It was so nice talking to you again." Natalie led Dee away, sliding her arm around her waist.

"Thank you," Dee whispered.

"Anything for my future daughter-in-law," Natalie said, squeezing her.

"Your mother is amazing," Dee said as they headed for the door.

"Yes," Ben said. "She sure is. Is there anything else you want to do this evening? We can dance the night away if you'd like."

"Let's go to your place," Dee suggested.

He hesitated. "I don't know that you would be safe at my place."

"I think I'll take my chances."

When they stepped off the elevator, she led him to the sofa and sat on his lap. "I had a good time. I felt like a princess."

"You're more beautiful than any princess could ever be," he said. "I had to fight to keep my hands off of you tonight. I felt like I was going insane."

She giggled. "It's the dress."

"No, you make the dress look good."

She nipped his top lip and felt him stir beneath her. She nipped his top lip again, then the bottom, sliding her tongue in his mouth.

He looked into her eyes. "You are the sexiest, most desirable woman I've ever met," he said, his breathing labored.

She looked at him lovingly and kissing him again. "I want to be with you," she said.

He looked into her eyes. "Are you sure?" he asked.

"Yes." She nodded.

He picked her up and carried her into his bedroom, laying her on the bed. Standing, he took off his jacket and tie. Dee lay on the bed, looking up at him. He unbuttoned his shirt, removing it slowly and revealing his muscular chest and arms. His washboard abs and smooth, tanned skin excited her. He was devastatingly handsome. Pulling her up to stand in front of him, he took the straps of her dress off her shoulders and let it fall to the floor. Then, letting his fingers trail down her arms, he brought her hands to his lips and kissed each one.

He moved his hands to her hips and up to her breasts, letting his fingers trace the outline of her nipples. Reaching behind her, he unclasped her bra then eased the straps down her shoulders, dropping it to the floor on top of her dress. She nervously covered her breasts with her arm.

"Please," he said, his voice raspy. "Don't."

Taking her hand, he kissed her palm and moved her arm to her side. "You take my breath away. I've never seen a more beautiful woman." He drew her to him. His lips brushed her cheek as he spoke. "I love you, Dee." His mouth covered hers.

She felt her knees weaken. Gently, he eased her down on the bed. Lying beside her, his lips traced a line from her mouth to her breast. His hot mouth moved to her nipple. She shivered as his tongue tantalized her bud. She moaned.

He pulled back to look at her. His eyes were burning with passion. "Are you sure?" She whimpered from deep within her throat, wanting—needing—his touch. She nodded. As his hand brushed over her small waist and taunt belly, the contrast of their skin tones suddenly excited him, causing the fire burning in his emerald eyes to intensify. He kissed her softly, then more deeply, moving his hands down to her thighs. He parted her legs, his hand gliding to the thatch between them. She closed her eyes, biting her lower lip in ecstasy, moving her hips in rhythm with his hand. "You're so wet," he whispered. He felt a tightening between his legs as he said it. He bent down and nibbled her breast, kissing a trail from her breast to her navel to the warm, wet spot between her legs. She whimpered.

"Ssh, I won't hurt you, sweetheart," he said, sliding the satin panties down her silky thighs, discarding them as he parted her legs further. Licking slowly, he closed his eyes, letting his senses become electrified by her essence, using his fingers to massage her clit.

She moved uncontrollably, grabbing his soft hair. "Oh, God!" she cried. He sucked until he felt her juices flow, sending waves rippling through her. He then stood, removing his pants and boxers in one swift move. His manhood sprang to life. She gazed at his hard body and then his beautiful face. She couldn't take her eyes from his. He reached into the nightstand and removed a small, square plastic packet, tearing it open with his teeth. He reached for her hand.

"Here, help me." Holding his erection with one hand, she delicately put the condom on the tip. He gasped as her fingers touched him, and then slowly rolled the condom down. As he lowered himself onto her, she gasped. "Ssh, it's okay. If you want me to stop, just say so." She closed her eyes. "Open your eyes," he whispered. "I want you to look at me. I want to see the love in your eyes. I want to see your desire for me."

He put his hand under her right leg and kissed her knee; then he did the same with the left. "Breathe slowly; I'm going to take my time." Unable to speak, she nodded. He put himself on her moist opening, rubbing it a little. Then he eased it in and out a little at a time.

"Ah," she gasped.

"Okay?" he asked. She nodded.

"Oh yeah, you're so tight." It took everything within him not to thrust hard. He kept moving slowly, going a little deeper each time.

"Are you with me?" he whispered sometime later.

She moaned, saying, "Yes."

"We're almost there, sweetheart." He couldn't hold back much longer. She moaned again. And he plunged in.

"Oh, God!" she cried.

He went faster, not able to control himself any longer. She dug her fingers deeply into his shoulders, raking his back with her nails. "Oh, yes," she cried. He released, and they both soared together among the stars.

Ben woke up, reaching for Dee. When he found her missing, he looked at the clock on the nightstand. "Dee?"

"I'm in here."

He left the bed and went into the bathroom. She was sitting in a warm tub.

"Are you okay?"

She smiled. "Fine, just a little sore."

He stepped into the tub, sitting behind her.

"I'm sorry, sweetheart." He kissed the top of her head. She leaned back, taking his hand and kissing it. Then, looking up she kissed him.

"I love you," she whispered.

His heart swelled along with his erection. "I love you too."

He woke again, this time to the soft sound of Dee's breathing. Propping a pillow under his head, he watched her sleep. Her lips were slightly parted, her thick lashes looking like soft feathers. She looked so innocent. He was the happiest he had ever been, and it was mostly because of her. She had found Heather and Kyle in order to help Lisa, but most of all she had found his heart. He had made his decision last night, and he now knew there was no turning back. He would call

Jill and have her make the arrangements for his trip—he needed to do this before he lost his nerve. He needed to do it before Christmas; he wanted her Christmas to be special.

Leaning close, he smelled her hair. "What are you doing?" she asked, her eyes still closed.

"Nothing, just admiring your beauty."

"I must look terrible," she said, pulling the sheet over her head.

"No, you don't. You look perfect." He gently pulled the sheet down, stroking her cheek. "What are you going to do today?" he asked.

She stretched. "I thought I'd do some more Christmas shopping."

"It's Sunday—a day of rest."

"Yes, but Christmas is getting close, and I still have a lot to do. Why, what did you have in mind?"

"I was thinking," he said as he moved the sheet down her body, "we could stay in bed and I could feed you breakfast and lunch—and in between, you could be my brunch." He ran his hand up her inner thigh, tickling her. She laughed. "Then," he continued, "We could have each other for dinner."

"I don't know," she said. "How about we skip the breakfast part and go right to brunch. Then I'll go shopping and we can meet at my place for *dinner.*"

"That sounds good to me," he said, pulling her under him.

* * * *

Dee leaned against the door, unlocking it while continuing to hold her shopping bags. She dropped three as she pushed the door open. "Shoot," she said, pushing the bags inside with her foot and closing the door. She walked into the bedroom quickly to put the few she hadn't dropped on her bed, returning to the living room for the rest. As she bent over to pick up the remaining packages, she heard the front door unlocking. She looked up to see Janet standing there, with her hands on her hips, smiling at her.

"Hello, do you need a hand?"

Dee stood up slowly. "How the hell did you get in here?"

Janet shook the keys at her.

"Give those to me."

Janet smiled, putting the keys in her pocket and folding her arms across her chest. "After today, I won't have to deal with you again, so I guess I might as well give them to you."

"Why are you going somewhere?" Dee asked.

"No," Janet said, sure of herself, "but you are."

"Ah, and just where am I going?"

"Anywhere that Ben isn't!" Janet barked.

Dee smiled. "Am I now?"

"Yes. Look," Janet began, "Ben is in love with me, and we are going to be married and spend the rest of our lives together."

Dee tilted her head to the side, examining Janet.

"You seem like a smart woman," Janet continued. "Why would you allow yourself to be used by a man?"

"Used?" Dee asked.

"Yes, surely you know you're being used? Ben can't possibly be serious about you. You're just jungle... something or other," she said, waving her hand dramatically. "A white man can't want anything from a black woman but sex." Dee couldn't help but laugh. "He can't be with you," Janet went on. "He has too much at stake."

"You know what?" Dee said, "I'm not going to do this. I'm not going to have this conversation with you. Get out."

"You poor fool. I can't believe you really think he wants you."

"No it's not me who's the fool; it's you. You steal my key, come to my house looking like some pathetic loser, and think you can convince me that Ben doesn't care about me? He's a strong man with a mind of his own. You're just some nut who scared him away."

Janet took a step toward Dee. "Why, you little bitch."

"Don't do it lady. Don't be stupid," Dee said, squaring her shoulders. Janet bit her lip and decided to use another angle.

"Okay, I'm going to be honest with you. I love Ben, and I want to be with him, and I'm asking you, from one woman to another, to step aside."

"What makes you think that if Ben and I weren't seeing each other he would go back to you?"

"Because we are meant to be together."

Dee looked at her closely. "Now I see it clearly."

Janet smiled. "I thought you would see things my way."

"You haven't been taking your medicine, have you? Only a psycho would do the things that you've done. You know, like coming to Ben's home half-naked. Didn't think I noticed that, did you?" she said, smiling. "Then, coming here when you don't even know what kind of person I am," Dee said, scrutinizing the woman standing across from her. "You're downright certifiable!"

Janet glared at her. "Ben knows what he wants, and that happens to be me."

Dee heard keys jiggling in the door; she threw up her arms. "What is this, freaking Grand Central Station?"

Ben stepped inside the doorway and saw Janet. "What the hell are you doing here?" he said, frowning.

"Hello, lover," Janet said, smiling at Dee.

He walked over to Dee and kissed her. "Are you all right?"

"Sure, we were just talking about how you two are going to get married and ride off into the sunset. And by the way, she let herself in—with a key, I might add."

Ben glared at Janet, who smiled back. Ben turned back to Dee.

"Can you leave us alone for a moment?"

"Hell no! This is my home. Take her crazy ass outside, where it belongs."

He took her hand. "Please, sweetheart?"

She looked at Ben, then at Janet, her eyes shooting daggers. Janet beamed. Snatching the remaining shopping bags from the floor, Dee marched into her bedroom, slamming the door.

"You want to take me right here?" Janet purred, putting her arms around Ben's neck.

He grabbed her wrist and flung her away.

"Give me the damn key," he demanded. She pouted then smiled. "Now!" his voice boomed. She reached into her pocket and pulled the key out, dropping it in his hand. "Janet, have you no pride?"

Her expression changed from amusement to hate. "Don't talk to me like that. I'm not your little nigger whore."

Ben's jaw tightened. "What is wrong with you? I don't even know who you are."

"Yes, you do."

"No, I don't. The Janet I knew would never have degraded herself like this."

"I'm fighting for what's mine."

"No, Janet, that's the problem—I'm not yours to fight for. I never was and never will be. I don't want to hurt you, but we need to stop this. I don't love you." He took a deep breath. "I never have, and I never will."

Tears welled in the rims of her eyes and her lip trembled.

Ben bit his lip, waiting for what he had said to sink in. "I'm in love with Dee. And one day, I hope to make her my wife. I'm sorry, but I don't want you to believe in something that will never be."

"It's her fault! She did this to us!"

"No, it isn't. I decided to stop seeing you before I ever met Dee. Every time I told you it was over, you didn't hear me. Janet, it's over it's been over for a very long time."

She squared her shoulders and forced a shaky smile. "You're going to be sorry you chose *that,*" she said, gesturing toward the bedroom, "over me. And when you want me, I *might* consider taking you back." She stepped out the door, slamming it behind her. Ben glanced around the room, making sure Janet didn't leave anything behind, before he walked down the hall to the bedroom. He knocked. Dee snatched the door open, causing him to jump.

"What?"

"Can I come in?"

"Did your girlfriend leave?" she asked, marching to the center of the room.

"That's not fair."

"And sending me out of the room was?" she said, her arms folded defensively.

"I'm sorry, but if you stayed, you would have only added fuel to the fire."

"Mm-hmm" she said, tapping her foot.

Ben smiled, walking toward her. "You know, you're sexy when you're angry— the way your eyes scrunch up—"

"That's not going to get you off the hook."

"And when you grit your teeth, you can just see those dimples I love so much," he said, brushing her cheek.

"I'm still mad at you," she said, smiling.

"Oh, you make me so hot."

She walked by him, punching him playfully in the stomach. "You're an ass."

"And you have a cute one," he said, following her.

Chapter 14

Dee set her fork down and looked across the table at Ben. He was deep in thought. "Is there something wrong. Hey?" she said, placing her hand on his.

"Hmm?" He met her gaze. "Oh, I'm sorry."

"Are you okay?" she asked.

"Sure." He smiled half-heartedly, setting down his fork. "I have to go on a trip," Ben said. "It will only be for a few days." He breathed out heavily. "I wish you could come with me."

"Wish I could too, but I have to work," she said, placing her hand on his cheek. "When will you be leaving?"

"Tomorrow."

"What are you doing tonight?" she asked.

"Why?" He smiled. "What do you have in mind?"

"Hmm," she said, pulling her bottom lip between her teeth. "Maybe we can go to your place and pack your bags; then you can come to my place and we can play captain and stewardess?" She looked at him, smiling mischievously.

"Oh yeah, I like being the captain," he said, leaning over and nibbling her earlobe.

"Oh no, baby—you're going to be the stewardess."

"Mmm, yes, Captain. Anything you want," he whispered.

She growled. "You shouldn't do that, or we may not make it to your place, let alone mine."

"You promise?" he asked, as he continued nibbling.

She giggled, turning to kiss his chin. She sighed, whispering, "I love you."

He drew his head back, gazing into her eyes. "I love you more."

After dinner, they drove back to the penthouse. "Where are you off too?" Dee asked, sitting on the bed watching Ben pack.

"Europe."

"How exciting. I wish I could take off. I'd like to see Europe." She turned, pulling her legs under her. "Which part?"

His back was to her as he answered. "Finland."

She watched as he took a few pairs of socks out of the drawer. If she had learned anything in her profession, it was how to sniff out a lie—the curtness of his answer, the avoidance of eye contact—all the signs were there. She tilted her head and watched him closely.

"Is something wrong?"

"No, sweetheart, why do you ask?"

"I mean, with your trip. Do you need any help? If you do—"

"No, everything's fine. It's a standard meeting. I'll only be away for a couple of days, then I'll head back home to you." He walked to the closet, holding up ties against shirts, deciding which to take.

"I'm going to get a drink. Do you want something?"

"No, I'm almost done here."

In the kitchen, she reached into the refrigerator and got a bottle of water. Then she walked into the living room, crossing to the window. She hoped everything was all right. Ben had said there was nothing wrong, but she just didn't know.

Then, something caught her eye. She walked over to the recliner and picked up a blue blouse as Ben walked out of the bedroom carrying his luggage. She looked at him, holding the blouse.

"I was going to bring that to you," he said, setting the bag down. He walked toward her, taking the water out of her hand and taking a sip.

"Where did you find this?" she asked.

"The housekeeper found it under the bed. She washed it for you." He saw a slight frown on her face.

"What's wrong?"

"Nothing," she said, shaking her head. "I just can't remember the last time I wore this."

He saw doubt in her eyes. It couldn't have been Janet's, not after all this time.

"I must have had it in my overnight bag and forgot." She smiled. "Thanks for giving it back."

"Are you ready to leave?" he asked, rubbing her arm. She nodded slowly. When he turned toward the door, she scanned the room quickly then followed him out.

"My plane will be landing in twenty minutes. I should be at the hotel at around two. Okay, I'll meet you there." Ben hung up his cell phone, scrolling down on his laptop, checking the stock market. He rotated his neck, trying to loosen the muscles, and then he massaged his eyes. He signed off and closed the computer, then reached forward to close the pull-down tray. He missed Dee already. However, although it would have been nice to have her with him, he understood that she had to work. Moreover, he might not have been able to get things done if she had come along. The flight attendant walked down the aisle.

"Can I get you something, sir? Maybe a pillow or something to drink?"

"No, I'm fine, thanks," Ben said. She was a pretty brunette, about thirty, with beautiful hazel eyes. She smiled, displaying perfect teeth.

"If you need anything, just let me know."

"Thank you," Ben said, turning to the window. She stood watching him for a moment then continued down the aisle. The fasten-seatbelt sign lit up as the captain announced, "We will be landing shortly at Schiphol Airport, Amsterdam."

"Hi, babe," Terry said, standing in the open door of the hotel room. "Come on in," she said, leaning seductively against the door. Slowly and methodically, she licked her top lip. "I missed you."

"I missed you too, sweetheart," he said, taking her into his arms.

"Did you bring me something?"

"Me," he said, smiling.

She pouted. "Nothing else?"

He reached in his pocket, pulling out two theater tickets.

"I got tickets to *Cats.*"

She frowned. "Cats? I didn't travel this far to see a cat."

"I thought you might enjoy it."

"When is it?" she asked, sighing.

"Tonight."

"Can we go shopping first?"

"Sure, anything you want." He bent his head kissing her neck.

"Did you tell her yet?"

He stopped. "No, not yet."

"What are you waiting for?"

"The right time." Terry stood on her toes, kissing him, letting her tongue tickle the roof of his mouth. Then she drew back, her eyes meeting his.

"Call her and tell her tomorrow." She nipped his lip, "or I won't see you anymore—and you know you don't want that." She nipped his lip again. "Do you?"

He moaned. "What will you give me if I do?"

She led him to the bed, then, facing him, she dropped her robe. "What do you want?"

He moved closer to her. "I'll tell her when we get back—I promise," he said, taking her in his arms, kissing her with all the passion he felt.

"I'm better for you than she is," she said, her breathing heavy. "I'm a real woman, and that's what you need." *She always gets what she wants,* Terry thought, *but not this time. It's my turn, and I'm going to have it all.*

Lying on the bed, she opened her cell phone. She waited until she heard him turning the bathroom doorknob before she pretended to speak. "Okay, I'll be there as soon as I can." Then she quickly snapped the phone shut. "Babe, I have to leave," she said, holding up the phone. "I just got a call. There's an emergency, and I have to go home tomorrow."

"I hope it's not serious."

"Oh no, it's nothing like that. It's just something I need to take care of."

"Okay, we can leave tomorrow."

"No, I want you to stay and have some fun. All you ever do is work. Why don't you stay for a couple of days, and I'll see you when you get back."

"You're so considerate—that's why I love you."

"I know. I love you too." She smiled, glad that things were going as planned.

Holly and Edmond walked in just as Terry was telling Dee her news. "Holly, hi!" Terry said, walking over to her and giving her a hug. Holly kept her arms at her sides, stiffening. "I haven't seen you in a while. You look good. Hi, Edmond. How are you?"

"Hi Terry." Edmond watched Holly's reaction. Holly didn't say anything, merely bit the inside of her mouth as she watched Terry.

"I was just about to tell Dee my good news. Come, sit down. I want to tell you all at the same time."

Edmond walked over to the sofa. Holly stayed where she was, glaring at Terry.

"Well," Terry began, "I'm in love." No one said anything; they just looked at one another. "No, really—this time it's for real."

Dee smiled and embraced Terry. "I'm happy for you."

"Congratulations," Edmond said.

"Holly?" Terry smiled, looking at her. "Aren't you going to say anything?"

"Nothing that can be said in mixed company," Holly spat.

"Oh well. Anyway," Terry said, smiling, "I am so happy."

"Then I am too," Dee said, meaning it. "So, tell us about him."

"Well," Terry said, looking at Dee intently, "he's rich and handsome, and his name is Benjamin. He's wonderful and sweet—he even calls me 'sweetheart.' I just love that."

"What?" Dee asked, the pit of her stomach sinking fast.

"I'm sure he's going to ask me to move into his penthouse with him. He has plenty of room."

No, Dee thought, she had to be hearing things.

"What did you say his name was again?"

"Oh, you know him, Dee. He's one of your clients. Ben Harrison." Dee felt as though her world had just collapsed in on itself. She felt cold and hot at the same time. *Don't let her see you fall apart,* she told herself.

"Um, Terry, I just remembered something that I need to take care of. I'm going to have to talk to you later." Dee turned around, walking mindlessly toward her bedroom.

"I'll talk to you tomorrow," Terry called to her retreating back.

Dee walked into her room, closing the door and leaning against it for support. *This can't be happening. It has to be a mistake.* She couldn't breathe. She put her hand over her mouth and closed her eyes. Thinking back, she remembered the box of lingerie in the car and the scarf that he had given her, saying she had left it under his seat. *No, it can't be true.* She picked up the phone before remembering that Ben was away on business. "Oh God," she moaned, dropping the phone and sinking to the floor.

"You whore," Holly hissed.

Terry looked at her with an amused expression. "What?"

"Get the hell out."

"What are you talking about?"

"I said get out!" Holly was shaking.

Terry took her coat off the coat tree. She gave Holly a knowing smile and left, closing the door behind her.

"Oh my God. This can't be happening."

"You don't think it's Ben, do you?" Edmond asked.

"Oh, my God. Oh, my God," Holly said, putting her hands to her face, pacing back and forth. They heard a loud crash. It sounded as though a tornado were going through Dee's room.

Edmond and Holly rushed down the hall, and Edmond grabbed the doorknob.

"No!" Holly rested her hand on his forearm. "You go on home. I'll take care of her."

"Are you sure you don't need me?"

"We'll be okay," she said, nodding.

After walking Edmond to the door, Holly walked down the hall. She rested her head against the door. She waited until she didn't hear any noise in the room then tapped lightly on the door. "Honey, can I come in?" Dee didn't answer. She turned the doorknob, stepping through the doorway. Dee was lying across the bed, sobbing.

Holly walked across the room and lay across the bed, putting her left arm around Dee and sliding her right arm under her head. She lay with her, letting her cry.

"I can't believe he would do this. He told me he loved me."

"I know, honey," Holly cooed, reaching up and stroking Dee's hair with her fingers. "I'm so sorry."

"But I love him," she said through sobs. "I gave myself to him, and he used me."

"Don't jump to conclusions. Maybe it's a mistake."

"How can it be?" She told her about the clues. "Terry just confirmed that she was seeing him."

"I wouldn't put too much stock in anything she has to say."

"How could I have been so stupid? Oh God," Dee sobbed. Holly felt Dee's body tremble, felt her tears trickle onto her arm. Tears welled up and ran from her eyes as well. She held Dee tightly, rocking her back and forth.

Once Dee had finally cried herself to sleep, Holly moved so as not to wake her. After covering her with her blanket, she went into the living room and began looking through their phone book. She picked up the phone and dialed the number. "Hi, it's Holly," she said, barely able to contain a sob. "We need you."

* * * *

Holly woke feeling like she hadn't slept at all. She walked toward the kitchen with the intention of making coffee when she heard a knock on the door. Listlessly, she dragged herself to the door, only to be slapped in the face by Terry's smug expression.

"What do you want?" she spat.

Terry pushed past her, walking into the apartment.

"I want to see Dee."

"No. Get out."

Terry turned, looking at Holly from head to toe as if she were something foul. "Who are you to speak to me that way?"

"How could you be so vile? Dee's your cousin, and she has always looked out for you."

"Please, honey. Self-preservation and all that crap," Terry said, fanning her hand.

"You knew that Dee was seeing Ben?"

"And?"

"And you set out to get him, knowing that she was with him."

Terry pursed her lips, looking down at her manicured nails.

"You know what, I'm going to let you in on a little secret. I'm sure you haven't figured it out yet, but I always get what I want. I wanted David, and I got him. I get my bills paid, I have a car, and I don't have to work. I wanted Ben, and I got him too. And there's not a damn thing anybody can do to stop me."

"Tell me, did you stalk him, throwing yourself at him like a bitch in heat until he gave in?"

"No, I came here and got his home and office addresses from the file. I sent him a few gifts, we met and went out, and the rest is history."

"I guess that was the day you poked holes in my condoms."

Terry looked at her smugly. "And one day we'll get married. I'll remember to invite you to the wedding."

"Ben might be stupid enough to mess around on Dee, but he can't be stupid enough to think he can turn a whore into a housewife."

Terry laughed. "Like Edmond thought he could do with you? Oh, but he hasn't even married you now has he?"

"You know what? One of these days, you're going to get yours."

"Nope. Don't think so, because, you see, I'm smarter than most. They just don't know it, which gives me the upper hand. All this brains and beauty in one package—what man wouldn't want me...?" Terry stopped, sensing another presence in the room. She turned, and her mouth dropped.

"Don't let us interrupt," a voice came from the open door.

"Mom, grandma." Holly crossed the room, giving Jean and Harriett big hugs. "I've missed you," Holly said, then she looked at Terry and asked. "How long have you been standing there?"

"Long enough," Harriett said, glaring at Terry.

"Hi, Aunt Jean," Terry said, pulling her too-short dress down.

Jean looked at her niece with dismay. "Terry Ann Meyers," she demanded.

"What have you been doing?"

Terry looked defiantly at her aunt. "Just taking care of business."

"Yeah, I just bet you are," Harriett said, looking at Terry, her gaze cold and piercing, her contempt becoming more evident on her face with each passing moment.
"Mama, Dee needs you" Jean said, gently placing a hand on her mother's shoulder.
Harriett turned to Holly. "Where's *my granddaughter?*"

"She's in her room," Holly told her.

Harriett headed down the hall. She knocked softly on the door. "I don't want to talk now," Dee called. Harriett opened the door. Dee looked up; seeing her grandmother, she rose from the bed and rushed to her, then she cried all over again.

"Oh baby, it's going to be all right."

"Terry, for the life of me, I can't figure out what goes on in that head of yours."

"Aunt Jean, I'm looking out for my son and me.

"Terry, you don't treat family like this. I'm really disappointed in you."

"Yeah, whatever," Terry said, dropping an envelope on the coffee table. "Give this to Dee," she said, walking out the door. Holly picked up the envelope and dropped it in the wastebasket.

Harriett stood at the stove making breakfast for everyone.

"I'm not hungry, grandma," Dee said.

"I want you to eat something, both of you." She looked at Holly. "Since it seems there's going to be a baby around here soon, you need to take better care of yourself." She directed that at Holly. "And that means no skipping meals."

"Yes, grandma," Holly said humbly. Jean, who had been cleaning up some of the things Dee had thrown around in her room, walked into the kitchen.

"I'm sorry about the mess, Mom. Do you need any help?" she asked.

"No, baby," she said kissing her daughter's head. She stepped to the counter, picked up two of the plates with ham, eggs, and toast, and placed one in front of Dee and one in front of Holly. "Eat."

"I don't know where we went wrong with that girl," Jean said, shaking her head. "We gave her the best life we could. We raised both of you the same—I just don't know what happened."

"I told you that girl would be nothing but trouble," Harriett said. "You should have let her live with her mother's people. She was always trouble, that one."

"She seemed to be headed for trouble when she was younger," Jean said. "William and I should have been stricter on her. We thought she would grow out of her rebelliousness if we gave her time."

"I think you shoulda taken a paddle to her behind."

"Mama, I don't think that would have changed anything."

"It would have given her something to think about," Harriett huffed. "I tell you that."

"So, what you going to do, child?" Harriett said to Dee.

"I don't know, grandma. I guess I need to try to move on."

"Have you tried to call your young man?"

"He's not my man, grandma."

"Just call him, Dee. Talk to him and find out what's going on," Jean said, patting Dee's hand.

"That's the problem with you young folks," Harriett said, shaking her head. "Just taking stuff for granted."

"I remember back in my day," Jean said, teasing her mother.

Harriett looked at her. "You know you're not too old for a paddling neither."

Jean laughed. "Yes ma'am."

Harriett looked at her granddaughter. "So, call him."

"He went away for a few days on a business trip."

"So? This is important," her grandmother said.

"I don't think so."

"Why not?" Holly asked. Dee rubbed her eyes, feeling a monster headache coming on.

"I can't talk to him about this on the phone. We need to handle this face to face. And as for Terry, I don't know what to do about her."

"I asked her why she was doing all this," Jean said.

Dee looked at her mother. "When did you talk to her?"

"She was here when we got here," her mother answered.

"She came to leave something for you," Holly said. "Some card. Do you want it?"

Dee shook her head.

"Give it to me," Harriett said. Holly rose and brought the card to Harriett. She tore it open. "It's an invitation."

"To what?" Jean asked, leaning close to get a look.

"It says that the two of them are having a dinner party at some restaurant and they want all of us to come."

"Oh, that's just great." Dee threw her hands up and left the table. She went into her room and slammed the door.

Dee let the answering machine pick up all her calls. She was hoping it wasn't Ben. She couldn't talk to him, not now. Why was this happening to her? What the hell was wrong with Terry? She had always tried to treat her well, to treat her like a little sister. Sometimes she got on her case, but always with the best of intentions, always to steer her in the right direction. She thought back, remembering the signs. "I do this for a living, damn it. I know this stuff. I should have seen this coming." She put her pillow over her face. *What am I going to do now?* "Ugh!" she yelled in the pillow to muffle her scream. The phone rang. She let the machine pick it up.

"Hi, Dee. It's Chris." She reached over and picked up the phone.

"Hey, Chris."

"You okay?"

"I'm not feeling well today."

"Wow, that's a first. You're never sick. Do you need anything?"

"No, I'm fine. Hold down the fort for me. I should be there in a day or two."

"Will do, boss. You sound pretty bad."

"I can't possibly sound any worse then I feel."

"Take care of yourself."

She hung up. *I should have stuck to my guns. I should have never gotten involved with him.*

Angry with herself, she let out a piercing scream, throwing her pillow across the room and knocking a picture off the wall. Jean came to the door. "Dee, are you all right?"

"I'm fine, mom." A few moments later, she heard her mother walk away. I need to start over again, she thought. I need to start fresh. The phone rang a second time. She reached for it, paused, and then pulled her hand back. The machine picked up.

"Hello, sweetheart," she heard Ben's sexy voice say into the machine. "I called your office and Kimmy said you were out sick. I tried your cell too. I hope it's nothing serious and you're just lovesick for me. Call me when you get a chance. I love you. Bye."

Dee brushed her hair from her forehead.

"I'm not going to cry," she told herself, reaching over and turning on the radio. Brian McKnight's "One Last Cry" blared through the speaker. She grabbed another pillow and cried anyway.

* * * *

"Hi, sis," Ben said anxiously into the phone.

"Hi. How's your trip going?"

"Good, but I need you to do me a favor."

"Sure, what is it?"

"Is either Kyle or Heather around?"

"Heather's here with me now."

"Can you send her over to Dee's to check on her? I've been calling, and she hasn't answered. I'm a little concerned."

"Sure. I'll send her right away. Bye," Lisa said, hanging up the phone.

"Is everything all right?" Heather asked, setting her magazine down.

"We need to go check on Dee," Lisa said

"May I help you?"

"Hi, my name's Lisa Harrison. This is my sister, Heather. Is Dee in?" Holly looked at the young women, seeing a greater family resemblance to Ben in the younger of the two.

"Sure, come on in."

"We're sorry for disturbing you like this, but Ben was concerned and asked us to check on her."

"No problem, have a seat," Holly said, walking down the hall. She tapped on the door. "Dee, someone's here to see you."

"Tell them to go away."

Holly opened the door, stepping inside. "It's Ben's sisters."

Dee sighed, getting off the bed.

"Are you all right?" Lisa asked, watching Dee walk down the hall toward them.

"I'm fine. Just a little bug." Her eyes were red and her face drawn.

"Is something wrong? You look as though you've been crying."

Dee took a deep breath and sat on the arm of the couch. "No, I'm fine."

"Ben has been calling you—he's worried." Dee looked down, trying to hide her pain. "Tell me what's wrong," Lisa said, taking her hand.

Dee bit the side of her mouth, trying to hold back the tears, but they spilled from her eyes. "Thank you both for being concerned, but it's nothing."

Lisa looked over at Heather, nodding. "Okay, but if you need us, you just call."

"I will," Dee said, giving both women a hug before they left.

Lisa dialed her cell phone as Heather drove. "Hello."

"Hi, it's me. Something's really wrong. You need to come home."

"I'll be there tomorrow."

"Good. See you then."

As Holly walked toward the mall entrance, she heard someone call her name. She turned around and saw Terry walking in her direction. She walked over to Holly, her eyes sparkling like a child at a candy store. "Holly, I'd like you to meet my boyfriend, Benjamin Harrison," Terry said with a pompous smile on her face. Holly stared at him, her mouth hanging open. "Well, dummy, aren't you going to say something?"

"Hello," Holly said, extending her hand.

"We've just come from Lord and Taylor. I bought the sweetest dress ever. But you'll see it tonight." Terry said smugly. She waited for Holly to comment, and when she didn't, Terry continued, "We'll we have to go. We're on our way to Little Italy for lunch. See you later." Holly watched as they walked away.

"Whoa," she whispered to herself. She turned and began walking toward her car, and then she started running. *Oh, my God! This couldn't have turned out better if I'd planned it myself.* She started the car, driving home as fast as she could, her heart racing. "Calm down, girl. Just calm down," she said as she patted her midsection. "Little one, we have a big surprise for Auntie Dee—and an even bigger surprise for that witch."

"Dee!" Holly called, walking into the apartment. Dee walked out of her room with her robe on and a towel around her head.

"What's up?"

"We're going to dinner tonight."

"I'm not up to it, Hol."

"No, we're going to Terry's dinner."

"Are you crazy? You couldn't pay me to go."

"Look, Dee, we've been friends for twenty years. Have I ever steered you wrong?"

"No."

"Do you trust me?"

"Yes."

"Then trust me on this—you have to go."

"Why?"

Holly bit her lip, thinking of an answer. "If you don't go, Terry will think she has beaten you."

"But she has."

"No, she thinks she has, but this game isn't over yet."

"Hol, I don't know if I can do this."

"Yes, you can. I'll be there, and so will mom, grandma, and Edmond. We will all be there to support you. Trust me, Dee, if you've never trusted anyone before, you need to trust me on this."

Dee sighed. "Okay, I guess so."

"Good. I want you to wear your red silk dress. It looks great on you, and Ben will love it."

"Ben's not important anymore."

"Just trust me." Dee went back in her room and closed the door as the phone rang.

Holly grabbed the cordless phone on the second ring. "Hello?" she said.

"Holly, what the hell is going on there?"

"Boy, am I glad you called," Holly said, walking into her room and closing the door.

* * * *

Dee applied her eyeliner for the third time. "You are not going to cry again," she chastised herself. She wore her hair up to accent her slim neck, letting wisps of curls hang delicately around her face. She decided that she would take a couple weeks off, go to Atlanta and spend some time with her mother and grandmother. When she returned she would expand the company, throw herself into her work. She would hire a few more investigators, maybe open a second office. Tomorrow she would set things in motion. She nodded to herself, approving of her decision. Sticking chopsticks in her hair, she sighed heavily. "I'm not going to let them beat me. I am strong. I can do this." She fought back the despair that threatened to overcome her. Closing her eyes and taking a deep breath, she stood, turned off the lights, and left the apartment.

* * * *

Holly and Edmond were waiting at the door when Dee arrived. She gave the valet her keys and walked inside slowly. "You look amazing," Holly said, taking her hand.

"I don't know why. I feel like garbage," Dee said as the trio walked to the table where their party waited. Terry was sitting with her back to the door. Jean was sitting across from her and Harriett was next to Jean.

"Well, it's about damn time," Terry said once she saw Dee. "You mother has been driving me crazy."

"Terry Ann, I'm trying to talk sense into that head of yours. Why must you be so self-destructive?"

Terry turned to Jean. "Look, I am not self destructive. I just see what I want, and I get it."

"And to heck with whoever gets hurt, right?" Jean added.

"Life's tough, Aunt Jean. Deal with it."

Jean turned away, talking to no one in particular. Throwing her hands up, she said, "What are you going to do?"

"I want to talk to all of you before Ben gets here," Terry said. "Have a seat." She looked at Dee, Edmond, and Holly. "Go on, have a seat." She waited until they were seated before she continued. "First of all, I want to thank you for coming."

"Cut the crap, Terry," Dee said. "What is this really about?"

"Always trying to steal my thunder," Terry mocked. "Not this time. I have the floor. Now, like I was saying. Thank you for coming. I want to say a few things." She looked down. "I'd like to tell you that I'm sorry for what happened between Ben and me." She paused for a moment. "But I can't."

"What?" Jean said, not believing that she had actually raised this girl herself.

"The truth is, I wanted him, and I got him," Terry said, smiling at everyone. Dee couldn't believe what she was hearing.

"Terry, why would you do that?" Jean asked.

"Because I'm tired of her always getting everything. You got everything, even when we were young."

"Oh my gosh! I'm not going to sit here and listen to this lunatic," Dee said, standing.

"Sit down," Holly whispered, placing a hand on Dee's arm.

"No, I'm leaving. I've had enough."

Holly looked at Dee, her eyes pleading. "Please," she whispered. Dee shook her head slightly in disgust, sitting down.

"Whatever Dee wants, Dee gets," Terry said, raising her voice.

"Terry, we gave you everything we gave Dee. And when that wasn't enough for you, she gave you what she had."

"I've said this before and I'll say it again—you're a real piece of work," Harriett spat. "Your problem is you're greedy—always have been."

"I deserve everything I get and then some," Terry threw back.

"You only deserve what you *earn,* little girl," Harriett said, pointing her bony finger. "And one of these days, you'll get what you've earned, mark my words."

"Why are you talking to me, old lady? You don't even like me."

"Terry, don't speak to your grandmother like that," Jean said.

"She's not my grandmother."

"You're right. I don't like you. I saw you were a spawn from hell when you were fifteen, stealing this and taking that. I knew back then that you were trifling, just trifling. Dee's a better woman than me, 'cause back when I was a girl I would've whooped you good," Harriett said, her voice slow and steady. "She's got a big ol' soft heart, like her mama and grandpa. I'd a given you what for—you can believe that." Harriett was silent a moment, and then she finished, "You're the one your mama should have swallowed."

"Mama," Jean said, looking at her mother with surprise.

"Don't *Mama* me," Harriett scolded.

"You people don't know how hard it's been for me!" Terry cried. "I could have had my daddy growing up if it weren't for *her* stupid husband." She jerked her head in Jean's direction. "If he hadn't worked for him, he would still be here."

Jean covered her mouth, shocked at Terry's statement. "Terry, your father wanted to work with his brother," Jean said tearfully. "He loved what he did."

"Yeah right. Dee had a father and I lost mine, and now she owes me and I think this about makes us even."

"What about what you did to Holly?" Jean asked. "Did she also owe you too?"

Edmond looked at Holly. "What did she do to you?"

"We'll talk about it later." Holly squeezed his hand. He looked at Terry, now feeling a personal sense of scorn for the girl.

"She deserved it. She shouldn't have pissed me off."

Dee shook her head. "You're certifiable."

"I may be, but in the end, I win. I get the man, the fancy house, and all the money."

"What Ben and I had wasn't about money," Dee said softly. "It was about love."

"Terry laughed without a trace of humor in her voice. "You're so naïve. You probably weren't giving him any, and that's why he turned to a real woman."

That stung Dee to the core. Terry couldn't have loved Ben, Dee thought. She didn't even know what love was. How could he be so foolish?

Holly looked at the entrance. "Oh, this is about to get good," she said, squirming in her seat from excitement. "Damn, I wish I had me some popcorn." Terry's man walked to the table. He slowed his pace when he saw Dee.

"Terry, what's going on?"

"I told you I had a surprise for you. I wanted you to meet my family." He looked very pale.

"Everyone, this is Ben Harrison."

Dee was shocked.

"Hi," he said, his eyes meeting hers.

Dee hesitated, blinking in bafflement. "Hello, Mike."

"Hot damn." Holly yelled, clapping her hands. Edmond jumped, looking at her. Unable to contain her excitement, Holly pointed at Terry. "Keep watching, keep watching."

Terry looked at Dee then back at the man she thought was Ben. "Why did she call you 'Mike', baby?"

"Because," she heard a deep voice say from behind her, "his name is Mike, Mike Kellan. He's my driver." Terry looked confused.

"Sweet ... uh, baby, we need to go somewhere and talk." Mike stepped close to Terry, taking her hand.

Terry snatched her hand away. "The hell we do! I want to know what's going on right now!"

"I don't think you want to do this here."

"Bullshit. I sure as hell do!" Terry yelled. Everyone in the restaurant turned to watch.

"Look, you know I love you. I was going to tell you tonight."

"Tell me what?"

He hesitated, looking at everyone sitting around the table. "My name *is* Mike Kellam." He sighed. "When you sent Mr. Harrison those gifts and those letters I... I read them, and I thought you were someone I'd like to meet. Then, when we talked and finally met, and you thought I was Ben Harrison, I couldn't tell you the truth—not until I knew you felt the same way about me that I felt about you."

"What about the car and the penthouse?"

"Sometimes, Mr. Harrison lets me use his car. And I kind of... borrowed the penthouse too," he said, glancing at Ben, embarrassed.

"But all those gifts and dinners."

"I make pretty good money, and I live with my mother so I can help her out. So I can splurge sometimes. I'm sorry for lying to you. I did all this because I wanted to be with you."

"Get away from me," she said, backing away.

"Sweetheart, listen to me."

"Don't call me that! I can't believe you would do this to me. You humiliated me in front of my family." She snatched her purse, tucking it under her arm. Holding her head high, she walked away from the table, looking back at Mike. "Don't call me, and don't come near me again. Ever."

"I'm sorry, Mr. Harrison," Mike said, turning to Ben. "I know I shouldn't have done this, but she seemed so special, and things just got out of hand."

Ben didn't know what to say. He sighed. "Don't worry about it, Mike," Ben said, putting his hand on the man's shoulder. He stepped in front of Dee. "What is this I hear about you thinking that I was seeing someone else?" Dee looked down, fidgeting. "I was worried sick about you until this afternoon, when I called and Holly told me what was going on. Why didn't you talk to me?"

"I didn't want to do this on the phone."

"You should have said something. All you had to do was say the word, and I would have hopped on the first flight back." He took her hand, pulling her from her seat.

She smiled at him. "I'm sorry for doubting you."

"You should be," he said, taking her in his arms, brushing her cheek. "I love you. Never doubt that."

"I won't. I promise," she said. "I love you too."

Holly squealed and Edmond jumped again. "Baby, you need to stop doing that," he said.

* * * *

"Mom, what time does your flight leave?" Dee asked as they walked through the airport looking for a seat.

"Ten forty-five," Jean said, picking up a magazine and leafing through it. Dee watched her grandmother talking to Ben. He was looking at her intently, smiling at her every word. "I like him," Jean said, glancing up from the article she was reading. "He's a good man."

"Yes, he is."

Dee and Ben walked the women to the gate. After saying their goodbyes, they returned to his car.

"Your place or mine?" he asked, starting the car.

"Yours," she said, placing her hand on his. "I really missed you."

He turned his hand over, embracing hers.

"I missed you too." She stared at his profile for a moment. He glanced over at her.

"Are you okay?" he asked, squeezing her hand.

She inhaled deeply. "Yes. Thank you."

"For what?"

"For being you."

He brought her hand to his lips and kissed it. They rode in silence. Dee thought about the last couple of days. She had never realized how much Terry wanted to hurt her and to what lengths she would go to do it. Did her own cousin hate her that much? She loved Terry, and she always would—they were family—but things would never be the same. She felt tears run down her face. Brushing them away quickly, she turned to the window. Ben pulled the car to the side of the road and put it in park.

He got out and walked to the passenger-side door. He then opened the door, helped Dee out of the car, and took her in his arms. She sobbed for the loss of her cousin. "I don't understand why she hates me," Dee said, sobbing.

"She doesn't hate you, sweetheart. She envies you."

They continued to stand at the side of the road holding each other as the cold December air enveloped them.

* * * *

"Dee, can you get that?" Holly called from her bedroom. Dee walked out of the kitchen to the door.

"How much?" she asked as she opened the door, expecting the pizza deliveryman. She was surprised to see Terry.

"Hi, can I come in?" The look on Dee's face provided the answer. "Just for a minute." Dee hesitated, then nodded and opened the door.

Holly walked out of her bedroom. "Good, I'm starving..." She froze when she saw Terry.

"Hey. Holly."

"What does *she* want?"

"I just want to talk to you guys."

Holly turned, heading down the hall.

"Please, just hear me out."

She turned, crossing her arms. "What?"

"I just wanted to apologize for what I did to you."

"Oh yeah?"

"Yeah, I know that I shouldn't have poked holes in the condoms, and I wanted to say I'm sorry. Will you accept my apology?"

"No."

"What do you mean 'no'? How can you just say no after I come up here, practically groveling?"

"You changed my life. It wasn't your place to decide whether I needed children or not. It wasn't your job to alter my future. Dee might forgive you because she's family, but I can never forgive you." She went in her room and closed her door.

"I guess I deserve that," Terry said, shifting her weight from one foot to the other. She looked at Dee. "Dee, I'm sorry. I don't know what came over me."

"Can you just tell me why?"

"When I started seeing him, he told me not to tell you. I wanted to—I swear I did."

"No, Terry. Go home."

"Why? Just let me explain."

"No, if you can't tell me the truth, I don't want to hear anything you have to say," she said, pushing her toward the door.

"Okay," Terry said, removing Dee's hand from her shoulder. "Okay, I don't know why I did it. It just seemed like a good idea. I figured he was rich, and I wanted him."

"Terry, you thought he was Ben, and you knew I was seeing him."

"Not at first." She paused. "But after a while, I got caught up in it, and it just didn't seem to matter. Things just always seem to go your way. You went to college and then inherited the business from Uncle Will."

"Stop," Dee said, holding her hand up. "You had the opportunity to go to college too—we had the same amount of money set aside for it—but you decided you needed to go to France for a year instead," she said, shaking her head. "I even offered to help you pay your way through college so you could come and work for the company, but you wouldn't hear of it. So don't you dare stand there and tell me that I've had it easy. I'm sick of it. From the time you moved in with us, all I ever did was give, and you just kept taking."

"I know, Dee. You're right. I wish I could change it, but I can't. Please forgive me."

Dee massaged her eyes, trying to ease the tension. "Terry, I do forgive you, because you're my family and I'll always love you. But you can't be part of my life."

"Dee, I'll make it up to you. I promise."

"Terry, I've never been anything but fair to you, and I've always been there for you. But you take too much out of me. I can't do it anymore."

"I can't believe you're going to treat me this way," Terry cried out, shoving her hands in the pockets of her coat.

Dee opened the door. "Goodbye, Terry."

Chapter 15

She walked into the smoke-filled pub and looked around. She was nervous. She had never done anything like this before; in fact, she had never even been in a place like this before. She spotted an empty seat at the bar and sat down. The bartender walked over, cleaning his hands on his brown sweatshirt. "What can I get you?"

"I'd like a dry martini."

He gave her a crooked grin and shook his head. "We got beer, whisky, and wine. Which do you want?"

She shifted her weight on the stool, trying to get comfortable.

"Give me a white wine then." He walked away and returned with a glass a moment later. He replaced the ten she had set on the bar with the glass.

"Is this seat taken?" said the man standing next to her. His long brown hair hung past his shoulders, his beard was neatly trimmed, and his eyes were dark and unexpressive.

"Depends?"

"On what?" he asked.

"On what your name is?"

"Jake."

She nodded. As he sat down, she examined his profile. He wasn't what she had expected. He was handsome, in a rugged sort of way. She might have even dated him under different circumstances. "Okay, lady," he said, not wasting any time. "Let's talk business."

* * * *

Ben let himself into Dee's apartment. "Hi, babe," she said, walking out of the bedroom, carrying an overnight bag.

"I thought we were spending the evening with Holly and Edmond?" he said, eyeing the bag.

"We are. We're going to have dinner and exchange gifts here, then we're going to your place. I want us to spend some time together alone." She smiled, setting the bag on the floor.

Dee and Holly made a baked glazed ham, sugar snap peas, scalloped potatoes with cheddar and, for dessert, carrot cake with coconut frosting. Dee had also bought an apple pie from the bakery. After exchanging gifts, they wished each other Merry Christmas, and then Dee and Ben left for his penthouse.

As she got out of the elevator and took off her coat, Dee said, "I got you something special for Christmas. Well, actually, I have two gifts for you. But I want to give you the special one now and the other one in the morning."

Ben looked at the shopping bag she was carrying. "Okay," he said, nodding as he sat down.

"Wait here. I'll be right back," she said, walking into the bedroom. The timer made a clicking sound, and the Christmas tree switched on. He sat watching the lights twinkle. He smiled, remembering the time Dee took him to the roof of the movie theater to stargaze.

"Merry Christmas," Dee said.

He turned to look at her, and his mouth went dry.

She was wearing the sexiest outfit he had ever seen—a red "Santa" mini-dress with white marabou trim, red fishnet stockings, and four-inch white slippers with marabou trim. A red and white Santa hat completed the outfit. Ben was speechless. "Well, do you like it?"

"Yes, Lord," he said once he found his voice. She walked to the stereo and turned it on, then danced around in front of him.

"Mrs. Claus has a special gift for you, because you have been such a good boy," she said, taking his hand and pulling him from the chair. "Do you want it?"

"Oh yes," he said, unable to contain his excitement. Dee pulled him along with her as she swayed toward the bedroom. She turned with him, pushing him on the bed, and standing in front of him.

"Merry Christmas, baby," she said, dropping her hat on the floor.

"Good morning, sweetheart," Ben said, holding Dee tight.

"Good morning," she said. "Merry Christmas."

"Merry Christmas." He reached under his side of the bed, pulled out a gift, and placed it on her lap. It was wrapped in gold and had a bright red bow on it.

She smiled. "Can I open it now?"

"Sure." She sat up and tore the box open, finding a platinum Japanese pearl and diamond bracelet.

"It's beautiful," she said, gently taking it out of the box. She handed it to him and he slipped it on her wrist.

"I thought it could make up for the one you lost."

"I love it," she said, kissing him. "Thank you." She slid off the bed, crossed the room, and looked into the bag she had brought with her. She took out a box, which she brought to him. "I didn't know what to get you," she said, sitting next to him.

"I have all I need now."

"I know," she said, laughing at herself, "but I got you something else anyway." He looked at the large silver box with the blue ribbon around it. "Go ahead and open it." He tore the paper from the box.

"Hmm..." he said, looking at it.

"It's a remote-control boat—you know, like the one the kids on the beach had. You had so much fun with it, I thought you might like to have one." He looked at her, seeing the sparkle in her eyes, and smiled.

"You are so thoughtful. It's the best gift I've ever gotten. Well, almost the best gift," he corrected.

"So, what was the best?" she asked slowly.

"I can't really describe it to you—I'll have to show you."

"Oh yeah?" She smiled, biting her lip.

"Yeah," he dropped the box next to the bed and pulled the covers over their heads.

She giggled. "Oh yeah, I remember that."

"Merry Christmas, everyone," Dee and Ben said, entering the living room.

"Merry Christmas, my darlings," Natalie greeted them, hugging them both. "Come, sit down," she said, pulling Dee toward the couch.

Before sitting down, Dee passed out her gifts, rubbing her hands together in anticipation. "I hope you all like them."

She saved Lisa's gift for last. "This is for you. I hope you like it," she said, passing her the flat box. Lisa opened the box and pulled back the paper. It was a certificate in a gold frame. "I had a star named after you," Dee said. "I've met a lot of people in my life, but I've never met one that shined as brightly as a star—not until I met you." Lisa threw her arms around Dee, while Natalie smiled and quickly brushed away a tear. Ben couldn't speak because of the lump in his throat.

"Excuse me," he said, leaving the room. He went into the kitchen and began pacing back and forth, trying to work up his nerve. Stopping, he leaned on the sink and drew a glass of water. He reached into his pocket and pulled out the black box; he stood there a moment, looking at it. Then he took a deep breath and walked back into the living room, where Dee and Natalie were sitting on the sofa, holding hands and talking. Ben walked over and sat on the other side of Dee.

"Dee was telling me that you two are going to see her family tomorrow. I was thinking that maybe we could have an intimate party on New Year's Eve."

"That sounds good," he said, taking Dee's hand and breathing deeply.

"What's wrong?" Dee asked, looking at him. He looked around at everyone. Then, standing, he pulled her to her feet.

"Come with me." They walked into the study, closing the door behind them.

"Come, sit down." He led her to the chair. She sat, looking confused.

"What's wrong?" she asked nervously.

"Deanna," he said, taking her hand. "When I look at you, I see the most beautiful, most caring, most exciting woman in the world. Before you, I only existed—I didn't live. You give me joy. You give me inspiration. But the greatest thing you have given me is your heart." He got down on one knee and reached into his pocket. Dee gasped as she touched her face. They heard a screech from the hallway. "I know we haven't known each other long, but I also know that I want to spend the rest of my life with you." With shaking hands, he opened the velvet black box, revealing a 2.0-carat marquise-cut diamond ring surrounded by four round-cut diamonds. "Will you marry me?" he asked, holding up the ring.

"Yes!" Natalie yelled from the hall which made Dee laugh.

"Yes!" she said, jumping into his arms. Natalie, Lisa, and Heather barged into the room, hugging Dee and Ben. Kyle walked in behind them.

"It was all I could do to keep these three from breaking down the door," he said, smiling. "Congratulations," he said, shaking Ben's hand.

"Thanks," Ben said, smiling at the women.

* * * *

"Yes, mom. We'll be there soon. I have to tell you something. No, I don't want to tell you on the phone. No, it's nothing bad. Okay, I'll see you soon. I love you too." After hanging up, she resumed her packing. Remembering the sweater Lisa had given her for Christmas, she left the apartment and went out to her car to get it.

She walked to the back of the car and opened the trunk, then froze. The hairs on the back of her neck rose, and she looked around. There was a man walking in her direction, looking around suspiciously as he walked. She closed the trunk and walked to the apartment door.

"Excuse me, miss." She picked up her pace. "Miss!" he called, jogging to catch up to her.

She turned around, assuming a defensive posture. "Yeah?"

He stopped, and seemed to assess her demeanor. "I wanted to know if you knew Tammy Davidson?"

"No," Dee said, looking at him suspiciously.

"She lives in this building. I was just wondering if you saw her today?"

Dee took a step back instinctively, making a mental note of his appearance. Although he was large, he didn't seem aggressive. She still had a bad feeling about him.

"I'm sorry. I don't know her." She backed up, trying to put some distance between them before she turned and walked away.

He rushed toward her, grabbing her arm, trying to cover her mouth and drag her at the same time. She dropped down, trying to wiggle from his hold, but he bent with her, holding her tightly. She brought her fist down, hitting his knee. The pain made him loosen his grip, but he didn't let go, hoisting her up off her feet. As he began dragging her away, she reached above her head and raked his eyes. He dropped her, grabbed his eyes, then felt her booted foot slam into his midsection, slightly knocking the wind out of him.

Dee turned and ran for the door, not looking behind her but listening for the sound of his footsteps. When she reached the door, she took the steps two at a time, running breathlessly into the apartment, closing the door behind her, and locking it. She ran to the closet to grab the baseball bat she kept there for protection, and then snatched up the phone.

"Nine-one-one. What is the nature of your emergency?"

"Hello, I need help. Someone just tried to assault me."

* * * *

Ben ran into the apartment when he saw the two uniformed police officers. He rushed to Dee's side. "Are you all right?" he asked, looking her over.

"Yes, I'm fine," she said. She went over her statement with the officer again. As Ben listened, he became agitated.

"Excuse me," he said. He walked into her bedroom and began pacing, waiting for her to come in. "I should have been here," he said, reprimanding himself. He closed his eyes and his mind began to entertain all sorts of terrible scenarios, from crazed subjects she had followed before to pervert stalkers.

"Hey," she said as she walked through the doorway. She wrapped her arms around his neck and said calmly, "I'm fine."

He held her so tightly he thought she would break. He then let go and took a step back. "I want you to come home with me."

"We're leaving to go to Atlanta soon," she said.

"No, I mean when we come back. I mean for good."

"I can't do that."

"Why not?"

"What about Holly?"

"I don't want either of you here—it's too dangerous. I'll help her get another place."

"But we have a lease."

"I'll take care of it. I don't want you living here anymore. I'm afraid for you."

"But it's my home."

"It's not safe, Dee."

"I think he's right," she heard from the door. She looked over her shoulder and saw Edmond and Holly. Holly walked into the room and hugged Dee.

"Are you okay?"

"Yeah, I'm fine."

"I think Ben's right. Ed and I have been taking about getting a place together anyway. This way I won't have to worry about you here alone." Dee looked around her bedroom and let out a sigh.

"Then it's settled," Ben said with finality. "When we get back, you'll move in with me "

* * * *

Jake pulled his car next to hers then got out and sat in her passenger seat.

"Did you get her?"

"No." Jake answered tightly.

"What do you mean 'no'?"

"I had a little problem."

"What problem?"

"*I had a little problem,*" he said slowly and clearly.

Oh God, she said to herself, covering her eyes. *I would have to get the dumbest hit man in the world.*

"How hard can it be?" she mumbled. "There's not much to her." She shook her head, looking out the window. "Okay, now what?" she asked, not looking at him.

"I'll try to catch her in a confined place, so she can't run away."

She looked at him. "And just how in the world are you going to do that?"

"Let me take care of that. You just make sure you have my fifty thousand."

"You mean forty thousand?"

"No, I mean fifty—an extra ten for aggravation, and because you didn't tell me all there was to tell about this broad."

She rolled her eyes, wanting to scream. It was hard enough to part with the forty, let alone another ten. She would practically have to live on crumbs until the money that went into her trust fund built back up. *It doesn't matter,* she thought. *When we're married, I will have more than enough money.* She looked back at him.

"Okay, when are you going to do it?"

"I'll let you know," he said, opening the door. She watched as his car drove away, placing her hands on the steering wheel. She then closed her eyes, imagining that the steering wheel was the neck of the idiot who had just left her car. She twisted and squeezed with all her might, letting her rage flow out of her. Then, taking a deep breath, she calmed herself. She pulled out of the parking lot.

Soon it'll be all over and we can be together. Soon she won't be there to come between us, and you'll be free to love me. I know that you think about me, that you miss me. I can tell by the way you look at me. I can feel it.

She parked at the curb a half a block from Dee's apartment. Watching the apartment, she noticed that his car was next to hers. Her heart raced at the thought of seeing him, even at such a distance. They walked out of the apartment building together, he carrying a suitcase with one hand and placing the other on her back. "Don't touch her," she said aloud. "*Don't!*" She hit the steering wheel, sucking in large, panicky breaths. She continued to watch as they got in his car and drove away.

She sat there for a long time, overwhelmed with grief. It was then that she devised her plan. "I'm not going to let you get away with this." She nodded. "Your time will come—real soon." She started the car and drove to the airport.

* * * *

"Merry Christmas!" they said as they walked into her grandmother's house.

"Merry Christmas!" Jean hugged her daughter, then Ben.

"Where's grandma?"

"She'll be down shortly. So, how was your Christmas?" she asked Ben.

"The best ever." He smiled.

She looked at Dee and then back at him. "What's going on?"

"Nothing. Come sit down. We want to give you your gifts when grandma comes down."

"Merry Christmas!" Harriett yelled as she made her way down the steps.

"Merry Christmas, grandma," Dee said, hugging her. When Harriett was seated, Dee looked at Ben who handed Harriett an envelope with a receipt and a contract in it.

"It's for the both of you—a new dishwasher and microwave." Dee said.

"The deliveryman will be here the day after tomorrow to install them," Ben added.

"This is wonderful. Thank you both." Jean rose, hugging her daughter and Ben.

"Child, I ain't going to know how to act with a dishwasher. I'm liable to cook a whole lot of food just so I can use it," Harriett said, laughing at herself. She then stopped suddenly and looked at Dee. "Hey, what's that on your finger?" she said, squinting. "Is that what I think it is?" Dee held her hand out for her grandmother to see.

"We' re engaged."

Jean and Harriett were elated. Dee told them they would decide on the details of the wedding after Natalie's New Year's Eve gathering, and then Ben suggested that they all take a cruise together and have the wedding on the ship. Finally, they toasted their engagement, and the holiday, with eggnog and Christmas cookies.

Later, in the kitchen, Harriett and Dee were alone, washing dishes. "Mom told me that Terry is planning to come?" Dee said.

"Yeah," Harriett said dryly. "Your mama felt sorry for the child and invited her down." She looked at her granddaughter. "How you feel about that?"

Dee thought for a moment. "I'm all right with it. I don't want her to be alone on the holidays because of me. She needs her family."

Harriett shook her head, turning back to the counter. "No, it's not because of you she did what she did because she wanted to." She grunted. "You get your compassion from your mother... get your spunk from me," she boasted, glancing at Dee. "Don't be taken in by her. You're a smart girl. Don't be fooled by them crocodile tears, or she'll be drying her tears with one hand and picking your pocket with the other."

"Okay, grandma," Dee said, hugging her.

"Merry Christmas, Dee," Terry said meekly.

"Merry Christmas, Terry," Dee replied. They hugged awkwardly, then Terry turned away, walking quickly into the living room after giving her greetings.

"Hi," Terry said to Ben, avoiding eye contact.

Ben nodded. "Terry."

"Where's the baby?" Jean asked.

"I let him spend the week with David; I thought it might be best."

"I know it must be hard not having him for Christmas."

"Yes, but I went to David's apartment for a few hours yesterday morning to spend time with Little David—you know, watch him open his gifts."

Harriett saw the looked that Dee gave her cousin. She walked over and pinched her.

"Ouch!" Dee yelled, looking at her grandmother. Harriett smiled.

"Well," she said, "Ben made reservations at La Grotta Ravinia for dinner, so we'd best be getting ready to go."

As the five of them walked into the restaurant, Ben approached the hostess. "Reservations for Harrison," he said, and the hostess led them to their table.

As they perused their menus, Jean took in the surroundings. "This is really nice."

"I'm going for the king salmon with grilled asparagus," Harriett said, her enthusiasm hinting at her still robust appetite.

Ben laughed. "I think I'll have the same."

As they ordered, they made small talk.

"What a lovely ring," the waitress said as she brought the drinks.

"Thank you." Dee smiled, holding it up so the waitress could get a better look. Terry looked at the ring and then at Ben.

"They just got engaged," Jean said to the waitress.

"Congratulations," she said to both Dee and Ben. Although Dee knew Terry was watching as well, she didn't want to look at her. She also felt sorry for her, however, and the conflicting emotions made her feel uncomfortable.

"Congratulations, Dee, Ben," Terry said, her voice solemn.

Dee smiled at her. "Thanks."

After dinner, Jean thanked Ben.

"My pleasure. I hope you don't have plans for the evening," he said, "I got tickets for the Lion King at Cadillac Palace, if anyone wants to go."

"That sounds like fun," Jean said.

"I don't know if I should," Terry said, looking at Dee.

"Why not?"

"After all the things that have happened, maybe I should meet you guys back at the house."

"No," Dee said. "Ben got tickets for all of us—that includes you."

Terry nodded, following them to the car.

Ben lay on the sleep sofa, trying to find a place where a spring didn't poke him in the back, like a shake following his every move.

Dee crept down the steps. "Hey," she said, peeking around the corner.

"Hey."

She walked over, lying next to him on the bed. "How's it going?" she asked, looking at him sympathetically.

"Not so good, I'm afraid. This isn't the most comfortable place I've ever tried to sleep."

"Poor baby. I'm sorry," she said humorously. "I would have suggested we share the bedroom and let Terry sleep down here, but there's enough friction between us already. I know how she thinks, and she would have taken it the wrong way."

"That's okay." He gave her an understanding smile. "Having you here makes it better." She moved closer, laying her head on his chest. He absentmindedly stroked her arm.

"Today was a wonderful day. Thank you."

"I'd do anything in the world to see that smile. I love you, sweetheart."

"I love you too." She said, snuggling close to him. He kissed the top of her head, then closed his eyes and drifted off to sleep.

She stood in the shadows of the dining room with her back pressed against the wall, listening as their voices drifted down the hall. As she heard them confess their love for each other, tears welled in her eyes. She shook her head, trying to chase away her feelings—feelings of despair, loneliness, and failure. Things had not gone as she planned; she hadn't thought things through. She turned and walked quietly up the stairs and into the bedroom. Sitting on the bed, she took a calming breath. She had to set things right, put them on the right track. She lay on her side, sighing heavily at the thought of failing again. Her plan had to work, she told herself.

"Here's Ben's home number," Dee said, as she wrote it down for her mother. "Okay," Jean said, looking at the piece of paper. She then she looked at her daughter with questioning eyes.

"I'm moving in with him when we get home."

"That's sudden," her mother said, looking from Dee to Ben.

"We thought it might be a good idea, since—" Ben started to say.

"Since Holly and Ed are getting a place together," Dee interjected. "I thought it would be good."

"Mm-hmm," Jean said. She then looked at Ben. "Is there anything else you want to tell me?"

He looked at Dee, who looked back at him, pleading with him silently not to tell them about the near abduction. He didn't want to hide this from her family, and he thought they should know, but he wanted to respect Dee's wishes. He dropped his gaze to the floor.

"No, ma'am."

She looked at Dee, disbelieving her look of innocence; she had seen it too often to be fooled. "I know there's something going on, girl. You'd better not get into anymore trouble at work. Holly and Craig can't keep your butt out of jail forever."

"I know, mom."

Harriett gave her granddaughter a hug; then, turning to Ben, she hugged him and said, "You know you're going to have to put your foot down with her, don't you?" He laughed. "If you don't, she'll have you in a mess of trouble."

Dee looked at her grandmother and then her mother. "Mom!"

* * * *

"The moving van should be here any minute," Dee said, looking up from the box she was taping. "Are you sure you don't want any of the furniture in my bedroom before I give it to Kimmy?"

"No. Ed and I have more than we can use as it is," Holly said, leaning against the doorframe. "I'm going to miss seeing you every day," she said.

"I'm going to miss you too, but we can get together once a week and have lunch or dinner—or both." That didn't seem to make either of them feel better. Dee set the tape next to her on the table. "Have you guys found a place yet?"

"No. We're going to stay at Ed's place until we find an apartment with two bedrooms."

"Why don't you keep this place?"

"I think it's time to get a new place. With Maurice breaking in, and then some guy trying to grab you, I don't think it's as safe as it once was. Plus, Ed doesn't want me here alone, in case someone's watching the place."

Dee nodded. "I really do think it was a random attack; I mean, if he was a stalker, he had to have known that I would at least put up a fight."

Holly sat down. "What if he *wanted* you to fight him? What if that's how he gets his kicks?"

"Yeah, that could be the case, but then why would he take the chance to let me see him and then get away."

"I guess that's true," Holly said. "Something just doesn't seem right, though. He can't be a pro. If he is, he would have planned better. But I still can't help but believe that there's something more to this." She looked at the door. "But better safe than sorry," she added.

She sat in her usual spot, a block away, watching as the moving truck pulled up. She saw her walk out of the building and talk to the driver. "What's going on?" she said softly. She watched her walk back inside, and then walk back down a few minutes later carrying a box. She was so elated that she screamed with glee. *She's moving away. Maybe when Jake grabbed her, he scared her away.* She rocked glee- fully, clapping her hands like a child and smiling so wide she thought her face would crack. She started her car, planning to drive away, when out of the corner of her eye she saw *his* car drive by.

She watched as he pulled behind the truck, then got out of the car and walked around to open his trunk. He approached one of the movers, talking as if he was giving him instructions. The driver nodded, went up the stairs, and brought down several boxes, putting them in the trunk and on the back seat of his car. Then they did the same to her car. After the truck was loaded, the three vehicles left. She started her car, following slowly, staying a block behind but watching as the truck made a left on Maple Avenue and the two cars kept going straight. She had a nauseous feeling in the pit of her stomach. "Oh God, no," she said. "No, please don't let this be happening." She watched as her car turned into his parking garage, with his following. She drove by, watching them pull up the ramp, not seeing the car in front of her. She saw it at the last second and managed to slam on her brakes before crashing into it.

The driver leaned out of his window. "Hey, lady! You need to wake up. You almost hit me."

She was startled. She rubbed her eyes with the palms of her hands, trying to brush away the confusion.

"Hey, lady, are you listening to me? Are you stupid or something?" the driver yelled, hanging out of his car.

She sped around him, stopping long enough to flip him the bird. Her breathing was labored, her eyes welling up; she angrily wiped them, clearing her vision.

Pulling into a nearby park, she turned off her car. "I can't believe this is happening." She shook her head, unable to breathe. She stretched the collar of her turtleneck to help ease the choking sensation. "No!" she cried, shaking her head violently, trying to erase the vision of him coming home to her, going to bed and waking up with her. She let out a blood-curdling scream, throwing the contents of her handbag around the car. She grabbed a metal nail file and stabbed the passenger seat. "I hate her! I hate her!" she said with each stab. When she was spent, she took a deep breath, sat back, and closed her eyes. She pulled down the visor to check her makeup and then searched the car until she found her cell phone. "Hello, Jake. Change of plans. She's moved, and I know how to get you in."

* * * *

"I have a surprise for you." Ben reached for her hand, pulling her closer to him.

"What is it?"

"Come with me." He took her hand as the door opened, leading her off the elevator and down the hall to the bedroom. He pushed the door open and Dee walked in to see that everything was gone, except the bed. There were carpet and fabric samples spread out on the floor, while paint charts and furniture catalogs lined one wall "What's all this about?"

"I had a decorator send this over. When you decide what you want, they'll come in and redo everything to your liking."

"It was fine the way it was," she said, looking at him.

"This is your home, too." He pulled her close, placing his chin on the top of her head.

"I want you to be happy and comfortable here."

"I will be."

"No, I mean really comfortable."

"I'm comfortable anywhere as long as you're there." He smiled. "I'll tell you what," she said, leading him back to the living room. "When the movers finish bringing everything up, why don't we look through all that stuff and design the room together. It will be our own haven."

* * * *

"Why, hello, Mrs. Feldon. How nice to see you." The woman turned to see the young woman approach her. She regarded her with slight suspicion. "Do you need any help with your bags?"

"Why, yes, I suppose I could use a little help. Thank you." She walked the elderly woman to her car, chatting about her recent holiday.

"Starbucks is around the corner. Can I buy you a cup of coffee, maybe a bite to eat? We could catch up."

Mrs. Feldon looked at the younger woman, not quite remembering where she knew her from. The other woman seemed to know her, though, and Ester Feldon was not the sort of woman to turn down a free meal.

"Sure, why not?"

The young woman took her arm, and together they walked to Starbucks.

* * * *

Jake sat on the steps of the abandoned factory. He hated when people made him wait. He had been waiting for half an hour for this chick, and he was furious. He flicked his cigarette butt, and watched it spiral in the dark.

He was starting to get a bad feeling about this job. Usually when he got a job, he completed it within a few days, got his cash, and got out of there. He got a lot of work. Although some guys wouldn't think of hurting a female or a kid, hell, he thought, if the money's green, that was all that mattered. But this was different. This time he had to kidnap some broad and take her to a cabin in the mountains.

That was a little too hands-on for him. He liked to keep it nice and simple. *Pop!* One shot to the back of the head and he was gone. Plus, there was something weird about the chick he was doing the job for.

She wasn't like the people he usually worked with. That made him kind of nervous, but there was something else, something deep inside that kept telling him to cut his losses. But when he thought about the fifty Gs, he couldn't say no. Her car pulled up and Jake stood up, taking long strides as he walked to the car.

"Why the hell did you have me waiting here so long?"

She gave him a quick look. "I'm here, aren't I?"

He eyed her. Yeah, she was a crazy one all right. *Walk away, man,* his subconscious yelled. He shook his head at the unheard voice and leaned into the car. "What the hell happened to your seat? Looks like a tiger crawled in here and went nuts."

She glared at him speaking with no emotion. "None of your damn business." He looked at her, at the blank eyes that looked back at him. They made him uneasy, and he had to fight to maintain eye contact. He fidgeted before he spoke. "So, what's up?"

She passed him the card for the garage gate, as well as a piece of paper with an address printed on it. "You'll have to get a truck that can't be traced to you. Go there before dawn and wait for her. There's a surveillance camera—I wrote its location on that slip of paper—so you'll have to cover the camera or do something with it."

He stood up, putting his hands in his coat pocket.

"So, when are you going to do it?" she asked, looking straight ahead.

He looked down at her profile—her expression was still blank, but he saw her slim hands gripping the steering wheel tightly.

"I'll give you a call," he said, turning around and walking around the building to his car.

Turning into the driveway, Jake put the car in park and looked at the small bungalow. It was only 9:30 P.M. and already all the lights in the house we off. Peggy must be asleep. Since she gave birth, it seemed to him that that was all she ever did anymore. Sleep, or take care of those dammed babies. When she told him she was going to have a baby he was pissed, but he learned to deal with it. She said that things wouldn't change all that much; that they would still spend time together. But things did change, in a major way.

He would never forget the day he walked into that hospital room. Peg was sitting on the bed, with a stupid grin on her face, and his gut told him to turn around and leave, but he didn't. When he walked further into the room, he saw Peg's mother and a nurse there; Peg's mother said, "Congratulations, Jake, you are the proud father three beautiful baby girls." He couldn't believe it; Peg couldn't have just one, or even two kids. No, not her; she had to go have three. Hell that was a litter. Jake was so angry, he could have pulled his gun from under his jacket, and killed Peg, her mother, and the nurse, right on the spot.

Jake shook his head, and got out of the car. Going quietly into the house, he crept into the bedroom and took his gym bag out of the closest He looked in the bottom of the closet and removed a large cardboard box. He had told Peg they were mementos from his childhood, so she wouldn't look in it. The top half of the box had old comic books, a baseball, a cap, and an array of other things. All of which meant nothing to him, except what he had hidden at the bottom. He took out a large white box marked "baseball cards," opened it, threw the cards on the floor, and took out the three stacks of money. He put the money in his bag, and went to the dresser from which he took out only one change of clothes.

"What's going on?"

He turned, to see Peg leaning on her elbow, looking at him. He stepped to the foot of the bed and looked down at her. Even after gaining all that weight she was still a looker. Too bad.

He reached behind his back feeling the butt of his .45. One of the babies stirred, making a small whimper. He looked at the three bassinets lined against the wall next to the bed, then stepped next to them, glancing down at his daughters. It was Baby Jade that was stirring in her sleep, or maybe it was Amber or Pearl. Who the hell know, he thought to himself, and why would someone give their kids such names. Peg said that the babies were their jewels. He thought she gave them such names because she was an idiot. He looked at Peg then back at his sleeping daughters.

Sighing, he removed his hand from his gun, and went back to pick up his gym bag. Reaching inside the bag, he grabbed one of the stacks of money. "Here." He tossed it on the bed. "Use this for you, and those kids." He turned, and headed for the door. "I won't be back" he said leaving the bedroom.

CHAPTER 16

"Have a good day, babe," Dee said, kissing him.

"Where are you going?"

"I have to leave for work."

"Wait, I'll walk out with you."

"No, I'll be fine. I'll get Mac to walk me to my car."

"Give me a moment," he said, slipping on his shoes.

"Don't be silly," she said, kissing him again and walking across the room. "I love you," she called to him, picking up her bag and walking out of the bedroom toward the elevator.

On the ride down, a feeling of dread nearly overcame her. She shook it off, convinced that Ben's paranoia was rubbing off on her.

"Hey, Ernie, how's it going?"

"Fine, Ms. Meyers. How about yourself?"

"Good. Can one of your guys walk me to my car?"

"Mac went to help Mrs. Feldon in 3B. She lost her card for the garage gate. He should be back soon."

Dee nodded and asked, "How are the kids?"

"Great, Cindy got a bike for Christmas, and she's learned to ride already."

"Cool," she said looking around. "You know what? I'm just going to go."

"You sure you don't want to wait? He shouldn't be much longer."

"No, I'll be fine," she said, walking out the side door to the parking garage. She walked up the ramp to the second level, where Ben's private parking spaces were, reaching into her purse as she walked and pulling out her keys. As she approached the car, she had an uneasy feeling and slowed down. Looking around, she didn't see anyone, but her instincts kicked in and she turned, heading back to the door. She heard footsteps behind her and started running. Then she felt a sharp pain before darkness overtook her.

* * * *

When she woke up, she was in a dark room. Her head hurt and her arms and legs were tied. She moaned from the pain as the skin on the back of her head was stretched tight from the swelling. She lay back, trying to get her bearings and collect her thoughts. Holding her head up and looking around, she felt nauseated and her head began to spin. She heard a noise on the other side of the door, then a sudden bright light blinded her. She snapped her eyes shut against the glare, and opened them slowly, trying to adjust to the light and see the face of the person standing in front of her.

* * * *

Ben walked out of the elevator.

"Good morning, sir," Ernie said.

"Morning, Ernie. Did Mac see Ms. Meyers to her car safely?"

"Mac was taking care of something for one of the other tenants, so she decided to go alone.

Ben became angry. "Damn it!" he said, walking to the side door. "I told her I didn't want her to go out there alone." He walked briskly to their parking level and walked to Dee's car, expecting to see her sitting in the driver's seat. It was empty. Panic gripped him, and he looked frantically around the garage.

"Oh my God!"

He raced to the entrance of the lobby. "Call the police!" he cried with a look of dread on his face. "Something has happened to Dee."

* * * *

She focused on the man going through her purse.

"Jake, I think you should have put the handcuffs on her before she woke up."

Dee looked across the room at Janet who was sitting on a table happily swinging her legs.

"I'll get to it. It won't be a problem." He dropped the purse on the floor and walked toward Dee. She rolled on her back, moving close to the wall. When he got close enough, she kicked him in the gut with both feet then started kicking frantically, trying to loosen the rope on her ankles before he could reach her again. As he raced in her direction, she jumped to her feet and tried to ram him with her head. He moved, hitting her in the stomach, causing her to slump forward. Then, grabbing her hair and pulling her upright, he tossed her on the bed.

"Sit still. I don't want to hurt you, but I will."

He put his knee in the small of her back, bending her arm back to put on the handcuffs. After cuffing her hands, he flipped her on her back and began struggling to get another set of cuffs on her ankles. He removed her ankle boots, as she kicked violently. He punched her on her right hip to still her. The pain slowed her, but she didn't stop her kicking.

"Why the hell are you doing this?" she yelled at Janet.

"I told you to leave Ben alone, didn't I? You wouldn't listen, and now you have to pay." Janet sneered.

Dee moved her wrist, trying to free herself.

"It's no use. That's why we used handcuffs, so you can't escape. You might as well save your energy. You're going to need it."

"Look, Janet, let's talk about this."

"No." She jumped to her feet. "When I wanted to talk, you wouldn't listen. It's too late for talking. I told you I loved him. Why didn't you just go away?" She was pacing like a caged animal.

Jake sat Dee up, bending to check her ankles. "Is that too tight?" he asked, squatting in front of her.

She head-butted him in the face.

"Ah, my nose!" he screamed, falling back.

"Imbecile," Janet mumbled under her breath, shaking her head in disgust.

He scrambled to his feet and walked into the bathroom while catching the blood leaking from his nose.

"What are you going to do, Janet? Kill me?"

"No, of course not. We're just going to leave you here to die."

"Janet, you can't do this."

"Yes, I can. No one comes here anymore, and my parents haven't been here in years. We'll leave the door open, and you'll freeze to death. Then some wild animal will come and drag you away. In a few months, I'll send Jake here, and he'll get rid of anything that might be left behind."

"This is crazy."

"Not really. It's a good plan. Ben will be grief stricken, and I'll go to him—as a friend, of course. I'll even tell him I'll help him find you, and when we don't, he'll turn to me. Then we'll be married." She looked pleased with herself. She looked at the ring on her finger, then held it up in the light. "This is a nice ring, exquisite even, but the one he's going to give me will be much nicer."

"Janet, don't do this. No man is worth going to jail for, or worth killing for."

Janet turned to her. "Tell me you wouldn't do anything you had to do to be with him."

"No, I wouldn't. Not something like this."

"Liar," Janet yelled, shaking all over. "I know you would. I've been watching you, you bitch." She talked through clinched teeth, spit forming at the corner of her mouth. "I watched you put your dirty hands on him when the two of you went to get a Christmas tree, the tree that should have been mine. You took my first Christmas with him away. And then he took you ice skating with his sister. *We* were supposed to take her out together—he said we would—but you took that away from me. That was supposed to be me!" she screamed, tears filling her eyes.

Then, abruptly, she stopped. Closing her eyes, she took a breath, and then reopened them. Her tone changed; she spoke softly now. "But that doesn't matter. You were just a whim." She was thoughtful. "No, more like a virus that I had to get rid of. He loves me, and he wants to be with me."

After watching Janet's transformation, Dee knew this was no game. She was in serious trouble.

* * * *

Ben sat on the sofa in his penthouse feeling completely isolated and helpless. His head was pounding. He needed to do something. He needed to find her! He had talked to the police and the FBI for hours. Now, a young man in a gray suit walked off the elevator. He talked to one of the policemen, who directed him to Ben.

"Mr. Harrison," he said, "I' m Agent Blackstone." He reached out to shake Ben's hand. "I'm with the FBI's kidnapping task force. Can I ask you some questions?"

"I've answered all of your questions repeatedly. Can you please find Dee?"

"Mr. Harrison, we've checked the security cameras, and there's not much there. We caught a glimpse of the assailant from the inside camera, and the make, model and tag number of a van that was reported stolen yesterday We're just trying to figure all this out, trying to decide if this is a kidnap for ransom. If it is, as long as they know they can get money, she should be safe, at least for a while. How long would you say she's been missing?"

"I don't know!" he yelled. "Six, seven hours maybe." Ben put his face in his hands.

"Can you think of anyone who might have wanted to harm her?"

Ben thought of the man in the restaurant and the welder. No, he said to himself. They wouldn't have done that.

"I don't think so. She's not the sort of person who would deliberately hurt someone."

"But," Edmond said, "she does have an uncanny knack for pissing people off."

Agent Blackstone looked at him. "And you are?"

"Detective Edmond James."

The two men shook hands.

"Detective Lawson," Holly said, extending her hand.

"What can you tell me?" Blackstone asked.

"What about Terry?" Edmond added.

"No." Holly shook her head. "Terry's a parasite, but she wouldn't have done this."

"What about that Maurice guy?" Ben said.

"Would he want to see her hurt?" Blackstone asked.

"He's her ex-boyfriend, and he has attacked her before," Ben said, looking at Holly.

"That was the first thing I checked," she said. "He's in Las Vegas. He's been there for a few weeks."

"Russell Pemberton," Ben said. "He was an employee at Harrison." He told agent Blackstone about the incident with Russell. "Then there's Janet Summers. She was an ex-girlfriend of mine."

"Would she have a reason to hurt Ms. Meyers?"

"She was angry when we broke up." Ben shook his head. "But I don't think she would have done this." Edmond and Holly exchanged looks, which didn't escape Ben. "What?"

Holly sighed, looking at Ben. He saw the dread on her face.

"I didn't want to say this, because I don't want you to panic, but often those who fight their captors get hurt."

"Yes," Blackstone said, "that is very true."

"Dee's a fighter, and I'm afraid of what could happen." Holly added.

Ben felt his stomach turn over. He looked down at his shoes, trying to keep the nausea at bay.

Jean and Harriett stepped off the elevator, looking frantic. "Where's my baby?" Jean said calmly. "I want to know where my baby is."

Holly walked over and hugged her. "Mom, we're doing everything we can." Jean looked around the room searching for Ben. She found him, taking his hand in hers, touching his cheek.

"Ben, I know you love my baby. You're going to make them find her, right?"

"Yes, ma'am," he said as she stepped close to him.

"Please," she whispered, "find my baby."

He hugged her and said, "I will."

* * * *

"I'm going to leave now. I have to get my alibi together," Janet said as she stood and put on her coat. "I'll be back soon."

Dee listened for her car. She heard it start, then drive away.

"Jake. That's your name, right?"

He turned, glaring at her. His nose was the size of a softball, and both eyes were an ugly color purple.

"Sorry about the nose thing." She tried to sound demure. "It was just reflex."

"Yeah, sure it was."

"You know she's crazy, don't you? She could be setting you up to take the fall."

He ignored her.

"Hey, whatever she's paying you. I can make sure you get double."

He looked at her. "What? Do you think I'm stupid? Soon as I let you go, you'll go straight to the cops."

"No, I won't. I just want to go home."

"No, lady. I ain't that dumb."

"Well, you're certainly not proving it by doing this," she said sarcastically.

"You're a real smartass, aren't you?" he barked as he walked to the bed, pulling a gun from under his shirt.

"Hey, buddy," she said, backing up on the bed, "I was just joking."

"I need to cuff you to the bed. If you hurt me, I swear I'll shoot you."

She pondered her situation for a moment. *I should kick him in the face—maybe I'd knock him out—but if he shoots me, I could bleed to death before help comes.* She moved her feet to the bed frame slowly, allowing him to hook her ankles to the bed.

"Come on, Jake. How much is she paying you?"

"Fifty Gs."

"You're kidding, right? You're going to go to jail for murder for fifty thousand dollars?" She lay on her back, shaking her head. "My fiancé would pay you much more to get me back."

Jake watched her, then asked slowly, "Who is this fiancé you two keep talking about?"

She tried to reason with him. "Ben Harrison, of Harrison Enterprises. Think about it, Jake. You could get maybe a half million in ransom and leave the country. The cops probably know who you are already anyway. They have security cameras both inside and outside that building, you know. You'll need the extra money to flee the country. Janet's measly fifty thousand won't do it."

Jake walked to the window on the other side of the room, looking out at the snow. He thought about the ring Janet had pried from Dee's hand when he had brought her into the cabin. How she had been careful not to let him see it, thinking he would take it. He grunted. That rock had to have cost about twenty or thirty grand, easy. He sucked his teeth and turned back to Dee. "Ben Harrison, huh?"

* * * *

Unlocking the door, Janet walked quietly into her parents' house. She went up the stairs and into her old bedroom. Quickly, she removed her clothes, put on a robe, and walked down to the sitting room. Hillary Summers' bridge party was underway. Her mother looked up at her.

"Good afternoon," her mother said. Then, as she realized her daughter was still in her robe, she added, "Janet, it's almost three! Why are you not dressed?"

"I haven't been feeling very well."

"You should have told me. I could have had Teresa bring you up some soup. How long have you been here?"

"I spent the night."

"Really?" Hillary sounded surprised.

"Yes, when I came in, you and Daddy were busy and I didn't want to disturb you."

"Well, go back upstairs and rest, and I'll have some soup and orange juice brought right up "

"You know, mother, that's not necessary. I'm feeling a lot better; I'm sure I just needed to rest." She looked at the other ladies sitting around the table and smiled. "I think I'm going to go home. I have a few things I need to take care of." She leaned down, giving her mother and hug and kiss.

"Are you sure?"

"Yes." She turned and left the room. Walking briskly back upstairs, she grabbed her clothes and slipped them on. She walked downstairs to her father's office, looked around then stepped inside, and closed the door behind her. A moment later, she walked out of the office, leaving the house and going home to change clothes.

* * * *

Ben walked out of the kitchen and headed for the elevator. Edmond stood quickly, following him. "Where are you going?" he asked Ben. "I'm going to find Dee."

"Man, you don't know where to look."

"I'm going to talk to Russell Pemberton."

"I can't let you do that," Edmond said, placing a hand on Ben's arm.

"You can't stop me."

"Let the FBI handle this."

"If it were Holly, would you leave it to someone else?"

Edmond looked back at all the people milling around. "Okay then—but I'm going with you." They arrived at Russell's home a half-hour later. "Don't do anything foolish," Edmond said. When Ben stopped the car, he added, "We're only here to question this guy."

Ben nodded. They got out of the car and walked up the steps to ring the bell.

Russell opened the door. "Benjamin, I've already talked to the police—" Before he could finish his sentence, Ben hit him. Russell fell back, hitting the table behind the sofa.

Edmond grabbed Ben. "Calm down, man."

"Where's Dee?" Ben yelled, taking a step closer. A young woman walked out of the kitchen and froze when she saw the scene. Screaming, she dropped the glass she was carrying and ran upstairs.

"What the hell are you talking about?" Russell cried, trying to move away.

"Did you have anything to do with her disappearance?" Ben said, stepping toward him. "Answer me!"

"I told the police I didn't know anything! I swear I don't!"

Just then, the FBI rushed in, seizing Ben and taking control of the situation. Russell went over his statement for the FBI a second time. He said that he hadn't seen Dee since he resigned for Harrison and that he had been with his new girlfriend, Bridget, for the past two days. The terrified woman corroborated his alibi.

Ben stormed out of the house with Edmond in tow. Once in the car, Ben yelled, hitting the steering wheel.

"Man, you need to calm down. This isn't going to help Dee, us running around half-blind."

Ben lay his forehead on the steering wheel, trying to calm down. Then he sat up, started the car, and drove to Janet's apartment.

The FBI was there when they arrived. Ben walked down the hall with Edmond following him. Janet was talking to agent Blackstone.

"No, I haven't seen Ms. Meyers." She looked at Ben, who was standing by the door. Her eyes remained on him as she talked to the agent. "No, I saw her a week or so before Christmas, when she told me about her engagement, but I haven't seen her since."

Ben turned his back, listening to her talk to the FBI. "I was at my parents' home yesterday. No, I stayed the night. We had dinner, and I was under the weather, so I stayed there." Ben looked at Edmond and said, "Can you catch a ride back to the apartment with agent Blackstone? I need to be alone."

"Are you going to be all right?"

Ben nodded and walked out of the apartment to his car.

* * * *

Her cell phone rang. She answered it before the second ring.

"Hello, Ben."

"Change of plans, babes," Jake said.

"What? What do you mean change of plans?"

"I want more money."

"You can't do that."

"Yes, I can," Jake said, looking at his nose in his mirror. "I deserve another ten grand for my troubles—like my broken nose."

"No, we agreed on fifty thousand dollars. That's what you're going to get."

"You didn't tell me I might get hurt."

"That's not my fault!" Janet yelled.

"I could go let her go. She said she would give me double."

"She's a PI. She doesn't have that kind of money."

"Yeah, but maybe that fiancé of hers does. I could get it from him. She's a pretty little thing. I bet he would pay a lot to get her back."

Janet fumed. "How much do you want?"

"Sixty... no, better yet, seventy-five."

She closed her eyes, picturing Ben's face. "Okay, fine. But after I give you the money, you can't come back asking for more."

"Sure. And by the way, bring it with you," he said before hanging up. He then sat back and thought, *She was willing to do anything to keep that Meyers bitch away. I bet that Harrison would do anything to get her back.* Walking out of the bathroom, he looked at Dee. "What's this fiancé's phone number?" he said, taking a piece of paper and pen from the table. Dee gave him the number. "What's this to?"

"His home," she said.

He nodded. "You'd better hope he's willing to pay for you." He walked to the door, looking back at Dee and smiling. "Sit tight."

"Yeah, like I'm going somewhere," she mumbled.

* * * *

Jake drove twenty miles in the opposite direction, stopping at a large discount store. He strolled inside and walked to the counter.

"Hey, man, do you guys have those throwaway cell phones?" The clerk pointed to the phones on the shelf. "Give me two of 'em," he said, thrusting his chin in the direction of the phones. After paying for the phones, he sat in his car to make the call.

* * * *

"Hello?" Ben said, knocking the base of the phone off the table as he grabbed the headset.

"Harrison, I have your fiancée."

Ben sat up straight. "Who is this?"

Everyone rushed to his side. One of the FBI agents turned on a tape recorder, switched the call to speaker, and immediately tried to trace the call. "Keep him on the line," Blackstone whispered.

"What do you want?" Ben demanded.

"Five million dollars."

"Oh my God," Jean cried. "We don't have that kind of money." "I want to talk to Dee," he said. "We aren't going to discuss anything until I know that she's all right."

"I'll call you back in two hours. You can talk to her for a minute, and then you tell me you got my money."

"I don't know if I can get that much in two hours."

There was a pause.

"Figure it out. Two hours." He hung up.

Ben looked at Blackstone.

"We couldn't get him. He used one of those disposable phones."

Ben dropped his head, running his hands through his hair.

"What are we going to do, Mama?" Jean said, looking at Harriett. "We don't have that kind of money. Even if we sell the house and use the cash in my retirement fund, it won't make a dent."

Ben looked up. He stood and stroked her back. "Don't worry about it. I'll take care of everything."

He walked to the elevator with one of the FBI agents accompanying him. He could get the money. It would be a little tricky, given the narrow window they had, but he could manage it. He needed to go home and talk to his mother and Lisa before he got the money. They all had to agree, but he knew it wouldn't be a problem. He also wanted to talk to them before all this leaked to the press—he didn't want them to find out like that.

When he walked through the lobby, Mike was there talking to Ernie. Mike nodded to the man in front of him and then walked over to Ben. "Sir, I'm sorry about Ms. Meyers. She's a good lady. Is there anything I can do?"

"No, Mike. Thanks." He patted the man's shoulder.

"Do you need me to drive you anywhere? I can do that."

Ben started to say no, but he could tell Mike needed to help. He gave him his keys. "Can you drive us to my mother's?"

"Sure thing."

* * * *

Janet walked into the bank and withdrew all the money she had from her checking and savings accounts—a little more than fifty thousand dollars. She pulled the check from her purse and looked at it. It was a check from one of her parents' various accounts, which she had taken from one of the checkbooks in her father's desk. Reaching for a pen, she paused, thinking about what she was going to do. No one would notice the missing money for months, meaning she would have enough time to get back together with Ben and get married before replacing it. If her parents discovered the missing money, she would tell her father that she had needed it for an emergency. He would be upset, but she was his little girl—he would get over it.

She frowned, thinking about her trust fund. If only the deposits didn't come in such small increments, she wouldn't have to stoop to committing such acts. She started writing, quickly scrawling $25,000 on the check and forging her father's signature, then walked to the bank manager to get him to cash it.

* * * *

Natalie and Lisa were hysterical, unable to believe that someone could have done this to Dee. "You don't need to ask us about the money," Natalie said. "Dee's family now. I think we should be at the penthouse with everyone else." Lisa nodded in agreement, rising from her seat.

Ben and Mike waited by the door for the women and then drove to the bank. Natalie went inside with Ben, and within fifteen minutes they were walking out of the bank with the money.

As they headed for the penthouse, the air in the car was heavy with worry. Natalie took her son's hand and squeezed it, giving him support. Mike stopped at the front door.

"Mike, you go ahead inside."

Mike looked at Ben and nodded.

"Are you coming in?" Natalie asked.

"I'll be in soon," he answered.

She leaned over and kissed her son's cheek.

"She'll be fine. She's strong, a fighter."

Once they got out of the car Ben watched them get inside safely. *Yes, she is a fighter,* he thought. *That's what I'm afraid of.*

He drove around to the side of the building and up the ramp to his parking spot next to Dee's car. He looked at her car, imagining her fear as some jerk grabbed her, forcing her into his van.

He got out of his car and walked to the front. Squatting down, he threw up.

* * * *

Jake walked back and went into the cabin. He grabbed the chair from the table and carried it over to the bed. Spinning it around, he sat backwards on it.

"Look, bitch, I'm going to make a phone call. You've got one minute to talk. If you tell him where you are or give him any kind of hint, I will cut your throat and walk out that door." He dialed the number. Ben answered on the first ring. Jake held the phone up to Dee's ear.

"Hello," she said.

"Dee, sweetheart, are you all right?"

"Yes, I'm fine."

"Did he hurt you?"

"No, I'm not hurt. Actually I'm quite comfortable. At least I can rest, and it's not like my apartment—you know, Grand Central Station."

"I never should have let you go downstairs alone. I'm going to give him the money, sweetheart. I'm going to bring you home."

"It's not what you think, Ben."

Jake snatched the phone. "Do you have the money?"

"Yes," Ben said slowly.

"Okay, I'll call you back at seven A.M. to tell you where to leave it."

"What about Dee?"

"I'll let you know everything then." He hung up. "What the hell was all that about?" He rose up, towering over her angrily. "What?" she said, trying to sound afraid. "That 'it's not what you think' shit?"

"I wanted him to know that you hadn't hurt me." He scrutinized her with doubt in his eyes. She hadn't said anything about him or where she was. He nodded, sitting back down. "So," he said, leaning on the back of the chair. "What does the lunatic have against you?" Dee laughed and opened her mouth to speak just as Janet walked through the front door.

"What the hell is going on?"

Jake stood up. "Nothing. Where's my money?"

Janet crossed the room to him. "Here," she said, shoving the tote she was carrying towards him.

"There's been a change of plans."

"You told me," she said, folding her arms.

"Well, I changed them again. I'm going to give her back to him for five million dollars."

"What?"

"I have it all worked out. I just talked to him, and he has the money. All I have to do is call him in the morning, pick up my cash, hop on a plane out of the country, and I'll be scot-free," he said, displaying his even white teeth.

"No!" Janet screamed. "We made a deal! You can't do this to me! I won't let you. This bitch ruined my life. You can't just let her go." She took a deep breath and spoke in a calm voice. "If you let her go. She'll tell them who you are."

"I don't care. I'll be long gone."

"What about me? I'll go to jail."

Jake gave her an incredulous look and shook his head. "I don't give a shit."

"This can't be happening," she said, shaking her head. "Why can't you just kill her anyway? You can keep the money I gave you. Then you can get the ransom and get away."

Jake rubbed his chin. "Hmm, maybe."

"Hey, Jake? Jake?" Dee called.

"Shut up!" Janet yelled.

"No, you shut up," Jake said, glaring at Janet. "She's the one who gave me the idea about the ransom. You tried to hide the fact that her fiancé was loaded, just like you tried to hide that ring. Well, I trust her a whole helluva lot more than I trust you right now." He looked at Dee. "Go ahead and talk."

"If you kill me, Ben will be upset—so upset he will do everything in his power to find you. With the kind of money he has, he's sure to find you."

He nodded, looking at Janet. "That's right. There's no need to kill her," he said. "Anyway, if I let her go, I have a better chance of getting away."

"Why are you doing this?" Janet cried.

"Because this is how I want it. I'm in charge now. I call all the shots, and I get to keep all the money," he said, jabbing his thumb in his chest.

Dee noticed that the veins on Janet's neck looked like they would erupt at any second.

"I'm going to let the bitch go," he said, thrusting his thumb toward Dee.

"Wait a minute," Dee said, wagging her head. "My name is not bitch, it's Dee."

"Oh, shut up!" Janet screamed, her face blood red.

Jake laughed as he looked from Janet to Dee. "I like you," he told Dee.

"You know what?" Dee said trying to sit up. "I like you too. We could have been friends, but this kidnapping thing kinda kills it for me—you know what I'm saying?"

He smiled at her and nodded.

"Oh, for crying out loud!" Janet yelled, throwing her purse on the table.

Chapter 17

I have to think of something. That fool is going to ruin everything, Janet thought as she paced behind the cabin. The lightly falling snow stuck to her lashes, and her cheeks were red from the cold, but she didn't seem to notice it. *I've come too far to let this happen. I'm so close to getting what I want. Just a little further.*

After running through her plan one final time, she walked back into the cabin. She looked at Jake, who was sitting across from Dee; they were chatting as if they were long-lost buddies.

God, he's such a fool.

She went into the other room for a minute then walked back in the room where Jake and Dee were.

"Uh, Jake," Dee said, "do you think I could get something to eat?"

"Yeah, that's a good idea. I could go for something to eat."

Janet smiled. This was perfect. "Yes," she said, "that sounds like a great idea. Let's go, Jake."

"We have to bring something back for her," Jake said, tilting his head toward Dee.

"Yes, of course," Janet said, putting on her coat and gloves. "We'll bring something back."

"Do you want to take your car?" Jake asked, walking toward Janet's car.

"No," she said, "I would rather take yours."

He nodded and walked to the car. "Whew, it's cold as a bitch," he said, starting the car.

"Yes, it is," she said, pulling the collar of her coat around her neck. After they had driven a few miles, she turned to him. "Jake, why haven't you tried to hit on me?" He grunted. "Well?" she asked.

"Not my type."

"What do you mean, I'm not your type?" she said sourly.

"I mean, you're not my type. You're kind of cute, but not what I'm attracted to."

"I was hoping you would feel differently."

He glanced at her. "I don't mix business and pleasure."

"It could be fun," she said, smiling. Then she took his hand and placed it on her leg. "When we first met I thought you were very handsome, and I was just thinking..."

He smiled, moving his hand further up her thigh. "Why don't you pull over up ahead?" she said, reaching over and tracing her fingers along the seam of his fly.

He looked her over again. "Okay, why the hell not?" he said pulling the car over.

She pointed to a dark spot off the road where the car wouldn't be seen. "Pull over there; we don't want someone thinking the car broke down."

He pulled in farther, turning off the headlights.

"Let's get out," she said.

"Hell, no—it's too cold."

"Come on," she said, giving his crotch a gentle squeeze.

He felt himself becoming hard but said again, "Hell no. I ain't doing it in the snow."

"It's kinky."

"You don't seem like the kinky type to me."

She took off her glove and unzipped his pants, freeing him from his confines.

Then, bending, she slowly licked him, her tongue circling his tip, sending shivers of delight down his thighs. A sense of urgency surged through him.

She sat back, looking at him. "If we go outside, it'll be something you'll never forget."

He breathed hard, adjusting his crotch. Then he opened the door and stepped from the car. After putting on her gloves, she opened the door, got out, and followed him as he went to the rear of the car. Stopping eight feet away from him, she slipped her hand in her pocket.

"You know, I really don't want to kill you, but you give me no choice," she said, glaring at him.

"Yeah, sure. You want to spank me first." He laughed and then stopped abruptly. At first, he had thought she was playing some sort of kinky sex game, but then he saw the hate in her eyes. He reached in his jacket pocket.

"Are you looking for this?" she asked, pulling the gun out of hers.

"Wait a minute. Just hold on," he said, raising his hands. "You don't want to do that."

"Don't tell me what I want to do!" she screamed. "Everything was going fine until you had to go and get greedy on me! This is all *her* fault!"

"Look, if you want, we can go back to the old plan. Anything you want. You're the boss."

"No," she said. "She turned you against me, just like she did with Ben, and I'm not going to let her turn you against me too."

As he turned and ran, she shot him in the back. Walking closer, she shot him three more times. After standing over him for a moment to make sure he wasn't moving, she put the gun back in her pocket, got in the car, and headed back to the cabin.

She walked in smiling, clearly very pleased with herself as she dropped her coat on the chair.

Dee asked, "Where's Jake?"

"He's gone," Janet said merrily.

"What do you mean 'gone'?"

"Gone as in gone for good."

Oh my God, Dee thought. "You killed him?"

"I had to," Janet said. "He was messing up my plan, and I couldn't have that."

Dee lay with her eyes closed for a moment, trying to think. "Janet, now you have to let me go. When they find him, they'll trace things back to you."

"No. I've never touched his car. For now, I'll leave it here, and I'll pay someone to dispose of it later. When the police find the car, they'll find traces of you in it and will assume Jake was the kidnapper. More than likely, they will think that he had a partner and that something went wrong, that his partner killed him and got away killing you in the process, I might add."

"Why are you going through all this trouble? Why not just kill me right now?"

"Because I want you to suffer, like I suffered without Ben." Janet grabbed her coat off the chair. "Goodbye, Deanna," she said, smiling sweetly. "I'll make sure I take real good care of Ben."

"You know, Janet, even if you do convince Ben to take you back, which I doubt he will, when he hears your voice, he'll be comparing it to mine; when you touch him, he'll pretend that it's my hand he's feeling. And every time he has sex with you, he will be making love to me."

Janet rocked on her heels, grabbing the doorframe to keep from falling. Dee laughed, taunting her. Janet reached for the light switch and turned it off, leaving the door open as she turned and left the cabin. Dee stopped laughing when she heard Janet drive away.

"Shit, shit, shit!" she said. She lay back, trying to figure out her next move. "Think, Dee, think." She tried to kick the bedpost loose. It didn't budge. Resigning herself to the fact that escape was impossible, she lay back and prayed that someone would find her.

* * * * *

He was growing weary of the sympathetic looks. Grabbing his keys, he walked to the elevator, passing the dozens of people who had invaded his home. *No, our home,* he thought, *Dee's and mine.*

He drove to the park and sat in his car looking at the stars. "Where are you, sweetheart?" He closed his eyes and said a prayer, pleading for her safe return. He was terrified. If Holly was right and Dee had fought her captors, she could very well be hurt. His cell phone rang. He answered it after the first ring.

"Hello, Ben, it's Janet. I wanted to call to make sure you were all right."

"I am, thank you."

"Do you want to come over? I can wait with you, if you like?"

"No."

"I know I've been acting crazy. I was upset that we broke up, but I'm so sorry about Deanna." She paused. "If you came over, maybe we could come up with something, some idea on how to find her."

"The FBI is handling it."

"Okay. I hope you find her, Ben. I'm here if you need me."

"Thanks for calling, Janet," he said hanging up.

She hung up and smiled. With her arms folded tightly, she sat on the arm of the sofa, rocking back and forth. *Everything is going as planned. I just need to remember to be patient Don't be too eager Janet. Just take it slow*

* * * *

Lying on the bed, Dee tried to think of anything but the cold. She'd tried to break the bed frame again, but it hadn't budged. She couldn't tell what time it was, but it was dark. She curled up, trying to keep warm, licking her lips to moisten them. Her mouth was dry; she needed water and she couldn't feel her fingers. She thought of Ben, remembering the look on his face when she had convinced him to try an Italian veal sandwich with hot peppers, and the feeling of his arms around her the first time they danced. She then thought of her mother and grandmother and how happy they would be planning the wedding—all the flowers her mother would want and the big reception they would have. She smiled as she imagined the dress she would wear, one that she would ask her grandmother to make and Natalie to help design.

Grandma will like Natalie, she thought. *They are a lot alike. And Holly will be my maid of honor, of course, and Lisa and Heather will be matrons of honor, and maybe Terry and I will patch things up and she'll be in the wedding too...*

Her thoughts then began to jumble, and she felt her consciousness begin to slip. She shook her head, trying to clear it. *Must be the cold,* she said to herself. "Ben," she whispered, "Come on, baby. I'm waiting for you." She looked down, trying to kick the metal bed frame again, but she was too tired. "Don't go to sleep, Dee," she said, but as hard as she tried, she could not stay awake. *I'll just rest for a little while,* she thought, drifting off as soon as she had thought it.

* * * *

Walking off the elevator, Ben saw that the FBI was setting up additional equipment on the coffee table. Everywhere he looked, there were police. He walked into the living room as the colorful lights on the Christmas tree came on with a click. The twinkling lights looked like hundreds of new stars. In the seven years he had lived here, he had never had a Christmas tree.

Walking to it, he removed one of the ornaments, thinking about the day they went out in search for the perfect tree. Dee had been like a child, so excited and eager to pick just the right one. They had the tree delivered while they went shopping for ornaments. Then they came back to the penthouse and decorated it while Burl Ives and Nat King Cole serenaded them with Christmas carols. Afterwards, he had it the fireplace and they had made love next to the tree.

The ornament suddenly felt heavy, and he hung it back on the tree. He looked around the room; everyone seemed to be doing something, but they weren't doing what they needed to do. They weren't finding Dee. He walked to the mantel and let his fingers brush the stockings. He picked up the one Dee had filled for him and looked inside. She had filled it with candy and other useless things that he would never use but that he would keep forever because she had given them to him. He saw a two-by-two-inch card with a red heart on it. He took it out and read it:

My life was so bare, my existence so empty,
Until you came along,
My love, my world, my everything.

He closed his eyes to blink back the tears as Lisa walked next to him. "Are you all right?"

"Yes," he whispered. Putting the card in his shirt pocket, he hung the stocking back in its place. He then walked into the bedroom and closed the door. When he entered the room, he sensed Dee's presence, as if she were still there. He struggled to breathe, walking to the bed and picking up the sweater she had worn the day before her kidnapping. He breathed in deeply, drawing in her fragrance. His heart swelled, and he sat on the side of the bed feeling as though he was going to fall apart.

There was a light tap at the door. "Yes," he answered.

"Can I come in?" Harriett asked, peeking in. He nodded. She walked to the bed and sat next to him. "Everybody keeps saying about how Dee's a fighter and how she might get hurt." She looked him in the eyes. "She's also smart, and she wouldn't do anything to get herself hurt, so you don't fret none. I know my granddaughter better than most, and I know she's a survivor. She knows you're looking for her, and she's waiting for you."

Ben smiled at the woman as tears threatened to spill from his eyes.

"And if you want to cry, well then, you just go ahead and do it. My husband cried many a day, and he was as strong as they come." She smiled weakly at him as she stood, kissing his cheek before she left and quietly closing the door behind her.

Ben paced nervously, waiting for the phone to ring. He looked at the clock. It was two hours past the time that the kidnapper said he would call. He heard Blackstone call Holly and Edmond into the kitchen, and he followed.

"Mr. Harrison, I think you should go into the other room."

"No, I won't," Ben said. "You're going to tell me what the hell is going on."

Blackstone sighed. "We definitely have a problem."

"What is that?"

"You didn't give the kidnapper any reason to think that you wouldn't pay the ransom, but he hasn't called. I think something is wrong."

Ben shook his head. "No, it can't be," he said, his voice on the verge of panic. "I can't believe this."

Holly looked at Edmond. "That's what she meant when she said that this wasn't what we thought it was. She was trying to tell us that whoever took her didn't do it for the money. How could I have been so dumb?"

Ben felt like screaming. He sat down, covering his face with his hands.

"Okay," Blackstone said. "We need to look at any cases she might have had in the last few months, then go back and talk to these people on the list you gave us again."

"Edmond, can I talk to you for a moment?" Ben said, turning to leave the kitchen.

Edmond followed him down the hall. "What's up?"

"I want to talk to Terry, and I'd like you to come with me."

Edmond rubbed his chin. "Holly thinks she has nothing to do with this, but I agree with you. I think maybe we should—just to be on the safe side."

Ben nodded and they walked back into the kitchen.

"Hey, babe, I'm going out with Ben for a while," Edmond told Holly.

"Where are you going?"

"Just to get some air." He leaned close, letting his lips brush hers.

She eyed them suspiciously. "Don't get in trouble."

"We won't." Edmond smiled.

* * * *

Terry lived in an apartment house on the fourth floor. They walked up the steps and knocked on the door. There was no answer. Ben knocked again, this time much harder.

"What are you doing here?" they heard from behind them.

Ben turned to see Terry walking up the steps with a little boy.

"Hello, Terry."

"Terry," Edmond said with a nod.

She stopped on the landing and looked at them. "Like I said, what are you doing here?"

"We need to talk to you," Ben said, looking at the child. "Is that your son?"

"Yeah," she said, stepping around them and opening the door. "Davie, go in your room and play. I'll fix your lunch soon."

The boy looked at Ben. "Who is that?"

"He's Dee's fiancé."

"What's a fun say?"

"No, honey, fiancé—that means he's going to marry her."

"You're going to marry Aunt Dee?"

"Yes," Ben said.

"Good, then I can have a cousin."

"Go to your room, Davie," Terry demanded. He started down the hall and then turned back to Ben.

"Can you try to make my cousin a boy?" he said, tugging at his ear.

Ben laughed. "I'll see what I can do."

Terry turned back to the two men. "Now, what do you want?"

"We're trying to find Dee," Edmond said

"She's not here. I haven't seen her since we were in Atlanta."

"No," Ben said, "something has happened to her."

Terry had a blank look on her face. "What do you mean something's happened to her?"

"She's been kidnapped."

"What? Oh my God," Terry said, shaking her head.

"We wanted to see if you knew anything about it?"

It was then that she realized what was happening. "You think I would do something like this?"

"We just wanted to check."

"I can't believe you. You come into my house and accuse me of hurting my own family," she yelled.

Edmond put his hands up. "Calm down, Terry. We don't want to upset you. We just wanted to talk to you."

"You don't come up in my house accusing me of anything," she said, shaking her head.

"Wait a minute, lady," Ben said, pointing his finger at her. "You have no right to be offended about anything. I know what you're capable of. Your theatrics won't work on me, so save your performance for someone else."

Terry was quiet for a moment. She looked at Ben. "I honestly don't know anything. She doesn't even talk to me anymore."

"Well, when you two still *were* speaking, did she say anything about someone wanting to hurt her?"

"No. Look, I can understand you thinking I might do something like this—I know I do dumb stuff sometimes," she said, meeting Ben's glare. "Okay, a lot. But I do love Dee. I was just jealous of her," she admitted honestly. "I'm giving my relationship with my son's father another chance, and I signed up for college. I want to make things right."

They heard the sound of a key in the door. "Hey," Terry said walking to the door. "David, this is Dee's fiancé, Ben, and you know Edmond. Something has happened to Dee, and I want to go with them." She looked at Ben and Edmond. "If they'll let me."

Edmond looked at Ben and nodded.

* * * *

Ben had slept only a few hours here and there. Harriett kept forcing him to eat. She told him that it was her way of dealing with the situation, by taking care of others. Natalie watched him with worried eyes. Lisa had called Heather and Kyle in Portland, and they had come immediately.

Walking into the living room, Ben looked out the window. He couldn't shake the feeling that he had missed something, something he couldn't put his finger on, something about Janet.

"I'm going out, mother," he said. "I'll be back soon."

Lisa followed him to the elevator and asked, "Do you need me to go with you? Maybe you shouldn't be alone."

"I'll be fine. I have something I need to do," he said, giving her a brief hug.

Kyle walked next to Lisa's side. "I'll go with you," he said, looking to Ben for confirmation.

Ben nodded.

* * * *

"Where are we going?" Kyle asked, looking at Ben.

"To see Janet, a woman I used to date."

"Do you think she has something to do with Dee's disappearance?"

"I don't know. She said something that doesn't make sense." He thought back to the last time he had talked to Dee, about the odd comment she had made about Grand Central Station. Why would she say that? He knew it was a clue, but he couldn't figure it out. He parked the car in front of Janet's apartment.

They walked inside and took the elevator to the second floor. Ben rapped on the door with his keys, waiting impatiently for her to answer. She opened the door wearing a robe, looking as if she had just gotten out of the shower.

"Hi," she said, smiling. "I didn't know you were coming over. Come in." She stepped out of the way, allowing them to enter the apartment. "Who's your friend?"

"He's my brother," he said as he strode into the living room, scanning the room and looking for any sign of Dee.

"Have you heard anything yet?"

"No."

"I'm sorry," she said. "Can I make you two some coffee?"

"No, thanks," Kyle said.

"Janet," Ben said, turning to her. "I need to ask you about something you said to the FBI yesterday."

"Sure," she said, studying his face.

"You said that Dee told you we were getting married a few weeks ago?"

She nodded.

"But I didn't ask her to marry me until Christmas."

"Oh, maybe she knew you were going to ask her," she said casually. Ben watched her. Kyle walked to the sofa.

"No, that's not possible. We had never even discussed it," he said, putting his hands in his coat pockets, feeling the single key he had taken from Janet earlier. It brought back the memory of walking into Dee's apartment and seeing Janet there—and Dee saying something about Grand Central Station. Kyle sat down, knocking Janet's purse over. He instinctively reached to put the contents back in it.

"No, let me do that!" Janet said, rushing to the sofa. Dee's ring fell out of the purse, landing with a thud on the carpet. She placed her hand over it, trying to hide it. Ben walked over and pulled her upright, prying the ring out of her hand.

"Where is she?' he said, trying to contain his rage.

"What are you talking about?"

"You know what I'm talking about." She glared at him, her jaw locked. "Where is she, damn it!" he said, grabbing her throat.

Kyle rushed to his side. "Ben, don't do this, man. If you hurt her, we may never find Dee."

"We can be together now that she's out of the way. We can be together forever," she said, her fingers clawing at his wrist as he tightened his grip.

Kyle took a step back.

"Tell me!" he demanded.

"She's at my parents' cabin," she whispered. He pushed her away and she fell on the floor, gasping for air. He pulled his cell phone out of his pocket and dialed Holly's number. "Holly, she's at Janet's family cabin." Ben gave her the location, and then they hurried to the door.

"It's probably too late," Janet said between gasps. Ben turned, looking at her with such hate that she cringed. He stepped toward her, and Kyle grabbed his arm. "Come on, man, lets' go."

"You'd better hope not," Ben said, pointing at her. "If something happens to her, there will be no hole you can slither into where I won't find you." As they walked out the door, he slammed it behind them.

* * * *

Ben jumped from the helicopter into the powdery snow, hitting the ground running toward the cabin. Holly, Edmond, and Kyle were close behind. The door was open, and snow had blown inside, covering the floor. They ran to the back room. Dee was lying on the bed in the fetal position with her hands cuffed behind her and her legs cuffed to the bed. Ben froze, feeling like part of him had just died. He ran to the bed, trying to lift her without hurting her. Edmond used the key to un-cuff her, while Holly stood by the door crying. The paramedics walked in. "We need to check her."

"No," Ben said, holding her. "Don't touch her." He rocked her, talking to her. "Sweetheart, can you hear me? Please don't leave me. I can't live without you." Holly wept at the sight. "If you die, I'll die too." He sobbed.

"Ben," Kyle said, touching his shoulder. "You need to let them check her." Ben felt that if he let go, he would be letting go forever. He nodded, telling them that they had to check her while he held her.

"She has a pulse, but it's weak," the paramedic said. "We need to warm her and get her to the hospital."

* * * *

Natalie and Jean sat outside the hospital room door. When they saw Holly and Edmond walking toward them, they stood. "Any change?"

"Not yet."

They looked in the window. "How's he doing?" Edmond asked.

"Mama got him to eat something before she went to the chapel," Jean said. "He's been sitting there for three days now."

"He won't go home or even to the lounge to take a nap," Natalie added.

"I'll try talking to him," Holly said. She pushed the door open and walked into the room. "Hey," she said.

He looked up. "Hey."

"Are you okay?" He nodded then turned his attention back to Dee. "Why don't you take a break while I sit with her?"

"No, I'm fine."

"You should take a rest. Maybe get some coffee."

"I can't. I have to be here when she wakes up."

"If she wakes up, I'll call you."

"No." His voice was sharp; he looked at her, his eyes were bloodshot and he clearly hadn't shaved in a couple of days. "I'm sorry," he whispered. "I can't leave."

Holly rubbed his back. "Your mom and Jean are worried about you."

"I'll rest when Dee wakes up. She's going to wake up soon. I can tell..."

Holly nodded. "I'm going to get you some coffee. I'll be back." She left the room. He laid his head on Dee's arm, closing his eyes.

"I know you can hear me, sweetheart," he whispered. "It's time to wake up now. We need to go to Europe, and to the beach so I can sail my boat. I can't do it without you. We have to plan our wedding." He took her hand, squeezing it. "I need you here with me. You're my world. You make me whole." He sobbed. "Please, wake up, sweetheart."

He felt fingers stroking his hair. He looked up at her.

"Hey," she said.

"Hi." He smiled, tears in the rims of his eyes. "I missed you," he whispered.

"I missed you too."

"How do you feel?"

"Hungry."

He laughed, stroking her cheek. "You scared me," he said, tears spilling from his eyes.

"I'm sorry," she said, wiping them with the back of her fingers. "I knew you would come for me," she said. "You're my everything."

He reached into his pocket and pulled out her ring. After placing it back where it belonged, he kissed her hand. "I love you."

"I love you, too."

Epilogue

When Ben walked into Dee's office, she was on the phone. It had been three months since the kidnapping, and things were finally getting back to normal. Holly and Edmond had held a small wedding ceremony in Ben and Dee's penthouse for close friends and family. Edmond's sister, Karen, had even helped with the wedding. Dee and Ben gave them a trip to Rome as a wedding gift. Dee told Holly that she needed to have all the fun she could before the baby came, and her aunt Dee spoiled her, making her unbearable.

Kyle was tested and was found to a match for Lisa's bone marrow. The transplant went well, and Lisa and Heather were as close as sisters could be. Ben asked Kyle to be his best man. The twins spent time with their mother, and their new family, and it seemed to work for them. Jean and Natalie planned the wedding; it went from 300 guests to 400 once Harriett got a hand in it. Dee talked to Terry once a week. Terry was going to school full time and even got a job, who would have figured? She moved in with David and they are planning to get married; Dee couldn't wait to see how that turned out.

Janet is serving time for kidnapping and murder. She told the FBI that it was all Jake's idea, and that she shot him in self-defense. But Dee made sure they heard the truth, including how Jake was going to let her go and how Janet killed him because of it. "Hey," she said, hanging up. "Hi Sweetheart," he said, kissing her. She stood up, facing him.

"Do you have any appointments for this afternoon?"

"No, I have a little time; what did you have in mind?" he asked, taking her in his arms.

"Chris was supposed to be going on this surveillance with me; some woman cheating on her husband with some guy who owns a boat; it's down on the pier." Ben frowned.

"What is it that you need me to do?"

"I need you to help me sneak on the boat."

"Oh no, I'm not doing that."

"Come on, it'll be a piece of cake."

"Oh boy," he said as she pulled him out the door.

Here's how you can order books directly from Denise Skelton:

Denise Skelton
P.O. Box 60 Lutherville, MD 21094
U.S.A.

Please add $2.50 for shipping and handling for the first book and $.75 for each additional book. Maryland residents, add appropriate sales tax. No cash, stamps, or CODs. Canadian orders require $5.00 for shipping and handling and must be paid in U.S. dollars. Prices and availability are subject to change. Payment must accompany all orders.

Name: ____
Address: ____
City: ______________________State: _____ ZIP: __________
E-mail: ____

I have enclosed $________ in payment for the checked books(s).

- ❑ Forgotten Promises
- ❑ My Angel
- ❑ My Everything

For more information, check out
www.deniseskelton.com.